# SINS OF OMISSION

IRINA SHAPIRO

Storm
PUBLISHING

Copyright © Irina Shapiro, 2016, 2023

The moral right of the author has been asserted.

To request permissions, contact the publisher at rights@stormpublishing.co

Ebook ISBN: 978-1-80508-150-0
Paperback ISBN: 978-1-80508-151-7

Previously published in 2016 by Merlin Press LLC.

Cover design: Debbie Clement
Cover images: Shutterstock

Published by Storm Publishing.
For further information, visit:
www.stormpublishing.co

ALSO BY IRINA SHAPIRO

**Wonderland Series**

*The Passage*

*Wonderland*

*Sins of Omission*

*The Queen's Gambit*

*Comes the Dawn*

# ONE

## JANUARY 1, 1686

**Barbados, West Indies**

The deck of the ship was drenched in golden sunshine, the sea a startling shade of turquoise, and the sky a cloudless dome of azure; the whole scene reminiscent of the inside of a snow globe, the type people brought back from a holiday to remind them of the fun they'd had, Max Everly mused as he pried his eyes open to gaze around. He could barely see after being in near darkness for close to two months, but the warmth felt good on his shoulders, and the briny smell of the sea carried on the gentle breeze was heavenly after the stink of men cooped up in a wooden cell without the benefit of sanitation or even water for washing.

The calamitous voyage had been plagued by storms; the ship tossed on the waves like a child's toy, riding the huge swells until Max had nothing in his stomach left to vomit. He had been so seasick, he'd often wished that he would just die and be done with it, but somehow both he and the ship had survived, and eventually sailed into the calmer waters of the Caribbean.

Max's once-short hair brushed his collar, and his thick beard scratched liked the devil and was infested with lice. *What I wouldn't give for a bath and a shave,* he thought with intense longing. He'd always been lean, but now he was downright skeletal, having survived on meager rations completely devoid of any nutritional value for weeks. Max's shabby clothes were stiff with dried sweat, vomit, and other bodily fluids he didn't care to think of. Whatever was to come couldn't be any worse than this. At least he would now be on land, hopefully have a cot or mattress of his own, and not have to shit and eat in the same fetid space.

Max's optimism was short-lived as he was herded off the ship and onto a busy quay. People darted all around, commands were shouted, and downtrodden Negro slaves with sweat-glistened backs carried crate after crate to and from vessels being loaded and unloaded. Max heard snatches of conversation in several languages, ranging from English to Dutch.

"Where are we?" Max asked the quartermaster, who escorted the line of men into town with two armed sailors bringing up the rear. The quartermaster's mouth was stretched into a thin line; his eyes fixed on some distant point straight ahead, his hand on the hilt of his sword. Max couldn't account for the tension the man felt, but clearly he didn't relish this part of his job. Few would.

"Bridgetown," the man replied curtly. "Barbados."

A dim memory of a sunlit classroom sprang to Max's mind, making his eyes fill with angry tears as he remembered those carefree days. He'd been too busy passing notes to his friend Jack and making plans to go to the arcade after school to pay much attention to the droning of Mr. Peters, the history teacher, who went on at length about the establishing of the first British colony in the West Indies. How Max wished he had listened that day; for, now, some of the information he'd so carelessly disregarded as being boring and irrelevant might be useful in helping him survive this ordeal. He did recall that many

Englishmen and Irishmen who toiled at the tobacco and sugar plantations had been sent down by Oliver Cromwell, as well as George Jeffreys, the man responsible for his own sentence, giving rise to the term "barbadosed." Max had thought it a funny-sounding word at the time, but he wasn't laughing now.

They passed several low buildings painted in a dazzling shade of white, their windows closed against the blazing sun and the verandas shaded by overhanging awnings. Here and there, a house slave hurried along, shoulders stooped, and eyes glued to the ground for fear of attracting unnecessary attention, but otherwise the streets were empty, since the sun was riding high in the sky, and this was likely the hottest part of the day.

The quartermaster herded the men into an enclosed courtyard, where at least a dozen men, women, and children huddled in a queue, waiting for their turn on the auction block. Several children cried, but the adults just stared straight ahead, their eyes hollow as they waited to find out their fate. Despite the stink of unwashed bodies coming off the slaves, what Max smelled was the reek of fear and defeat. These people were too broken to fight back, as their demeanor and the scars on some of their backs suggested. There was not a glimmer of hope among them, just a resignation and mute acceptance of their lot in life.

A number of prosperous-looking white men stood before the block, assessing the merchandise with undisguised interest. They were dressed in suits of light fabric and wore wide-brimmed hats to keep out the sun, but were still sweating; their faces red and glistening from the heat. The men talked among themselves, made jokes, and displayed general signs of camaraderie, completely oblivious to the plight of the people in front of them. For them, this was a commonplace occurrence, something that they'd seen and participated in numerous times. They were probably looking forward to a cool drink and a good meal once their business was done and the new slaves were paid for and delivered to the plantations.

Max and his compatriots were ordered to join the queue as the quartermaster joined the gaggle of buyers, his face creased with annoyance. He clearly didn't want to do this, but the captain had given his orders, and he couldn't disobey without facing punishment. Perhaps he was an abolitionist, if there was such a thing in the seventeenth century. Most people of the time saw slavery as part of the natural order, an institution sanctioned by God, and they quoted the Bible to justify the selling and buying of human beings. Max felt as if he were having an out-of-body experience as the queue moved forward. Was it really possible that he was here, at a slave auction, awaiting his turn to be bid on when only a few months ago he had been contemplating a political career in the twenty-first century, and was a man of wealth, position, and rank?

Max watched as one person after another mounted the block and was sold with the minimum of fuss, then taken out of the courtyard to a waiting wagon which would transport them to their new home. He tried to steel his heart as he saw a mother separated from her howling child, but felt an overwhelming pity for the woman as the boy was torn from her embrace. The buyer didn't want the woman, just the boy, who was about eight but already showed signs of physical strength and good health. The boy screamed for his mother as she cried softly, knowing that nothing she said or did would appeal to the hardened hearts of the slave owners. She barely had a moment to say goodbye before the boy was led away and told to shut his mouth if he knew what was good for him.

It was finally Max's turn, and he stepped up on the platform and stood facing the buyers, shoulders back, legs apart, head held high. He wouldn't let these people break him, not on his first day. He was filthy, and smelled like a man who hadn't bathed in months, but he was still Lord Everly, and he had his pride.

The auctioneer waited until the men quieted down before presenting Max.

"Lord Hugo Everly, sent down for high treason and attempted murder. Despite his less than groomed appearance," the auctioneer added with a smirk, "he's in fine health and would make a welcome addition to any plantation. Do I have any offers, gentlemen?"

A few men shrugged, indicating that they had no interest in a disgraced lord. They needed workers, not traitors who might use their leadership abilities to rile their men against them. There had already been two island-wide slave rebellions, and they didn't need a third.

One man stepped forward, his jowly face full of curiosity. He was squat and overweight, his stomach straining against his beige coat, his face flushed from the heat. He pushed up the brim of his hat and studied Max as if he were an animal at the zoo.

"I reckon having a chastened lord among my slaves might give me something of a leg-up, socially," he said quietly but with a sneer to a large, blond man who came up beside him.

The blond man had bushy whiskers, which only served to accentuate his high cheekbones and slanted light eyes, which were openly appraising Max. He looked as strong as a bull and slapped a riding crop against his thigh as he waited for the other man to make a decision.

"The governor takes an interest in men sent down for treason, especially those involved in the Monmouth Rebellion. Perhaps he's under orders to make sure they never return," the fat man speculated, still watching Max. "Having a convicted traitor might give me some leverage," the man mused.

"He looks strong and healthy," the blond man said, encouraging his associate, who opened the bidding.

Another man stepped forward to make a bid, but he was too late.

"Sold," the auctioneer said before he pushed Max off the platform.

Max watched as the quartermaster handed over his indenture contract to the man and accepted the payment. Max briefly wondered who'd get the money, but it didn't really matter.

The auctioneer's eyes briefly rested on Max, and he thought he saw a twinge of pity, but then he looked back toward the platform as John took his place.

"I'll take that one as well," his new master said before tossing a purse of coin to his associate and turning to leave the auction. "Johansson, take them to the plantation. I have some business in town. Tell Dido that I will be back for supper, and I have an appetite for honey-glazed pork tonight," he said and walked away. He moved quite briskly for a man of his size, and Max couldn't help noticing the air of well-being emanating from him. This was a person well pleased with his lot in life, and very much aware of it.

"I'm Erik Johansson, the overseer at the Palms sugar plantation. You are now the property of Master Jessop Greene until such time as you work off your indenture contracts, *ja*?" He laughed at that point, as if the possibility of them regaining their freedom was some great joke. He was trying to intimidate them, Max realized, but John just shrank under the scrutiny, his eyes darting around with anxiety as Johansson stopped in front of the wagon and stared them down. "Forget whatever life you had in England," he said gruffly. "You will work twelve-hour days cutting sugar cane for Master Greene. Any slave or indenture who slacks off will know the sting of my whip on his back and will remember it long after the scars heal. You are here to work and to pay your debt to His Majesty. Now get in the wagon and keep your mouths shut."

Max and John silently climbed into the wagon, only the rattling of their chains audible over their ragged breathing. They stared out over the azure expanse of the sea as the wagon pulled away from the building and drove through the narrow streets of Bridgetown into the hills. The ride lasted several hours—hours of baking in the hot sun without so much as a cup of water or an inch of shade.

John hardly looked around as they finally reached the plantation and passed the two-storied house with wide verandas and a garden ablaze with colorful, tropical flowers. A middle-aged woman, presumably Mistress Greene, stood on the veranda, gazing at them as the wagon passed by. She smiled, but her smile was not one of compassion, but of pride. They were two more slaves whom she now owned; two more men who increased the value of her property and elevated her status in society.

# TWO

## FEBRUARY 1686

**Paris, France**

Huge flakes of snow twirled silently and settled on the flower beds of the forlorn garden, blanketing everything in sight in a soft comforter of white with a hint of lavender. Branches of trees suddenly looked festive as the snow transformed them from bare sticks to whimsical creations against the pale winter sky, which was just purpling with twilight, the darkness beginning to pool in hollows and corners. There wasn't a human being in sight as I gazed out the window at the pristine street below. Soft light could be seen from neighboring homes, but I preferred to sit in the dark, content with the glow of the fire in the hearth. This was my favorite time of day, when real life seemed momentarily suspended between day and night, sun and shadow.

I leaned against the windowpane, its cold glass smooth beneath my forehead. I was always hot these days, my hormones playing havoc with my body. The baby wasn't due for almost another month, but I felt as if I'd been pregnant forever, my body no longer my own, but controlled by the little being, thoughts of whom dominated my every waking hour. I finally left the window and settled in front of the fireplace, feeling somnolent and content. It was so nice to have a home again after living like nomads for months.

The journey from Le Havre to Paris had taken over a week and left me tired and cranky. Traveling by carriage wasn't comfortable on the best of days, but we'd been plagued by rain and flooding, and my advanced pregnancy didn't help, since I needed to stop often to relieve my bladder and stretch my legs, which tended to cramp. Frances and Jem had quickly grown tired of traveling and were bickering and complaining about the rain and the discomfort, which had left Hugo and Archie grinding their teeth with frustration. All in all, I was very happy when we finally got to Paris. Hugo had found us a suitable inn, and once we were all settled and fed, left us to go on some mysterious errand. I was so tired, I was glad to stretch out on the soft bed and get a few hours of sleep, which soothed my aching back and strained nerves. Archie made sure to keep Frances and Jem out of my way per Hugo's instructions.

Hugo had returned a few hours later, tired and wet, but satisfied with the day's work. He had stripped off his sodden garments and climbed into bed next to me, making me squeal as he pressed his cold feet against my warm ones.

"Are you feeling rested, *mon coeur?*" he asked as he placed his hand on my belly in a proprietary manner.

"Are you going native already?" I asked, surprised by the endearment. Hugo spoke fluent French but had never called me "my heart" before.

"I thought I'd try it out. I overheard it today and thought it had a nice ring to it," Hugo confessed as he snuggled closer to me for warmth.

"So, where have you been? You look half-frozen, but strangely pleased with yourself."

"I paid a visit to an old friend from London. I might have

mentioned him—Luke Marsden. We shared a Greek and Latin tutor while living at Court with our fathers."

"Is he not the same friend who took up with Margaret, lured her to London, and then dropped her like a stone when he grew tired of her?" I asked, my voice suspicious. I'd never met Margaret. She'd died a year before I met Hugo, but she had been Jemmy's mother, and I felt angry at the man for behaving as he had. In this day and age, a woman didn't recover easily from such treatment, particularly if she had no family to turn to or income to fall back on. Margaret had eventually returned to Cranley, but only after Hugo had come upon her in the street, prostituting herself to survive. Hugo had brought her back and helped her get back on her feet, but the girl who'd left and the woman who'd returned were not the same person.

"No, that was his cousin, Nicholas Marsden," Hugo clarified. "Luke is here with Sir William Trumbull, the English envoy. I think James II sent Luke to keep Sir William in check, as he's a zealous opponent of Catholicism and seeks to improve the conditions of Protestants in France after the Edict of Fontainebleau."

"Which is?" I asked, not really wanting to know.

"The Edict of Fontainebleau revoked the Edict of Nantes, which granted French Protestants substantial religious freedoms. Louis XIV felt that it was an affront to him, as a Catholic king, to have heretics practicing their religion openly in his country. The Huguenots are being persecuted once again, something that Sir Trumbull vehemently opposes."

"Why does everything always come down to religion?" I asked, annoyed. "Why can no one just let anyone worship as they see fit?" I knew I was being ridiculous but blamed it on pregnancy hormones. This was seventeenth-century Europe, the hotbed of religious intolerance and persecution, not twenty-first-century England, which, incidentally, had its own share of problems. As much as the world had changed, it hadn't changed all that much. In the twenty-first century, religious intolerance was still very much alive in some parts of the world, but slightly more subtle due to the veneer of civilization that cloaked the hatred that still seethed beneath the surface. True, Catholics and Protestants were no longer slaughtering each other en masse, but now the world was fixated on problems in the Middle East, especially since the region seemed to grow more unstable by the day.

Hugo dismissed the question and pulled me closer, nibbling on my ear. "Luke was very glad to see me, although it took him some time to recognize me. I do look a fright," Hugo said with a sigh.

I didn't argue. The handsome nobleman I'd met last year now had dirty-blond hair with two-inch-long black roots, clothes that had seen better days, and boots that were practically worn through. To anyone who didn't know him, he looked like a down-on-his-luck merchant, not a scion of a noble, titled family.

"I trust Luke got over his confusion?"

"Yes, he did, and he's offered to help us. He will call on us tomorrow with his tailor. The first order of business is the state of our wardrobe," Hugo said as he glanced at my one gown, which hung over the chair in all its parts. "We cannot do anything until we are all properly attired. Everyone will be fitted for new clothes tomorrow."

"What about a place to live?" I had asked, voicing my greatest concern. I didn't care as much for new gowns as I wanted a place to call home. We'd been staying at inns since the beginning of September, and I had wanted a place of our own, even if it was tiny and unfashionable. Hugo and I had barely had any privacy since leaving London and had to share our room with Jem and Frances more often than not on the way to Paris. Archie had chosen to stay in communal quarters, where he'd shared a bed with other travelers, but he didn't mind; he wasn't fussy. At this point, a room of my own with a bed made up with clean linens had been my idea of heaven.

"That might take a little longer, but have patience, my sweet. I promise you a home where we can be happy and comfortable."

\* \* \*

Luke Marsden arrived at noon on the following day, as promised, and whatever resentment I might have felt toward his philandering cousin did very little to stop me from liking him. Luke was in his early thirties, with a mane of dark-blond wavy hair, which he chose not to cover with a wig, and dark blue eyes that crinkled with humor and wit. He was tall, lean, and tastefully dressed, something that wasn't easy to accomplish in Louis XIV's France. Most men looked like overly groomed poodles, with lace, bows, high heels, and waist-length curls coifed in outlandish styles.

I was glad to see that he shunned the forced formality of Court and instead acted like an old friend. "Lady Everly, what an utter delight to meet you. I honestly believed that no woman would ever ensnare Hugo again, but I'm glad to have been wrong." He kissed my hand and smiled into my eyes as his lips stretched into a warm smile. "I'm so pleased to see him happy at last, even if he is homeless and dressed like a beggar, but we will see to that. I've brought my tailor, who is setting up in your room even as we speak. Perhaps you will join me for a drink while Hugo is being measured."

"Thank you," I said as I accepted a cup of wine I had no intention of drinking. Now in my last trimester, I couldn't abide any alcohol and drank only milk and tea, when available. Tea was impossible to find in the small towns, but now that we were in Paris, Hugo had been able to buy a pound of tea leaves, which I brewed in our room with hot water procured from the kitchens. "How do you like Paris?" I asked, wondering exactly what his function was.

"It's very French," Luke confided with a wicked grin, "but it has its charms. I act as secretary and confidant to Sir Trumbull—not an easy task, believe me. He's a brilliant politician, but something of a zealot when it comes to questions of religion. He can be quite outspoken on the subject of the Huguenots, which rankles His Majesty James II to no end. One of my many jobs is to rein him in whenever he gets too passionate about his cause. After all, Louis must not get wind of Sir Trumbull's views or our diplomatic mission here will be jeopardized—not something that would be viewed favorably in London."

I was just about to respond when Frances and Jem entered the parlor, having been expelled from our room to await their turn with the tailor. They both appeared bedraggled, but unlike myself, who looked wan and tired after weeks of travel, they looked fresh as daisies, and just as beautiful.

"Master Marsden, allow me to present Frances Morley and Jem, Hugo's page."

Luke Marsden jumped to his feet and bowed to Frances as if she were the Queen of France, his eyes round with admiration. Frances blushed prettily and accepted a chair and a cup of wine which Luke poured for her. His eyes never left her face as he struggled to get himself under control. He was clearly overcome by Frances's loveliness, a condition that afflicted most men when they came face to face with our ward. Unlike the ornamental ladies of the Court, Frances was naturally beautiful, with curling golden hair and eyes the color of a summer sky. Her delicate features and natural shyness brought out people's protective instincts, which always struck me as ironic, considering what she'd suffered at the hands of her husband, who was now thankfully dead. Frances had been so scarred by her marriage, that she refused to use her husband's name and reverted to calling herself Frances Morley, the name she'd been born with.

"Mistress Morley, how wonderful to meet you. Hugo told me that he's now your guardian, but I'm afraid he never mentioned how lovely you are. And Jem, a pleasure to meet you," Luke said, looking intently at the boy who was now standing in front of him. I wasn't sure why he seemed so taken aback, but he studied Jem with open curiosity.

"Master Marsden," Jem replied and fled, eager to get out of the parlor and away from boring adult conversation. He had already charmed the innkeeper's wife, who supplied him with hot buns and cups of chocolate which made him hyper.

I could see questions forming in Luke's mind, mostly those having to do with Jem's relationship to Hugo, but I pretended not to notice and asked him to tell us something of life at the Court of Louis XIV. Frances listened intently, eager for every morsel of information about a life she'd only heard about, but never seen with her own eyes.

"The French Court is vastly different from the English one," Luke explained, his eyes never leaving Frances. "There are the usual intrigues, love affairs, and feuds, but in France, everything is gay, colorful, and utterly glorious. Most courtiers devote their lives to the pursuit of pleasure and go from one glittering dream to another. The fashions are utterly outlandish, and the degree of extravagance is staggering. The Court of James II is much more somber by comparison. He's nothing like his brother, who could have rivaled Louis in his hunger for pleasure. I must admit that it does grow over-whelming after a time, and I long for the quiet pleasures of life in the country. I look forward to returning home," he added wistfully.

"Where is your home?" Frances asked, clearly wanting to know more.

"My family comes from Devon. We have a great big house

near Exmouth. There's a view of the sea that would take your breath away, Mistress Morley. I miss it dreadfully."

"It must be nice to live by the sea," Frances mused.

"It's like nothing else in the world. Once you've lived by the sea, anyplace else feels suffocating, even the Court of a great king."

Frances was about to question Luke further when Hugo finally came down and informed her that it was her turn. Frances departed with a pretty curtsy and Hugo joined us for a drink, glad to be finished with the tedious task of being fitted for a new suit.

"Hugo, I've made some inquiries, and I think I've found something that might be quite perfect for you. An acquaintance of mine has recently lost a large sum at cards and has reluctantly decamped to his family chateau in the Loire Valley to lick his wounds. Considering his dire predicament, he was more than happy to entertain the notion of leasing his Paris residence, complete with all its furnishings and staff. The house is on Rue de Surène, which is not too far from the Jardin des Tuileries and the Louvre Palace," Luke explained, assuming we didn't know Paris very well. "It's a three-story building with five bedchambers, reception rooms on the ground floor, several rooms for servants on the top floor, and a small garden at the back. And the asking price is very reasonable. I think it would be quite suitable. Would you like to see it?"

I glanced at Hugo to see his reaction. A house in the center of Paris was bound to cost more than we could afford, but Hugo seemed eager to see it, so I readily agreed.

"Splendid. We can go as soon as Monsieur Jacques is finished," he suggested, "and then I invite you all to my house for supper. I've asked Cook to prepare some English specialties to remind you of home."

Hugo inclined his head in thanks, his smile full of the things he couldn't say. It was nice to have a friend, especially one as

charming as Luke. In some ways, he reminded me of Bradford
Nash. We wouldn't hear anything from Bradford until the
spring, when the ships started sailing again. Hugo longed for
news of home, particularly of his sister with whom he'd parted
on terrible terms. There was no hope of a reconciliation after
what Jane had done, but Hugo hoped that in time he might at
least be able to see his nephew, Clarence.

# THREE

The décor at 14 Rue de Surène was ostentatious, and the staff not overly friendly, but I was thrilled to have a permanent residence at last. I looked around, smiling. There wasn't a straight line in the place; every surface and piece of furniture was either curved, gilded, or curlicued. Even the polished wooden mantels were scalloped and rounded, avoiding harsh edges. Ancient tapestries and paintings decorated the walls, and the heavy velvet drapes kept out the worst of the drafts. The best part, however, was the cook. Madame Claudette was a wonder in the kitchen, and although she spoke not a word of English, we quickly found the common language of food.

Her old master had suffered from an ulcer, likely brought on by frequent losses at cards, so the fare had been bland and boring. Madame Claudette explained this by holding on to her stomach, grimacing, and bending over in pretend pain. Now that she had people who actually liked to eat, she was in heaven, whipping up succulent dishes every day for our pleasure.

There were also two maids, Marthe and Elodie. Neither spoke any English and harbored an instinctive dislike of foreigners, but they were afraid to lose their positions, so had no choice but to put up with us. I'd actually overheard Marthe, who seemed to be the more outspoken of the two, referring to Archie as *"Diable,"* French for the devil, because of his red hair; it being a sure sign of degeneracy in the eyes of a devout Catholic. I'd been infuriated by their ignorance, but Archie found it to be amusing and shrugged it off the way he did most things that were unimportant. The maids communicated only with Hugo, who spoke French and was a Catholic like them. The rest of us were tolerated with stoic resolve. I didn't care as long as they did their work and kept their opinions to themselves.

"Why are you sitting in the dark?" Hugo asked as he came into the parlor carrying a brace of candles. After two months in France, he looked like his old self again, with dark hair and the well-tailored clothes of a nobleman. He set down the candles and sat down next to me, clearly exasperated. Hugo spent two hours every afternoon tutoring Frances and Jem in reading, writing, and simple mathematics. Jem was only nine, but Frances, who'd turned fifteen in December, was woefully uneducated. Her father never saw any necessity in wasting money on educating a girl, so Frances could read, but had never been taught to write, add, or subtract. By the end of the sessions, Hugo was usually frustrated, and Frances and Jem eager to escape and pursue something more enjoyable, like a game of cards.

While Hugo worked with Frances and Jem, I usually retired to the parlor to do a bit of reading. I found a few books in the library which appealed to me and spent at least an hour reading in French and jotting down words that were unfamiliar to me in order to ask Hugo their meaning later. I'd made a little progress, but the past few weeks, I'd found myself daydreaming more than reading. I simply couldn't put my mind to anything now that the birth of our baby was rapidly approaching.

A reputable physician, Doctor Durant, had come to visit me twice. He was an older gentleman whose manner I found to be reassuring, if not his advice. Of course, he expected me to go into confinement, but that was not something I was prepared to do. To spend a month lying prone in total darkness, with no one for company except a maid who took out the chamber pot and brought my food was out of the question. I would stay indoors, as propriety demanded, but I would not be locked in a room. I even ventured out into the garden on fine days to get a little air and exercise, which scandalized the maids and relegated me to the same satanic status as Archie.

Frances usually came with me, partially for companionship, and partially to make sure that I was all right. She treated me as if I were her mother, and worried about me day and night. I found her devotion endearing, if a trifle misplaced, but I suppose casting me in the role of a parent filled some need in her heart. I worried how she would react once the baby was born, having lost her one-day-old son in October. Frances seemed to be over the worst of her grief, but a new baby might be a reminder of the child she had lost so recently.

Since I couldn't go out, Archie often escorted Frances about town, with Jem tagging along. They needed to get out, and the three of them spent hours exploring Paris together. When they returned, Jem told me of their latest adventure and described everything in detail, and then made off for the kitchen in the hope of getting something to eat. Frances always looked happy, her eyes sparkling and her cheeks rosy from the cold, but Archie was more silent than usual, and eager to escape to his own room. I couldn't quite figure out the relationship between those two, but as long as it was platonic, I felt no need for concern. Hugo, however, wasn't as easily put off. The subject came up when we were in bed, cozy in our curtained world as snow fell outside.

"In time, I'd like to introduce Frances to Paris society," Hugo announced, surprising me. Hugo was slowly expanding his circle of acquaintances, thanks to Luke, but few people were willing to socialize with a man who'd been branded a traitor and believed to be serving out his sentence in the West Indies. To acknowledge Hugo was to expose themselves to scorn and possible censure, and no one wished to be the first to take that risk. Only Luke invited Hugo to card parties and various soirees in the hope that his presence would become a matter of routine. I, of course, couldn't attend due to my advanced pregnancy, but I encouraged him to go. Hugo usually went alone, but now he seemed eager to take Frances.

"Yes, I suppose she'd like a bit of entertainment. It would be nice for her to meet girls her age," I replied.

"It's not girls I want her to meet," Hugo said, smiling at my naiveté. "She needs to be married."

"What?!" I exclaimed. "She's fifteen, and she's already been married to that monster. Hasn't she suffered enough for now?"

"Neve," Hugo replied patiently, "this is not the twenty-first century where Frances can go to university, have a career, and then date for a decade or two while she decides if she's ready to commit to a lifelong partner. This is seventeenth-century France, and the only option for a gentlewoman is marriage. What will Frances do once her beauty fades? Besides, she might want to have another child."

Hugo refrained from mentioning that, at twenty-six, I was practically geriatric, and having a child at my age was considered a great risk. Most girls were married off before eighteen and finished having children by twenty-five. There were some women who still bore children into their thirties, but they'd had multiple children before, so it wasn't seen as being as much of a risk. Frances was young, but in a few years her window of opportunity would begin to shrink.

"Hugo, you said yourself that she might be frightened of men after what Lionel did to her. How can you talk of marrying her off?" I chided him.

"I won't let her marry just anyone," Hugo objected hotly. "I will make sure he's a good man and will be kind to her. She must get back on the horse sometime, and I'd rather she did it after she was safely married," he finished, giving me a glimpse into his thoughts.

"What exactly are you implying with that ludicrous equestrian metaphor?" I asked, amused by Hugo's choice of words.

Hugo's eyebrows shot up in amazement, making me laugh. "What am I implying?" he asked. "Are you blind, woman?" I knew he was referring to Archie, and I had to agree. I wasn't sure that Archie had any romantic feelings for Frances, but I was beginning to suspect that Frances was harboring a secret flame for Archie.

"Don't you trust Archie?" I asked, watching Hugo's reaction.

"With my life, but not with Frances's virtue. He's a man, Neve," he stated, as if that explained everything.

"And have you shared your plan with Frances?" I asked. I couldn't begin to imagine her reaction to the suggestion of marriage.

"Not yet, but I will. I'm waiting for the right time."

"Have you someone in mind?" I inquired, suddenly suspicious. Hugo was up to something; his eyes slid away from mine, confirming my suspicions. He had a candidate.

"Luke is besotted with her," Hugo replied, swiftly moving away before I swatted him.

"Are you insane?" I demanded. "Luke Marsden is at least thirty."

"So what? He's a good man, and he's English. He will take good care of her, emotionally and financially. And, Frances will be able to return to England once Trumbull is recalled. I don't think she'd want to marry a Frenchman and remain here for the duration."

I had to admit that after giving it some thought it didn't seem like such a bad idea. Luke was a handsome man; he had a gentle manner and a good sense of humor, which never hurt in a relationship. Luke had invited Frances for a ride in his carriage on several occasions but had to deal with Hugo as chaperone since I wasn't allowed to show my face in public. Frances had enjoyed the outings, but I hadn't noticed any particular interest in Luke.

"I think Frances would be more receptive if it came from you," Hugo suggested, his eyes twinkling with humor. "She worships you."

"Which is exactly why I don't feel comfortable pushing her into anything. She deserves to be in love, Hugo."

"Who says she can't be in love with Luke?"

"You have it all figured out, don't you? Does she have no say in this? People don't fall in love on demand."

"I think we'd better leave this for another time, my sweet," Hugo said as he drew me to him and kissed me thoroughly. "Nothing needs to be decided today, tomorrow, or next week. It was just a thought."

I couldn't help admiring his tactic. It was just a thought, which he had carefully planted in my head in the hope that I would do the same with Frances.

"Clever clogs," I said and smacked Hugo with a pillow.

"Honor forbids me to retaliate against a pregnant woman, but no one says I can't use other means to bring you to submission."

I let out a squeal as Hugo flipped me onto my back and pinned my wrists to the bed, his expression going from one of laughter to one of desire. A woman in my condition was forbidden from making love, but Hugo knew better, having visited the future. These last few months, my body had grown extra sensitive; every nerve ending zapping with electricity around the clock. My breasts were tender, my nipples growing hard from the slightest touch, and the skin stretched tight across my stomach, but having Hugo inside me never felt as delicious as it did now that extra blood was flowing to my nether regions.

I arched my back as he slid into me, moving slowly and deliberately as I cried out with exquisite pleasure. All thought fled from my mind as I lifted my hips to meet his until I was lost in a maelstrom of sensation.

I opened my eyes to find Hugo smiling down at me.

"You are so beautiful right now," he whispered. "I'm in awe. I wish I could capture that expression on your face and keep it with me forever."

"How do I look?"

"Blissful."

I took his face in my hands and met his gaze. He didn't say it straight out, but I knew he was worried about how the baby's arrival would change us. He feared that I wouldn't want him anymore and give all my love to our child. I suppose his worries were not unfounded, in this time or any time. Relationships changed once babies came along, and no relationship, no matter how close, remained exactly the same after birth. I hoped that I would still feel as I did now, but I could offer no guarantees. I couldn't even guarantee that I would survive the birth, a thought that I pushed to the back of my mind every day as my due date grew nearer.

# FOUR

Hugo blew out the candle and adjusted the coverlet around Neve to keep out the creeping chill of the February night. The fire had burned down, and soon the meager warmth from the glowing ashes would be replaced by the cold air of a slumbering house in winter. Hugo placed his hand on Neve's belly, enjoying the silent communion with his child. When Neve was awake, the baby often slept, but when she finally fell asleep at night, the child seemed to become active and push in all directions, as if it were looking for a way out.

*Soon enough, little one*, Hugo thought as what he assumed to be the head pushed stubbornly against his hand. Or perhaps it was the bottom. Doctor Durant said that babies got into position several weeks before the birth, their head at the entrance of the birth canal in readiness.

Hugo didn't share his worries with Neve, but he'd spent hours on his knees in church, praying for a safe delivery. He kept his fears in check around his wife, but deep down, he was absolutely terrified. Roughly fifty percent of women died in childbirth; sometimes during the actual labor, and many times within a few days of delivery. Countless newborns died with them. Neve had made her decision to go back to the past with him, but he couldn't help blaming himself for taking her away from the miracles of modern medicine that were the norm in the twenty-first century. What he wouldn't give to have Neve give birth in a hospital with a trained staff, an operating theater should anything go wrong, and various drugs to ease the pain.

Hugo dragged his mind away from the impending birth as Neve's stomach suddenly bulged just beneath her ribs, a protrusion the size of a small fist just visible under the skin. *Knee or foot?* Hugo wondered as he gently pushed back. He felt a ripple deep within as the baby shifted position, and Neve's belly went back to normal. How did she sleep through all these acrobatics? He wished he could sleep, but his mind buzzed like a beehive; thoughts, ideas, and worries colliding, multiplying, and morphing into new concerns. Hugo hadn't shared these particular worries with Neve, since despite agreeing to her not going into confinement, he strongly believed that she should feel as serene and untroubled as possible during this delicate time. Sooner or later, he'd have to divulge what was on his mind, but not until after Neve was safely delivered.

Hugo stared at the darkened canopy of the four-poster, trying to make out the fauna and flora so elaborately embroidered on the apple-green damask, which appeared to be a deep gray in the darkness of the room. The matching bed hangings kept out the worst of the drafts, and created a comforting cocoon around his little family, but Hugo's mind was still awhirl. The conversation about Frances was only part of what was on his mind these days, a very small part. He'd naively thought that getting away from England would solve most of their problems, but there were particulars that he hadn't properly taken into consideration, and they had been pointed out to him by Luke shortly after their move into the new house.

Unlike Bradford Nash, who was Hugo's closest friend, and the one person Hugo would trust not only with his own life, but those of his wife and future child, Luke had been more of a partner in crime. They'd had some epic adventures while at Court as teenage boys, and there had been a healthy rivalry between them. Hugo always suspected that Luke had flirted with Margaret simply because he knew that Hugo had residual feelings for her from the time when he was a boy. But it had been Nicholas Marsden, who was several years older than Hugo, who had sweet-talked Margaret into following him to London from Cranley after visiting the Everlys in Surrey, then had ultimately tired of her and cast her aside. And now Hugo was foster father to Margaret's child, whom everyone perceived to be his own. Hugo had noticed Luke watching Jem when he came into the room, seeing the ghost of his mother in the child's face. He'd had a speculative look on his face but said nothing as he waited for Jem to leave so that he could address what he'd come to discuss with Hugo.

"How's your lady, Hugo?" he'd asked, starting from afar. "Is she pleased with her new home?"

"Yes, Neve is settling in very well. Thank you for recommending Doctor Durant; he's due to call tomorrow," Hugo had replied, wondering why Luke had asked to speak with him privately. He'd never before seemed to mind the company of Neve, and especially not that of Frances, who'd left him nearly speechless with admiration.

"I'm very happy that everyone is comfortable and safe," Luke had replied smoothly, accepting a snifter of cognac from Hugo. "I wouldn't like to think that anything was worrying Lady Everly so close to the birth."

"Luke, what are you getting at?" Hugo had asked as he took a seat across from Luke, his right side pleasantly warmed by the roaring fire, but his hands cold in his lap as he anticipated some unpleasant news, which Luke was sure to deliver within the next few minutes. He'd known Luke since the former was twelve, and he was well acquainted with the pained look that

Luke had on his handsome face. He was wearing an elaborate wig, and his face was powdered and rouged, but beneath the mask of the courtier was still the mischievous boy, who'd sworn eternal friendship to his older counterpart.

"Hugo, I hate to be the bearer of bad news, but I feel that I must warn you of certain aspects of your current situation."

"Such as?" Hugo had asked warily. He didn't think this was about money, since Hugo had paid for everything in full. Their financial situation would eventually become strained, since, like most landowners, Hugo's wealth was tied up in property and not readily available in coin, but for now there was enough money to last until the estate manager collected the rents from Hugo's tenants, and Bradford sent a sum drawn on Hugo's account in London. He would do so in the spring, and include news of home, and Jane; something that Hugo almost dreaded.

"Hugo, your situation is somewhat more complex than you might have originally imagined," Luke had begun as he crossed his legs. He always did that when he was not altogether comfortable with the topic. "Being a representative of the Crown, Sir Trumbull cannot openly acknowledge you as being Lord Everly, since he would be challenging the verdict of George Jeffreys and sending a clear message back home that the man convicted of treason was indeed innocent. Such an action might have repercussions, since to ignore the fact that the English envoy is convinced of your identity is to silently acknowledge the injustice of the trial, and *that* the Crown will never do."

"I see. Is that all? I feel there's more," Hugo had said, taking a sip of his cognac to steady his nerves. Judging from Luke's fidgeting, this was only the tip of the iceberg.

"There is, old friend. There's the question of your allegiance and how it might best be addressed. Being a Catholic who worked to undermine the Protestant Rebellion of the Duke of Monmouth, you would, of course, be welcomed by Louis

XIV into his Court. You'd risked your life to preserve the monarchy of James II, which makes you seem devout and courageous in the eyes of a Catholic king. However, should James II's marriage bear no fruit, and a Protestant succession be the result, your re-entry into England might be compromised by the open admission of your part in the rebellion. Should a Protestant king sit on the throne, he will not welcome back a nobleman who openly tried to thwart the efforts of a Protestant hopeful. So, if you are seen as the traitor who supported Monmouth in his efforts to overthrow a Catholic king, you will not be welcomed in the French Court. But, if you openly admit to your true role and religion, you will not be welcomed back should you wish to return home. And, of course, I must act based on whatever you decide. I'm here as a politician first and your friend second. My reputation must not be tarnished by an association with a known traitor."

"A conundrum, indeed," Hugo had replied, his head cocked to the side and his eyes hooded as he considered this impasse. Of course, Luke had no way of knowing that in less than three years, James II would be overthrown in what the English people referred to as the Glorious Revolution, and Protestant William and Mary were going to take the throne of England. Hugo had every intention of returning to England and reclaiming the position he'd been forced from by accusations of treason. He'd have to pay court to a Protestant king, so to openly admit to his Catholicism and part in the rebellion was tantamount to political suicide.

He would have to give this a great deal of consideration before deciding on how to proceed. At this time, he was virtually invisible since he hadn't been introduced into French society or invited to the Court of Louis XIV. He could remain that way, but wasn't sure he'd like to exist on the fringes of society. He'd done that since escaping arrest in May of the previous year, and he didn't at all care for the way it felt.

"I'd like to have a word with you about Frances as well," Luke had said, uncrossing his legs and changing the topic to something much more pleasant, at least to him. "As you know, I lost my wife nearly three years ago," Luke had confided. Hugo had known that Luke was a widower, but wasn't sure what his relationship with his wife had been like. He'd never met her. "Eleanor had been my father's choice, but I'd come to love her," he said, his eyes clouding over with the memory of his dead wife. "I hadn't realized how much until she was taken from me."

"I am very sorry for your loss, Luke. I'm sure she was lovely."

"She was beautiful, inside and out. You probably won't believe me, but I have been completely alone since," Luke had confided, blushing slightly beneath the rouge. "There were a few drunken visits to an exclusive brothel, but I haven't taken a mistress, since I just couldn't bring myself to care for anyone."

"And what bearing does this have on my ward?" Hugo had asked carefully. He knew where this was going, but he needed to hear it from Luke, and be able to judge the degree of his sincerity.

"Frances is..." Luke had grown silent as words failed him. "She's someone I can truly love," he'd finished at last. "I know that she's young, and I would be willing to wait if I knew there was hope of her accepting my suit. I would be devoted to her, Hugo," Luke had said earnestly. "Do you think you might prevail on her to consider me? It would help you to have her future assured as well," he'd continued. "You have enough to contend with without worrying about the future of a young girl. I would provide for her handsomely, and her position would be assured as my wife, both here and in England."

"Luke, I must tell you that Frances has suffered some emotional and physical trauma in the recent past. She is very fragile, and I would never permit anyone I felt to be unsuitable to attempt to court her," Hugo had said, watching Luke. If Luke were seeking a complete innocent, he would instantly renege on his offer, but Luke had looked shattered as he gazed at Hugo.

"I would dedicate myself to making her happy, Hugo. We've known each other for many years, and I think you will agree when I say that I'm not an unkind or an insensitive man. Frances would never have cause to regret becoming my wife, emotionally or physically," he'd added carefully. Luke didn't want to be indelicate, but he wanted Hugo to know that he was a gentle and considerate lover, not some brute who would use her without any regard for her feelings. Hugo did believe him on that score. Luke had been mischievous, but never cruel, not like his cousin who'd seduced women and discarded them without any thought to their future.

"All right, Luke. I will broach the subject with Neve, since she has much more influence with Frances than I do. You have my word that I will not stand in your way should Frances be willing."

"And I will do everything in my power to help you navigate your way through French society and find a happy medium which would pave the way for you here, and, in time, ease your return from exile."

So, Luke could do something to help, but he expected something in return, and that something was Frances. Hugo angrily turned onto his side, aware of his precarious position. He didn't want to use Frances as a pawn in this game of politics and identity, but he needed a way in, and Luke was the only person who could offer him that. He seemed to genuinely like Frances, so at least that was something to ease Hugo's conscience after he'd presented the idea to Neve.

# FIVE

## FEBRUARY 1686

**Barbados, West Indies**

Max squinted at the brutal sun holding court in the cloudless blue sky, grateful that it was only about a half-hour till the midday meal. He was hungry and terribly thirsty; his lips chapped from dehydration. Most days, his mind was numb as he cut the cane, but today his thoughts were in a whirl, probably because of the punishment that was to be administered to one of the slaves at the end of the workday. The overseer, Erik Johansson, prudently administered punishments in the evening, so as not to incapacitate a slave during working hours and diminish productivity. He was a hard man, one who always erred on the side of cruelty. Every transgression was punished, especially if the offender was black.

Johansson was much harder on the Negro slaves than the indentures; partially because he was a racist, and partially because he could get away with it. The plantation owner, Jessop Greene, rarely came this far afield and left all disciplinary action to his overseer. Max had not seen Greene since the day he'd been taken to the plantation, and likely wouldn't until his indenture contract was up; if he lived that long. Very few people survived the seven years, and even fewer had the means to go home. Max couldn't even think that far. He had only one objective—survival.

Whatever discomfort Max had suffered aboard the vessel was nothing compared to the humiliation and injustice he had to deal with at the hands of Erik Johansson. Max worked four-teen-hour days, never got enough to eat or drink, and hadn't had anything resembling a bath in months. There was a water barrel by the barracks, and each man was allowed ten seconds once a week before being forced to move on. Max had become accustomed to his own stink, and the only thing he looked forward to during the course of the day were a few hours of oblivion between supper and breakfast.

Most men managed to forge friendships to sustain them in their hardship, but Max kept himself to himself, wary of getting too close with anyone. The only person he ever spoke to was John, one of the men who'd come over with him and was purchased by Greene on the same day. John was an older man, gruff and taciturn, but he was the type of man who'd come to your aid when you needed it and share his last hunk of bread or cup of ale with a hungry friend. Max had learned to rely on him and even shared something of his story, although he kept back some pertinent details, such as the fact that he was born in the twentieth century and had traveled back in time, only to be arrested for a crime he didn't commit in place of a man who was his ancestor and now archenemy.

John had been sent down for stealing—a story that reminded Max of *Les Misérables*. Years of hard labor for a stolen loaf of bread, or, in this case, a deer that John had poached from his master's land. John had left behind a wife and four daughters, all under the age of fifteen, and there wasn't a night that he didn't pray for them before going to sleep. Max had long since stopped praying. He was godless, angry, and hard. If there had ever been any vulnerability or humor in him, it was long gone, replaced by a feral need to survive.

Night after night, he dreamed of the gentle rains of England and the comfortable life he'd left behind. His inner voice of reason told him that he'd never see that life again, but Max refused to accept defeat. He needed something to keep him going, and this was the only thing that meant anything at this juncture. At thirty-eight, he had no family, no money, no friends, and no freedom. Things were bleak, but not as bleak as they were for the poor boy who would get flogged tonight for going to the privy too many times during the course of the day. The poor kid was obviously ill, but Johansson wanted to prevent him setting an example to others who might decide to claim illness to take a few minutes' break from the backbreaking labor.

Max would rather avoid seeing the boy punished, but everyone was required to attend. If they didn't, they'd get a flogging as well, not something that anyone wanted to risk. Max straightened as he heard the gong summoning them to their meal. Greene was a stingy bastard, but he realized a simple truth: well-fed slaves had more energy and therefore did better work, so he fed them almost adequately, at least during the day. Supper was never plentiful, and as Johansson was fond of reminding them, it was healthier not to sleep on a full stomach. He roared with laughter every time he imparted this bit of wisdom. Max was fairly sure that going to bed on a full stomach never did Johansson any harm. The man was strong as an ox.

Max wiped his glistening forehead with a kerchief, splashed some warm water from a barrel on his face, and hastily washed his hands before being shoved out of the way by the next man. Max took his seat on a long bench next to John and closed his eyes before opening them to Dido, the kitchen slave, who was

doling out a thin stew, followed by a young, frightened girl who
handed out chunks of day-old brown bread. The men mutely
held out their bowls and accepted the bread, tucking in as soon
as they were served.

Dido was about the only thing on the godforsaken plantation that made Max smile. She was about twenty-five, with skin
the color of molasses and light green eyes fringed by ridiculously long lashes. Dido always wore a colorful turban on her
head, but strands of dark hair escaped the tightly wound cloth,
its texture not like the rest of the Negro slaves. *She has to be a
mulatto*, Max thought as he accepted his bowl of food. Most
likely, she'd had a white father and a black mother, and had
been taken away by her mother's owner and sold on. She was
truly beautiful, inside and out, and Max wished that he could
express to her the gratitude he felt for the occasional smile or
kind word that she bestowed on him, but Max didn't dare to
even look at her for more than a second.

Johansson had a fondness for the girl, and would punish
Max for ogling her. Max often wondered if Dido was Johansson's mistress, but couldn't be sure. The overseer had a young,
pretty wife, who looked almost as frightened as the slaves. She
was hardly older than eighteen and seemed to speak only
Dutch. Someone had said that Elsa had been sent to Barbados
to marry Erik Johansson without ever meeting him, and Max
thought that had a ring of truth to it. He might have felt sorry
for the girl had he any energy left to care.

Dido poured a cup of ale for Max and gave him one of her
heart-stopping smiles. "Thank you," he breathed before she
moved on to John, but he knew she'd heard him.

Strangely, there was something about Dido that reminded
Max of Neve. Of course, they were as physically different as
two women could be, but there was a vulnerability and gentle-
ness that brought Neve to mind.

*If only Neve had never found the passage,* he thought for the thousandth time; how different his life would be. He would be back in his own time, preparing his campaign for an upcoming seat in Parliament, enjoying various pursuits, and playing lord of the manor. Instead, he was here, in Barbados, a virtual slave with no avenue of escape, and it was all Neve's fault.

# SIX

Max tried to remain on the fringes of the crowd as the unfortunate boy was tied to a stake in the ground by his hands. He was shaking with fear, his eyes huge and pleading as he tried to swivel around to get a look at Johansson. "Please, sir," he begged. "I was ill. I wasn't trying to get out of working. Please. It won't happen again."

Johansson remained deaf to the boy's pleas, slapping the whip against his thigh as he allowed tension to build among the gathered slaves. The group was huddled together and completely silent, their fear palpable as they tensely waited for Johansson to begin.

Max stared straight ahead but forced his mind to roam free; removing himself from the horrible screams that pierced the air as the overseer began to mete out the punishment. Max heard sharp intakes of breath, his nostrils burning with the acrid smell of the spectator's terror. A woman wept quietly at the back, but otherwise all was quiet.

The whip whistled through the air and made contact with the boy's back with a sickening crack, bits of flesh flying in all directions and rivulets of blood trickling down the boy's back and into his waistband. Max tried not to look, but he felt a gaze on his face that drew his eyes like a magnet. Dido was on the other side of the clearing, her turban rising above the heads of the other women. Her green eyes bore into him with an expression he couldn't quite make out. Her usual soft manner was gone, and there was an intensity in her gaze that sent shivers down his spine. Her eyes were sending him a message, but he couldn't decipher the code. Dido's shoulders were squared, and her mouth pressed into a thin line; she seemed to be challenging him to do something, but he wasn't sure what.

Max's attention strayed from Dido when the boy lost consciousness and hung suspended by his wrists from the pole, his cheek scraping against the wood. The crowd let out a collective gasp, which was quickly silenced by Johansson's snort of disgust. "Take him down," he barked and strode off toward his quarters.

The boy's mother began to wail. Someone put their arms around her and steadied her as the boy was taken down and carried away. Dido hadn't moved, but her posture had relaxed somewhat, and she leaned into a big man who was standing just behind her. He was at least two heads taller, but he had the same mocha skin and green eyes. The man put his hands on Dido's shoulders and leaned down to say something in her ear. She stirred to life and hurried away toward the kitchens. The man met Max's gaze above the heads of the crowd. His expression was hard to read. There was no open challenge, as there had been in Dido's eyes, more an appraisal.

Max had noticed the man several times before, although they never worked in the same area of the field or sat on the same side during meals. The black and the white workers were separated at all times, so very little contact was made. Max had, however, noticed that most Negro slaves seemed to show this man deference, and he carried himself like a leader despite his slave status. Perhaps he was one of their priests. Max had heard

rumors about what went on during the night. The white indentures whispered among themselves of demonic rituals that took
place at midnight, with the Negro slaves communing with the
devil and casting evil spells.

"If they can cast evil spells, why don't they cast one on
Johansson?" Max asked John as they lay side by side in their
sweltering hut that evening. "Surely they can turn him into a
toad or, better yet, have him eaten by a crocodile." Max was
being sarcastic, but John took him at his word, seriously considering such an act.

"Do you really think their black magic can accomplish such
a feat?" he asked. "Maybe they just haven't thought of it yet. I
do know that Johansson seems to be indisposed every time they
have one of their ritual gatherings, so he's never caught them in
the act. Mayhap they put some curse on him." He scratched his
beard, making a rasping noise as nails met skin. "They summon
the devil, I tell you. They dance around the fire and make
incantations until they are not human anymore. They become
his vessels of sin; that's why they are so black."

"Is that so?" Max asked, annoyed by the man's ignorance. If
these people could summon the devil, surely they could do
something to help themselves, rather than be enslaved by the
thousands and brought over from Africa to be abused by their
white masters. "But they go to Sunday service," Max remarked,
more to continue the conversation than because he was really
interested.

"Oh, aye, they do. They've been baptized into the Church
of England, but it's their own gods they worship," John
explained, his voice harsh with emotion. "They worship Vodun
and are guided by the Loa."

"And how do you come to know all this?"

"I hear them talking," John replied vaguely.

"Do they not speak in their own language?" Max asked,
surprised. Most of the black slaves spoke some English, but they

conversed between themselves in whatever dialect they'd spoken in their native land.

"Believe me or not, but that's the truth of it. You can see for yourself if you like. They'll be at it come the full moon, and mark my words, Johansson will be ill that night."

"But they are locked in for the night, how can they perform their rituals?" Max asked, still clinging to practical details and refusing to credit what John was telling him.

John just snorted in the darkness, letting Max know that he was an ignoramus who failed to acknowledge the powers of the devil and the dark magic that summoned him.

Max turned over on his side and pondered this information. He had noticed that Johansson was ill from time to time, and left several of his deputies to oversee the slaves while he retreated to his house to recover. Max just assumed that the man had some kind of recurring gastric trouble, since he tended to turn white and clammy and ran for the privy clutching his stomach, but he hadn't noticed that his bouts of illness corresponded to the cycles of the moon.

Max snorted with disgust. Why was he even thinking about this? What difference did it make? If Johansson managed to shit himself senseless, he would only rejoice, as would the rest of the population of the plantation.

Max rolled back onto his back annoyed with himself for even entertaining such thoughts. Perhaps he was just searching for something to focus on to take his mind off the unbearable and relentless drudgery his life had become. He'd been at the plantation for less than two months, but already he felt his body wasting away as he toiled in the fields with insufficient food and rest, and not enough water. His skin was tanned to a deep brown, and whatever little body fat he'd once had had melted away, leaving him thin as a whippet, his forearms bulging with ropey muscle.

*Perhaps people in the twenty-first century should go work on sugar plantations instead of going to fat farms or gyms to lose weight,* he thought grimly—*results guaranteed.*

Max gritted his teeth as he acknowledged to himself that which he could never say out loud. The veneer of civilization had been stripped from him, slowly robbing him of his humanity, and he didn't much like the person that was left behind.

# SEVEN

## FEBRUARY 14, 1686

**Paris, France**

I stood back and surveyed Frances as she turned this way and that, displaying her new gown. It was made of pale blue damask threaded with silver and worn over a cream-colored underskirt with matching lace frothing at the cuffs and decorating the top of the bodice. Frances had matching blue slippers and silk hose that tied mid-thigh with pale blue ribbons. Her golden curls had been swept up with a few ringlets left loose to artfully frame her face. She was a picture of teenage loveliness as she smiled at me shyly in search of approval.

"You look beautiful, Frances," I gushed, eager to make her happy.

"I've never owned anything so fine."

Hugo made sure that Frances had several gowns suitable for attending social functions, such as the one that was being held tonight at Luke Marsden's residence. Luke had decided to commemorate Valentine's Day with a musical soiree, promising a singer of unparalleled talent to entertain his guests. Hugo had considered refusing the invitation, but I implored him to go, if only for Frances's sake. The girl needed a reason to get dressed up and leave the house and bringing her into Luke's orbit could only be beneficial under the circumstances.

I'd had my reservations at first, but, having had the opportunity to get to know Luke better over the past two months, had to admit that Hugo knew what he was about. Luke seemed like a genuinely decent man, one who would make a good husband and father. Hugo hadn't told him much of what had happened to Frances back in England, but just enough to make him understand that she was fragile and in need of tenderness and understanding. I had a sneaking suspicion that Luke was the type of person who liked to mend broken things, and when the thing in question was a beautiful young girl who craved love and attention, it was a match made in heaven.

Frances blushed furiously as Archie poked his head into the room and froze at the sight of her, his mouth opening in appreciation. Frances averted her eyes, but continued to gaze at Archie from beneath her lashes, making the young man momentarily forget what he'd come for.

"Eh, his lordship requires your presence, my lady," he finally uttered before hastily leaving the room.

I turned to go, but not before I saw a secret smile that lit up Frances's face. She clapped her hands as she twirled once more before the cheval glass and gingerly touched a crescent-shaped patch on her cheekbone. I had never thought patches to be anything other than silly, but I had to admit that the crescent made Frances look charmingly whimsical rather than foolish.

Hugo was already dressed, but not preening quite as much as Frances. He frowned at the mirror as he adjusted his new coat, which was splendid, and gently pulled on the lacy cuffs of his shirt, which intentionally protruded from the turned back sleeves.

"Will you help me?" he asked shyly.

"Have a seat."

Hugo hated this part with a passion, but he couldn't show his face in polite society without first being properly made up. I dusted his face with rice powder until it resembled a pale moon, then touched a sachet filled with rouge to Hugo's lips and cheeks, tinting them just enough to appear rosy. A beauty patch completed the transformation.

I laughed as Hugo scowled at himself in the mirror while I adorned his head with his new periwig, which was longer and curlier than the one he'd had in England.

"I can't bear to look at myself," Hugo spat out and turned from the looking glass. "I shudder to think what people of the future will make of these fashions."

"They will find them utterly ridiculous and effeminate, but you must look like a proper seventeenth-century fop if you expect to enter French society. One more patch?" I asked innocently as he growled at me. "You are very pretty, *mon amour*," I said sweetly and jumped out of the way as Hugo tried to catch me. Jumping was a bit of an overstatement since I was so unwieldy, I could barely shift my bulk, but I eventually let him catch me and give me a kiss. "I've never kissed a man wearing rouge before," I mused as I wiped my lips. "Have a good time. And keep an eye on Frances," I admonished. "Perhaps Luke's intentions are not as honorable as you think."

"Luke Marsden will only lay a finger on Frances if he wishes to be gelded," Hugo replied. He was in a foul mood indeed, so perhaps an outing would do him good. He'd been brooding since we'd moved into the house, a fact he tried to hide from me, but I noticed, nonetheless.

I was sure that Hugo wasn't telling me the whole truth of our situation, but I made a conscious decision to put off all heavy conversations and life-changing decisions until after the birth. Sometimes ignorance *was* bliss, and although I was feeling far from blissful, I was more at peace than I had been in months.

"Are you sure you will be all right on your own?" Hugo asked yet again.

"I will be just fine. Besides, I won't be alone; Archie will be here, and so will the servants."

Hugo rolled his eyes at the mention of the servants, but he knew I would be safe with Archie.

During the long winter evenings, we had discovered that we shared a love of chess, so Archie and I were looking forward to a game with no interruptions, and maybe a couple of snacks pilfered from the kitchen. I found that I got awfully hungry at bedtime, and Archie had a sweet tooth that I liked to tease him about. He was as bad as Jem, who would sell his soul for a sweetie.

I watched through the window as Hugo escorted Frances to the waiting carriage sent around by Luke. The snow of a few days ago had melted, but it was still slushy and wet, so Frances wore wooden pattens over her slippers to keep them from getting wet, and a fur-lined cloak with a trimmed hood. She looked a picture. Hugo handed her into the carriage and looked up at the window, blowing me a kiss before following Frances into the vehicle.

I'd put on a brave face, but, secretly, I would have given anything to attend this musical evening. I was so tired of being cooped up in the house, hidden from view. I hadn't heard music since a few sailors had played some old French songs aboard the ship and danced on deck. What I wouldn't give for an iPod, or even an old-fashioned record player. I longed to hear something besides the howling of the wind or the crackling of the fire. Archie had a lovely baritone, but he wouldn't sing if I asked him. I'd heard him singing once in the stables, and it had been beautiful. He had sung some haunting old folk song about love and loss, but had clammed up as soon as he realized I'd been listening. Archie was not one to appreciate an audience.

There were so many things I missed about the modern

world, especially now that my due date was almost upon me. Had we been back in the twenty-first century, we would be picking out a layette and decorating a nursery. Countless little outfits would fill the dresser drawers, a shiny new pram would be standing in the corridor, and there would be toys, and books on the shelf. I would have weekly appointments to monitor the baby's and my health before delivery, safe in the hands of trained professionals who would do everything in their power to save us should anything go wrong. And I missed food. I had such cravings. I would give anything for some fish and chips, or Indian takeaway.

I tried not to dwell on what could never be, knowing it to be pointless, but there were moments when I felt as if I would burst if I didn't go for a walk, or do something to get out of my own head for a few hours. I drew the curtains and turned from the window, determined to make the most of my evening. I set up the chess set and sat in my favorite armchair by the fire waiting for Archie.

"Can I watch you play?" Jem asked as he sauntered into the parlor and perched on the other chair. "I wish I could go to a musical evening as well," he complained.

"You and me both," I agreed and gave him a smile. "You can watch until it's time for bed. Or, perhaps, you can read a little and make his lordship happy tomorrow when you dazzle him with your newfound knowledge."

"No, I'd rather watch," Jem replied happily. Dazzling Hugo wasn't high on his list of priorities. He jumped up and pulled open the door as Archie carefully maneuvered his way in without upsetting his laden tray. "Ooh, what did you bring?" Jem asked, jumping up and down to see what was on offer.

"Cook has gone for the night and Elodie was feeling generous. She's much easier to deal with when Marthe isn't around," Archie said as he set the tray on a low table. "I have some madeleines, almond biscuits, poached pears, and we'll make mulled wine."

Jem grabbed a madeleine while Archie inserted a poker into the fire. The wine was already spiced with bits of fruit and raisins added to the mixture, but a hot poker would make it warm and melt the honey that had been added to the brew. I thought I might take a cup to lift my sagging spirits.

Archie pulled the poker out of the fire and used it to stir the wine. The iron hissed as it met with the cool liquid, and a lovely smell wafted into the air, suddenly reminding me of Max. He had offered me mulled wine when I'd stayed at Everly Manor for a few days while on assignment for the production company. I had never had it before and thought it to be an old-fashioned drink no longer served in the age of coffee and tea, but had found it to be surprisingly delicious, the spices and honey ensuring the warm wine slid easily down my throat and making me feel pleasantly drowsy and content. I was hoping for the same effect tonight.

Archie laid the poker down and poured me a cup of wine. He handed a cup to Jem and took one for himself. I wasn't sure if the French celebrated Valentine's Day in the seventeenth-century despite the fact that it had been around since Roman times, but I was sure it was celebrated in England, so I raised my cup in a toast. "Happy Valentine's Day, Archie and Jemmy."

"And to you, my lady," they replied in unison.

Jem was already slurping his wine as Archie handed him an almond biscuit, which he dipped in his cup. It still set my teeth on edge to see a child drinking wine, but there wasn't much I could do to stop it. Children drank wine the way modern kids drank juice, so to object would be out of character for a woman of the time. All I could hope to do was limit the damage. I was actually shocked that with all the alcohol women and children consumed, there weren't more raging cases of alcoholism and liver failure. Hugo had assured me that drinking wine and ale was actually safer than drinking water, but my twenty-first-century brain still couldn't accept the rationale and longed for a glass of water when I was thirsty.

"One cup of wine and then it's off to bed with you," I said sternly, knowing that Jem would argue like a trial lawyer to stay up and watch us play chess.

Archie popped a biscuit into his mouth and took a sip of wine, savoring the aroma. The firelight played on his face, setting his hair ablaze and casting shadows that gave him a chiseled look, like a Roman statue. *Oh, Frances*, I thought as I covertly studied him, *you don't stand a chance*. If I were a young girl of fifteen, I'd be blushing too. Of course, Luke wasn't without charms. He didn't have the brute strength or the masculine aura that Archie possessed, but Luke had a pleasant manner and a smile that could light up a room. He could probably charm a woman right out of her clothes and into bed with very little effort.

I set down my cup and took my seat across from Archie. It was time to get my raging hormones under control.

Archie made his usual opening move, and I pretended to think about what to do next when I already had the first half of the game planned out. Archie tended to be predictable, until he'd suddenly do something unexpected and totally demolish my strategy. Jem was peering at the board from his chair, but his eyes were already a little glazed from wine and sleepiness, his face covered with crumbs from the almond biscuits, and his fingers probably sticky to boot.

Archie had just taken my bishop when Jem nearly fell off the chair as he tried to turn over in his sleep. He momentarily woke up, mumbled something, and fell back asleep, his lips stretching into a happy smile as he returned to the world of dreams.

"I'd better take him to his bed," Archie said as his eyes scanned the board, memorizing the position of the pieces. As if I were going to cheat! He scooped Jem up in his arms and carried him from the room, leaving me to contemplate my next move.

I had to admit that I was having difficulty concentrating. I was tired and achy, and despite the calming properties of the wine, I felt cranky and inexplicably annoyed. I had no reason to feel so unsettled, but something was eating away at me. I rose to my feet to stretch my legs when something warm trickled down my thighs and onto the floor beneath me. I stared down at the puddle at my feet just as Archie came back into the room. There was a moment of stunned silence as I frantically wondered if I had peed on myself without realizing it. It took a second for my dazed mind to comprehend that my water had broken.

"I'll go for Doctor Durant, shall I?" Archie said as he approached me. "Let me help you to your room first."

"I'm all right," I stammered. "I can go up by myself. Go get the doctor, please. And hurry."

Archie vanished without another word, and I laboriously trudged up the stairs. I wasn't experiencing any contractions yet, but my body felt unusually sluggish, my reflexes slow. I unlaced my bodice and skirt and took everything off until I was in my shift. It was wet, so I changed and was about to wash my face when a sharp pain sliced through my lower abdomen. It took me so completely by surprise that I just grabbed on to the bed post to steady myself. The pain hadn't felt like what I'd expected a contraction to feel like, so I took a moment to calm myself and went back to my task. First babies took a long time, or so everyone said, so I just had to hold on until the doctor got here.

The second pain came as swiftly as the first, leaving me breathless with its intensity. My belly had suddenly grown hard, and the skin felt so sensitive that even the thin fabric of the shift felt as if it were steel wool.

Suddenly, I was scared. I wished that Sister Angela was

with me as she had been with Frances when her time had come. Her calming manner would be a great help right now, even if she couldn't do much to stop the pain. I just wanted a mother figure to help me through this.

*And what if something is wrong?* I thought. Contractions were supposed to start out with dull pain that was far apart and grow closer and stronger, not come on so unexpectedly. What if this wasn't labor, but an indication that something was amiss? This pain was reminiscent of what I'd felt when I suffered a miscarriage.

I doubled over as a terrible pain tore through me. I was shaking and sweating by the time it was over, though it couldn't have lasted more than thirty seconds. I climbed into bed and grabbed on to a pillow as if it were a life raft.

*Archie, please hurry*, I thought frantically as my body tensed in anticipation of another attack. It came quickly, tearing me from the inside and making me gasp with shock. My hands flew to my belly, and I wrapped my arms around myself as if I could hold back the pain that seemed to reverberate all through me. It seemed to circle my belly and travel up my spine, making my lower back and shoulders stiff with tension.

I curled into a fetal position and wrapped my body around my belly as I waited for the doctor. I hadn't even realized that I was praying. My lips were moving of their own accord, begging God to let everything be all right and to allow both me and my baby to survive.

I nearly screamed with relief when I heard the opening of the front door. Archie was back. I let out a low moan as another pain sliced through me, leaving me breathless. I tried to breathe through the pain, but my breath stilled when I saw Archie's face. He was still wearing his cape which was dusted with fresh snow. His lashes seemed to glitter as the snowflakes melted and turned to water, and his cheeks were ruddy with cold.

"Where's Doctor Durant?" I moaned.

"He's not coming, my lady. He's been taken ill. I asked his housekeeper if she might know of a midwife in the area, but she just scoffed at me and said the good doctor didn't associate with those ignorant creatures."

Archie threw off his cape and came toward me as I let out a low wail of despair.

"Archie, I'm scared," I cried. "It hurts; oh, it really hurts."

"Shall I go fetch his lordship?" Archie asked as I grabbed his hand.

"Don't leave me, please. I don't know what to do."

"Let me get the girls," Archie said as he reclaimed his hand, which was red from my hard grip. "They'll know what to do; they are women after all."

That was not reassuring in the least, but I let him go. Those girls were young and ignorant. What could they possibly know? Perhaps the cook might be of help, but she didn't live at the house. She went home in the evenings to her husband and returned in the morning to prepare our *petit dejeuner*.

I rocked back and forth as another contraction seized me. I was suddenly very warm, my cheeks burning while my forehead was covered in cold sweat. Somewhere, a clock chimed ten o'clock. Hugo wouldn't be home until at least midnight.

Archie came back into the room, his face full of determination.

"Where are the girls?" I whined.

"Marthe is afraid, and Elodie went to the kitchen to prepare some hot water and towels. She'll be up shortly. I don't think she knows much, but she said her sister recently had a baby."

And Archie had recently saddled a horse, but that didn't mean that I knew how to do it by association. Elodie would be useless.

I looked at Archie in surprise as he unbuckled his sword, removed his dagger, and began to roll up his sleeves. He washed his hands in the basin of water and then wet a towel and brought it over to the bed. Archie wiped my brow with the cool towel, then pulled me to my feet and turned me around to face the bed.

"Bend down," he said as he began to massage my back. He stopped for the duration of another contraction, but then went back to work.

"What are you doing?" I asked, shocked.

"I remember my sister's husband saying that it helped when he massaged her back during labor. He said it eased the tension. I don't know what else to do, and I need to do something," he replied as he continued to knead my lower back. I had to admit that it did help somewhat. "Try to relax," he advised, which made me want to kill him.

"Can you relax when you are in acute pain?" I growled as another contraction silenced me.

"I'm sorry, my lady, I'm only trying to help."

"I know you are." I was about to say something else, but I simply couldn't form the words. The pain was so intense that my knees buckled, and I slid to the floor screaming. I barely registered as Elodie came into the room carrying a bucket of hot water and a stack of clean towels. She looked shocked but didn't say anything as she pulled back the bedding and covered the mattress with a layer of towels to keep it from being ruined.

I wanted to keep quiet, but I no longer had any control. The pain subsided for only a short while before coming again and again in relentless waves of torture. I was screaming and rocking back and forth on the floor as Archie tried to get me back onto the bed.

"Come now, you need to lie down. You don't want your baby to fall on the floor," he said soothingly as he finally managed to help me onto the high bed.

I arched my back and spread my legs as the pain dictated. The sweat running down my face stung my eyes, and Elodie tried to dab at it with a damp towel as she bent over me. Her light eyes were round with worry, but she kept smiling reassuringly and prattling in French. I grabbed her hand and held on for dear life until she began to scream with pain.

"I'm sorry," I whispered.

"Here, take mine," Archie offered, and I grabbed onto his hand with all my strength.

I could barely see or hear anything by that point. All my awareness was concentrated on what was happening inside my body, all my senses attuned to my womb. My belly was heaving, and suddenly I let out a primal, low scream. My pelvic bones felt as if they were being pried apart. The pain was so unbearable that I could no longer even speak. I was roaring with agony as I bore down to keep my bones from breaking. Archie's arm was covered in scratches, but he didn't peep as he tried to talk to me.

"It can't be long now. It must be coming." I stared at him in alarm. Was it really possible for the baby to come so quickly? Labor usually lasted for hours, but I couldn't survive hours of this; it was too intense. My back felt as if it would snap from the tension, and the acute pain of the contractions seemed to have morphed into pressure.

I slid my free hand between my legs and felt the hard, smooth curve of the baby's skull. It was just the top of the head, but it was obviously time to push. My body knew what to do, and I pushed as hard as I could. I felt terrible pressure building up in my body as nothing happened. I continued to push, but the head seemed to be firmly lodged in the perineum. I didn't know it was possible to feel such pain. I was being torn apart, eviscerated. I was no longer screaming, but growling, which scared Elodie, who fled the room in tears.

I wasn't even aware of Hugo until his face loomed above me. He was white to the roots of his hair, but it wasn't rice powder; it was shock. He was talking to me, but I couldn't hear him above the roaring in my ears. I was dying; I knew it. I was a throbbing, raging nucleus of unbearable pain. I was completely incoherent as my body heaved with every push. Archie was behind me now, supporting my back, as Hugo pushed my legs apart. His hands were slick with blood as I arched my back and roared, giving this push everything I had.

The baby slithered out of my body into Hugo's waiting hands as I collapsed back against Archie, crying and shaking. The pain had receded somewhat, but my tender tissues were on fire from being stretched so much. I couldn't even move my legs. They were bouncing on the bed from the strain that my body needed to release. I felt as if my spine had been broken in two, and my head ached terribly from the pressure of pushing.

Hugo left the baby between my legs as he reached for Archie's dagger and cut the umbilical cord, severing the child from me. He wrapped the baby in a blanket and held it, unsure of what to do next.

"You must clean its mouth and nose," Frances said forcefully as she swept into the room. She took the baby from Hugo and went about gently cleaning its face with a damp handkerchief. Only a moment ago, I had been relieved to feel less pain, but now my heart was hammering, tears running down my face as I tried to see around Frances.

"It's not crying," I wailed. My voice was raspy from screaming, so my cry came out as a whisper, but I didn't care. "It's not crying. Please make it cry." I was thrashing again, trying to get to my baby.

Frances looked terrified, confirming my worst suspicions. I watched, horrified as she unwrapped the blanket and slapped the baby on the bottom. There was a stunned moment of silence before the baby began to scream in outrage, its face turning purple from crying. Mucus flew from its nostrils and mouth as it screamed, but I didn't care. It was alive, blessedly alive. Frances threw me a look of apology as she wrapped the baby back up and handed it to me. I held it close to me as it calmed down and seemed to settle. A tiny hand escaped from the blanket and pushed against my breast. I was sobbing with relief as I felt the baby's stomach rise and fall as it sucked air into its lungs. The tiny mouth was moving, but the eyes were closed against the light of the candles.

Frances's bodice was covered with bloodstains, but she looked on happily, proud to have been able to help. Hugo's shirt was utterly ruined, and his hands were still covered in blood as he sank onto the bed, just staring at me as his mind finally accepted that it was over, and we were both alive. Archie tactfully removed himself and went to stand by the window where he wasn't in the way.

I suddenly realized that I no longer felt any pain. All I felt was an overwhelming sense of wonder and a fierce love, the kind I'd never experienced in all my life. The tiny baby had been in the world for roughly two minutes, but everything that had been important just fell away and nothing mattered except the tiny being that now snuggled against my breast. I felt an all-encompassing joy, which could only be described as euphoria as I carefully pushed aside the blanket. I had been so terrified that the baby was dead that I hadn't even noticed if it was a boy or a girl. I took a peek and smiled.

"Hello, my funny little valentine," I whispered to her and kissed the warm little head.

"So, that's it then?" Hugo asked with a smile as he drew closer and cupped the baby's head. He looked overcome with love as he beheld his daughter. "Is she to be Valentine?"

We'd discussed several names over the past couple of months, but none of the names we picked seemed to fit now that we were looking at our baby. We'd come up with several good male names, but the female names just didn't appeal to me at all. It was customary to give women traditional names, such as Elizabeth, Anne, or Catherine. Most women named their daughters after whatever queen happened to be on the throne, but I felt no such compulsion, wanting my child to have a name that was even a little unique.

"Yes, I think that's it. Valentine Elise Everly. What do you think?"

"I think I love it," Hugo replied as he reached out and accepted the baby from my arms. Elise had been his mother's name, and although he'd never mentioned it, I thought it was nice to acknowledge the woman who had given him life and died at a young age in childbirth. He held the baby close, studying her little face. "I've never seen a newborn baby before. Are they always this little?"

"You wouldn't call her little if she'd just emerged from your body," I retorted. "I feel as if I just gave birth to a cannonball."

"What happened to Doctor Durant?" Hugo asked Archie as the younger man made to leave the room.

"He's very ill."

"God, of all the days to get ill," Hugo remarked, exasperated. "I'm so sorry you were alone," he said to me.

"I wasn't alone; Archie was with me. He was a great midwife."

"Thank you, Archie," Hugo said emotionally as he clapped Archie on the shoulder.

"It was nothing; just don't expect me to do it again," he replied with a smile. "I might never recover."

# EIGHT

Hugo removed his bloodstained shirt, wadded it into a ball, and threw it into the corner to be rescued by one of the maids tomorrow. Right now, he couldn't think about practicalities. Elodie had finally gone, taking with her a pile of bloodied linens and rags that she'd used to clean up the afterbirth. Neve was asleep in the big bed, her face flushed, and her forehead covered with perspiration. Her hair clung to her face, and there were dark smudges beneath her eyes, but to Hugo she'd never looked as beautiful as she did at that moment. He picked up the candle and walked closer to the bed to make sure she was sleeping peacefully. Hugo touched his hand to her forehead. She was warm, but not too hot, praise God. Frances said that she'd also felt fevered when the milk first began to come in, so this was normal.

Hugo left Neve to sleep and turned to the baby who was lying in a cot they'd found a few weeks ago in one of the attic bedrooms. It was lined with fresh linens, and the little girl who was swaddled tightly in a soft blanket was sleeping soundly. Now that no one was around, Hugo could finally drop the façade of calm and allow himself a moment of pure panic. He'd never expected to find Neve in labor when he came home tonight, and her screams had terrified him as he ran up the stairs and into their bedroom. The baby was a few weeks early, but the fact that Doctor Durant was not in attendance was what had frightened Hugo more. Doctor Durant was the most respected *accoucheur* in Paris, but that meant little if he couldn't attend the birth. Hugo supposed it might have been worse had the doctor managed to attend and brought an infection with him which might have carried off both mother and child. Thank God for Archie and his quick thinking. Hugo had no doubt that had he and Frances not returned home in time, Archie would have managed to deliver the baby in the quiet, competent way he did everything.

Hugo returned to his chair by the fire and rested his head in his hands. He'd heard women in labor but had never been present during a birth. His mind could hardly accept that a human being went through such unspeakable suffering to bring a child into the world. Neve's agony had been indescribable, and he'd momentarily frozen, unable to think of what to do. Thank God for Frances, who seemed to know more than him, having given birth only a few months ago. Hugo had a new respect for the girl when he realized that she'd gone through the same torture only to lose her child in less than a day. How painful it must have been for her to see their baby and know that her Gabriel was lost to her forever, his grave miles away at a secret convent in the woods.

Hugo hadn't realized that he was crying, but hot tears snaked down his cheeks. He wiped them away, angry with himself for being weak, but his heart thumped painfully, reminding him with every thud just how close he'd come to losing both Neve and the baby tonight, just as he had nearly lost them less than six months ago when Neve had been carted off to Newgate Prison. He suddenly felt utterly exhausted and emotionally drained. Was there never going to be a time when everyone was just safe? Even now, anything could still happen. Countless babies died every day, as did their mothers, who developed fevers and infections after the birth. He had to find a physician come morning and make sure that everything was progressing normally.

The baby began to fuss, making noises of discontent, and turning her head from side to side, her mouth opening and closing like a landed fish. Her eyes flew open as Hugo bent over the cot, gazing at her father in the dim light of the bedroom. Hugo carefully scooped up the child, remembering to support the head, and held her against him. Father and daughter stared at each other for a moment before Valentine filled her tiny lungs with air and let out a cry of protest. She kicked her legs and managed to work her arms out of the swaddling, shaking her little fists. Hugo held her tighter, suddenly afraid of dropping the infant. Were they all so feisty within hours of being born?

"Give her to me," Neve called from the bed. "I think she must be hungry."

Hugo eagerly surrendered the writhing, squirming bundle and watched as Neve put the baby to her breast. Valentine instantly quieted and began to suck, her cheeks puffing out like those of a chipmunk. Her eyes were closed in concentration, but she seemed to be content for the moment. Neve grimaced as the baby latched on, but bit back her gasp of pain.

"It hurts?" Hugo asked, surprised. Nursing was so natural, yet Neve seemed to be squirming as well.

"My nipples are tender," she replied, "and she's gumming them very hard. It's painful."

"I'm sorry you suffered so," Hugo said as he brushed back a curl of Neve's golden hair. "I would have gladly taken your pain if I could."

"And I would have gladly given it to you," Neve replied with a chuckle. "I don't know how some women do this again and again. I felt as if I were being torn apart. Don't ever touch me again," she said with mock seriousness. "Well, at least not for a year or so."

"I don't think I'll be able to without remembering what I put you through," Hugo replied.

"How is Frances? Is she all right?" Neve asked as she shifted the baby to the other breast.

"Frances was wonderful, actually. She made quite an impression at Luke's soiree. There wasn't a man there who was immune to her charms. Luke got quite territorial; he hardly left her side."

"And what did Frances think of that?"

"She was gracious, but I think she was glad to leave. She'd never attended this kind of gathering before and felt quite overwhelmed by all the attention."

"I hope you didn't hover over her shoulder the entire evening, scaring away eager young men," Neve said with a raised eyebrow. She knew him too well.

"No, I spent the evening indulging in mindless chatter, false flattery, and vicious gossip. I was on my best behavior," Hugo replied with an impish grin. "But when it's time for Valentine to be introduced into society, I will be armed to the teeth and ready to challenge any man who so much as looks at her."

"Oh, God," Neve moaned, "don't even talk to me about marrying her off. She's two hours old. Let me enjoy her before you start playing the overprotective papa who's plotting an advantageous match."

Hugo just laughed joyfully. He was suddenly unbearably happy. Neve seemed to be feeling much stronger, and the baby was sucking vigorously, ravenous after her ordeal. She seemed robust, which was all he could ask for at this moment.

# NINE

The church clock chimed 2 a.m., but Frances couldn't get to sleep. She pushed aside the bed hangings and threw open the shutters, watching as thick flakes of snow fell from a strangely colorless sky onto the rooftops just visible from her window. The night was eerily quiet, only the chimes of the clock disturbing the deep peace that had settled onto the city as it often did when it snowed.

Tonight had been a surprise on many counts, and Frances had experienced feelings that were foreign to her, having spent most of her young life shut away from society. Normally, she felt sorrow and pain, but never joy.

The gathering at Luke Marsden's house had been a glittering affair with beautifully attired guests, delicious tidbits passed around by liveried servants, and a singer whose sublime voice transported Frances to an unfamiliar emotional plane. She had no idea what the woman was singing about, but her throaty voice had carried Frances off to another place, a place where anything was possible, and a heart could soar to the heavens, freed of its constraints. She hadn't realized that she was crying until Luke had gently wiped her tears away with his handkerchief. He'd reached out and taken her gloved hand, planting a feather-light kiss on the inch of exposed wrist as his eyes caressed hers. Frances smiled at the memory of Hugo's indignant scowl, but he hadn't said a word and allowed Luke to woo her, which was surprising.

Frances supposed that it was natural for Lord Everly to wish her to wed. After all, she wasn't his kin, and he had no obligation to her, past whatever he chose to accept. He wouldn't force her, she was sure of that, but he wanted her future assured. So did she. Of course, marriage was the only way forward for someone like her, but she wouldn't enter into anything without being sure of her intended's character; not after Lionel. Was Hugo steering her toward Luke Marsden? she wondered. His endorsement would mean the world to her, since Hugo Everly was the one man she trusted implicitly: him and Archie.

Frances closed her eyes and pictured Luke's face. He'd been elaborately coifed and attired for his soiree, but no amount of rice powder or rouge could disguise his masculinity. Luke was an impressive man, with eyes that were like bits of melted chocolate, warm and inviting. Beneath his wig, he wore his hair cut short, and it was a dark blond, streaked with gold from time spent outdoors. His touch had been gentle, as if she were a porcelain doll that he was afraid to break. Luke was wealthy and well-connected due to his position. Did he really wish to court her, or were his overtures just the opening act in a game of seduction intended to make her his mistress?

*Lord Everly would never approve of that,* Frances thought. If Luke was paying court to her, it had to be with honorable intentions.

The thought of marrying again made good sense, but the reality of what it entailed made Frances shake with nerves. The memory of Lionel was still fresh, her skin recoiling from any contact that hinted at pain. How could she possibly consent to be any man's wife when she couldn't bear the thought of being touched? What if a man who appeared to be gentle dropped the mask as soon as they were wed and subjected her to the same humiliation and brutality that Lionel had?

Frances had been pondering all these things when they had arrived at home, only to hear the heartrending screams coming from upstairs. She had been galvanized into action, desperate to help Neve, but seeing that sweet baby nearly tore her heart to pieces. She'd wanted to hold it and pretend for just a moment that it was her Gabriel, but instead she had turned away and allowed Neve and Hugo their moment of parental joy.

*They deserve this baby a lot more than I deserved Gabriel,* she thought bitterly. Valentine had been created in love and joy, while Gabriel had been a product of violence and fear, a child of hatred, not meant to thrive. But he had been so beautiful, so innocent, and so vulnerable. Surely there had been some measure of redemption in his birth, which had ended in further heartbreak. No physical pain that Lionel had inflicted on Frances hurt as much as holding her lifeless son in her arms, knowing that he was gone from her forever, and that, in time, she would forget his face and the way he smelled, the weight of him in her arms, and the joy she felt for one fleeting moment in time.

She would like another baby eventually, but getting with child involved bedding, the thought of which made her heart skip a beat with anxiety.

Frances flopped onto her stomach and hugged the pillow. What was it like to feel desire and freely give yourself to a man? She'd noticed the glances exchanged between Hugo and Neve, had seen him kiss her, and her melt into him as he pulled her closer. She trusted him completely, and he accepted her trust and made himself worthy of it. Neve wanted Hugo's baby, and had not felt the soul-crushing resentment that Frances had endured while carrying a child of the man she'd despised. She thought she'd despise the baby as well, but oh, what a surprise he had been. When she got with child again, she wanted it to be with a man she loved and trusted, a man who cherished her the way Hugo cherished Neve.

Of course, there was one man Frances trusted, and that was Archie.

Frances rolled onto her back and threw off the covers, suddenly hot. Archie. He was her friend, her protector, and her guard, as per Hugo's instructions.

An idea began to form in Frances's mind as she considered her future. It was several hours before she was finally able to sleep, but the terrible restlessness had subsided, and by the time her eyes finally closed, there was a secret little smile on her face.

# TEN

## FEBRUARY 1686

**Barbados, West Indies**

The sound of dirt hitting the plain wooden coffin echoed in Max's memory as he mindlessly cut the cane. His back burned with tension, and the cotton shirt he'd been issued was plastered to his back with sweat, but it was still hours until quitting time. They'd started an hour later this morning, having been herded to the low building that served as a chapel. Djimon, the boy who'd been flogged last week, had died the day before and a brief funeral was held, followed by burial in the adjacent grave-yard. Djimon's relations had stood together, hands held, as the coffin was lowered into the ground. Johansson stated that Djimon died of an illness, but everyone knew the truth. He'd died of infection following the flogging. Max thought it might have been sepsis, but he was no doctor. The boy's mother had applied some kind of salve to the wounds, but Lord only knew what it contained. Several women had begun to sing in their native tongue, the tune mournful and eerie in the silence of the morning.

Johansson had ordered them all to work as soon as the first

shovelful of dirt hit the coffin, but the pall had remained as the crowd dispersed. Dido had stood next to the boy's mother, her green eyes narrowed in anger and grief; the color accentuated by the green streaks in her yellow and orange turban. She'd stared at him again, one eyebrow raised in an unspoken challenge. What was it she'd been thinking as her eyes met his? She was a beautiful, proud woman, not meek and frightened like the rest of the female slaves. The one word that Max would use to describe Dido was "defiant." He liked that about her, although her demeanor might be the result of certain knowledge that Johansson would protect her. Rumor had it that she was his creature, but somehow Max doubted that; she didn't seem the type to prostitute herself, at least not willingly. He'd seen Johansson eyeing her speculatively, but it wasn't a look of possession or even desire, more fear, if Max had to put a name to it. Truth be told, there was something about the woman that inspired trepidation, but, unlike most men, Max found that attractive, or at least he would have, had he been free to feel.

Max hadn't felt anything resembling sexual desire since he'd been arrested in Cranley, but when he looked at Dido, he felt faint stirrings of arousal. It felt so odd after all this time that he was almost frightened by the feelings. He preferred to remain numb; that was the only way to survive. He was too exhausted to masturbate, much less actually expend energy on sex, not that it was on offer. He supposed some of the slaves copulated, but there were no white women among the indentures, and the Negro women never interacted with white men.

Max stopped cutting cane for a minute, but remained bent for fear that Johansson would notice that he wasn't working. He would give his right arm for a pint of cold beer right now, or even a cup of iced water, but the best he could hope for was warm water with dead insects swimming in it. His tongue was stuck to the roof of his mouth, and his hands slick with sweat on his machete as he raised his arm and cut a few more stalks. The machete felt heavy in his hand, the blade glinting in the sunlight as it came down.

There were nearly two hundred workers in the field, all wielding sharp weapons. Strange that no one ever thought to use them to regain their freedom. How easy it would be to butcher the few men who were in charge, Max mused, but the problem wasn't overpowering the men. The problem was the next step. Killing Johansson and his minions would be easy enough, but the Negro slaves had nowhere to go and would be recaptured by the authorities as soon as they tried to flee, and the indentures had no means of getting back home to Europe unless they burglarized the plantation house and took care of Greene and his family in the process. Still, even with money enough to buy passage home, they'd be executed if caught, so the risk was not worth it. They were trapped here, and so was he. The only way out was to turn the weapon on himself, but Max pushed the idea out of his mind. He wasn't a coward, nor was he a quitter. He would survive, he swore to himself as he hacked at the cane viciously. He would survive.

# ELEVEN

## Paris

I polished off a plate of eggs, accompanied by fresh bread liberally spread with butter, and a tankard of ale. I'd been starving since giving birth four days ago. It was as if my body had turned on itself, devouring every bit of nutrition I was giving it. The doctor Hugo found assured me that it was normal for a nursing mother to be hungry and advised me to drink ale since it aided the production of milk. He was a very young man, one who considered himself to be on the cutting edge of medicine. I couldn't help smiling at his self-assurance and pomp. He carefully examined me and pronounced me to be recovering from the birth admirably. I held my breath as he bent over Valentine.

"I don't see anything wrong with her," he proclaimed as he handed the baby back to me with a mild look of revulsion. "You must keep her completely isolated until the baptism to avoid evil spirits," he advised Hugo, who stood off to the side now that he was allowed back into the room. "Of course, your wife must lie in for a minimum of thirty days, and then be churched before re-entering society. She's considered unclean until then. I've no doubt you'll see to that, milord. It's regrettable that Doctor Durant could not attend the birth; he's gravely ill, I hear, poor man. I've no doubt it's the result of a curse invoked by one of the witches he'd evicted from assisting during a birth. Your wife and child are that much safer having been delivered from being attended by a midwife. They deal in evil and superstition."

I nearly gagged at that, considering what the young fool had just said, but rearranged my face into an expression of utmost respect.

"These women try to reduce the pain and ease the birth," he went on, "when it is the Lord's will that a woman should suffer in childbirth to atone for the sins of Eve."

"Isn't it true, Doctor, that one in two women die in child-birth?" I asked, wondering if he believed that to be God's will.

"It is, madam, but we still have plenty of women to go around."

My reaction to this statement was to want to grab a hot poker and shove it up the man's pompous ass, but Hugo gave me a warning look. He knew what I was thinking.

"Well, we do appreciate your visit, Doctor," Hugo said as he took the man by the arm and practically shoved him out the room. "We'll be sure to call on you again, should the need arise." Hugo's tone suggested that he would sooner call on a coven of witches to cast out evil spirits, but the doctor preened with pride and gave Hugo an elaborate bow.

"Glad to be of service to you and your lady, milord."

"If you ever let that man near me again, I will divorce you," I said as I put Valentine to my breast. That was the worst threat I could think of to issue to a Catholic man. "Wherever did you find him?"

"He came highly recommended," Hugo replied as he sat

down to watch me nurse. "You will need to be churched, as he said," he added carefully.

"And what exactly does that entail?" I would not submit to some barbaric ritual. I'd read somewhere that in medieval times, the birth canal had been packed with earth as part of a cleansing process after giving birth. I couldn't imagine anything less hygienic or misguided. I had no idea what churching meant but couldn't imagine that times had changed much where the Church was concerned.

"It's nothing invasive, Neve. Being churched refers to going to church after the lying-in to be blessed by a priest before you start accepting sacraments again. We should have Valentine baptized as soon as possible as well," Hugo added.

He tried to sound casual, but I knew exactly what he was thinking, and it sent a chill down my spine, although I under-stood his reasoning. A child who died before being baptized into the Church was denied a proper burial, relegated to either being buried in some remote spot or secretly placed into someone else's coffin. Some women tried to bury their stillborn children and infants by the cemetery wall in an effort to have them lie as close to consecrated ground as possible. The Church's position was cruel and unfair, but it wouldn't change for centuries to come. The thought of losing my little girl was more than I could bear, but Hugo dealt in practicalities; that was his nature.

"May I hold you?" he asked as Valentine finished nursing and fell asleep with a sigh of contentment.

I was surprised by the question but allowed him to take the baby from me and put her in her cot.

"I miss you," Hugo said simply. He pulled off his boots, climbed into bed with me, and pulled me into his arms.

It felt good to be held, but my body recoiled when Hugo bent his head to kiss my breast. I wasn't ready for anything more than a hug. Fifty percent of women died in childbirth, and I had survived. It was a miracle, but one that wouldn't necessarily happen next time. I wanted to be free to love Hugo, but another pregnancy was not in the cards as far as I was concerned, not anytime soon. Hugo was besotted with his daughter, but he still wanted a son. He hadn't said as much, but I knew that was his heart's desire. Only a son would carry on the family name and inherit the title he'd fought so hard not to have to forfeit, and the Catholic Church's views on birth control were clear. I would make my feelings known but wasn't ready to broach the subject just yet.

# TWELVE

A somnolent silence descended upon the house, the only sounds coming from the crackling of wood in the fireplaces, the ticking of a clock in the parlor, and the scurrying of mice in the attic. If one listened carefully, a rhythmic drip-drip could be heard from the melting icicles in the eaves of the house. The past two days had been a little warmer, melting the snow in those out-of-the-way spots that weak winter sunshine hadn't been able to reach, and turning the roads into ribbons of mud. February was the dreariest month; that last stretch of darkness before the promise of spring, which lifted the spirits and dispelled the gloom of the long winter months.

Frances listened intently for any sounds coming from down the hall. Neve had fed Valentine only an hour ago, so everyone should be asleep until the baby woke up howling for another feeding. Frances hadn't realized how often babies needed to be fed. Normally, noblewomen turned over their children to wet-nurses who breastfed the babies without disturbing the mother, but Neve wouldn't hear of it. She wanted to nurse Valentine herself, and barely let the baby out of her sight. It was endearing, if a little unorthodox, but Frances understood only too well.

She'd have kept Gabriel with her also, had he lived, and not wanted to miss a moment with him.

Frances tiptoed down the corridor and up the stairs. Archie's room was on the top floor, next to the servants, who each had a small garret with a dormer window overlooking the rooftops of Paris. There were empty bedrooms down on the second floor, but Archie felt that it wouldn't be appropriate for him to sleep on the same floor as the family. Frances carefully turned the doorknob and entered the monastic room. Archie's clothes were neatly folded and left on a chair; his dagger on the floor by his bed, and his sword—his prized possession—in its scabbard, laid reverently atop the clothes. There were no other personal possessions to speak of. Frances suspected that Archie never made any place a home, for fear of getting too emotionally attached.

Archie was stretched out on his bed, his bright hair fanned across the pillow, and his bare chest silvery in the moonlight.

*Good thing the window isn't shuttered or it would be completely dark,* Frances thought as she advanced into the room slowly so as not to startle Archie out of a deep sleep.

She stood for a minute just drinking him in. Archie really was handsome, in a real-man kind of way. He didn't need curly wigs or rouged lips to be attractive.

Frances sucked in her breath. She could still leave and save herself the humiliation, but she'd made up her mind. She would never accept another man until she knew exactly what it was she was agreeing to.

"Archie," she whispered.

Archie sat bolt upright and stared at her for a moment before realizing that she wasn't a restless spirit wandering the halls. Well, actually she was, but not in the way he might have thought.

"Frances, what's amiss?" he asked urgently, as he took her in and decided there was no need to go for the dagger. "Are you all right?"

"Yes; sorry to wake you, Archie," Frances muttered. She wasn't sure how to broach the subject now that she was here. She'd had a speech carefully prepared, had thought the whole scheme through, but the words had fled, leaving her tongue-tied and embarrassed. Frances shifted from foot to foot and wrapped her arms around herself as she stood mutely over Archie's bed.

"What are you doing in my room?" Archie leaned back against the pillows and surveyed her, a slow smile spreading across his face. "Have you come to seduce me?" he joked, thinking that would put her at ease.

Frances nearly bolted, but mortification rooted her to the spot. She hoped Archie would say something, but he just watched her, his expression blank as he waited for her to state the purpose of her visit. His eyes, which were a cornflower blue, appeared almost black in the shadows of the room, making him look strangely forbidding.

"Archie," she began at last, "I think Lord Everly wishes me to marry."

"That wouldn't be unreasonable, would it?" Archie asked. "What else would you do with your life?"

"No, it's not unreasonable, and I'm not opposed to the idea, but after the last time..." Frances's voice trailed off. There was no need to say any more; Archie was well aware of her history.

"Frances, I know you are frightened, but Lord Everly would never allow you to wed someone he thought would be unkind to you. You can trust him; he has your best interests at heart." Archie patted the space on the bed, inviting Frances to sit. She perched on the edge, wondering how to blurt out what she'd come to ask.

"It's not that, exactly."

"Well, what is it then?"

"I won't agree to marry anyone until I know what to expect," she stammered, "you know, in the bedchamber."

"And what is it that you think I can do to help? And in the middle of the night?" Archie asked carefully, beginning to realize that this nocturnal visit wasn't as innocent as it might seem.

"I want you to show me," Frances blurted out, her cheeks turning crimson. Good thing Archie couldn't see in the darkness.

"Show you?" Archie asked, dumbfounded. "You want me to lie with you?"

"Yes," Frances said simply.

"Are you mad? Lord Everly would castrate me with a dull knife if he found out, and he would be right to do so. You are his ward, not some serving wench. Go back to your room," Archie said with feeling.

"Archie, please, don't send me away. You are the only person I trust, and I know you wouldn't hurt me. I just want to know what it's supposed to feel like when it's not done to inflict pain. No man has ever touched me in love, and I can't agree to a marriage until I know that the person I'm going to marry is capable of loving me like that."

"And how will you know? Do you plan to lie with every man who courts you?" Archie asked, exasperated by Frances's request.

"Of course not, but I'll be able to see how I feel when he touches my hand or kisses me. I'll be able to imagine the rest."

"I can't say that I fully comprehend your logic, but I suppose I can understand your fear. Frances, I'd like to help you, but it wouldn't be right for me to do what you ask. We are not even courting."

"Have you never made love to women you weren't courting?" Frances asked innocently. She knew perfectly well that Archie wasn't the courting type. He liked experienced, willing women, who only wanted a few hours of pleasure and nothing more.

"Frances, turn around and go back to your room. This conversation is over," Archie hissed.

Frances made to leave, but there was one more thing she could do. It was daring, but it might show him what he was missing. Frances pulled at the strings keeping her shift closed, but Archie was quicker than she anticipated. He grabbed the strings, expertly tied them, took her by the shoulders and pushed her out of his room, locking the door firmly behind her.

Frances let out a sob of despair as she pressed herself against the cold wall of the corridor. She had never felt so humiliated. In a way, it was almost worse than being abused by Lionel. She never expected any affection or kindness from him, but she had from Archie.

She sank to the floor and rested her head against her drawn-up knees as hot tears of shame ran down her cheeks. What was wrong with her? Did Archie find her repugnant? Would it be such a hardship to do it once just to put her mind at rest?

Frances was so wrapped up in her own misery that she didn't hear the door open or Archie step into the corridor. He lifted her to her feet and held her until the worst of the crying subsided, patting her on the back as if she were a child. He was warm and solid and smelled, as usual, of horses, leather, and his own musky scent, which Frances found strangely reassuring ever since the night they had spent together in the barn outside Portsmouth. Archie had never laid a finger on her, but he made her feel safe and cared for.

"You silly, silly goose," he murmured as he wiped the tears from her cheeks with his thumbs. "I didn't reject you because I don't find you alluring; I'm only trying to do what's right. Can't you see that?"

Frances raised her tear-stained face to his, her eyes full of incomprehension. He was so perverse sometimes. He behaved as if he cared for her, but he wouldn't take what she was offering so freely. She didn't expect anything in return, didn't he understand that?

"I'm sorry I asked," she mumbled. "Goodnight, Archie. Please, do let us forget this ever happened."

Archie stared down at her. Frances was bathed in a beam of moonlight shining through the dormer window of the corridor, her face a study in lavender and silver, her eyes sparkling like sapphires. Her lips were parted as she gazed up at him, and her cheeks were damp from her tears of humiliation. Archie's mind hollered for him to stop, but his instinct was stronger. He bent down and kissed Frances lightly on the lips. He meant it to be a kiss of tenderness and reassurance, but instead she leaned into him and wrapped her arms around his neck, finally breaking through his hard-won control.

The kiss deepened as Frances tried to respond in a way she thought a woman should. She was more like a blind, helpless kitten than an instrument of seduction, but Archie's heart turned over at her innocence. She'd likely never even been kissed. He hardly realized what he was doing as he slid his tongue inside her mouth and felt her stiffen in his arms. Frances balked for just a moment, then allowed Archie to explore her mouth as his hand came up to cup her breast. She moaned delicately, grinding her hips against his in a gesture of pure instinct rather than intention to seduce.

Archie grabbed Frances by the shoulders and pushed her away, panting. His loose cotton drawers did little to hide his arousal, which Frances's eyes were drawn to. She appeared torn between satisfaction and wariness, no doubt slightly frightened by his reaction to the kiss.

"Go to your room," Archie ordered her gruffly, "and don't ever come to me in the middle of the night again. Ever." He disappeared inside his room and locked the door, leaving Frances baffled.

She touched her lips with trembling fingers, unsure of how to feel about what had just taken place. Archie had said no, but then kissed her more passionately than she would have expected, like Hugo kissed Neve when he thought no one was looking. Perhaps he cared for her after all. He certainly wanted her just a moment ago.

Frances shuffled down the corridor toward the stairs, still bemused. He'd told her to leave him alone, but his body had told her something else entirely. *Why are men so difficult to understand?* she mused.

Frances re-entered her room and climbed into bed, pulling the coverlet to her chin to stave off the cold. Her feet were freezing from wandering the corridors, but there was a warm glow radiating from within. A slow smile spread across her face as she replayed the kiss over and over in her mind, amazed by the feelings it invoked. She felt tenderness, desire, wonder, and fear all at once. How was it possible for one kiss to render her so helpless, yet make her feel so alive? Would it feel like that with everyone, or just with Archie? Frances wondered. She had a lot to learn about the relations between women and men, she decided as she closed her eyes.

# THIRTEEN

After several hours of tossing and turning, Archie finally gave up, pulled on his clothes, and crept from the house. He couldn't stand to be confined a moment longer, and needed a breath of fresh air to clear his head.

The morning was cold, and the mud that had squelched beneath his boots yesterday had frozen into a slippery crust, forcing him to walk more carefully, otherwise he would have half ran toward the river. A barely visible band of peachy-pink was just appearing above the horizon, the sun not far behind as the city began to wake all around him. Several boats appeared on the river, and a coach drove past, likely carrying some fop home after a night of debauchery.

Archie strode along the riverbank, oblivious to the cold breeze coming off the water. The early-morning air was fresh, his breath coming out in white puffs as he hurried along. He had no particular destination, just needed to walk until he burned off the nervous energy that was coursing through his veins.

What had Frances been playing at, coming to his room like that? Did she think he had no honor? Archie wondered angrily, and immediately berated himself. Of course he didn't—he'd done the right thing, and then immediately went back on his word and kissed her. And it wasn't just a kiss of affection, but a kiss of desire, driven by blind need.

Archie angrily kicked a mound of snow, making the bits fly in all directions and giving him some small measure of satisfaction. He was so ashamed of himself. Frances was his to protect, not to lust after. She was just a child, hardly older than Jem. Yes, she was probably more beautiful than any girl he'd even seen, and the trust in her eyes lowered his defenses, but he'd had no right to touch her. She needed him to stay strong and honorable, not burn with a desire he had no right to satisfy.

Archie's nose was red with cold, and his fingers grew stiff since he'd not taken his gloves. Thankfully, his traitorous cock was also reacting to the cold and was now flaccid in his breeches, beaten into submission by the weather and Archie's fury. Frances deserved better than him, no matter how much he cared for her, and he would behave like a gentleman and not do anything—*anything*—to ruin her chance of happiness. He had nothing to offer her, save protection and devotion, not nearly enough. Frances deserved a better life than a mere man-at-arms could give.

Archie stopped walking and stared out over the river, stunned by his thoughts. He'd never considered a future with any woman and was shocked to find that he was talking himself out of loving Frances when he'd never realized he did until this very night.

He turned back, but not before he drove his fist into a stone parapet, nearly breaking his hand in the process. The impact brought him back to his senses, and he took a deep breath and cradled his injured fist in his left hand, sobered by the pain. It had been a moment of weakness, and it wouldn't happen again, he resolved as he marched back home. Not if he could help it.

# FOURTEEN

## MARCH 1686

**Paris, France**

Hugo pressed his signet ring into the blob of wax on the seam of the letter, marking it with his personal seal. There, it was done. He'd thought long and hard about taking this course of action, but there didn't seem to be much choice. When he'd originally planned to take refuge in France, Max had been safely going about his business in the twenty-first century, not wreaking havoc in seventeenth-century London. Now that Max had been tried and sentenced to indentured servitude in the West Indies, everything had changed. Hugo Everly couldn't exist in two places, so his tenuous position in France depended entirely on him proving his identity and being publicly accepted. If he failed to accomplish this feat, he would have virtually no chance of returning to England in 1688 and reclaiming his old life, or a place at the Court of William and Mary. He had to make a move, and it had to be a bold one.

Hugo had considered discussing the situation with Neve but decided not to distress her. She was preoccupied with the baby, and needed no additional worries. Neve was just beginning to realize that unlike in the future, where political issues were hotly discussed and played out in the media, seventeenth-century politics happened mostly behind closed doors between a handful of powerful individuals. In the future, the common person was not as directly affected by what transpired as they were in the present. A change of policy, a death of a monarch, or an unexpected alliance could alter the course of someone's life and instantly turn them from a dutiful citizen into an enemy of the state, a heretic, or an exile. Neve's realization that their position was almost as precarious as it had been in England would do nothing to make her life with him easier. He'd promised to take care of her and their child, and he would, even if it meant selling his soul to the devil. And, there was no guarantee that the devil would even be interested in acquiring his soul, for what he was proposing to offer could only be described as fantastical.

Hugo stowed the letter in his coat pocket and headed downstairs. He was due to chaperone yet another of Frances and Luke's outings. He had better things to do, but there was no one else who could accompany the pair, and ultimately, it served his purpose. Besides, Frances looked pale and forlorn, and it would do her good to get out of the house and enjoy something of the city. Thankfully, the snow had melted and the intoxicating smell of spring was in the air, making the prospect somewhat more pleasant.

Frances liked to get out of the carriage and take a walk by the Seine, where she could watch the boats crisscrossing the river and admire the forbidding outline of Notre Dame. Luke, who'd never been a great advocate of walking, was only too happy to squire Frances around town and dazzle her with his knowledge of architecture and French history, all the while gazing at her as if she were the Holy Mother herself, come to life. It was amusing to see his old friend so utterly bewitched by a mere slip of a girl.

Hugo usually walked discreetly behind the couple, thinking his own thoughts and enjoying the fresh air. He missed the country and the natural order of things that were to be found in nature. Paris was a beautiful city, a worthy counterpart to London, but it would never feel like home, nor make him feel as if he were welcome here. He often dreamed of Everly Manor and the surrounding countryside, his dream-self galloping over the open countryside on Aamir, the wind fragrant with the smell of churned earth and growing things. How he wished they could go home so that Valentine could grow up in a place that was rightfully hers; a home in which generations of Everlys had lived, loved, and schemed, as she would, if he played his cards right.

Of course, thoughts of Cranley invariably reminded Hugo of Jane, and his heart constricted painfully at the memory of his last meeting with his sister. Soon, there would be news from home, but he wasn't sure what he wished to hear. He supposed he hoped that Jane and Clarence were well, but in his heart, his sister was dead to him. He'd never see her again, even if he managed to return to England and pick up the threads of his former life. Perhaps in time he might find it in his heart to forgive her for the evil she'd brought into his life, but for now he allowed himself to remain angry, if no longer vengeful.

Hugo obediently accompanied Frances and Luke to a coffeehouse overlooking the banks of the Seine. Frances beamed like a joyful child as Luke ordered her a flaky pastry filled with rose-petal custard and sprinkled with powdered sugar, which looked like freshly fallen snow. Hugo refused the pastry, but accepted a cup of strong coffee. He'd normally be hungry at this time, but the letter in his pocket was making him feel a bit queasy. He could still change his mind, and he happily would if he could only think of another alternative to his present situation.

Frances delicately licked the sugar from her fingers, leaving Luke staring at her open-mouthed like a smitten youth.

"Would you like another, my sweet?" Luke asked, his eyes glued to Frances's sugar-dusted lips.

"No, thank you, but it was wonderful," Frances breathed. "I'd never eaten anything so sinfully delicious back in England. I do so enjoy these outings, Master Marsden. Perhaps once the spring is truly here, you can take me on a cruise down the river. I would so enjoy that."

If Hugo didn't know better, he'd think that Frances was enjoying her power over Luke. She was playing him like a particularly fine-tuned instrument and making beautiful music. Was it possible for a sheltered, frightened girl to change so much in the space of a few months? Hugo wondered. She seemed more aware somehow, more in control, as if all this was a part of some elaborate plan and not an innocent outing with an admirer.

"I will hire a barge and some players, and we will make a day of it. Perhaps by that time Lady Everly will be able to join us. Wouldn't that be delightful? I know how you enjoy her company."

"Yes, I think Neve would enjoy that very much," Hugo chimed in, thinking of how long it'd been since Neve had had a few hours of pleasure. He suddenly felt like a failure for not being in a position to offer that to her. Perhaps if his plan succeeded, everything would change, and they would be able to finally have the life they were meant to have, not live like disgraced exiles.

Hugo was glad when it was time to go back; he'd had enough of chaperoning and longed to spend a little time with Neve between feedings. He adored the baby, but at times felt left out of the intense mother-child bond that seemed to consume Neve and leave no room for him. It'd been nearly a month since the birth, but Neve hadn't so much as allowed him to kiss her. She seemed frightened almost, as if he would hurt her or force her to do anything she wasn't ready for. Surely she knew that he would never force the issue.

Hugo sighed and climbed into the carriage, suddenly no longer as eager to return home, his mood sour.

Hugo waited until Frances entered the house before speaking with Luke. "I wonder if I might prevail on you to do me a favor," he said as he invited Luke back into the carriage for more privacy. Luke was still smiling happily, so this was probably the best time to ask him.

"Of course. What can I do for you, Hugo?"

Hugo withdrew the letter and passed it to Luke. "Can you please deliver this in person?"

Luke gazed at the name on the letter in some consternation. "Hugo, what possible business do you have with the Marquis de Chartres?" he asked, the smile no longer on his face, Frances forgotten.

"The kind of business I'd like to keep private, old friend," Hugo replied smoothly. He'd known that Luke would be full of questions, but he was the only person who could get close enough to the Marquis de Chartres to deliver the message, so trusting him was a necessary evil.

"I'm sure you know what you are doing, but please be careful, Hugo. De Chartres is one of the most dangerous men in France. His word is enough to make someone disappear without a trace, sometimes into the bowels of the Bastille, but often into the murky waters of the Seine or an unmarked grave."

"Luke, I appreciate your concern, and value your advice; however, there are some things that I would prefer to keep private, if you have no objection," Hugo replied, hoping Luke would desist and simply deliver his letter. He had enough reservations about this course of action without Luke carrying on like a nervous old woman.

"As you wish," Luke replied, tucking the letter away for safekeeping. "I will be at Versailles at the end of the week, and will make sure to deliver the letter in person." He gave Hugo a stiff bow, indicating that the interview was over.

"Thank you, Luke. I appreciate your help and discretion." Hugo alighted from the carriage with a heavy heart, aware that he had until Luke left for Versailles to change his mind, and knowing that he wouldn't.

# FIFTEEN

## MARCH 1686

**Barbados, West Indies**

The merciless sun beat down on the fields of sugar cane, the humidity in the air making the heat that much more unbearable. Nothing stirred, not even the leafy palm trees at the edge of the field, their shaggy heads bent in submission to the impenetrable stillness in the air. Johansson ordered several women to walk around with buckets of water to prevent the workers from getting sunstroke. They ladled out the water carefully, giving each man only a cupful before moving on.

Max straightened laboriously as Dido approached, her ladle already full. He drank greedily, his eyes never leaving her face. She looked calm and cool despite the heat, the gay colors of her turban making her appear festive—a striking contrast to the impassive expression on her face. Their eyes met, and she blessed him with a rare smile, showing even white teeth. Dido might have gotten in trouble, but she dipped her ladle into the bucket and offered Max a second cup of water, instantly elevating herself to divine status in his books.

"Thank you," Max breathed, but Dido had already moved

on to the next man. She slowly made her way down the line, her turban just visible above the tall stalks of uncut cane. Most of the slave women looked fearful, but Dido looked imperious. It was as if the events of each day didn't touch her, but merely swirled around her in a gossamer cloud, leaving her unaffected. Was it strength of character, or was Dido's lot easier than that of the other women? Max wondered. The slave women seemed deferential to her, but perhaps it was just his imagination.

Max bent down to cut the next batch when he saw Johansson running away from the field, his hand on his stomach, and his face blanched to the color of flour. He stopped, doubled over, retched into a bush, and staggered away toward the privy. Max was surprised to see him walk straight into a tree. The man could barely see where he was going, he was so ill. Had he been anyone else, Max might have felt a twinge of pity, but he took grim pleasure in the overseer's misfortune, as did the men around him. No one looked up, but he felt a tremor of satisfaction pass down the line, small smiles hidden beneath the brims of wide hats that made the men look like mushrooms.

"Full moon tonight," John mouthed as he turned to face Max.

And so it was.

Max wiped his perspiring forehead and glanced over to the section of field allocated to the Negro slaves. They all appeared to be working, but a current passed from man to man as their eyes followed Johansson's back. They were up to something.

Max went back to work before he drew unwanted attention, but his mind refused to stay uninvolved. He'd been numb for months, just managing to survive from day to day, but if he were to survive, he had to be aware of what was happening around him. What had these people done to Johansson, and to what end?

By quitting time, Max was trembling with exhaustion and thirst, his arms burning from the strain of cutting cane. He was grateful for the long-sleeved cotton tunic, trousers, and hat that he'd been issued by the overseer, or he would have third-degree burns by now, his light skin unused to the brutal sun, especially without the benefit of sun cream.

Max ate his meal in silence and stumbled back to his hut, desperate to stretch out on his pallet. The hut was hot as hell after a day of baking in the sun, but it was still much cooler than the outdoors. Max fell into a deep sleep, grateful for the oblivion it provided from the soul-crushing reality of his life.

He was nudged awake some hours later. Moonlight streamed through the window, painting the sleeping men in a silvery glow. Some faces were lost in shadow, but some looked grim even in sleep, the lines etched deep, mouths slack with discontent.

John crouched next to Max, his eyes wide open, and his teeth pearly in the dark bush of his beard. "Listen," he whispered.

Max strained to listen, but heard only a rustling of palm leaves moving gently in the breeze that had dispelled the oppressive humidity of the afternoon.

"What am I listening for?" he asked, deeply annoyed at being woken out of a deep sleep.

"They are on the move," John replied.

Max pushed open the door of the hut and looked out. All seemed quiet and peaceful. The tropical night was full of the usual nocturnal sounds: insects chirped, palm trees whispered to each other, and something slithered through the grass a few feet from where Max stood.

Max was just about to go back in when he noticed movement out of the corner of his eye. He peered into the darkness. Several figures disappeared into the jungle, moving so stealthily as to be almost invisible. Max gazed after them in surprise. The slave barracks were locked for the night, unlike the hut of the indentures. He wasn't sure why that was, but he'd seen

Johansson sliding the bar into its brackets at night and shutting the slaves in. How had they gotten out?

*Don't get involved*, Max's mind warned, but he was suddenly wide awake and curious. The bar was clearly visible in the moonlight, still firmly in its place. The building was securely locked, and the windows were not nearly wide enough for a human being to climb through, not even a child.

Max began to walk in the direction the slaves had taken, followed by John, who seemed to be hanging back just in case. All was quiet, but he was sure something was happening.

"Where are you going?" John hissed behind him.

"I want to see what they are about," Max replied without breaking his stride. "Wasn't that why you woke me?"

"Don't be daft. I only woke you to show you that they were up to something. I never meant for you to follow them. They're dangerous; no better than savages. Ever heard of human sacrifice? It's a common enough practice in darkest Africa." John grabbed Max's arm in an effort to prevent him from going into the jungle, but Max was undeterred.

"And what do you know of darkest Africa?" he demanded in a loud whisper, annoyed with the man's ignorance.

"Enough to have the good sense not to put myself in danger. You go on then, but leave me out of it."

John fell back, still clicking his tongue in disapproval behind Max. He was probably bursting with curiosity, but too much of a coward to see what was going on for himself. John had woken Max up for a reason; Max was sure of that. John was a lot more cunning than people gave him credit for. He knew Max well enough by now to know that he would rise to the challenge, and do what John himself would rather not. No matter; he wasn't doing this to assuage John's curiosity, but his own.

As he plunged into the jungle, Max felt more alive than he had since the trial, suddenly keenly aware of his surroundings, and cognizant of the fact that his life might be affected by whatever he saw tonight.

Max must have walked for about a mile, but there was no sign of the slaves. He had no idea how large the plantation actually was since he'd never been allowed to go anywhere but to the fields, but Jessop Greene likely owned all the land hereabouts. The jungle was alive around him, menacing in the darkness. Max tried not to think of all the lethal creatures that could feast on him as he ambled into their sanctuary, but he continued to walk, careful not to step on anything sharp with his bare feet, too determined to stop and turn back now. Could the slaves be escaping? He wondered, but John had implied that something sinister happened at every full moon, so an organized escape was unlikely.

Just as Max thought he'd imagined the whole thing and no one actually left the camp, he noticed a flicker of firelight in the darkness up ahead. He got a little closer and crouched down behind a leafy bush. He had a good view from his vantage point, but was well hidden should anyone become wise to his presence. There was a small clearing in the jungle with a fire burning in the center. Dark shadows surrounded the flames, but light flickered over their faces and Max recognized a few of the slaves. What shocked him was their demeanor. Gone was the subservience and fear they displayed in front of Johansson, replaced by fervor and purpose. The same men who cowered in front of the overseer now stood tall, their shoulders back, and their heads held high. Their eyes were no longer downcast, but staring into the flames, their expressions exultant and full of expectation. There were women too. They appeared relaxed and unafraid, their lips stretched into mysterious half-smiles that held a world of meaning as they took their places in the circle.

The slaves seemed to be preparing for some sort of ceremony. They began stomping their feet, clapping, and chanting softly, their voices rising in unison. Both Dido and the man she resembled were inside the circle, close to the flames. The man— Max thought he was a priest—had a rattle in his hands and was intoning a chant, while Dido appeared to be in a trance, her eyes open and staring at everything and nothing. The chanting got louder and more frenzied, and Max watched in astonishment as Dido's body suddenly went rigid as a wooden plank, then began to convulse as she uttered something in her own language. He had no idea what she was saying, but the voice that came out of the woman sounded like one of those recordings people played backward to hear the voice of Satan. She was writhing like a snake, waving her arms above her head and bellowing something, which set the rest of the slaves into spasms of frenzied excitement.

Dido eventually exhausted herself and collapsed onto the ground, where she remained for a tense moment before coming back to her senses. She sat up and looked around, her face full of confusion until she felt the adulation of her people and smiled serenely. Max thought the ritual to be over, but the man in the center looked around the group, said something that seemed to rouse them from their trance, and held up a chicken. The chicken was clucking and squirming desperately, instinctively aware that it wasn't getting away alive. The man held it by its neck and threw some herbs into the outer rim of the fire. A pungent, medicinal odor rose from the flames as the priest thrust the chicken's head into the rising smoke. The chicken struggled for a few more moments but eventually grew quiet, as if it were drugged. Its body went limp, but its eyes were still swiveling in their sockets, the bird clearly alive. The priest held up the chicken, then withdrew a long blade and cut its neck, allowing the blood to drip into the fire. The blood made a hissing sound as it met with flame, and the priest intoned a prayer or blessing before tossing the chicken into the fire. Max smelled singed feathers before the odor of roasting meat filled the clearing.

The slaves seemed to be spent, their shoulders slumped and faces relaxed into an expression of contentment. Whatever this was had to be coming to an end, and it was time for Max to make himself scarce. He returned the way he had come, pondering what he had seen. Of course, it had been voodoo, and the chicken had been a blood sacrifice. What it was meant to achieve, he had no idea, but he was certain that Johansson's illness wasn't random. Had they cursed him in some way, or was there a simpler explanation for his gastric attacks, which according to John happened about once a month?

Max returned to the hut undetected, lowered himself to his pallet, and closed his eyes. Suddenly, he felt a poignant wave of envy toward the slaves. They were in captivity, at the mercy of their masters, and without any control over their lives, but at least they had each other. They had the sense of belonging and family, as well as their religion for comfort. Max had felt a sense of belonging when he'd been at school, but he'd never had a close family or any connection to the religion he'd been brought up in. He'd gone through the motions, just like his parents, showing his face at St. Nicolas's Church on holidays, and for funerals and weddings. He'd never felt the slightest connection to God or the teachings of the Bible, and now he was completely alone, a man without anything to tether him to this world, save his desire to stay alive.

Max wiped away a bitter tear as it slid down his stubbly cheek. He longed to go back to feeling numb, but he couldn't find a way to return to that mindless state of being. He was feeling so much yearning, loneliness, hopelessness, and regret, but most of all, he felt a desire for revenge against the only person he could think to blame—Hugo Bloody Everly.

# SIXTEEN

## MARCH 1686

**Paris, France**

The summons to see the Marquis de Chartres came two weeks later, after Hugo had nearly given up on the idea of getting close enough to the man to present his case. Hugo had gone fishing when he'd written to de Chartres, but caught nothing, or so he'd thought. He would have requested an audience with the king but would, without question, be denied. Louis XIV was a man who was careful of his reputation and fond of compliments and adulation. He was a fine statesman, and a monarch who would never knowingly put himself in a situation that might be misinterpreted by others. To meet with a man who'd been accused of plotting against a fellow Catholic monarch would be seen as an act of betrayal, and Louis would find it wise to distance himself from anything that might tarnish his glowing image.

The Marquis de Chartres, however, was not as high-handed as his master. He was Louis's spymaster, and at times, judge, jury, and executioner. He met with members of the lowest orders of society, and believed that he couldn't carry out his job properly without getting his hands not only dirty, but absolutely filthy. He was a man who despised the phony patina of respectability and believed that people, women included, would be truer to themselves if they embraced their baser urges more openly and stopped suppressing that which came naturally, such as greed, lust, and ruthless ambition.

Few people knew of de Chartres's true purpose since he operated in the shadows, appearing the idle and consummate courtier in public, but Hugo had been privy to his real occupation through his own association with the Duke of Monmouth, who feared de Chartres's influence on Louis XIV, and therefore, France's possible involvement should Monmouth's rebellion succeed and oust a Catholic monarch. Monmouth was long dead, but his concerns about de Chartres were fresh in Hugo's mind since he needed to use what he knew of the man to further his own cause.

The note from de Chartres was delivered by a young man who wasn't wearing any kind of livery or insignia. He looked like a pickpocket, not the representative of a man who ran countless spies in every country of Europe and beyond, or perhaps he looked precisely just as the representative of such a man should. He was inconspicuous, easily lost in a crowd, and completely forgettable; in other words, the perfect choice of messenger. Hugo was to accompany him to an unspecified location the following day. He was to come alone and unarmed.

The man came to collect Hugo close to 5 p.m., patted him down to make sure he wasn't carrying any concealed weapons, and wordlessly led him in the general direction of Louvre Palace. Hugo expected to meet with de Chartres at the palace, but his messenger made several turns and continued walking for a good half-hour before leading Hugo into a street he'd never visited before. The houses here weren't as grand as those closer to the palace, and the general atmosphere was one of genteel shabbiness. Grubby children played in the street, and harried women rushed past in an effort to get home in time to cook their family's supper. They passed several taverns which were doing a brisk business, catering to men who were on their way home from work and had stopped off at their local establishment to have a drink.

The messenger didn't bother to make any small talk or learn anything that might be helpful to his master as he led Hugo to a tavern in an alley that branched off the wider street they'd been following for some time. The tavern was small and cozy, a welcoming glow from the fire and numerous candles lighting the taproom, which was already filled with patrons who were drinking and talking loudly. A few men smelled of the river and held their tankards in calloused hands, giving away their occupation as ferrymen or fishermen. A few others were covered in fine dust, likely masons or builders. There was not a gentleman in sight, and no courtier would be found here unless he wished to have his pocket picked or his throat slit, after he drunkenly made his exit into the night and found himself in a neighborhood filled with pickpockets and thieves.

Appetizing smells drifted from the back, the aroma of roasted duck prevalent among the smell of vegetables, freshly baked bread, and something sweet that reminded Hugo of the smell of stewed blackcurrant.

The messenger motioned him toward the staircase, but didn't follow as Hugo ascended the dimly lit steps. A door to a private room was slightly ajar, so Hugo poked his head in to make sure he was in the right place. The Marquis de Chartres sat at a table, a flagon of wine before him and a merry fire burning in the grate. The windows were shuttered against the slowly settling dusk of the March evening, and a leather-bound book lay open but seemingly forgotten next to the wine.

"Ah, do come in, Monsieur Everly," de Chartres invited, purposely not using Hugo's title. He was making a point, which wasn't lost on Hugo. "Please, join me in some wine. This is my favorite vintage, a Pinot Noir from a vintner in Burgundy. The man is an absolute imbecile, but his wine is beyond compare, so I forgive him his idiocy."

Hugo accepted a cup and took a sip. The wine was good, but nothing special. Perhaps de Chartres was testing him. Hugo gave a nod of appreciation and set down his cup.

He'd met de Chartres once many years ago at the Court of Charles II, but time had taken its toll. The man had to be in his fifties now, but he looked more like a man who was at least a decade older. His shoulders were stooped, and his skin waxy above the unrelieved black of his suit. His graying beard was pointy and sparse, his eyebrows bushy above shifty dark eyes, which probably missed nothing. He was much thinner than the last time they'd met, almost cadaverous, but Hugo was certain that de Chartres was one of those men who wouldn't die until he decided to do so. Death had nothing on men like him.

"Thank you for seeing me," he said by way of opening. The rest was really up to de Chartres.

"I must admit that I was intrigued by your letter. You implied much, but divulged little," de Chartres said. His eyes never left Hugo's face, which was to be expected. He was searching for any sign of weakness he might exploit, but Hugo was giving nothing away, not yet, not until the time was right.

"I'm well aware of the folly of setting incriminating information on paper," Hugo replied smoothly. He wasn't in the best situation, but hopefully did not belong to the same category as the imbecile winemaker.

"Of course, you would be, or we'd know more about your activities. How may I be of service to you, and why do you assume I'd be willing to render assistance?" de Chartres asked as he took a sip of wine.

Straight to the point, as expected. Hugo had no choice but to tell de Chartres the truth, or a version of the truth he'd edited in his mind to gain the man's interest, but not allow too deep of a glimpse inside his soul. Hugo spoke of his faith, his commitment to His Majesty James II, and the unexpected arrest of Max Everly, which led to his present difficulty. Marquis de Chartres had to understand exactly where Hugo stood, and why.

The older man nodded as he listened but didn't interrupt until Hugo had finished his narrative. Hugo had made the opening move; now it was time for de Chartres to make his.

"I understand what you desire from me, *monsieur*, but I'm not certain that I comprehend what it is you're willing to offer in return. I'm sure you're intelligent enough to understand that anything that happens here will be a business transaction, not an act of kindness or a granting of a favor. I have no reason to help you whatsoever."

"Nor should you, but you are a man whose currency is information, and I have information which might come as a surprise to someone even as well informed as yourself," Hugo countered, inwardly taking a deep breath. Once he shared what he knew with de Chartres, there'd be no going back.

"Do go on," de Chartres replied. "Despite your reasons and oaths to the contrary, you committed treason against your sovereign; a transgression that will not be easily overlooked by a Catholic king, and a cousin of the man you plotted against. I would need to present something quite extraordinary to His Majesty for him to consider inviting you to his Court."

"I have it on good authority that James II will not sit on the throne of England for much longer. Once he has a son, which he will, a Catholic succession will be assured. The Protestant bishops will invite William, the Prince of Orange, to depose James and take the throne, restoring a Protestant monarchy once and for all."

Hugo paused for a moment to see whether he had de Chartres's undivided attention. The older man was regarding him with those shrewd eyes, no doubt testing Hugo's theory for flaws. Of course, Hugo could hardly tell him that James would have a son in two years and that William would take the throne in November of 1688, but it was within the realm of possibility, so couldn't be discounted. De Chartres had taken the bait.

"Now, considering the bitter hatred William of Orange bears toward your sovereign," Hugo continued, "who invaded his homeland only three years ago and murdered countless Protestants, I would think that any foothold Louis could find in the Court of William would be worth seizing."

"And what, in your estimation, will happen to James?" de Chartres asked, his face impassive.

"James II will eventually flee to France and seek assistance from your king, who will grant it. He will not, however, assist James in any attempt to recapture the throne. Once James is deposed, the face of European politics will change once again, and Louis XIV will no longer have a fellow Catholic on the throne of England—a development which will have important consequences for France."

De Chartres listened carefully, then gave Hugo a wolfish smile. "Sir, unless you are a warlock and can see into the future, your charming little fable is nothing more than conjecture. It's utterly worthless."

"Is it?" Hugo replied, undaunted. "I have no doubt that your spies in England are keeping you well abreast of the undercurrents and discontent of the Protestant population. Is my little fable really so far-fetched? You might dispute the validity of my information, but there will be a son, and what will follow is not so difficult to imagine."

"How do you know this?" de Chartres asked carefully.

"I know a woman who has the Sight. She's proved herself to be infallible."

"And who is this woman, *monsieur*?" de Chartres asked, his eyes lighting up with an unholy fire.

"Alas, I cannot reveal her identity," Hugo replied, meeting the marquis's gaze head-on.

"Because you fear that I will have the Church examine her for signs of witchcraft?"

"Exactly so," Hugo said. "She's a gifted Seer who has not made a covenant with the Devil. She's a pious Christian who keeps her great gift a secret for fear of persecution."

"Hmm, it would seem that your great Seer might have warned you of the outcome of Monmouth's rebellion," de Chartres said, his eyes twinkling with humor.

"She had. She told me exactly what would happen and when, which is precisely how I was able to avoid capture and execution. I'm the only known associate of the Duke of Monmouth who hasn't been arrested," Hugo countered.

"There are some who'd disagree. Lord Hugo Everly has been sent down to the West Indies as an indentured servant, or so I hear," de Chartres taunted him. "I wonder how long he'll last before being sent back to England in a pine box. Or perhaps they'll just bury him with all the other dead slaves, leaving him exiled from his homeland for all eternity."

"If you truly believed that to be the case I wouldn't be sitting here," Hugo replied. "You know full well that I am the real Hugo Everly and not the man who's serving an unjust sentence for a crime he didn't commit."

"Yes, you are correct; I remember you, although you were hardly more than a boy when we first met," the marquis mused. "I will share something with you if I may. I would dismiss your predictions as the ravings of a madman, but I have heard corresponding reports coming out of England. Of course, my sources are not trying to dazzle me with the visions of a Seer, but the unrest you speak of is real, so it's not too difficult to imagine that what you are predicting might actually take place. However, your information is not enough to buy you recognition from His Majesty," de Chartres said carefully, watching Hugo like a cat about to devour the canary it had been toying with.

Hugo wasn't surprised; he'd been expecting this and had

made his decision long before he wrote the letter. The information about the Glorious Revolution was just a juicy tidbit, nothing more. It wouldn't get him what he wanted, but what de Chartres was about to ask of him would.

"Once you return to England and present yourself at the Court of the new Protestant monarch, you will be welcomed as a hero, a man who'd risked his life to put a Protestant back on the throne, but I'm sure you know that already. You will be in an enviable position, milord, a position which might even make it possible for you to be invited to sit on the Privy Council—an invitation I'm sure you'd happily accept. Were you an agent of France, you would be a most valuable commodity to His Majesty; an asset he would be willing to support and entertain at Court."

"You want me to be your spy," Hugo stated unnecessarily, still astounded by the harsh sound of the word despite knowing exactly what would be offered when he came to see de Chartres.

"Of course—as you well knew when you wrote to me. Do you accept, Lord Everly?" he asked, pronouncing the title with emphasis.

"I think an agent of the French Crown might need monetary compensation to finance his entrance into society in a manner befitting a nobleman," Hugo countered. He was going to lose this chess game, but he wanted to make sure he took down as many pieces as he could before surrendering his king. It wasn't about who won or lost, it was how you played the game, and ultimately, Hugo had no intention of pledging his loyalty to Louis of France. His acquiescence was nothing more than a misdirection, but one de Chartres couldn't be aware of until the right time.

"I believe a stipend could be arranged to promote your smooth entrance into His Majesty's orbit."

"A generous stipend," Hugo replied, taking a sip of his wine and leaning back in his chair.

"Generous enough to quiet any misgivings you might have about redirecting your allegiance to someone who will actually appreciate it."

Hugo rose to his feet and bowed to the Marquis de Chartres, eager to take his leave.

"You will be hearing from me shortly, milord," de Chartres said in parting as he poured himself more wine. "*Au revoir*."

Hugo let himself out of the room and descended the stairs. The dining room was nearly full, patrons enjoying the roast duck and the wine that flowed freely as conversation buzzed all around him. The noise and the overpowering smell of unwashed bodies and overcooked duck made Hugo long for the cool air of the spring evening. He pushed his way through the throng and left the tavern, walking toward the Siene, where he strolled along the riverbank, oblivious to the stiff breeze that blew off the water and the breathtaking palette of color that was the sky at sunset. He needed time to think before he returned home.

The meeting had gone much as he had planned, with de Chartres pledging to Hugo what he needed now in exchange for what Louis would need later, but although Hugo knew the truth of his own intentions, he felt a hollowness deep inside, filling the space where his honor once resided. He might remain true to himself, but there would be those who'd see him as a traitor once again, and try to exploit his vulnerable position when he returned home. He had a few years to plan his strategy, but there would come a time when he'd be walking a fine line between patriotism and treason, and this time, Neve would not be able to save him from destruction, since she would have no prior knowledge. What he'd initiated hadn't happened yet, so there would be no warning and no escape.

# SEVENTEEN

## MARCH 1686

**Barbados, West Indies**

Erik Johansson seemed to recover from his bout of indisposition after a few days, but Max was now less inclined to ridicule John's assertion that the Negro slaves had done something to get him out of the way at the full moon. Perhaps they weren't as downtrodden and helpless as Max first took them to be. He had to admit that he had a new respect for the people who lived in such close proximity to him. He'd just dismissed them as being victims of circumstance but was glad to see that they had a few tricks up their sleeve. However, Max had grown wary of Dido. Before, he'd just thought of her as a beautiful woman who'd been dealt a terrible hand by fate, but now he wasn't so sure. Seeing her as she had been at the ceremony by the fire, he wondered what exactly she'd been up to, and if her channeling of whatever spirit she claimed to was in any way helpful to her situation. She certainly held a position of respect among the other slaves, as did the priest who'd offered the blood sacrifice.

Max put the whole incident from his mind after a few days, the routine of plantation life taking over once again. He was so worn out from the heat and the backbreaking work that it took all his determination just to eat supper and drag himself back to his hut in the evening. His life seemed to be one never-ending workday, interrupted by naps. Anything that had been important to him before had been eradicated from his mind, replaced by a need to survive. Having lived a life of privilege, Max sometimes marveled at the way all the trivialities of a modern life could be stripped away in a matter of weeks, leaving in their place a human being who was but one evolutionary step above an animal. Gone were the vanity, ambition, and greed. In their place were just the basic needs: food, water, shelter, and physical health.

What Max lacked utterly was hope. Hope was an integral part of survival, but whatever hope he'd felt while still awaiting trial back in England was long gone, replaced by bitterness and fatalism. Max went through the motions, but in his heart, he no longer believed that he could ever regain that which had been lost.

It was in the late afternoon several days after Max had witnessed the voodoo ceremony that the clouds began to gather, mercifully blocking the blazing sun and bringing with them a sudden wind that rippled through the sea of sugar cane and promised a welcome coolness. Fat drops of rain began to plop onto the parched ground, soaking the field in minutes. Max took off his hat and turned his face up to the sky, enjoying the downpour. The rain felt wonderful on his face and body, washing away months of sweat and dust.

The slaves looked around with some uncertainty, but Johansson yelled at them to keep working, as he took shelter from the storm in the hut at the edge of the field where he and his minions whiled away the afternoons, drinking, playing dice, and keeping an eye on the laboring slaves.

It wasn't long until the wind escalated from a strong breeze to a howling, raging force of nature, and the rain lashed against the ground, coming down almost horizontally and creating rivulets of water that pooled in the hollows and ran down any elevation in the otherwise flat ground. Rainwater streamed into the workers' eyes and made the stalks slick and hard to cut. Johansson eventually acknowledged the futility of making the laborers remain in the field and allowed everyone to return to their huts, locking in the slaves until supper.

As Max watched him slide the heavy bar into place, he finally understood why Johansson locked up the Negroes and not the whites. He wasn't as obtuse as he appeared to be and had some experience of island life. A runaway black slave would simply melt into the jungle and never be found once he lost himself among the native population of the island. A white man, however, wouldn't survive long before being either captured by a search party or perishing of whatever got to him first. He'd have no money to pay for passage back to England, nor would he be inconspicuous enough to avoid notice for long. Few whites bothered to escape.

John called to Max to come inside, but Max pulled off his wet shirt and stood in the yard, enjoying the drenching rain. He'd have loved some soap to wash with, but this was the closest he'd had to a shower in months. He washed his hair and then pulled off his loose trousers and washed them together with his shirt in a barrel of rainwater. What he wouldn't have given for a razor. He hated his beard; it was scratchy and probably crawling with lice, but the slaves weren't given shaving implements which could become weapons in their hands. Max managed to keep the length in check by simply slashing away a few inches at a time with his cane-cutting machete on the way to the field.

The storm picked up, and Max briefly wondered if they might be in the middle of a hurricane, but had no way of knowing.

None of Johansson's men were around, having gone back to their own lodgings to wait out the storm. Bits of dried palm leaves blew off the roofs of the huts, leaving unprotected spaces where the rain got in and dripped onto the heads of the men inside, but although awesome to behold, the storm wasn't wreaking too much destruction. Some repairs would be required, but nothing that couldn't be done in one morning. By tomorrow afternoon, there would be no trace left of the fury tearing through the jungle at that moment.

Max would have never been grateful for tropical rain before, but now he relished a few hours of cooler weather and a break from cutting the cane. He sat on the stoop of the hut and watched the horizon, wondering which way led to the sea.

A figure draped in colorful fabric detached itself from the slave quarters and braved the downpour to run toward him. Dido was soaked by the time she reached him, the fabric of her tunic clinging to her ample curves and glistening in her thick eyelashes. She'd never spoken to him before, but now she bent down to his ear and whispered, "Come with me."

Max glanced back at the door of the slave barracks, knowing before he even looked that the heavy bar would still be in place. He had no idea how she got out, but aside from being wet, she didn't appear to be dirty or disheveled. Her escape had been easy enough.

Max rose to his feet and followed the woman without question, driven by sheer curiosity. Whatever she wanted with him was well worth exploring. If she wanted a quick tryst in the bushes or a heart-to-heart, it was more female contact than he'd had since being arrested back in September. He would oblige her in whatever way she pleased.

He was surprised when Dido led him into the jungle behind the slave barracks and pushed aside some thick vegetation to reveal a trapdoor in the ground. So, that was how they got out to perform their rituals, leaving Johansson none the wiser. But why would she want to bring him here?

Max felt apprehensive, but obediently followed Dido into

the tunnel, which was lined with palm leaves to keep it dry. It wasn't that long, but having earth all around him gave Max the feeling of being entombed, so he rushed the last few feet after Dido, eager to get to wherever they were going. They finally emerged.

The hut was tightly packed with bodies, people sitting, lying, sleeping, or just staring into space. One woman was singing softly as she rocked a child to sleep. A single candle burned in the corner, illuminating the priest who was sitting with his back against the wall, eyes closed, his breathing shallow and even. He appeared to be asleep.

"Why did you bring me here?" Max asked as Dido beckoned him inside.

She just smiled and gestured for him to follow. The rest of the slaves seemed to shift without being told to do so, leaving a space around the priest, who was now seemingly awake and watching Max with those jade eyes that were so like Dido's.

"Please, sit down, Lord Everly," the priest said, indicating a space across from him.

Dido poured something from a clay vessel and handed it to Max without speaking. It smelled pleasantly familiar, but Max couldn't quite place it.

"What is that?" he asked warily, suddenly afraid. What did these people want with him?

"It's pineapple juice mixed with coconut milk. It's quite delicious," the man said as he took a sip of his own drink. "Do try it."

Max took a sip and closed his eyes in unexpected pleasure as the sweetness flooded his mouth, reminding him of all the things he was missing on this godforsaken plantation. The juice tasted like ambrosia, and Max gulped it down without spilling a drop, feeling like a thirsty man in a desert. Dido instantly refilled his cup and then melted into the corner of the hut.

"My name is Xeno," the man introduced himself. His voice

was melodious and pleasant, a smooth baritone which seemed to suit him perfectly.

Max stared at him, wondering if he was having him on. "Xeno" meant foreigner or alien in Greek. Would he know that? Had he been given the name at birth, or had he chosen it for himself as a symbol of his captivity? And "Dido" meant prank, although it wasn't a frequently used noun. Max was about to ask but thought better of it, instead waiting patiently to hear what the priest had to say.

Xeno seemed to be in no rush to state his purpose, instead choosing to tell Max something of how he came to be at the plantation. "Dido is my twin sister; you might have noticed the resemblance between us," he said, talking slowly, as if in a dream. "We were captured in Ghana when we were hardly more than children and brought here as slaves. We didn't know it at the time, but we fetched a higher price than the rest of the slaves we'd come over with due to our mixed lineage. Our father was a white man, a Dutch slaver, who kept our mother aside for himself. We'd like to think that he loved her, but that's not very likely, is it? After all, to him she was nothing more than a pretty plaything. He lusted after her, and she submitted to him willingly in the hope that he would take care of us. He protected her, and us, for as long as he lived, but he was carried off by a fever, leaving us powerless to defend ourselves."

Xeno took another sip of his juice and momentarily closed his eyes as if reliving the events of his youth.

"Dido and I were taken when we were out alone playing in the jungle. It was our father's brother who snatched us, our own uncle who'd viewed his brother's liaison with our mother as shameful and unholy. His only act of kindness was to allow us to stay together, for the sake of his late brother's memory. We don't know what happened to our mother or the rest of our family, but this is our family now, and we must protect it."

Max nodded, unsure of what response was expected of him.

It was a sad tale, but not a unique one. Many families had been torn apart, the children separated from their parents, siblings sold separately, never to see each other again. The fact that Dido and her brother had been sold by their uncle wasn't surprising either. A white man would never acknowledge a pair of Negro twins as family; if anything, he'd want to eradicate any reminder of a connection between his own bloodline and that of some lowly Negro woman, who was probably dead by now or pining for her children on some other island, some other plantation.

"I've been watching you since you got here, Lord Everly, as has my sister, and we've decided that you are the one to help us," Xeno said, still watching Max with that uncanny stillness.

"I appreciate your confidence in me, but I can barely help myself these days," Max replied, curious however as to what the man had in mind.

Xeno just studied him patiently, waiting for Max to ask the inevitable question.

"What is it that you need my help with?" he obliged.

"I'm glad you asked," Xeno said, smiling for the first time. He had strong white teeth, and the smile transformed his face from forbidding to strangely appealing. "Three slaves have died unnecessarily in the past several months due to Johansson's cruelty. Unfortunately, Jessop Greene will not address these deaths until a white man dies," he replied calmly.

Max felt cold fingers of dread walk up his spine. What the hell was the man suggesting?

"The death of a white man will cause Greene to either rein in his attack dog or replace him altogether. You see, you are worth much more than any of us, so it would be a financial loss to the owner, not to mention a source of gossip and censure among the plantation owners on this island. The governor turns a blind eye to most things that happen here, but if a white man is beaten to death for a minor infraction, word gets around."

Xeno leaned against the rough wall and folded his hands in front of his stomach, looking as relaxed as if he were sitting on the sofa, watching a film with a cold beer in front of him and a bag of crisps nearby.

"Are you proposing to kill me, Xeno?" Max asked carefully, his mouth dry with apprehension. Had there been something in the juice that Dido had given him? Was he already a dead man?

Xeno smiled indulgently as he saw Max's eyes dart to the carafe. "Killing you would serve absolutely no purpose, my lord. You have to die at the hands of Johansson in order for it to benefit my people."

"So, what is it that you want of me?" Max was terribly uneasy, but he couldn't leave this hut without finding out exactly what Xeno had in mind, so that he could be prepared for whatever came next. Would they invoke some kind of voodoo curse to kill him and blame it on the overseer?

"Lord Everly, by all accounts you are a brave man, a man who risked his life to follow his conscience, not someone who'd been sent down for a crime against a fellow human being; this is why I came to you. If you were to annoy Johansson in some way and be sentenced to a flogging, your death would serve a higher purpose." Xeno was gazing at Max in such a self-satisfied manner that it left Max stunned. It was as if he were offering for Max to be crucified so that he could be compared to Jesus.

Max suddenly felt laughter bubbling up inside his chest. He hadn't laughed since the day he'd found the key to opening the secret passage that had led him to the seventeenth century, but he found himself convulsing with mirth as he looked at the surprised face of the voodoo priest. He was laughing so hard that tears began to run down his face and his stomach muscles contracted painfully, but he couldn't stop.

It took Max some time to catch his breath, but he finally got hold of himself and faced the man. "You expect me to provoke Johansson into flogging me to death just as a little favor to you?"

Max chortled. "Are you completely mad, man? What kind of a fool would I have to be to agree to this crazy scheme? I might have hit rock bottom, but I'm not ready to just give up and die, not even for a good cause. Thank you for the juice," Max added as he got to his feet.

Xeno just watched him until Max turned away, then his voice stopped Max in his tracks.

"You haven't heard what I'm offering in return, Lord Everly. Freedom."

"If you mean that I will be free of this life, then I think I've got the point," Max threw back over his shoulder.

"No, I mean freedom—and life. Won't you hear me out?" Xeno's voice sounded like warm honey as it drew Max back. He was like a snake charmer and Max was the snake, unable to resist the lure of the siren call.

Max reluctantly sat back down and faced Xeno, his face all hard angles and lines. This man was playing games, and Max was no man's fool. However, something in Xeno's voice held him captive, and he needed to understand what was really happening here. Dido seemed to be hovering behind him, listening, and silently willing him to agree, but he ignored her seductive presence, focusing instead on her brother.

"Lord Everly, as I'm sure you already know, since you followed us a few nights ago and watched our ritual of blood sacrifice, we practice the ancient art of voodoo. Many people believe this to be black magic, but it has nothing to do with that. Voodoo is about the connection between all living things and a devotion to each other. We summon spirits to help those who are in need of guidance, and we offer sacrifice which symbolizes the cycle of life," Xeno began.

"That's very illuminating, but what has this got to do with me?" Max asked rudely.

"My sister is a priestess who has extensive knowledge of plants, herbs, and poisons. She uses her skill to heal, but there are other, more potent potions which can also be useful in our situation."

"You are still talking in riddles, Xeno," Max replied, growing more annoyed by the moment. What did any of this have to do with what Xeno had suggested?

"All right, I will come straight to the point. Johansson never flogs the white indentures as severely as the Negro slaves. There's no chance of you actually dying from a flogging. The only way you could die is from festering of the wounds which could be a result of the flogging. Once dead, you would be buried in the graveyard on the plantation and forgotten about, but your story would live on, at least for a little while," Xeno stated.

"Sounds about right, so I'll be on my way if you don't mind," Max retorted, angry for having allowed himself a tiny seed of hope.

"Dido can make a potion which would slow down your heart and cool your body, making you appear dead for several hours. You will be declared dead and buried, which will serve our purpose, but then you will wake up. My men will dig you up and take you through the jungle to the port, where you will board a vessel bound for France. The *La Belle* will be docking in a few days, and will be ready to return to France after it has been unloaded, re-provisioned, and reloaded with cargo for the return voyage. You can be on it."

Max just gaped at the man. He had to be stark raving mad to propose what he just had. "Let me see if I understand you correctly, Xeno. You wish me to get flogged, pretend to die of infection, and then consent to be buried alive in the faint hope that you might dig me back up. And, if that actually happens, you claim that you can get me off the plantation and onto a French ship? I have a few questions, if you will," Max said forcefully. He was getting really bloody fed up with this charade.

"If you have the power to drug people, why not drug Johansson and his minions and escape yourself? You could all escape into the jungle one night and no one would find you. How on earth could you know about the French vessel, and why would anyone allow you to bring me on board, even if you could smuggle me out? And even if I got as far as the French ship, I have no money to pay for my passage, and, I assume, neither do you. And, why would you help me escape once your objective had been met? You could just leave me buried alive, which would suit your purposes just as admirably. Why bother going through this charade of helping me escape to freedom? You must think me a real fool, Xeno," Max spat out.

"You have every right to be suspicious, but I will answer your questions one by one," Xeno replied. He didn't seem in the least annoyed or offended by Max's ire. Instead he inclined his head in acknowledgment of Max's concerns, almost eager to speak further of his plan. "We've given Johansson a small amount of water hemlock every time we needed him out of the way, but to actually kill him would have severe repercussions, since we would be instantly suspected of the crime. We need him reined in, not dead. A new overseer could be even more brutal, so we'd be right back where we started," Xeno explained.

"The reason we don't escape is because we have nowhere to go. One or two people have run off in the past, hence the bar on the door, but to rescue everyone would require a place to go where we could live in peace and freedom, and that doesn't exist on this island. There are currently less than one hundred free blacks on Barbados, and they live in perpetual fear of losing their freedom," Xeno said with disgust.

Max was sure that the day he lost his own freedom would be fresh in his mind till the day he died.

"To get off the island would invite the attention of the authorities, so we would all be recaptured and sent back to be severely punished and tormented for our crime. Some might even be killed to teach the rest a lesson. Most of us come from the same place, if not from the same village. We are family now, and we either all go together or stay together," Xeno said forcefully.

Max could see why he'd been chosen as leader. He had a certain charisma that was hard to refute.

"Now, you ask how I know of the vessel and how I could get you aboard. I will tell you. The captain of the *La Belle* is a smuggler and a pirate. I meet him whenever he's in port, as do some of the slaves from neighboring plantations. We exchange certain goods which don't concern you. It's a mutually lucrative enterprise which will continue as long as both parties continue to prosper. If I ask the captain to hide you on board, he will do so. He will not help you once you reach France, nor will he treat you like a nobleman, but he will fulfill his end of the bargain and get you away from Barbados, if that's what we agree to."

"What could you possibly have to smuggle out?" Max asked, his voice full of derision. These people were as poor as church mice. What on earth did they have to trade that would be worth anything to a French privateer?

"We have something of value to the French, but that must remain a secret until you are on board the ship," Xeno replied calmly.

"You don't need to go through the trouble of digging me up if I agree. You can just leave me to die in the graveyard," Max pointed out.

"I can, but I won't. I am a black man and a slave, but that doesn't mean I don't have honor, Lord Everly. Honor is not something anyone can take away from me, and I pride myself on being a man of my word. I'm sure that you've seen the amount of graves in the cemetery. There are many. What do you think your chances of survival are? How many actually return home? I've been here since I was sixteen years old, and there were only two men who regained their freedom. I believe they hired themselves out as part of the crew and were able to sail back to England, to an uncertain future. Hundreds, if not thousands, have died all over Barbados from yellow fever, being worked to death, or simply because they'd given up and taken their own lives. You won't see their graves in the cemetery, but they are all here.

"This is your chance to regain your freedom and eventually return home. I cannot get you on a vessel bound for England, since you will be immediately returned to Jessop Greene, but sailing to France will set you free. From there, you can return to England under a false name and go about reclaiming the life you left behind. You have my word, Lord Everly, that I will keep my part of the bargain if you agree to help us."

"And what, exactly, would you give me to make me appear dead to someone like Erik Johansson? He's no fool and would be on to you in moments, and I would pay the price for the deception," Max replied, curious despite his better judgment. "Have you ever done this before?"

Xeno was silent for a few moments as he considered Max's final question. So, this was it; he had nothing, Max realized. All this was just a clever ruse to get him to agree. Xeno likely never expected Max to ask exactly what would be used and didn't have a ready reply. He looked away from Max, his eyes searching out those of his sister who was hovering quietly behind Max, listening in on the conversation.

"You better tell him, Dido," Xeno finally said. "He has a right to know."

"Very well." Dido didn't sound pleased at being ordered to divulge her methods, but she obediently sat down next to the two men and spoke in a low whisper, so as to keep the information between only the three of them. A voodoo priestess needed to keep her secrets. "There is one substance which can produce the result we seek; it is the poison of the puffer fish. It's very deadly, but when administered in a tiny quantity can cause the slowing of the heart, undetectable breathing and pulse, and a paralysis of the body. The victims are totally senseless, and can remain so for several days, depending on the amount of poison used. They wake up once the poison wears off with no visible ill effects," Dido explained, her eyes never leaving Max's face, silently challenging him to question her knowledge.

"Has this ever been done before?" Max asked suspiciously. He'd heard of fatal cases of blowfish poisoning, which he supposed was in the same family as puffer fish, mostly in Japan, but had never read anything about puffer fish causing a death-like state from which a person could wake up without suffering brain damage.

"Puffer fish poison is often used in voodoo to make zombies," Dido replied defensively.

"Zombies?" Max almost choked on the word. He thought that zombies were an invention of the twentieth-century enter-tainment industry, so the term sounded surreal coming from Dido.

"I know you are not familiar with the term," Dido said patiently, "but zombification has been around for some time, particularly in Haiti. It's a punishment for severe crimes," she stated and grew quiet.

"And how exactly does this punishment work?" Max asked, still amazed that he was discussing zombies with an African slave in the seventeenth century.

"The victim is given enough puffer fish poison to appear dead and is buried alive," Dido replied, clearly uncomfortable with the subject. "He comes back to life after several days and is dug up, but the punishment is not over. Another potion is given to him, which induces a permanent state of delirium and confu-sion. When in this state, the person can be commanded to do anything, and they will. Their mental faculties are too impaired to think clearly. Eventually, this condition wears off, and the person returns to normal." Dido's eyes slid away from Max's in embarrassment. She didn't approve of this, he could tell, but she was ready to give him poison to make him appear dead.

"Have you ever zombified anyone?" Max asked, refusing to let Dido off the hook. He wanted to know the truth.

"I have never done that to anyone, nor would I, regardless of the crime they'd committed," Dido said hotly, "but I have experimented with puffer fish poison and am familiar with its effects. I know exactly how much to administer to get the desired result."

"So, how do you know about zombies then?" Max asked, still curious.

"There was a *bokur* from Haiti on the ship which took us from our home. A *bokur* is a Vodun sorcerer who practices black magic," she added, seeing Max's look of incomprehension. "He was very knowledgeable, and we talked during the voyage. He taught me many things, some of which I still practice. I do not use my skills to punish or cause suffering, only to help the people I serve," Dido stated, head held high and eyes blazing.

Max remained silent for a long while after Dido finished speaking, considering what he'd just learned. She got up and left him alone with Xeno, who sat silently on the floor, legs crossed, and eyes partially closed. If someone had told Max an hour ago that he would be considering temporary death and discussing zombies, he'd think them crazy, but nothing that had happened to him in the past six months had been even remotely sane, he mused bitterly. Time travel was the stuff of science-fiction movies, yet here he was, trapped and without hope of escape.

"You are asking me for complete trust, Xeno," Max said at last, watching the man for any hint of falseness or cunning.

"I am, but I'm offering you something just as precious in return. I don't expect you to give me an answer now, but please think about it. The *La Belle* will dock in a few days, and won't be ready to sail back to France for at least ten days. You have until then."

"I don't need until then. The answer is no."

Max rose to his feet, gave Xeno a mock bow, and disappeared into the tunnel. Having turned his back, he didn't see the look that passed between Xeno and his sister, but had he seen it, he would have been surprised.

It had grown dark while he was talking to Xeno, but the rain had stopped and the air was fresh and cool. Max gazed up at the heavens, surprised to see a sky full of stars; the heavens like black velvet strewn with diamonds, breathtaking as only a Caribbean sky could be. The air smelled of wet earth, tropical flowers, and a whiff of something spicy coming from the kitchen. No doubt Johansson and his men dined on different dishes than the workers.

Max returned to his hut, but didn't go in. He sat on the stoop until his clothes fully dried and the gong sounded for supper. He rose to his feet and followed the rest of the men to the open tent with trestle tables and benches where the meals were served, but his mind was a thousand miles away.

# EIGHTEEN

## MARCH 1686

**Paris, France**

It turned out that my worries about being churched had been unfounded. I suppose the term itself was what set my teeth on edge. It made me think of something associated with the Inquisition, but, in reality, the vicar said a prayer in the church porch, blessed both myself and Valentine, and proclaimed me ready to attend services. I breathed a sigh of relief as the ritual ended and we were free to return home.

Frances suggested to Archie that they take advantage of the fair weather and walk home, but he politely declined, which was thoroughly out of character since Archie usually enjoyed walking. It took Jem to change his mind. The boy begged and pleaded, eager to spend time outdoors. I felt sorry for Jem since he had no friends his age to play with and, except for his lessons with Hugo, spent most of his time hanging around Archie and driving him to distraction.

Archie was always patient and kind, allowing Jem to help him with the horses or letting him polish the scabbard while he cleaned his sword, but the boy needed something to keep him busy, as did Frances. She seemed listless and irritable, often sitting down only to jump up a moment later, wander toward the window, and then come right back to sit briefly before taking off again. As much as I secretly disapproved of the idea of her marriage, I had to admit that Frances was no longer a child and needed the pursuits of a woman to keep her occupied. She could no more go back to the schoolroom than I could return to being the woman I was before I'd recklessly plunged into the passage in the crypt. We were both irrevocably changed by our experiences and needed to look to the future. It pained Frances to be around Valentine, and the only cure was a family of her own, and a baby to dim the heartache of losing Gabriel.

I was feeling terribly thirsty, and more than a little hungry by the time we finally arrived at home. I was grateful for Valentine's hearty appetite, but she seemed to be draining me and leaving my body depleted of both hydration and nutrients. I'd lost the baby weight very rapidly and was actually thinner than I had been before getting pregnant—a fact that Hugo had remarked on only the day before. He was worried about me, but I felt physically well, especially when I made sure to include some protein with every meal, otherwise I became a bit shaky by midmorning, as I was now.

I stopped by the kitchen to have a cup of ale and whatever cook might offer me by way of a snack, while Hugo took the baby upstairs to be changed by Elodie before her feeding. I came upstairs to find Hugo seated in his favorite armchair by the hearth, staring at Valentine in a way that nearly made my heart stop. I thought I was familiar with all of Hugo's facial expressions, but this was one I hadn't seen before. It was a mixture of love, sorrow, regret, and something else I couldn't name.

"Hugo, is she all right?" I cried as I stumbled toward them, suddenly scared.

"Yes, of course," Hugo replied, looking up at me, his eyes

full of confusion. "Why would you think otherwise?"

I took the baby and sat down across from Hugo ready to nurse. Valentine appeared to be asleep, but latched on right away, never one to pass up on a meal. She was pleasantly plump, a solid little weight in my arms, which I always found reassuring. I breathed a sigh of relief as she began to suck, and discreetly checked her for any signs of a temperature. The baby seemed fine; it was Hugo who needed checking. He still looked as if he'd seen a ghost; his eyes fixed on Valentine as if he expected her to disappear at any moment.

"Hugo, what's wrong?" I asked carefully. He wasn't the type of man to wear his emotions on his sleeve, so the look of bereavement I had seen a few moments ago had to have been brought on by some strong sentiment. I had simply caught him in an unguarded moment.

"I've been thinking," he replied as his fingers drummed on the armrest of the chair. Hugo often did that when he was agitated, as he clearly was now.

"Always a dangerous pastime where you are concerned," I quipped, in the hope of making him smile, but my joke didn't go down as I'd intended, making him wince instead.

"Not in this case." He took a deep breath and leaned forward, resting his elbows on his thighs, his face in his hands. "Sometimes I wish you'd never shown me the future," he began. "Ignorance truly is bliss."

"Why, do you miss television, cars, and chips?" I knew that wasn't what he was referring to, but I still hoped that an attempt at humor would help him put his feelings into words.

"I do, actually, but that's not what I meant. Before I knew the future of my country, I had a reason to follow my conscience and do what I thought was right, but now, regardless of what I think or do, the outcome is already known to me, and it's shaping my actions."

"In what way?"

"With James II on the throne, I believed that there was a chance for a Catholic monarchy in England, and that gave me some modicum of hope, but now I know that there will never be another Catholic king, or queen, on the throne of England. That knowledge should have no bearing on my personal life, but it does; it changes everything."

"Hugo, what are you talking about?" I asked gently, seeing his obvious distress. He was skirting around something important, something he wasn't ready to say out loud, but needed to get off his chest; something that might have been brought on by the service we'd just attended since he seemed to be in much better spirits before we left for the church. I couldn't imagine what could have upset him, but he'd been nearly silent since leaving the church—a fact that I'd only just realized.

"I'm talking about Valentine, and our future son, should we have one. Knowing what I know, I find myself wondering if I might be doing my children a disservice by insisting on raising them in the Catholic Church." Hugo seemed to almost deflate as he uttered the words, his pallor worsening in the soft light of the room.

"But your faith means everything to you," I exclaimed. Hugo's faith was his moral compass; his anchor in a roiling sea of European politics, and his source of solace. For him to even bring this up was paramount to emotional suicide, and showed me just how deeply he'd been affected by learning what was to come.

"My faith will not change, but I want what's best for my children—and what's best for them, politically speaking, is to be Protestant. I don't want them to be a minority in their own country, viewed with suspicion and mistrust, and discriminated against because of how they choose to worship. I want them to be free to love, and not feel that they can't marry the person of their choice because they are of the wrong religion. I want them to belong," he finished hotly.

"Is that how you feel, that you don't belong?"

"I've been taught by my father from a young age to keep my faith a secret. I've masqueraded as a faithful Protestant at Court and at home. Revealing my true religion would have marked me as someone who was different and whose judgment was in question. Not all Catholics believe in thumbscrews and burning heretics at the stake, but that's how the English people view us. I've benefited from my deception, but I've also suffered for it, so why put my children in the same situation?"

"Hugo, are you saying what I think you're saying?" I couldn't believe that we were actually having this conversation, but I knew where Hugo was going with this.

"I would like to baptize Valentine in the Protestant Church, if that's all right with you," he said quietly.

"Oh, sweetheart, are you sure?" I asked, my heart going out to him. This was a huge sacrifice on his part, and there'd be no going back once the deed was done.

"Yes, I believe I am. We should do it as soon as possible. Now that you've been churched, we can make arrangements for the baptism. However, I'd like to do it privately—no guests."

"Why?"

"I have my reasons," Hugo replied cryptically and rose to his feet. "I need some air," he said and strode from the room, leaving me shaken and confused. He seemed sure of his decision, but the request for a private baptism left me with a sinking feeling. Hugo had tried to shelter me as much as he could during my confinement and after the birth, but I wasn't an ignorant girl who knew nothing of the undercurrents rippling beneath the surface of history. We were in a Catholic country, ruled by a Catholic king, and if Hugo meant to make a place for himself at the Court of Louis XIV, he needed to wear his

Catholicism like a badge as the price of admission. Baptizing our baby into the Protestant Church would spoil Hugo's plans, and if I knew my husband, his plans were not as straightforward as he'd have me believe.

# NINETEEN

By the time the church clock struck 2 a.m., Hugo had given up all pretense of sleep. He'd helped himself to several cups of brandy before retiring, but the alcohol had all the effect of water, leaving him wide awake and unbearably agitated. Telling Neve of his decision had been but a small part of what had been on his mind over the past few weeks, and although he was glad to have finally spoken the words out loud, he still felt as if he'd lost a part of himself this day.

It was all for the best, he knew that, but his faith was such an important part of him that he felt like Judas Iscariot. Not having Valentine baptized into the Catholic Church was a sin he'd have to live with for the rest of his life, but he'd already married a Protestant, and this was the next step on his path away from the Church.

Hugo glanced over at Neve, who was sleeping peacefully, having fed the baby an hour ago. He'd pretended to be asleep in order to hide the evidence of his frustrated desire, knowing that his advances would not be welcome. Neve had barely allowed him to touch her since the birth, leaving him confused and upset. She'd been so easily aroused while pregnant; a certain look, a fleeting touch, a sweet kiss, and she was reaching for his flies, ready and willing, and now she was as cold and remote as a block of ice. Hugo assumed that it was natural for women to feel a certain lack of interest after the birth, as they recovered and spent most of their waking hours caring for a baby, but it had been two months, and the doctor said that after thirty days it was reasonable to expect to resume marital relations. Most men would either just exercise their husbandly rights or slake their lust on a whore, but Hugo couldn't fathom doing either. He would never force himself on Neve, nor would he betray his marriage vows by visiting a brothel. He didn't want just anyone; he wanted his wife.

Hugo briefly wondered what his father would have advised, but deep down, he already knew. Joss Everly had been a harsh man, who brooked no disobedience from wife, children, or servants. He never spared the rod, never spoiled the child, and never gave any quarter to his wife. Hugo could almost hear the old man's voice, as full of derision as it had been when he was still alive.

"Do you never tire of your sentimental claptrap, boy?" the voice demanded. "Your wife is your property as much as your horse is. Do you ask your horse if you may ride it? No, I thought not, so why ask permission of your wife? Take her, and if she gives you any trouble, just show her the back of your hand. You're her master, and she should know it. Your mother never had the temerity to deny me; she knew better. I always said you were too soft."

Yes, perhaps he was, but he could never be the tyrant his father was. Strange how he still argued with the old man in his head so many years after his death, still torn between pleasing his sire and being true to himself. His father always said that he'd taken after his mother, who had been kind and loving, but whose spirit had been broken years before Hugo was even born.

His mother would have advised him to be patient and kind,

to try to understand what Neve was feeling rather than assert his power over her like some feudal overlord, and his mother's advice would be the one Hugo would take every time.

Hugo moved closer to Neve and pulled her into his arms, but even in sleep, she stiffened. *Has she stopped loving me?* He thought, suddenly realizing that the lack of desire could be stemming from a change of heart. Was she sorry that she'd followed him back in time, and could she be planning on returning to her old life and taking Valentine with her? He couldn't stop her, of course. If she chose to go back, he would not stand in her way.

He couldn't say with any honesty that he would have made the same sacrifice and chosen to go back to a time of violence and ignorance for a woman, but Neve had given him her love and her life, and he'd accepted them gratefully, and stupidly assumed that they were his for the duration of her lifetime. Had he failed her in some way? Had he done something to hurt or disrespect her?

Suddenly, the pain in Hugo's heart was too much for him to bear alone. He needed to know what was on Neve's mind, and he couldn't wait another minute. If she were making plans to leave him, he'd rather know and try to accept her decision than lie here in the dark second-guessing her motives.

Hugo gently shook Neve awake, holding his breath as her eyes flew open in panic. She sat bolt upright, her gaze going straight to the cradle on her side of the bed. The baby slept peacefully, her tiny mouth open in an O, just as it had been when she'd released Neve's nipple, already snoozing happily.

"What is it?" Neve asked, finally accepting that there was nothing wrong with Valentine and Hugo had woken her up for some reason of his own.

"Are you leaving me?" he blurted out, suddenly unsure that he wanted to hear the answer. He'd been heartbroken when Catherine had left him after two weeks of marriage, but if Neve left him now, he'd never recover. Nothing would matter anymore because she was the best part of him, the part that gave him a reason for being, the lifeblood that flowed through his heart and kept him alive.

"What?! Where did that come from?" She was wide awake now, looking at him with that frown of worry that caused a line to appear between her brows. Hugo could just make out her features in the glow from the dying embers of the fire, but he was relieved to see shock rather than the guilt of being found out. Neve looked genuinely perplexed.

"You haven't allowed me to touch you since the baby's birth. Have I done something to hurt you? Have you stopped loving me?" Hugo cringed at the pleading tone of his voice, his pathetic need to be reassured that he was still loved and needed. He felt like a dejected puppy, but he couldn't stop now. "Why are you rejecting me, Neve?"

"Because I'm scared," Neve replied simply.

"Of me?"

"No, of getting pregnant again. Hugo, this was my first baby, and I had no idea what to expect. I was so scared of giving birth, especially in this time and place, but I pacified myself with the idea that there would be a competent physician by my side, or even an experienced midwife. Their presence would not make up for the lack of hospital and an epidural, but at least there would be someone to guide me through the process and help me bring our baby into this world. Instead, I got Archie, who might have delivered a foal at some point in his life. There was a moment that night when I really believed that I was going to die," Neve said quietly, making Hugo feel like an utter ass for questioning her love for him. She'd risked her life—more than once—and here he was, whining about her not giving him the affection he needed. "I love you more than I've loved anyone in my life, but the thought of getting pregnant again terrifies me. I know how much you long for a son, and my heart breaks every time you reach for me, but I just can't bring myself to surrender this tiny bit of control I have over my destiny at this moment. Please forgive me," she cried softly. "I know I have been unfair to you."

"Is that all?" Hugo asked, feeling ridiculously relieved. "I thought you were planning to go back to the future with Valentine."

"It never even crossed my mind, you silly fool," she said and bent down to plant a kiss on his lips. "I will get over this fear, but I just need a little time."

"Neve, I do want another child, but I can't guarantee that you would have an easier time of it during delivery. I'm so terribly sorry for not being here when you needed me. I would have turned this city upside down to find help, but I failed you, through no fault of my own. I will respect your wishes, but there are other ways to avoid pregnancy than celibacy. I need you, and I want you, and I will do whatever it takes to avoid getting you with child, if you'll let me."

"What can you do? I know the Church's stance on birth control—not that there are any reliable methods available to us in this century."

"I don't care about the Church's stance; I will not lose you over doctrine. I will see to it," Hugo promised as he noted a softening of her face. Perhaps not all was lost. "In the meantime, there are other ways of loving," he whispered softly as he slid down between her legs. Hugo smiled to himself when Neve let out a whimper of pleasure as his tongue slid inside her, reclaiming what he believed to be rightfully his.

# TWENTY

I felt like a pincushion as three women circled me like vultures, measuring, pinning, tucking, and snipping. Sabine, my new lady's maid whom Hugo had insisted on, was looking critically from the side, making rapid comments in French to the seamstresses, clearly displeased with the progress of the fitting. I was completely ignoring them all, lost in my own thoughts.

The summons to come to Versailles had arrived a few days ago, and I was thrumming with nerves like a tuning fork. I would be completely out of my element, and everyone would know it. It would have been difficult enough for me to navigate the tumultuous waters of the English Court, but the French one was scarier than a shark tank. My French was good enough to purchase a loaf of bread or ask someone for directions if I took a wrong turn, but not enough to converse with French courtiers who would be sniggering at me behind their fans and gossiping about my gauche ways.

I found it somewhat puzzling that Hugo had engaged Sabine about a week before the summons came, and had arranged for the seamstresses to come calling with swaths of fabrics for me to choose from. It was as if he knew that we would be invited, which was odd, since French nobility had unanimously shunned us since our arrival in Paris. Hugo had made the acquaintance of several expats who were happy to receive him, but the French had closed ranks—until now. That seemed to brighten Hugo's spirits as well as the reconciliation which our night talk had inspired.

I was actually glad that I'd been able to confide my fears in Hugo, and he, in turn, had made good on his promise. I didn't ask where he'd gotten the condoms, but, according to him, they had been in use for a few hundred years, just not actively since the Church saw the prevention of conception as being immoral. Having been in the twenty-first century and seen firsthand that the Church had survived the crisis of widely used contraception, Hugo had put aside whatever reservations he might have had and procured a dozen sheaths made from sheep intestines, which had been cleaned and sewn at the ends. I was actually surprised by how much they resembled modern-day prophylactics.

It took us a few fumbling tries to get the sheaths on since they couldn't be rolled on like modern condoms, but eventually Hugo got the hang of it, and the peace of mind that this protection gave me was worth everything. Having that intimacy with Hugo again filled a hole in my heart that I didn't know was there, and I noticed that my weight loss seemed to slow down. I hadn't realized how anxious and high-strung I'd become, but now that the paralyzing fear of another pregnancy had been removed, I felt more like my normal self, and was able to be Hugo's wife again in every sense of the word. Hugo hadn't said anything more about future children, but I knew that he harbored hopes that I would get over my fear in time. Perhaps I would, but for now, I didn't have to think about it, and that in itself was liberating.

I looked in the mirror as Madame Marie asked for my opinion. I looked like a giant meringue with yards of butter-yellow damask swaying about my hooped hips and the stomacher coming to a point at the waist. The fabric was worked with barely noticeable silver thread made to look like little bursts of fireworks. Cream lace frothed at my wrists and décolletage, and an underskirt of embroidered cream silk peeked from underneath my overskirt.

Madame Marie turned me around to show me the train which billowed behind me like a sail. The gown looked like a frothy concoction, but it weighed a ton. I moved experimentally only to freeze when the hoops swayed, and the skirt with them. It felt as if a bronze bell was tolling around my bum. Madame Marie, her assistants, and Sabine were all clucking in approval, but I just wanted to flee. What I wouldn't give for a pair of leggings and a sweatshirt.

Sabine helped me undress, but another gown was already waiting to be tried on. This one was of dusty rose brocade with accents in a deeper shade of mauve. I sighed and resigned myself to this torture, half-hoping that Valentine would wake up and howl for a feeding.

Later, when I finally managed to escape, I called for a bath. I couldn't believe how exhausting a fitting could be, and since the baby was full and sleeping peacefully, I decided to do something nice for myself. Most ladies of the time bathed in some sort of garment, but I stripped naked and immersed myself in the hot water just up to my breasts. Lowering my breasts into hot water made the milk flow, which wasn't desirable when bathing. I leaned my head back and closed my eyes, suddenly wondering how this had become my life. I wasn't complaining by any stretch of the imagination, but the idea of coming face to face with the Sun King was intimidating.

Hugo quietly entered the room and sat down by the fire, watching me in the bath. He seemed tired, and had that closed look that I've so often seen when he was worried or upset. It was one of those things that was a dead giveaway that something was wrong, and I suddenly felt very tender toward him. He'd been through so much in the past year, but our trials and tribulations were far from over. Hugo was walking a tightrope, and any misstep would result in a deadly plunge, with myself and Valentine falling with him. That was a lot of pressure for anyone to bear, especially a man who understood the consequences of his actions.

"Darling, what is it?" I asked as he smiled at me ruefully. "You look done in."

"Your new gowns are beautiful," he said instead, clearly avoiding the question.

"Yes, they are, and I might even remain upright for a few hours before falling flat on my face from the sheer weight of those fabrics. Now, tell me what's on your mind."

Hugo turned away and stared into the flames for a few moments, his jaw working in a way that suggested that he was grinding his teeth. I hadn't seen him do that before and was suddenly nervous.

"Hugo?"

"I've had a letter from Brad," he finally admitted.

We'd had no word from Bradford Nash since we saw him in London after Max's trial, and hadn't expected any communication until later in the spring. Hugo had sent a letter as soon as the ships began sailing in March, but by the time the letter would reach Brad and he would reply, it would most likely be May. This was unexpected since Brad wouldn't know where to send his letter until receiving Hugo's first.

"Really? When?"

"While you were having your fitting. A messenger brought it. It was addressed to Luke and included in the diplomatic pouch to ensure delivery. Brad knew that Luke was in Paris and hoped the letter would reach me." Hugo grew quiet again, confirming my suspicions that the news from home wasn't good.

"How are the Nashes?" I asked in an effort to draw Hugo into conversation once more.

"They are well."

More silence. After the long winter, we were all a bit pale, but Hugo looked ashen as he stared into the leaping flames of the fire, his jaw still working. I wished I could go to him, but I was soaking wet, with water streaming from my freshly washed hair onto my breasts.

"Hugo, please tell me."

He'd have to tell me sooner or later, but he seemed reluctant to speak the words. I waited patiently, giving him a moment to compose himself. He just sat there, perfectly still and silent, as if keeping the words locked in his head would undo whatever had happened.

"Jane is dead," he finally uttered, turning at last to face me. His eyes were full of pain, and I could only imagine what he was feeling. Despite his anger and resentment, he still loved the girl Jane had been, and couldn't reconcile the bitter, angry woman with the sister he had adored. He still blamed himself, I knew that; imagining other possible scenarios in which Jane's life had turned out differently.

I couldn't be as generous, given what Jane had intended for me and our baby, but then again, I'd never known the girl, or the young woman, who'd been innocent and naïve. I was secretly relieved that the woman who'd plotted to have me thrown into Newgate on a trumped-up charge of witchcraft, and hoped that I would die there, was dead. Now Hugo would have no choice but to mourn and heal, rather than worry about a possible reunion in England and another attempt on my life. As long as we only had a daughter, Jane still had a chance at succeeding in her plans—a fact that Hugo was well aware of.

"From syphilis?" I asked, surprised that it had progressed so quickly. Jane had shown some signs of the disease, but she certainly hadn't been far gone. I assumed that she still had years ahead of her before the illness incapacitated and eventually killed her.

"No," Hugo replied stonily. "She was found by some gravediggers in a cemetery in London a few days after the trial. There was a letter to Clarence found on her person. The ink had been smudged since it rained the day before, but most of the message was still legible. She said goodbye and begged his forgiveness, so there was no doubt that it was suicide." Hugo winced as he said the word, still shocked that his deeply Catholic sister would commit the ultimate sin against God.

"How did she die?" I asked softly. I suppose it was morbid curiosity, but I wanted to know.

"It had to be by poison since there were no marks on her body. She was shipped back to Kent and buried at the cross-roads closest to Three Oaks. Clarence will pass her grave every time he so much as leaves the house," Hugo added bitterly.

"Where is he now? Surely he's not living alone." Clarence had recently turned fourteen, but he was still too young to live on his own in the house of his birth. He had a tutor, from whom he tried to escape at every possible opportunity, but he still needed adult supervision and help with running the estate. I couldn't help feeling sorry for the boy, given how close he'd been with his mother. The shame of her suicide would haunt him as well, especially if the grave was just outside the estate for all to see. Clarence had been a bit sullen, as most teenagers are, but he was a good lad, one who didn't deserve to be abandoned by his mother.

"Clarence is staying in London with his half-sister, Magdalen. In my absence, Magdalen's husband will be Clarence's guardian until he reaches maturity and is ready to assume the running of the estate. Brad said that the boy is heart-broken and confused. He will have to live with the stigma of his mother's suicide for the rest of his life. Thank God Magdalen has taken him in or he would be completely alone."

"I'm really sorry, Hugo." I wasn't sure what to say. Jane had ensured that she would not be buried in consecrated ground or go to Heaven. Was that her way of punishing herself for what she'd done, or was she in such a state that she simply hadn't thought about it? I would have liked to think that there was a grain of remorse in Jane, no matter how small, but couldn't be sure. By committing suicide, she'd hurt Hugo once again, making sure that there could be no forgiveness, even in death.

"I'm going to write to Clarence," Hugo said suddenly. "Jane might have poisoned him against me, but I'm still his uncle and would like to think that we can have a close relationship once we return to England."

"Clarence probably thinks that you are in the West Indies, serving your sentence," I replied, wondering what Hugo was going to tell the boy.

"Well, it's time he knew the truth. He's old enough to understand, and to judge for himself. I can't put everything in writing, but I will ask Brad to call on him and explain. Perhaps he'll hate me a little less then."

Hugo raked his hand through his hair in agitation. If I knew anything about teenage boys, it was that they weren't easy to reason with, especially when led to believe that the person in question was a traitor. It was anyone's guess what Jane had said to him about me, if anything, but if Clarence believed Hugo to be bewitched, he might be nursing a grudge against me as well. It was reasonable to assume that Clarence blamed Hugo for his mother's death, which was indirectly true, so his feelings wouldn't be easily soothed.

By the time we returned to England and Hugo could speak for himself, Clarence would be nearly eighteen, a grown man, and the master of Three Oaks. I hoped that his previous relationship with Hugo would speak for itself and he would welcome his uncle home, but it was hard to predict how he would feel and what influence his sister and her husband might have on Clarence while he remained with them. I had never met Magdalen, but from what Jane had told me, she'd never cared for her stepdaughter and had been happy to marry her off. Perhaps Magdalen would help Clarence deal with his loss, but then again, she wouldn't know the truth about Hugo or myself, and would naturally assume the worst.

The biggest issue, however, was that legally Clarence was still Hugo's heir—a fact which Hugo was acutely aware of. If anything befell Hugo, Valentine and I would be at Clarence's mercy for our survival, yet another reason why Hugo desperately needed a male heir. I looked away from his tense expression, suddenly feeling very vulnerable.

# TWENTY-ONE

Blood-red ribbons of a spring sunrise were just becoming visible above the rooftops of Paris as our carriage rolled into the city. We'd left Versailles sometime after 3 a.m. and had been traveling since. What would have taken less than an hour by car took several hours by carriage, and although we had been invited to spend the night at the palace, we had to politely refuse in order to be at home by the time Valentine woke up for her morning feeding.

I forced myself to unclench my fists and relax, which took something of an effort. I could practically hear the baby howling with hunger since she was usually up by this time, hungry and wet. All I wanted was to hold that sweet-smelling warm body against me, bury my face in her chubby shoulder and cry.

Hugo was dozing with his head against the padded side of the carriage; his features relaxed in sleep. He'd been unusually tense after we left the palace, but the motion of the carriage had finally lulled him to sleep. I didn't want to add to his anxiety, so I'd put on a brave face and told him it had been a magical evening, when, in fact, it had been one of the most humiliating experiences of my life. I'd dreaded the visit to

Versailles, knowing that I couldn't possibly hold my own among people who'd spent most of their lives as courtiers. I was a woman raised in the twenty-first century, taught to be independent, straightforward, and proud of my accomplishments, not a simpering, flattering, forked-tongued sycophant whose only goal in life was to get as much as I could from my position and sex appeal, not that those would have gotten me much here.

Luke had spent hours over a period of several days tutoring me in the ways of Louis's Court. I took copious quill-scratched notes on who was married to whom, who was sleeping with whom, who had discarded whom in favor of someone with more social-climbing potential, and who was scheming against whom in a military-worthy campaign of taking them down. Luke had warned me of topics which were not to be discussed for fear of appearing vulgar. Speaking of Valentine was completely off-limits.

"Most women farm out their children to a wet nurse and forget about them until they are at least two," Luke had admonished me with a stern look. "Maternal pride is unheard of, not to mention utterly misplaced at Court. Nor are you to gush about your husband. French women regard their husbands with barely hidden contempt. They marry to improve their prospects, not out of any sense of misguided affection, so your love for Hugo would be a source of derision to them, particularly since they would be jealous enough to scratch out your eyes."

"Versailles sounds like Heaven on earth," I had said sarcastically, "can't wait to visit."

Luke had ignored my cattiness and continued unperturbed. "You will not be seated next to Hugo at supper, nor will you be anywhere near him for most of the night, so you will be entirely on your own. The best you can do is respond when spoken to, but not too effusively, smile mysteriously, and, for God's sake, don't stare at anyone. Lower your eyes as often as possible, lest someone take offense at your gawking."

"Ease up, Luke," Hugo had drawled from his place by the fire. "She's not a simpleton."

"I do beg your pardon, Neve," Luke had said immediately. "I just want to spare you any unnecessary embarrassment. One mistake can seriously cost you at the Court of Louis XIV." Luke had turned to Hugo, eyeing him suspiciously. "I'd still like to know how you managed to wangle an invitation to Court. Sir Trumbull is fuming, you know. Now he will be forced to acknowledge you, despite his desire to behead you himself. Whatever favors you called in, Hugo, I hope it was worth it."

Hugo had just smiled indulgently but chose not to reply. I had to admit that I had been wondering the same thing myself. One moment we were virtually invisible, and suddenly we'd been summoned to Court to attend on one of Europe's greatest monarchs. The notion of being presented to the Sun King made me giddy with nerves, but a more detached part of me couldn't help gloating at meeting such a famous historical figure.

"What is he like, Luke?" I'd asked, suddenly realizing that all I knew of the man I'd learned from history books, which, if I had anything to go on, were not always accurate.

Luke had looked around to make sure we were quite alone and then shut the door to the parlor to be sure that he wasn't overheard by the servants. They didn't understand English, but Luke's position would be severely compromised if anyone heard him say anything even remotely negative about the king.

"Louis is a spoiled child," Luke had begun. "He adores flattery, and surrounds himself with people who gush over him at any opportunity. The clumsier the attempt, the more flattering he finds it, since he believes it to be more heartfelt. He particularly craves praise of his military prowess, and will gladly start a war if only to show off his skill as a leader. Of course, he also fancies himself quite the lover, and has bedded many of the women of the Court over the years. Many of them are now too old and undesirable to still be received, but there is plenty of new blood. If he takes a fancy to someone, a refusal is paramount to social suicide. The woman is simply expected to grace His Majesty's bed at the appointed hour. He doesn't bother with wooing or playing the gallant."

"Stay out of his way, Neve," Hugo had advised me with a wary glance. "I wouldn't want to have to call out the king of France."

The chances of Louis inviting me to share his bed were mercifully nonexistent, but the mere thought was abhorrent. Would Hugo stand aside and let a monarch bed his wife as other men did? I'd wondered.

"No, I wouldn't," Hugo had replied as if I'd spoken out loud. "You are mine for better or for worse, and mine you shall remain."

I liked the sentiment, but I didn't care for the tone. I'd given Hugo a withering glance as I continued to scratch away. "Ah, Luke, I have a rather delicate question," I'd stammered. This was something very basic, but I didn't think I would be able to ask one of the ladies, for fear of making a fool of myself. "Where does one answer the call of nature?"

"There are several rooms set aside for that very purpose. There are chamber pots behind screens for the ladies. The gentlemen don't require such measures since they don't share your delicate sensibilities," he had joked. "I will discreetly point out the room to you once we get to the palace."

"Am I allowed to seek you out, if I can't talk to my own husband?" I'd asked, feeling even more nervous.

"You and I may exchange some pleasantries, but you cannot appear to purposely attach yourself to me. You can casually stroll by and stop for a second should you need assistance, but otherwise, you're on your own, Neve."

Hugo had risen to his feet and took my clammy hands in

his. "I know you're nervous, and you have every right to be, but it's only for a few hours, and I know that you can hold your own among those women."

Hugo might know a great deal about politics and religion, but he knew very little about the cattiness and duplicity of women. I'd felt a little guilty for that stray thought when I remembered how Hugo had suffered at the hands of his sister. Perhaps he did know something of women's capacity for deceit now. I'd smiled into his eyes and nodded in what I hoped was a reassuring way. Yes, I would be all right no matter what, as long as I didn't get milk stains on my gown. I would have to put thick wads of folded linen into my bodice and change them every few hours to make sure that I didn't embarrass myself. The women of the Court didn't nurse their babies, so this was a problem unique only to me. At least there were screens in the ladies' rooms, so I could have a little privacy when I changed my milk-soaked pads.

I nearly tumbled from the coach when we reached the house and ran up the path, my skirts bunched in my hands. Hugo was right behind me, but I was already pounding on the door, desperate to get to Valentine. I could hear her cries as I flew up the stairs, my fingers tearing at the laces of my gown frantically.

Frances was still in bed, but Marthe was in our room, rocking the baby and singing to her in French as Valentine screamed, her face red, and her little fists shaking as if she were spoiling for a fight. Her toothless gums shook with rage as she tried to make her needs known.

I grabbed the baby from Marthe and put her to my one exposed breast, as the maid went about unlacing me and carefully removing the parts of the gown without disturbing the baby. Valentine gave me the gimlet eye as she latched on and began to suck furiously, her eyes closing in concentration.

"How long has she been crying?" I asked, not really wanting to know the answer.

"Not long, milady," Marthe answered. I knew she was lying.

Finally, I was free of the gown and able to sit down in my nursing chair. I leaned my head back and closed my eyes as hot tears slid down my cheeks. I didn't want to remember what I had overheard as I'd stood frozen behind the screen, but the tittering voices of the women were hard to forget.

"I must admit that he's rather handsome, in that typically English way," one woman had said. "He's powerfully built; I always like that in a man."

"Mm, he is indeed," another one had purred. "He's one I'd like to see without his wig," she'd giggled, clearly implying something else.

"He can keep on his wig as long as he takes off his breeches," the first one had replied.

"Oh, he will soon enough," a third woman had added. "Did you see that wife of his? What a disgrace. She's no better than a peasant. I hear they are recently married."

"Probably married her in the hopes that she would give him an heir, but I hear she had a girl. What a bitter disappointment it must have been for our charming Lord Everly. If he knows what's good for him, he'll get her full in the belly again soon and take a mistress. At least that silly cow won't be invited to Court if she's pregnant, so he can have free rein."

"Hmm, he'd have to actually lie with her to get her with child again. What a chore that must be. She's got the face of a pug. And that hair...."

I had refused to allow Sabine to do anything drastic, wearing it piled as high as my natural hair would allow. Some of the women had rather elaborate hairstyles, which were so high and powdered that a family of canaries could live in the depths, mistaking the hair for a nest.

"He doesn't need to look at her face. What possessed him?"

one of the women had asked. "She has no title, no family, and, from what I hear, no money."

"Perhaps he plucked her out of some brothel. A certain kind of talent goes a long way." The women had burst out laughing as they finally exited the room and made their way back to the musical performance which was in progress. I strongly suspected that they'd known I was there all along, which made their comments even more spiteful. I had no doubt that something along those lines would be expressed to Hugo in short order, if it hadn't been already.

I wiped away the tears with the back of my hand, suddenly angry with myself. I promised myself that I would remain above all that, but I'd let their cattiness get to me at the very first opportunity. Those women had accomplished precisely what they had set out to do; they'd made me doubt myself and my husband. The fact that I had no title, family, or money signaled to them that it was a love match—something none of them could claim—and it was enough to make their tiny little hearts burn with envy. Had Hugo been short, homely, and pasty-faced, no one would have given our marriage a thought, but his attractiveness was sure to get the attention of the women and make me a target.

I smiled brightly as Hugo came in; already divested of his evening clothes and looking like the Hugo I loved. His hair was disheveled, he needed a shave, and his shirt was open at the throat to reveal a glimpse of crisp black hairs curling on his chest. He reached out and took the now sleeping child from me and, after kissing her head, put her in her cradle. Valentine smiled in her sleep, a little dribble of milk still on her chin. Hugo wiped it away with his finger and licked it off, his eyes never leaving mine. I just walked into his arms and rested my head on his shoulder, my equilibrium finally restored.

"That bad?" he asked, already knowing the answer.

"It was fine, really."

"Neve, the king was seen watching you across the room. That's enough to make women despise you on sight. He was probably nothing more than curious about you, but any sign of interest is enough to mark you as competition. Don't take anything they said to heart."

"Are you disappointed that Valentine is a girl?" I blurted out. I knew it was a silly question, but I had to hear it from his lips. I knew he wanted a son but was sure that he loved Valentine as much as he would have a boy. Was I wrong?

Hugo held me away from himself and stared at me, his face incredulous. "Do you really believe that?"

"No, but I had to ask."

"Neve, I thank God every single day for sparing you from dying in childbirth and granting me a precious little girl. Of course I'm not disappointed. Besides, there's still time to have a boy."

"And if we don't?"

"Then Clarence will inherit, and perhaps history will go on as it was meant to, with me dying without producing a male heir."

Hugo carefully maneuvered me toward the bed, but I planted my hands on his chest, making him pause. "Hugo, I know that you hope I'll change my mind, but I'm not ready for another child, nor will I be for some time to come."

"I know," he replied in a soothing manner. "I would never go against your wishes. We will plan for it when the time is right."

"But we hadn't planned Valentine," I protested.

"No, but we had never *not* planned her," Hugo replied soothingly. "I think perhaps you wanted to get pregnant; it made it easier for you to justify staying with me."

I opened my mouth to protest but realized that perhaps Hugo was right. Choosing to stay with him and go back had not been an easy decision, and being pregnant certainly made it easier for me to justify leaving everything I knew behind and returning to a century rife with disease, religious intolerance, and a lack of plumbing. Baby or no baby, I would have stayed with Hugo, but perhaps, subconsciously, I needed that extra reassurance that we were meant to be together.

I climbed into bed and snuggled up against Hugo, who'd given up on the idea of getting me into an amorous mood. His eyes were half closed, his breathing even, but I wasn't done with him yet.

"Hugo?"

"Hmm?"

"Why were we really invited to Court? We'd been treated like lepers for months, and suddenly the king himself is welcoming us to Versailles. What's changed?" I wasn't fool enough to believe that Hugo didn't have a hand in whatever was going on, but he'd remained tight-lipped so far, no doubt to spare me worry. But I was worried, more than I was willing to admit.

"Go to sleep, my sweet," Hugo mumbled, even though I was sure he was still wide awake. I felt my stomach clench. I'd been in the seventeenth century long enough to understand something of the way things worked, although I was still a novice at anything having to do with politics. If Hugo was suddenly welcome at the Court of Louis XIV, it wasn't because the king felt like showing generosity toward a traitor in exile. A deal had been struck, but what did it entail, and how would it affect us if it didn't play out as planned? I was exhausted but lay awake for at least an hour before finally drifting off to sleep, my mind still in a whirl.

# TWENTY-TWO

Frances watched from her chair by the fireside as the door handle turned quietly, and Sabine poked her face into the room, her smile full of mischief. Frances felt tired and languid, and not really in the mood for company, but she pasted a smile of welcome onto her face, for fear of offending her friend.

Sabine quickly entered the room and shut the door behind her with her foot. She set a small carafe of brandy and two cups on the small table where Frances kept a book of poems and a flagon of perfume Neve had given her for her birthday in December. Frances loved the scent, but it was the book of poems that was a favorite, since it was a present from Archie. The book looked as good as new despite daily handling, the pages crisp and the binding intact. Frances turned the pages reverently when she read, and never opened the book all the way for fear of creasing the spine.

Frances jumped to her feet and snatched the book off the table before Sabine spilled brandy on it and slid it beneath her pillow for safekeeping.

"I didn't take too much, so he'll hardly notice it," Sabine said, referring to the brandy.

Frances didn't think Lord Everly kept a watchful eye on the brandy supply, but it wouldn't do to get caught.

Sabine poured a cup for Frances and one for herself and sprawled in the comfortable chair by the fire. She raised her cup in a toast to Frances before tossing back the drink and refilling her cup.

Frances took a dainty sip. Brandy was meant to be savored, not gulped down, but Sabine wouldn't know that; she had probably never had it before, judging by the look of appreciation on her elfin face. She was remarkably pretty, with thick chestnut hair and eyes that were almost golden, especially in the firelight. Her features were delicate, and her figure trim despite a voracious appetite.

"I do wish we had some cake," Sabine complained, but Frances wasn't hungry. She wasn't particularly thirsty either, but she usually enjoyed these late-night visits from the maid.

Lord Everly likely wouldn't approve of their friendship, which is why they kept it secret, but it suited them both. Frances genuinely liked Sabine. She wasn't sullen like Marthe, or shy like Elodie. Sabine was mischievous, chatty, and very well informed for a girl of seventeen. She'd worked hard to become a lady's maid, and prided herself on her ingenuity and quick wit. Frances harbored a suspicion that Sabine had done something to "assist" in the dismissal of the lady's maid whose position she had taken up at her previous employer's, but Sabine didn't elaborate and Frances didn't pry. She kept plenty of secrets herself, so Sabine was entitled to hers.

At fifteen, Frances had learned that the less she divulged, the better, realizing that once something had been said it could never be unsaid, and she preferred to keep her past to herself. She wasn't looking for a confessor, just a friend to spend a few hours with when she was feeling lonely. The girls usually stayed up well past midnight, talking, laughing, and drinking until it was time for Sabine to retire. She had to get up early to start her day, and it wouldn't do to look tired or disheveled.

"I'm not a lady of leisure who gets to sleep till noon, like some people I know," she teased Frances good-naturedly.

Frances finished her drink and held out her cup for more, laughing as Sabine shook the carafe to get the last drops out.

"Waste not, want not," she said as she finished her own drink with a sigh of regret. "Oh, I do like this stuff. I tell you, Frances, I was born into the wrong family. If I weren't, why would I be able to appreciate all the finer things in life like a true lady?" she mused. "If only I could have a life of comfort like you. Why, I would marry an old, wrinkled man if he'd have me, just to be rich and titled, and I wouldn't complain once. I would feed him, and dress him, and pleasure him, if required, while secretly waiting for him to die and leave me a rich widow." Sabine sighed dramatically, making Frances laugh. She had no idea what it was like to be trapped in a loveless marriage, but then again, Frances had no idea what it was like to have to work for a living and know that the best you could ever hope for was to have enough to live on, and maybe a little money put by for old age.

"Do you chat much with Elodie?" Frances asked carefully, so as not to give herself away. She'd seen Elodie talking to Archie in the kitchen, the young maid blushing prettily as Archie practiced his French on her. Frances had told herself over and over that she didn't care, and it was no business of hers what Archie did, or with whom, but seeing them laughing together had cut like a knife.

Archie was always polite and helpful, but their relationship had changed since the night she had visited his room. Gone was the friend, companion, and confidante whom Archie had become over the long winter months. They were awkward with each other now, and it was all her fault. She'd gambled and lost, and she hadn't realized how much until Archie was no longer there.

"Oh, Elodie is such a mouse," Sabine said, pouting. "We have nothing in common. All she cares about is going to visit her family on her afternoons off. She's never even had a lover," Sabine whispered as if she was sharing a scandalous bit of gossip. "Imagine that. Twenty-three years old, and as innocent as the day she was born."

"I think she fancies Archie," Frances mumbled, praying that Sabine would dispute her assumption.

"Oh, she does. She thinks the sun rises and sets on him, but Archie is not interested in the likes of her."

"How can you tell?" Frances asked, intrigued.

"You can always tell. It's the way he looks at her, like she's a piece of furniture. I declare, his eyes have never strayed below her face, and if he desired her, they would—and lower. Archie is a dark horse, isn't he?" Sabine asked, warming up to the subject. "You say you spent a night with him once in England? Did he try anything on? Ooh, I would have let him," she purred, smiling wickedly. "He does have a certain way about him, even if he is a ginger. Never did care for red-headed men, but I would make an exception for Archie."

"No, he didn't try anything. He was the perfect gentleman," Frances replied. "And what do you know about having a lover anyway?"

Sabine smiled like a cat that had just got at the cream. "I know plenty. I'm not a baby like you. But you wait and see; getting married will be an eye-opening experience for you, if your husband is a good lover. If not, you'll spend the rest of your days wondering about what you are missing. Or, you can always take a lover. I would, if I were married to a man who didn't please me. As a matter of fact, there's a groom next door who keeps making cow-eyes at me. Perhaps I'll give him a bit of encouragement, but I would prefer Archie," Sabine mused, her eyes dreamy as she imagined having a secret love affair. "Wouldn't it be delicious to have a lover?" she purred.

"I wouldn't know; I've never had one," Frances replied, suddenly wishing that Sabine would just leave. She didn't want to talk about Archie; it upset her. What she wouldn't give to have Archie's friendship back. The worst part was that she couldn't quite understand what had happened between them. He'd rejected her, but then he'd kissed her so passionately, as if he truly wanted her, and now he treated her as if she were a leper. Had she insulted him somehow? She would ask him, but she couldn't bear to degrade herself any further. She was lonely without him, though. Even Luke hadn't called on them in nearly two weeks, so she was stuck with Sabine for company. "I'm feeling rather tired," Frances said as she rose from her seat.

"And what have you done to get tired?" Sabine asked petulantly as she gathered up the carafe and cups and made for the door. "I've never known anyone who has it so easy. Well, goodnight then, Your Ladyship," she said, giving Frances an exaggerated bow. "I'll see you in the morning."

Frances didn't bother to reply. There was a lump in her throat that prevented her from speaking. She turned away from the closing door, hot tears running down her face. She wasn't even sure why she was crying, but she felt thoroughly wretched. Archie would have understood, since he knew more about her than anyone besides Lord and Lady Everly, but Archie wasn't there for her, so she had to deal with her misery alone.

Frances climbed into bed, pulled out the book of poems from under her pillow and hugged it to her chest. She knew the poems by heart, so she recited one to herself for comfort. It was "On a Certain Lady at Court," by Alexander Pope—the one she thought applied best to herself and Archie.

> I know the thing that's most uncommon;
> (Envy be silent and attend!)

I know a Reasonable Woman,
Handsome and witty, yet a Friend.

Not warp'd by Passion, aw'd by Rumour,
Not grave thro' Pride, or gay thro' Folly,
An equal Mixture of good Humour,
        And sensible soft Melancholy.

'Has she no Faults then (Envy says), Sir?'
        Yes she has one, I must aver:
When all the World conspires to praise her,
The Woman's deaf, and does not hear.

# TWENTY-THREE

## APRIL 1686

**Paris, France**

Luke Marsden refolded the letter and tossed it on his desk, then leaned back in his chair and gazed out the window of his study. A gentle April rain was falling from a pewter sky, the air blowing through the open window, bringing with it the smell of wet earth and greening grass. The room was chilly and lost in shadow, but Luke didn't bother to light a candle or poke the fire back into life. Instead, he poured himself a small brandy and resumed his contemplation of the wet garden. Several birds were perched on a still-bare branch and were singing their hearts out despite the miserable weather. Luke supposed that was a fine example of optimism, something he wasn't feeling at the moment since he had a decision to make; a decision which would change several lives, including that of Hugo Everly. Ordinarily, Luke wouldn't have been so cautious, but his feelings for Frances complicated matters, since Hugo might not be too pleased with what Luke was about to undertake.

The letter was from Nicholas Marsden, Luke's cousin and lifelong best friend. At one time, Hugo and Nicholas had been great friends as well, but Margaret had come between them, as she had between most men. By the time Nicholas had met Margaret in Cranley, her relationship with Hugo was long over, but Hugo was still fond of her since she'd been his first adolescent love. Hugo never spoke of it, but Luke suspected that Margaret had seduced a teenage Hugo and stole his heart for her growing collection. Hugo's father had threatened Hugo with the whip if he so much as looked at Margaret again, but they'd remained friends, even after she had left the manor to go work in the village.

By the time Nicholas met Margaret, she was nearly eighteen and in full bloom. Luke had to admit that the two of them were better suited than any couple he'd seen before or since, but not for the long term. Nicholas was a man who loved life. Despite the repressive teachings of the Church, he embraced his desires and acted on them whenever possible. Nicholas was the wildest, wittiest, and most adventurous of them all. He and Margaret had collided like two celestial beings, ripping each other to shreds emotionally, but making the type of love that few people ever experienced in their lifetime. Their relationship was torrid and volatile, and had left them both scarred for life. It would never have lasted had they stayed together and would have left them bitter and disillusioned once the passion wore off, but their love wasn't blessed (or cursed) with longevity. It had been like a comet in the sky: unexpected, beautiful, and fleeting.

Hugo had disapproved when Nicholas took Margaret back to London with him and set her up as his mistress; he knew how it would end and wanted to protect two people that he cared about, but Nicholas and Margaret had just laughed off his concerns and went off into the sunset together—that was until Nicholas's father chose a bride for him.

Tess was a sweet, innocent girl of eighteen, a girl who would make a dutiful wife and a loving mother, but would never be able to give Nicholas what he needed, especially in the bedroom. She would be compliant and obliging, but she would never set him on fire the way Margaret did. Nicholas had confided to Luke once that Margaret liked to play games, games which heightened their sexual pleasure. Margaret often provoked Nicholas into a burning rage, and taunted him until he took a strap to her, which seemed only to inflame her desire, and his. She liked to be tied up as well, and blindfolded, totally surrendering control and allowing Nicholas free rein over her body. No prim maiden would ever let him do that, but Nicholas had to do his duty, and it was not as if he could ever marry his lover.

Nicholas had sworn to Margaret that he didn't care for Tess, but Margaret had flown into a rage and left in the middle of the night, sending Nicholas on a month-long search for her, which had ended with him finding her in a brothel purely by accident. Seeing her with other men had cooled his ardor, but Nicholas had never quite got over Margaret. He had married Tess and resigned himself to being a good husband, and might have succeeded, had the poor girl not died in childbirth less than a year after the marriage, the baby with her.

Nicholas had grieved for his wife and son longer than anyone might have expected, and then had eventually married Anne. Anne was better suited to Nicholas in temperament and strength of character. They actually got on well together, finding things in common and slowly building on fondness and mutual respect until something resembling true love began to grow out of mere affection. For the first time in years, Nicholas was content. He'd cut down on his drinking and carousing, gave up gambling, and settled down to making a family and running his estate. Luke was a frequent guest at The Towers in Devon, and had been there when tragedy struck.

Luke wouldn't admit this to too many people, but he'd always believed God to be jealous of people's happiness. Prob-

ably because joy rarely led people down the path of right-
eousness. Nothing brought people to church like misery and
suffering, but happiness reduced God to a quaint notion that
they remembered at Sunday service. It seemed that Nicholas
had committed that unforgivable sin of finally finding peace
and purpose in his life.

It had been a drizzly April morning just like today when
Anne had insisted on going out for her morning ride. Nicholas
had asked her to reconsider, but she was feeling restless after
days of driving rain and needed a bit of air and exercise. The
drizzle had finally let up, and the sun was peeking through the
clouds, making every raindrop sparkle, and turning the world
into a kaleidoscope of light. Luke had offered to accompany
Anne, and she had eagerly accepted, glad of the company.
Nicholas had stayed behind to meet with his estate manager
regarding some minutiae concerning the tenants.

Luke could still see Anne galloping in front of him, her
unbound dark hair streaming behind her as the sunlight
dappled her face and drops of moisture rained from the
branches overhead. Anne had laughed as she'd spurred her
horse on to go faster. She wanted to jump a hedge up ahead. He
could see it all in his mind. It happened in slow motion again
and again; the accident that he might have prevented had he
insisted that she slow down. Although, knowing Anne, she
probably wouldn't have listened to him anyway.

Anne had approached the hedge at great speed, and her
horse had jumped, the hooves flying over the top of the
branches and landing gracefully on the other side. Luke was
just about to call out his praise when he saw the horse falter and
heard Anne scream as the horse's hooves slipped in the mud on
the other side of the hedge, and the horse fell hard, coming
down on top of Anne, who'd been riding side-saddle.

It had taken Luke nearly an hour to get back with help since
Anne couldn't possibly ride back with him. Nicholas and the

estate agent had returned with a wagon and gently lifted Anne onto the bed. Luke could still hear her desperate screams. She had survived, but her pelvic bone had been broken when the horse's weight came down on her. Anne had eventually learned how to walk again with the aid of two walking sticks, but she could never bear children—something that ate at her every single day until the spirited, lively woman became nothing more than a mere shell of her former self. Now, twelve years later, she was still an invalid, and a constant reminder to her husband of what could never be.

It wasn't until Luke had seen Jem in December that the idea had taken root, but he needed to make sure he wasn't seeing something that wasn't really there. He'd written to his cousin, asking as tactfully as he could if Nicholas had ever taken a mistress since Anne's accident, and if there might have been an encounter with Margaret. In his youth, Nicholas might have boasted of his conquests, but not today. He'd become reticent and more religious; a sure sign that he was in pain.

Luke reached for the letter again and reread the two sentences which made all the difference. *"I don't know what possible difference it can make now, since Margaret is long gone, but yes, I did see her in November of 1676. I thought that finding Margaret again might relieve some of the pain, but this wasn't the same girl whom I'd fallen in love with, nor was I the same man."*

November 1676. Nine months before Jem was born. Luke had seen traces of his cousin in the boy's face long before he knew that Margaret had been his mother, but now he was sure. Jem wasn't Hugo's son, as everyone mistakenly assumed, he was Nick's; the only son he was ever likely to have unless Anne died and Nicholas married again, which was unlikely.

So, now Luke had two choices. He could keep silent and let sleeping dogs lie, or he could reunite the boy with his father and transform him from a bastard into an heir to a profitable estate, and in the process tear Jem from a family he loved, separate Hugo from his foster son, and most of all, break Anne's heart all over again. Of course, in due time, Jem would adjust, and Hugo would surely want what was best for the boy, but would Anne ever forgive him for foisting another woman's bastard on her and watching as her husband fell in love, for anyone who met Jem was bound to love him, Luke thought.

Luke ran his hand through his hair and finished his brandy. He'd have to talk to Hugo before replying to Nick, but his mind was made up. Nicholas had a right to know about his son, especially since he'd truly loved Margaret and would have married her had she not been a penniless washerwoman.

Thinking of marrying for love brought him back to thoughts of Frances. She was sweet and charming toward him, but he'd seen very little change in her attitude since he'd spoken to Hugo of marriage. Perhaps it was time he went directly to the source.

# TWENTY-FOUR

## APRIL 1686

**Barbados, West Indies**

Max turned over irritably in an effort to get more comfortable but couldn't get back to sleep. He was tired, and his back throbbed painfully, but the stifling, stale air in the hut and the snoring of twenty sleeping men were enough to raise the dead. He gave up on sleep for the time being, and ventured outside, where he sat down on the stoop and gazed up at the star-strewn sky. The air was balmy and warm, the tang of the sea just discernable if one breathed deeply. What he wouldn't give for a swim. It hadn't rained since that last storm, and Max felt dirty, smelly, and hot. He'd broken out in some sort of rash all over his body, likely caused by lack of hygiene, and his beard and hair were crawling with lice. He scratched absentmindedly as he leaned against the doorframe of the hut.

It'd been over a week since his conversation with Xeno, and with every passing day, he felt more tormented by thoughts of escape. Before Xeno had summoned him, Max had grudgingly accepted his fate, trying to keep his head down and planning for what he would do once his indenture was up, but now that there was a glimmer of hope—if being buried alive could be construed as hope—he felt restless and torn. Xeno's plan was absolutely mad, and any rational person would dismiss it out of hand, as he had, but what if it worked? What if there actually was a chance of getting off this godforsaken island?

Xeno had struck a nerve, as he knew he would, when he'd spoken of Max dying before his sentence was up. The graveyard was full of people who'd never see freedom again. Many had died of overwork and poor nutrition, but a much greater number had been carried off by yellow fever, or Yellow Jack as the slaves called it. Perhaps Max's twenty-first-century immune system could fight off an attack of yellow fever, but he could just as easily contract malaria or some other kind of island disease. And even if by some miracle he remained healthy, he still had more than six and a half years of servitude before he could regain his freedom, and then what? How would he get back to England? Even if he managed to hire himself out as part of a crew on a ship bound for England, he'd be coming back more than seven years after his disappearance from the twenty-first century.

Would the passage still exist? Would it take him back to the time he left, or would he show up in Cranleigh nearly eight years later? Would he be able to reclaim his place? He wasn't quite sure, but he thought it took seven years to pronounce someone dead if there was no body. Even if he managed to get back home, he might be seen as an impostor, a fraud. And his mother... Lady Everly might not even be alive by the time he got back, so he would be returning to a house inhabited by someone else. Max had never made a Will, but the estate would go to his next of kin, which was a distant cousin from Newcastle who'd emigrated to Canada a few years back. These thoughts drove Max crazy, making him uncomfortably aware of the urgency of getting back home.

Max shook his head as if trying to dislodge his turbulent thoughts, but they kept coming back, refusing to leave him in peace. Could Xeno be trusted? What if he just left Max to die? Who would know? Who would even care? Of course, many of the slaves had heard Xeno's promise, but who was to say that they would condemn him for breaking it, or not encourage him to leave Max to his fate? Max was just a white man, a symbol of oppression, even if he himself was in a position of near-slavery. In their eyes, he was a man who had something to go back to, a life of luxury to reclaim where their lives had been stolen from them. They would never see their homeland again, or reunite with the people they'd been torn from. This was where they would live and where they would die, unless Jessop Greene decided to sell them on or give one of them as a gift, possibly one of their children.

And what in the world could Xeno be smuggling to France? Did the slaves steal sugarcane and use it to pay for whatever it was they got from the French captain? Max hadn't seen any items of luxury in the slave barracks—nothing at all, save a few clay pots and moth-eaten blankets. A few of the women wore colorful dresses and turbans, but everyone else wore the same linen pajamas like those issued to Max. Perhaps it was just a story Xeno had made up, thinking it would give his proposal greater credibility.

Max leaned his head back and looked up at the sky. A bright light streaked across the sky, and was gone as quickly as it came, but for some reason, Max suddenly felt a little more hopeful. Perhaps not all was lost. What if he could escape and get back to England? He'd have a lot of explaining to do, but eventually he would get back to his life and think of this nightmare as a distant memory, a bad dream that had troubled his sleep a long time ago. He allowed himself a moment of fantasy, thinking of all the things he would do if he ever got back, a slow smile spreading across his face at the thought of a bath. But was Xeno's plan worth the risk, or would he be hastening his own death?

# TWENTY-FIVE

## APRIL 1686

**Paris, France**

Archie was glad to escape the house to see to some errands for
Lord Everly. It was a lovely spring day, and the newly greening
trees and vibrant flower beds lifted his spirits, if only momentarily. He'd spent the past two weeks brooding, particularly
because he didn't have enough to do. Since the birth of the baby,
things had been relatively quiet, except for the invitation to
Versailles. Archie had enjoyed the outing, getting to see something of the countryside, and spending a few enjoyable hours
with other men-at-arms and grooms as they waited for their
masters to return. The Frenchmen had been unwelcoming at
first, but as more ale was consumed, Anglo-French relations
greatly improved. Archie smiled at the memory, hoping he'd get
to go back. There were a number of very comely serving girls as
well, and given enough time...

*Oh, who am I kidding?* Archie thought miserably. He hadn't
stopped thinking of Frances since she had so unexpectedly
showed up in his room. He'd had many lovers over the past
decade, but they had all been either married or widowed,

women who gave as freely as they took and expected nothing in return. They wanted a bit of affection and physical pleasure, as did he. Archie had never stayed long enough to develop any feelings for his partners, although he felt a fondness for them all, especially Margaret.

The affair with Margaret had lasted close to a year, although she had made it clear that Archie wasn't the only one and never would be. He didn't really care. Margaret was considerably older than him and had had enough emotional upheaval to last several lifetimes. He didn't wish to add to her troubles, and they had become close friends rather than just lovers. Truth be told, Margaret had been one of the closest friends Archie had ever had, and he missed their talks. Margaret would have been the perfect person to talk to about Frances. She'd tell him what to do, and she would likely be right. Most men remembered Margaret for her beauty and her voracious sexual appetite, but they never realized how smart and intuitive she had been, how in tune with human nature.

Archie often wondered if Hugo Everly suspected that Archie had been one of Margaret's conquests, but he never asked. He had no claim to her but, like most men who'd known Margaret, still nursed feelings for her, only in his case they were more sympathy than lingering lust. Archie had to admit that just like Hugo, he felt a certain responsibility toward Jem because of the bond he shared with his mother, and kept an eye on the boy at all times, teaching him whatever he could about life.

Jem had begun asking questions about romance of late, forcing Archie to confront some questions of his own. He hadn't been with anyone since the previous summer when he'd thought that Hugo Everly was gone, and found himself feeling listless and frustrated. The months spent on his father's farm had left him itching for something to do, and the unexpected summons from Lord Everly were a blessing, as well as a balm to his soul. Archie truly cared about the man, and to find him alive after all those months had nearly made him cry.

But then came Frances. Archie thought he'd never see her again after leaving her at the Convent of the Sacred Heart. He'd felt sorry for the girl, and would have laid down his life to protect her, but he had firmly put her out of his mind, especially after seeing her hours after giving birth and then witnessing her bereavement after the death of Gabriel. He had never expected her to accompany them to France, nor did he bet on being the one to fetch her.

His thoughts often turned to that night they'd spent in the barn when she was so clearly terrified of him, but desperate to trust him all the same. That night something had shifted in Archie's soul, and try as he might, he couldn't get Frances out of his head. She was different from anyone he'd ever cared for: so achingly young, vulnerable, and hopeful. He'd rather cut off his own arm than cause her any more pain. She'd suffered way too much for a girl of fifteen, and he prided himself on being her protector and friend.

Only it seemed that his heart wasn't completely in accord with his mind. Kissing her had been a dreadful mistake, a mistake that had opened up a flood of feelings that Archie had been keeping suppressed since he'd first met her in her husband's house. Archie would have gladly killed Lionel Finch with his bare hands had Hugo allowed him to, but he'd kept his temper in check and did his absolute best to come up with a place where Frances would be safe. But now she wasn't safe anymore; not safe from him. He thought of her day and night, and woke up throbbing with desire.

In her innocence, Frances had opened a door he'd kept firmly locked for months, but what did he have to offer her when she had the opportunity to marry someone like Luke Marsden, who had wealth and a respectable place in society? Archie had spent fruitless hours searching for some fault in the man, but Luke was handsome, charming, influential, and wealthy. He seemed smitten with Frances, who appeared to be somewhat frightened by his ardor. She just needed time, but Luke was willing to wait.

*Damn him*, Archie thought vengefully as he walked faster in his agitation. *Damn him.*

# TWENTY-SIX

Frances smiled in gratitude as Luke presented her with a box of marzipan exquisitely molded into various spring flowers and arranged like a miniature flower bed. They were too lovely to eat, but she dutifully selected one and took a dainty bite, making Luke glow with pleasure as she held the box out to him in invitation.

"Do have one," she insisted.

Luke selected a delicate red rose sprinkled with caramelized sugar in an artful imitation of drops of dew.

"They say red roses are a symbol of love," he said as he took a bite. "Would you have given it to me had I asked?"

"Perhaps you should have given it to me," she replied, avoiding the question.

"I'd give you dozens of red roses if you would give me the slightest bit of encouragement," Luke said, looking like a particularly forlorn puppy.

"I don't believe I've discouraged you, have I?" Frances asked coyly.

Luke grinned, taking her answer as a sign of favor. "Would you care for a stroll in the Jardin des Tuileries? It's simply glorious outside. Perhaps we can feed the ducks and then have a cup of chocolate at that brasserie you like."

"I would like that very much," Frances answered.

In truth, she was desperate to get out of the house. The tension between Archie and her was so thick you could cut it with a knife; Neve and Hugo were preoccupied with their squalling offspring; and Jem was just plain annoying, with his constant demands for attention. Perhaps Sabine could chaperone. She would be grateful for a break from her daily duties, and Luke would be less than a gentleman if he didn't invite her for a cup of chocolate and pastries as well—a treat that Sabine likely never had, at least not in a brasserie, like a lady. She would really enjoy that, and owe Frances a favor for the outing, something that might come in handy in the future.

Frances had to admit that she was feeling a little resentful of Sabine at the moment. She'd finally succumbed to the advances of the groom from next door and was sneaking out to see him after everyone retired, leaving Frances feeling even lonelier than she had before. She'd finally come to visit Frances last night and gushed about the hours her and Pierre spent in his little garret; their limbs intertwined as they lay together naked after making love.

What would it be like to feel so comfortable with someone? Frances wondered. Could she have that type of relationship with Luke? Somehow she doubted it, but his buttoned-up exterior could very well be just a façade for his political career. Would he be a passionate lover, or, more importantly, a kind one? She was sure Archie would have been, but he'd been ignoring her for weeks, his eyes sliding away from hers every time they were in the same room together.

Frances sighed at the thought of Archie. She missed him so much. They used to talk about nothing and everything, and laugh at Archie's silly jokes, but now he was stone-faced and rigid, a stranger.

Frances had finally shared her feelings with Sabine, believing that it was safe to confide in her now that she had a lover of her own and was no longer interested in Archie, but Sabine had just scoffed at her. "You need to learn to think like a French woman," she had said, her chest swelling with her perceived superiority.

"And what would a French woman do in my position?" Frances had asked, annoyed, but unbearably curious. Sabine's view of the world was so different from her own.

"French women are practical and passionate at the same time, like me," Sabine had added with pride. "Any woman in her right mind would marry Luke for his position and wealth and take Archie as a lover."

"Before or after the marriage?" Frances had asked, pondering this sage advice.

"Before, during, and after, you silly *petite enfant*," she had replied, her brown eyes sparkling with mischief and her curls bouncing as she'd laughed at France's look of shock. "Who says you can't have two men at once? Men sleep with as many women as they wish, so why should we be any different?"

"Have you ever had two lovers at once?"

"I'm not going to tell you," Sabine had replied self-importantly and put down the hairbrush. "A woman must always have secrets; that's what makes her mysterious and desirable."

*Oh, I have plenty of secrets*, Frances had thought sadly as remembered the tiny baby she'd buried in a graveyard in Surrey. Gabriel would always be her secret, partly because Lord and Lady Everly advised her not to tell anyone she'd had a child, and partly because she just couldn't bear to speak of him without falling to pieces. It had taken her a long time to get a grip on her grief, and now she would take Sabine's advice and be a practical, passionate woman who was swathed in mystique and in control of her emotions.

"I need a few moments with Lord Everly, if you don't

mind," Luke said as Frances turned to go upstairs to get her cape and hat. "Shall we meet in the foyer?"

"Of course; don't rush on my account," Frances called over her shoulder as she dashed up the stairs, suddenly feeling lighter than she had in weeks. An outing with Luke was just what she needed, and she would make the most of it and remind him just how much he wanted her, in case he had forgotten. But, judging by the look in his eyes, Luke was as enamored as ever, so perhaps it was time to throw him a bone.

\* \* \*

Luke found Hugo in the library, reading some correspondence which he hastily shoved into the drawer of the mother-of-pearl inlaid walnut desk. He'd seemed distressed, but the look of pain was instantly replaced by a warm smile of welcome.

"Luke, a pleasure to see you. Are you here to see me or Frances?"

"Both, actually," Luke began as he took the proffered seat. He was suddenly unsure of how to phrase what he'd come to say, but it had to be done. Nick's interests had to come first, as did Jemmy's. Luke knew that Hugo genuinely cared for the boy and was his self-appointed guardian, but Jem wasn't his natural son, so all he could ever hope to be in Hugo's household was a poor relation, of sorts. "Hugo, what would you say if I told you that I know who Jem's father is?" he asked carefully.

"I would tell you that I'm interested in what you have to say," Hugo replied smoothly.

Luke had seen a glimmer of unease in Hugo's eyes, but Hugo instantly rearranged his expression into one of polite interest. Did he know the truth? Luke wondered. Had Margaret told him before she died? Was that why he had taken the boy in, out of regard for both his mother and his friend?

"I know you said that his father was a groom on your estate, but I think you might be mistaken," Luke continued. Hugo looked mildly curious, but not upset, so Luke went on. "I believe Jem's father is Nicholas." There, it was out.

Hugo leaned back in his chair and smiled at Luke, something that the younger man hadn't expected. Did he wish to get rid of the boy?

"I know," Hugo replied smugly.

"But you said..."

"I know what I said," Hugo remarked. "It was Margaret's wish that Jem's father never know about the boy, so she put about the tale about a groom since he'd left our employ shortly after she found herself with child, but I suspected he might be Nick's from the moment I first saw him."

"He's the spitting image, isn't he?" Luke agreed. "Why didn't she want him to know?"

"Pride, spite, fear of losing Jem," Hugo said, shrugging his shoulders. "Who could ever truly understand Margaret? She was a law unto herself, full of her own ideas of how life should be lived."

"Yes, she was that. So, you are not surprised then?" Luke asked carefully, in preparation for the next portion of his speech.

"No. I did believe the tale of the groom for a while, but it was when I saw you watching Jem as if you'd seen a ghost that I suddenly realized that my suspicions were not unfounded. I was wondering if you'd write to Nicholas. I'm assuming you did."

"Hugo, you know Nick's situation," Luke said delicately, hoping that Hugo would infer the rest.

"Yes, I do. How is Anne?" Hugo asked. He hadn't seen her for many years, but they'd been friends once, and Hugo had always admired Anne's spirit and her ability to tame Nick's wild ways. But the accident had not only broken Anne's bones, it had broken Nick's spirit and destroyed their marriage. He'd never set foot in her bedchamber again, following doctor's orders, and they became two strangers living under the same room and drinking from the same cup of bitterness.

"Same as ever. She spends her days painting, reading, and sitting in the garden on fine days. Her and Nick barely see each other. They can't bear to be in the same room without their hurt and disappointment getting in the way of any possible affection."

"Has Nick never taken a mistress?" Hugo asked, curious about his old friend. The Nick he'd known would have slept with half the Court by now, but he hadn't heard any gossip for years. Nick was living quietly in the country, tending to his estate, and generally staying out of trouble. Of course, there were plenty of women in the country, if one was looking for a quick fling.

"He hasn't been celibate, if that's what you're asking, but he hasn't forged any relationships out of respect for Anne. It would kill her to know that he loves someone else."

"Poor Nick; life hasn't been kind to him, has it?"

"Life is hardly ever kind, especially to those who choose to live the way Nick had. He's paying for his sins, if you ask me."

"We all have sins," Hugo replied, his face closed.

"Judging by the position you find yourself in, I'd say you are paying for yours, my friend. I do think it was kind of you to take in Jem, especially knowing what you know. You've never forgiven Nick for Margaret, have you?"

"Margaret was a grown woman and made her own choice. I warned her that Nick would tire of her," Hugo replied, remembering the heated argument he'd had with Margaret when he'd heard that she'd be accompanying Nicholas back to London.

"He hadn't. Margaret left him when she found out he was getting married. She said she wouldn't share him with anyone," Luke revealed, amazed by the misguided passion of the woman.

"Did she think Nick would marry her? Had he made promises?" Hugo asked, amazed.

"Of course not. Nick's father would have skinned him alive if he'd married Margaret and would have killed her with his bare hands if Nick had refused an annulment. Nick knew better than to promise anything. He was a libertine, but not a liar. He truly loved Margaret; that's why finding out that he had a son by her might soothe his wounded soul."

"If Nicholas wants to legitimize Jem, I would be very happy for them both. He's a wonderful boy who deserves a better future than being my secretary. However, if that's not why you brought this up, I understand. Jem will always have a home with me, regardless."

"I'm glad you're not upset. I will write to Nicholas and pass on the happy news. I think he will be most anxious to meet Jem."

"I do hope so," Hugo replied, his face suddenly serious. "I will miss him if he goes. A man does need a son, doesn't he?"

"Yes, which brings me to my next point. Have you spoken any further with Frances?"

"Luke, Frances needs a little time, so you must be very patient. Don't push her. She's like a spirited filly that needs to be gentled and tamed. If you rush it, you will get thrown from the saddle."

"As much as I appreciate your equestrian metaphors, I do understand something of women," Luke replied with a laugh. "I will be the soul of patience."

"Good, now take that girl for a nice long walk and put some color into her cheeks—and not in the way you're thinking right now," Hugo added to a contrite Luke.

"Yes, *milord*," he replied tugging his forelock like an obedient servant.

# TWENTY-SEVEN

## APRIL 1686

**Barbados, West Indies**

The darkness was complete. Max heard his own panicked breathing as he awoke; first partially, then completely as he suddenly remembered where he was and why. He brought up his hands, but his palms rested on the rough wood only inches from his face. The heat inside the box was stifling, grains of sand falling onto his face and making his skin and eyes itch. Max tried to breathe, but his heart hammered inside his chest. He was dimly aware of the fact that he was on the verge of an anxiety attack, which would use up whatever air there was in the coffin very quickly. He tried to calm himself by thinking comforting thoughts, but his mind wouldn't cooperate. He was in complete panic mode, and no amount of trying to rationalize the situation would calm him even remotely.

Max's back was on fire, the scars from the recent flogging fresh and seeping blood. Salt from his sweat which ran into the open wounds made the pain unbearable. The flogging itself had been bad enough, with Johansson taking a short break between each stroke just to heighten the tension and prolong the agony, but the pain he'd been in since was even worse.

Max could still hear the swishing of the whip just before it met with the unblemished skin of his back, the pain so intense that he actually felt the tearing of the flesh as the knotted ends bit into his skin. It had been only thirty lashes for quitting work ten minutes before the end of day, but Max had felt every one of them. By the time Johansson was done, Max felt as if his back had been branded over and over with a hot iron until his flesh was seared and puckered. Squirming made the pain even worse, but Max couldn't possibly turn over since the box was just big enough for his body.

He was buried alive, six feet beneath the ground, another casualty of a system that put very little value on human life. By now, everyone would have gone, leaving the freshly dug mound with the crude cross sticking out of the ground. Sometimes, relatives or friends carved the name of the deceased into the crossbar, but for the most part, the crosses were unmarked since no one cared enough to remember the person who had died, or to visit their final resting place.

Max's would be just another grave with a nameless cross, a faceless victim. Did anyone besides his mother even remember him in his own life, or had everyone just moved on, assuming that he was dead? Well, he'd be dead in a few hours, and no one would ever know what had actually happened to him. He would vanish from the face of the earth, much as everyone thought Hugo Everly had, except there'd been an explanation for Hugo's disappearance, just as there was one for Max's, but no one would ever learn the truth. Max would become a family mystery, a scary bedtime story, a spooky tale to tell on Halloween—the man who vanished without a trace and was never heard from again.

Max's body began to shake violently, his mouth gasping for breath like a landed fish, his eyes bulging with lack of available oxygen as the anxiety attack rolled over him like a steam engine. Sweat poured down his face, and he could smell the acrid smell of fear overlaying the wood and earth that had swallowed him up. Max tried to concentrate on a single thought, but his thoughts raced around like rats in a maze, colliding with each other, banging against walls, and succumbing to blind panic. He tried pushing against the lid, but it was firmly in place, held down by several feet of packed earth and nailed shut.

Xeno had said that he would be hidden in the jungle by the time he awoke, but either Dido's potion had worn off too soon, or Xeno had no intention of keeping his promise. The shaking got worse, and Max gulped in more air, which didn't fill his lungs. He began banging on the lid, but who would hear him? They'd all have gone back to work, leaving him to die a slow, agonizing death. Grains of sand fell into Max's mouth, and he began to cough violently, banging his head on the wood every time his body spasmed. He couldn't breathe, couldn't see, couldn't stop the overwhelming anxiety that had taken over. Hot urine ran down his leg as his bladder let go. He thought he might soil himself, but it truly didn't matter. No one would ever see his shame.

Max began to see colored lights in front of his eyes as the lack of oxygen began to take its toll. He was thrashing and screaming, clawing at the lid of the coffin until he ripped off his nails, and his fingers became slick with blood. Something seemed to explode in Max's head as he went completely limp, his eyes rolling into the back of his head and his body stilling at last.

*I'm dying*, was the last thing Max thought before he lost consciousness.

# TWENTY-EIGHT

It was pitch black. Still. Max came awake with a shudder, recalling once again where he was. His heart pounded violently in his chest, and his throat was raw from inhaling sand and howling in terror. He drew a ragged breath, desperate for oxygen; more so because his mind knew he'd run out of air soon enough than because he couldn't breathe. He filled his lungs to capacity before suddenly realizing that the air wasn't hot and stale, but cool and plentiful. He lifted his hands before his face, praying that they wouldn't come up against the wooden lid of the coffin, when a gentle hand rested on his chest.

"Shh, Lord Everly. You're safe now," a man's voice said quietly, his accent unmistakable. Xeno.

"Where am I?" Max stammered.

"You're in the tunnel behind the barracks. Here, sit up and take a drink." Xeno held a cup of rum to his mouth, and Max drank greedily until he'd drained it.

"Is there any more?" he croaked. His heart was still racing, and he suddenly wondered if he might be having a hallucination. "Are you really here?"

"Of course I'm here, and so are you. Now, try to calm down.

We'll be taking you to the ship in a few hours. Are you hungry?" Xeno asked matter-of-factly, his hand still on Max's chest, an insignificant weight which kept him anchored to reality and blinding hope.

Max considered the question. His stomach was in knots, and bile rose in his irritated throat which burned from the rum. His eyes felt raw, and his hands were in agony where he'd torn off his nails. His back was on fire; the shirt glued to his flesh with sweat and blood. The thought of food made him feel nauseous, so he shook his head in the dark. "Maybe later."

"All right, you just rest awhile, and I will be back soon. I'll send Dido to sit with you."

Max nearly grabbed for Xeno in the darkness but restrained himself. The rum was taking effect, taking the edge off the pain and anxiety. *Am I really alive?* Max wondered as he listened to his labored breathing. *Is this a dream and I'll wake up in the coffin?*

He laid his hands flat against the ground and inhaled deeply. The air smelled of damp earth, rum, and his own sweat, but he didn't mind; these were the smells of life, of hope. Only a short while ago, he thought that his life was over. He'd been terrified of death, and bitter about all the missed opportunities and unfinished business, but he'd been given a second chance, a chance at a future. He'd cheated death twice in the past few months, he realized suddenly, smiling in the darkness. Perhaps he wasn't meant to die in the seventeenth-century, but in his own time when he was an old man.

His thoughts were interrupted by Dido, who glowed in the light from a candle she was carrying, her particular scent of womanliness and some kind of flower oil enveloping him. She crouched next to him and offered him another cup of rum, which he drank gratefully. He was by no means drunk, but he was now pleasantly tipsy, which was a vast improvement on unbridled panic.

"You are a brave man, Lord Everly, and a foolish one," she chided. "You could have died down there if your heart gave out. If Xeno says he'll get you out—he'll get you out. My brother is a man of his word."

"I hardly know your brother, but no one is happier that he's a man of his word than I. I thought I would die in that coffin," Max replied.

"And so you would have, if you hadn't passed out. You'd have worked yourself up into an apoplexy. Now, calm yourself and try to rest. It's a long walk to the harbor—many miles."

Dido put a warm hand on his face and caressed his cheek. It was a sensual gesture which wasn't lost on Max.

"I've seen you watching me," he remarked, hoping she would answer his unspoken question. He was in no condition to do anything more than hold her hand, but his vanity was alive and well, and he supposed he needed more than air and a cup of rum to feel as if he were back among the living. Funny how a person's reality shifted in the blink of an eye, Max mused. Only a few minutes ago he thought he was about to run out of oxygen and die, and now he was hoping that Dido would admit to her feelings for him.

"I was. Xeno wanted me to get a sense for the kind of man you are, and if you'd be brave enough to take the risk. He trusts my judgment," she added proudly.

"Was that the only reason?" Max asked. What did he have to lose?

"No. My mother lay down with a white man willingly. I was angry with her, and never forgave her, not even after she died," Dido confided. "She said she loved him. All I know of my father is that he had green eyes like Xeno and me. I suppose that until I saw you, I never knew how it was possible to want a white man, but now I know."

Dido leaned down and kissed Max. Her lips barely brushed his, but he felt a white-hot surge of desire. She smelled of spices, flower oil, and a tang of sweat, but he didn't care; he wanted her desperately. Blood rushed to his flaccid penis, suddenly reminding him what it was like to be sexually aroused. He hadn't felt anything other than despair and fatigue in months, so the feeling took him by surprise. Max reached up to pull Dido closer, but she drew back, her eyes laughing at him in her brown face.

"No, my man; I will not be having no white man's babies, or any babies," she said. "Not if I can't offer them a home and a family. You will be gone tonight, and I will remain here, so giving in to a mutual attraction is not wise."

Dido rose to her feet and retreated into the tunnel, leaving Max in the darkness once more. He was throbbing with frustrated desire, but he acknowledged the wisdom of her decision. He wanted her, but the thought of causing her any pain cooled his ardor. There was no escape for her; no future to look forward to other than remaining on the plantation or taking her chances in the jungle. She needed to exercise some control over her life, and he respected that. There would be other women in time.

# TWENTY-NINE

Max breathed a sigh of relief as he and Xeno finally emerged from the jungle after an arduous three-hour walk. Xeno seemed oblivious to insects, snakes, and gnarled roots, but Max was drained after the difficult trek, his breathing labored and his muscles sore from the strain. He'd felt ill before, but now he was ravenously hungry, his empty stomach rumbling in protest at the lack of food. He hadn't eaten anything in over twenty-four hours and wished he had accepted something when it had been offered.

Max could just make out the outline of the vessel, black against the midnight-blue sky sprinkled with stars and lit up by the gibbous moon. It shone as bright as a light bulb in the heavens, casting a silvery pall on the sleeping town and painting a glittering path on the dark waters of the sea.

A lone lantern glowed on the deck of the *La Belle,* swinging gently to and fro in a hypnotic fashion, reminding Max of just how tired he was.

Xeno drew a candle stub out of his pocket, lit it, and made some kind of circular signal, which he repeated several times. A few minutes later, a dinghy detached itself from the hull and made its way toward the beach, oars splashing in the still waters. Max gasped as two shadowy figures suddenly appeared next to them: one a fully grown man, the other, a small boy. The boy looked frightened, but the man said something to him in his own language and the child seemed to relax, his eyes drooping with fatigue as he watched the approaching dinghy. The man gave the child a bear hug, wordlessly shook Xeno's hand, then vanished into the shadows as suddenly as he had appeared, leaving the boy with them on the beach.

"Why is the child here?" Max asked as they waited for the boat.

"You asked me what we smuggle out of Barbados, and here's your answer. We smuggle out our children before they are branded as slaves."

Max balked at the idea but looked more closely at the boy. He was about five, with huge black eyes and full lips, which were now quivering with an urge to cry.

"What happens to them?" Max asked quietly, imagining all sorts of horrors in some French brothel. He'd read enough about human trafficking to know what happened to children who vanished off the face of the earth and died of abuse and neglect. Did these people really think that selling their children into sexual slavery was preferable to working on a sugar plantation where they were at least among their own people?

"The boys are placed with noble families as pages. Negro pages are all the rage in France these days," Xeno said bitterly. "They are treated almost as well as pets, and lead much more comfortable lives than slaves."

"And when they get older?"

"They either stay with the family as servants or leave and forge their own lives. At least they have a choice, and the family is usually generous to them after years of service. Captain Benoit brings word of the children when he comes back. Sometimes they even write letters to their parents. Most slaves can't read, but the white men can, so they read the letters for us."

Xeno took the boy by the shoulders and crouched in front of him so that their faces were only inches apart. The child wasn't crying, but he looked terrified. "Banjo, this is Lord Everly. He will be making the journey to France with you. You can trust him, and may keep him company if he wishes you to. Mind Captain Benoit and try to make yourself useful. The captain will see you settled in France. I know you're scared, but someday you will be glad you've been given this opportunity. I will tell your mother that you were very brave."

The boy swallowed hard and nodded, trying to smile. His smile was more of a grimace, but he seemed a little less frightened as he studied Max from beneath his thick lashes. He hesitantly reached for Max's hand as the boat reached the shore, and the men beckoned to them.

"Godspeed," Xeno said as he shook Max's hand.

"Are you not coming with us?" Max asked Xeno.

"I must get back before sunrise. Take care of each other on the journey. Captain Benoit is expecting you, and your voyage is paid for. Look after Banjo," he said, gave a small wave, and melted in the darkness.

"Well, it's you and me, kid," Max said to the little boy, who was clinging to him for dear life as they waded into the water toward the waiting dinghy. Max had few dealings with children in the past, but he felt a strange kinship with this frightened child who was being so brave in the face of separation from his family and a voyage to an unknown land and an uncertain future. He lifted Banjo into his arms and gave him a reassuring hug before passing him to the waiting sailor. He wasn't sure which one of them needed the hug more.

# THIRTY

**Paris, France**

Sir William Trumbull's pale gray eyes nailed Luke to his seat, and his mouth virtually disappeared as it compressed into a thin line. Sir Trumbull was not normally an amiable person when at home; he spent enough time smiling and flattering at Court to not feel the need to continue the charade in his private life. His home was the only place where he could wipe the forced smile off his face and have a moment of unguarded pique, but the moment he was having right now could be described more as a temper tantrum.

Luke cringed as his superior jumped to his feet and stood over him, jabbing his finger in Luke's chest as he enunciated every word for Luke's benefit.

"You absolute, total, brainless, thoughtless, gullible, moronic"—at this point Sir Trumbull paused, searching for just the right noun, but had to content himself with—"fool. I have a mind to send you back to England on the next boat, but that would look too suspicious to Louis's spies, so I have to keep you here despite my better judgment. I've turned a blind eye while you've welcomed your old friend to Paris, helped him find a place to live, and have actually been foolhardy enough to socialize with him, but now I must object. Do you honestly believe that a Catholic king, one who's as shrewd as Louis XIV, will suddenly welcome a convicted traitor, one who plotted against a fellow Catholic king and the king's own cousin, into his Court? Answer me," Trumbull roared in fury.

"No, my lord," Luke muttered as he tried to become one with the seat and suddenly wished that he could just vanish off the face of the earth.

"That's correct; the answer is no. If Louis has allowed Everly into his Court, it's because something of great value has been promised to him in exchange. And what do you think that might be, you worthless piece of dung? Well, I will tell you, since you clearly haven't worked this one out for yourself," Trumbull fumed, spraying Luke with spittle. "What does Everly have to offer? Intelligence. Intelligence that he will get from his good friend Luke Marsden. And how will he obtain it?" Trumbull thundered. "I'm glad you asked," Trumbull went on without giving Luke a chance to speak. "He will gather it through the offices of his comely ward, Mistress Frances Morley."

"Frances is an innocent," Luke protested, his face growing hot with humiliation and rage at the unfairness of the accusation against Frances. He was used to Trumbull's tirades against himself, but he would not sit by quietly and listen to his superior tarnish Frances's reputation.

"Is she, by God? And have you asked yourself exactly who she is? What's her relationship to Hugo Everly? Why has he taken her with him to France? Who are her people?"

"She's his ward," Luke replied hotly, suddenly aware of his own gullibility. Sir Trumbull was an arse, but in this instance, he was right. Luke knew very little about Frances, and Hugo had not been exactly forthcoming with information. Perhaps he should have dug deeper, but Frances appeared to be so angelically innocent that it was impossible to conceive of her doing something underhanded. She was a child—a charming child.

"Well, it might surprise you to learn that I've made inquiries into Mistress Morley in my last communication with England, and they had quite a lot to say on the subject in the return post which arrived only this morning. Morley is her maiden name—she's a Finch by marriage."

"Marriage?" Luke gasped, now fully cognizant of the magnitude of his idiocy.

"Yes, marriage," Sir Trumbull spat out, his jowls quivering with righteous indignation. "She was married to one Lionel Finch—the same Lionel Finch who accused Everly of abduction, attempted murder, and treason. It might surprise you even more to find out that Lionel Finch had been found dead at the side of the road to Portsmouth. Murdered. Think he did that to himself, do you? So, answer me, oh shrewd, devious, political animal that you are, what is her relationship to Everly? Is she his mistress? His spy? His illegitimate daughter? What?"

A shower of saliva flew from Sir Trumbull's mouth as he spat out that last question before finally exhausting himself and sinking into an armchair. He grabbed his glass of brandy and drained it in one gulp, his eyes never leaving Luke's flushed face.

"I will sever all ties to the Everly household, sir," Luke offered in an effort to pacify Trumbull, but the bulging of the eyes and the disappearance of the bushy eyebrows into the curls of the wig made Luke belatedly realize that he'd just made an even worse mistake. He had no intentions of severing ties with anyone, especially not now, when he needed access to Hugo's household more than ever, but he should have considered the suggestion more carefully before blundering forth.

"Sever ties?" Trumbull bellowed. "Sever ties? What kind of a fool are you, man? Why don't you just compose a formal declaration and present it to Everly? You must act like nothing is changed. You must give him no inkling that you know anything. Watch him like a hawk. See what you can learn from the little trollop. Feed him false information. And, for God's sake, don't let that transparent face of yours show any emotion other than bland courtesy. One misstep and you are going back to England in utter disgrace. You will never set foot at Court again if you so much as raise an eyebrow at Everly. Be his friend, court Frances Morley, and learn all you can. Now get out! I'm too vexed to suffer your presence a moment longer."

Luke got to his feet, bowed to his superior, who scoffed rather loudly, and made his way out of the room, feeling lower than a slug. His pride was deeply wounded, but not by Trumbull. The man was right in everything he said. Hugo had played Luke for a fool, had dangled Frances in front of him, knowing he couldn't resist a beautiful, fragile girl who needed protection. Or had he? Hugo had never encouraged his suit until he, himself, became persistent. Hugo had no choice but to introduce him to Frances since she was part of his family, but had he done anything to encourage the romance? Not really, if truth be told.

If anything, Hugo had advised Luke to bide his time and not rush Frances into any sort of commitment. Of course, Hugo had always been a clever bastard. It would be just like him to stand back and give Luke enough rope to hang himself with. There had to be a reason why the widow of Lionel Finch, who had met with a grisly end just days before Hugo had sailed for France, was now living with the very man whom her husband had accused of abduction.

And what was Hugo's wife's role in all of this? Hugo seemed devoted to her and their child, but there were plenty of men who played the loving husband while keeping a tasty morsel on the side—or, in this case, right down the corridor.

Somewhere at the back of his mind, Luke acknowledged

that Hugo had always been a man of honor and discretion. He wasn't a letch, nor was he someone who would take his marriage vows lightly, but Luke was too furious and humiliated to give his friend the benefit of the doubt. His stomach burned with anger, and his blood pounded in his temples as he stepped out into the street. He wanted retribution for the shame he'd suffered at Trumbull's hands, and he would have it.

But he had to tread carefully since he couldn't do anything until Trumbull trusted him again and was less likely to carry out the threat of sending him back to England, which would end his political career. Luke had plans for the future, and they didn't include going home in disgrace.

# THIRTY-ONE

## APRIL 1686

### Aboard the La Belle

Max gazed around the well-appointed cabin of Captain Benoit. The man obviously liked his comforts. The bed hangings were of rich burgundy brocade embroidered with gold thread, the desk was inlaid with an intricate pattern of flowers and leaves, and several potted plants were arranged by the window spanning the stern; their vibrant blooms muted in the candlelight. The bookcase was crammed with leather-bound volumes. One was lying open on the desk, revealing the pages of what appeared to be a medieval illuminated manuscript of some kind; a book, which would be worth millions in a few hundred years, carelessly tossed aside like a day-old newspaper.

Captain Benoit smiled with pleasure as the steward brought their supper. It was some kind of seafood stew which smelled strongly of fish and garlic. Max salivated as the aroma filled his senses, suddenly starved. He took a sip of the captain's fine claret and accepted a helping of the food, feeling very contented indeed. He never imagined that being clean, shaven, and fed would make him so happy, but at this moment, having shaved off his scratchy beard, taken the closest thing he'd had to a bath since leaving the twenty-first century and about to eat something that wasn't gruel, he was ecstatic.

The captain was a man in his forties, with graying dark hair and twinkling blue eyes. His face was tanned to the shade of leather hide, and his girth bespoke of a fondness for good food and wine, but what Max liked most about the man were the laugh lines around the eyes and mouth. Benoit was a man who smiled easily and obviously did not lack for a sense of humor. He appeared to be comfortable in his skin and always ready for a hearty meal and a good laugh. Max had spent so much time surrounded by cruelty and the dour expressions of slaves that he'd almost forgotten how to be courteous and charming.

Some part of Max expected the captain to order him to be shackled and locked up as soon as they were underway, in the hope of selling him on to another plantation owner or collecting some kind of a reward for his capture, but instead the captain had greeted Max jovially, invited him to dine, and ordered his steward to organize a bath and find Max a suit of clothes to replace the tattered linen pajamas he had still been wearing.

Max had luxuriated in the bath for as long as he could before the water became too cold and grimy for comfort, then reluctantly got out of the wooden tub and reached for the razor thoughtfully left by the steward along with a small mirror. Max had propped up the mirror and lathered his face, but didn't look at his reflection straight away. He hadn't seen his own face in over six months, and wasn't sure he was ready to confront the man who would look back. Max had shaved off most of the springy dark hair before finally allowing himself a peek. The man who glared back was a stranger, and Max had quickly glanced away before forcing himself to turn his eyes back to his reflection and study the damage his ordeal had inflicted.

Max had always been lean, but now the skin was stretched tightly over the bones of his face, and the eyes and mouth were bracketed by furrows that weren't there before. The bottom half of his face was eerily white compared to his tanned cheeks and forehead, having been covered by a thick beard, so he would need to grow a short beard to hide the difference until the tan faded somewhat, and he didn't look so grotesque. Max's eyes had a haunted look in them, accentuated by the gray which now dusted his temples. He looked like a man who'd drunk long and deep from the cup of sorrow, and the brew had left its mark. He was no longer the handsome, athletic thirty-something, but a haggard, mean-looking bastard who didn't look a day younger than forty. No one would mistake him for Hugo Everly again, not unless Hugo had enjoyed a similar experience in the past few months.

Max had finished shaving, then held the mirror to reflect parts of his body. He was thin, but stronger than he'd ever been, with not an ounce of fat on his lean stomach or muscular legs. He'd tossed the mirror onto the berth and donned the suit. An unfamiliar smell still lingered in the cloth, but otherwise the suit appeared to be clean. He had tightened the laces of the breeches as much as he could and tucked in the too-long shirt before putting on hose, well-worn boots, and a coat which was way too wide; grateful to be wearing something other than rags. The suit hung on Max as if he were a child wearing his father's clothes, but Max didn't mind; at least he no longer looked like a slave.

Max had briefly wondered how Banjo was getting on, but he wasn't worried. The boy had been welcomed aboard by the captain's steward, and invited to the galley for some food before being taken below deck to his hammock. He seemed happy enough, considering he'd just been separated from his parents, whom he'd likely never see again, and Max had seen him exploring the ship with one of the sailors as he followed the steward to a vacant cabin for his bath. He would check on Banjo tomorrow, Max had decided as he brushed his hair, which now hung down to his shoulders, and tied it back with a leather thong he'd found next to the razor. He'd given himself a last once-over before leaving the cabin to join the captain.

Captain Benoit sucked some garlicky sauce from the shell of a mussel and took a sip of claret, sighing with pleasure. His hands and lips were greasy from his efforts, but he seemed to be greatly enjoying his meal, as was Max. He hadn't had anything other than the plainest of food for months, so this was quite a treat.

Max wiped up the delicious sauce with a heel of bread and popped it into his mouth, wishing he could eat more, but he was absolutely bursting at the seams. His stomach had shrunk since being in Barbados, so he couldn't consume nearly as much.

"So, tell me, milord, what do you plan to do once you reach France?" the captain asked as he refilled Max's glass.

"Well, first of all, I'd like to thank you for offering me free passage, Captain," Max replied, suddenly realizing that he'd been so overcome with his impending freedom that he hadn't thanked the captain properly.

"Oh, it's not free, *mon ami*," the captain replied with a hearty laugh. "I owed Xeno a favor, and, to tell you the truth, I make such a sizeable profit off these boys that the least I could do was offer you passage when asked. You see, I can't offer Xeno his share of the profits since as a slave he'd have no use for the money. Instead, I bring some necessary goods, herbs for his sister, and news of their children. We all win in our own way."

"Are the children really well cared for, or is that just something you tell their parents to make them feel justified in their decision?" Max asked, curious as to what awaited Banjo in France.

"For the most part, they are happy. They are treated like exotic pets as long as they are small and pleasant to behold. They have splendid clothes, plenty to eat, and they accompany their masters to some of the most beautiful houses in all of France. Once the children get older, they don't fare as well. Some are relegated to the kitchens, others to the stables, and some are just thrown out into the street. But they still have a better life than they would have had on a plantation. Many of them would never even see ten years old, either due to disease or hard work. I'm not a slaver, milord, just a businessman with a soft spot for little children."

"You are very kind indeed," Max replied, deciding that it would be churlish of him to pass judgment on a man who was at the moment master of his fate. "And to answer your question, I don't have any plan. I will have to seek some kind of employment or try to join a crew of a vessel bound for England. I'd like to get back home, but, of course, I can't do so openly, or I will be re-arrested."

"Perhaps you can stay in France for a time. Your kinsman might offer you hospitality," the captain suggested, looking toward the door eagerly in anticipation of dessert. "Oh, where is that boy?" he bristled.

"My kinsman?" Max asked, confused. Who could Benoit possibly mean?

"Why, Lord Everly, of course. He's been in Paris these few months. I just assumed that he was your kinsman since you share the same name and title. He's Hugo as well, I believe. Family name?"

"Lord Hugo Everly is in Paris?" Max felt his heart begin to race as the implication of what the captain just said sank in. Was it really possible that Hugo had come back to the seventeenth century and had taken refuge in France while leaving Max to take the blame for his crimes?

"Oh, yes. He's in Paris with his family. I hear he's recently been received at Court, which is something of a feat, given our sovereign's dislike of Protestants. I suppose it's just the Huguenots whom he despises, not the English sort."

"How do you know that Hugo Everly is in Paris?" Max asked carefully. Perhaps the man was mistaken.

"I have it on good authority from a friend. Captain Lafitte was glowing with pride as he recounted the story in a tavern in Le Havre, having performed his very first marriage ceremony. He fancies himself a man of God now and an instrument of love," Captain Benoit laughed as he tucked into sliced pineapple that had been brought by the boy. The pineapple had been soaked in rum and sugar and grilled until it was soft and golden brown. It was quite delicious.

"Whom did he marry?" Max could barely contain his curiosity. Was all this merely a coincidence, or was fate handing him this chance for a particular reason?

"Why, Lord Everly, of course, and his lady. Lafitte said she was quite beautiful, with golden ringlets and warm brown eyes the color of good brandy, as he put it, but a bit on the heavy side," Benoit laughed again as he made an arc with his hand in front of his protruding belly.

"She is fat?" Max asked, surprised. That certainly didn't sound like Neve, although the rest of the description did. Had she really gone back to the past with Hugo? She wouldn't give Max the time of day in the twenty-first century, but she loved his ancestor enough to give up everything for him and follow him to the past, where he was hunted and despised for his role in the Monmouth Rebellion? The thought rankled him, but he pushed his injured pride aside for the moment and focused on Captain Benoit, who appeared to be amused by his question.

"She was with child, *mon ami*, very much so. Lord Everly was in quite a rush to marry, before the child was born."

Max nearly spat out his pineapple, suddenly unable to swallow.

"Has she had the baby? Did they both survive?" he asked carefully, trying not to appear too eager for the news.

"Oh, yes. They are both well, or so I hear. It's endearing

that you are so worried about them. Do you know his wife then?"

"Yes, I do. She's a lady of great beauty and charm," Max replied, realizing that he meant it. Neve was beautiful and charming, but she obviously lacked all common sense if she'd thrown in her lot with Hugo Everly.

"Indeed, but not as beautiful as his mistress," the captain cackled happily. "They say the girl is exquisite."

"Mistress?" Max couldn't have heard the captain correctly, but the mischievous twinkle in the captain's eyes told him that he had.

"Oh, yes. She's supposedly Lord Everly's ward, but she is no relation to the family, and he's very protective of her. The wife seems to accept the situation. Many men take mistresses while their wives are with child, and for some time after, but few of them parade them so openly."

"And who is this mistress?" Max asked, utterly scandalized. Hugo didn't seem like the type of man who'd be so callous, but then again, how well did he really know him? And was it possible that Neve loved him so much that she was willing to allow herself to be humiliated, or did she not know the truth? Max wondered.

"Frances something or other," the captain replied as he helped himself to more fruit.

"Frances?" Max nearly choked.

"You know her too?"

"She's the woman Hugo was said to have abducted after he nearly killed her husband."

"There, you see? Obviously his mistress," Benoit concluded as he let out a soft burp. "You English are something, and you say the French are immoral. I wish I had relatives who are half as interesting as yours."

*You don't know the half of it*, Max thought bitterly as he pushed away his plate. Hugo was supposed to be dead; gone without leaving an heir. According to family history, he'd vanished in the spring of 1685 just before being arrested for treason. Hugo had never married, and had never had a legitimate or illegitimate child, as far as anyone knew. And now, here he was, living in Paris with a wife who fit Neve's description, by whom he had a living child, and a mistress who could also conceive.

Max had promised himself that he would find his way back to England and return to his twenty-first-century life as soon as possible. He would be grateful for that life, and never again give Hugo Everly another thought, but fate was having a good laugh right about now, taunting Max with the knowledge that his enemy was not only within reach, but on the brink of changing history and writing Max out of the equation since Max was a descendant of Clarence Hiddleston, Hugo's nephew. If Hugo had a living child, Max would come back to the future to find himself disinherited and destitute, Everly Manor belonging to whomever was Hugo's descendant in the future. No, he couldn't allow this to happen; not after everything he'd been through.

"Tell me, Captain, how will Banjo get to Paris?" Max asked, keeping his voice casual as he cut up a piece of pineapple.

"Oh, I will personally take him to Paris and oversee his placement with a good family, for the boy's sake, of course," the captain replied with a sly smile, which led Max to believe that a "good family" was optional as long as the price was right and they took the child off his hands.

"Of course. Would it be at all possible to travel with you as far as Paris? I would very much like to see Hugo again. It's been ages; feels like centuries as a matter of fact," Max quipped as he studied the captain's well-fed face.

"Of course. I'd be glad of the company," the captain replied sleepily. His eyelids were drooping, and he seemed ready for his bed, which was just fine with Max. After spending so much time alone with his thoughts over the past six months, he was somewhat overwhelmed by this drawn-out social ritual and was ready for a bit of quiet.

"Thank you for the delicious dinner, Captain Benoit. I will leave you to rest now," Max said as he gave a slight bow and let himself out of the cabin. His stomach was pleasantly full, and his senses dulled by the excellent wine, but instead of going back to his cabin, Max went up on deck, desperate to walk off some of the agitation he was feeling after learning about Hugo. He needed a plan, and a good one.

# THIRTY-TWO

## Surrey, England

Simon Harding stood next to his mother in the church graveyard as Reverend Lambert droned on, extolling the virtues of Lady Naomi Everly, who had left them all too soon. In Simon's opinion, she hadn't left soon enough, but he kept his thoughts to himself. He wasn't a mean-spirited person by nature, but Naomi Everly had always treated him like a servant, as if the world were still divided into Upstairs and Downstairs. Now that he knew the truth of his parentage, he realized that perhaps the disdain Naomi Everly had felt for him was due less to the fact that he was the housekeeper's son, and more to the fact that he was her husband's by-blow. Lady Everly was not the type of woman to ever acknowledge the affair, or lower herself to confronting the other woman, but frosty as she had been, she must have felt hurt on some level, especially since Simon's mother had carried on with Lord Roland Everly for years.

Roland Everly hadn't limited himself to just his wife and his lover, of course, but had other affairs along the way. None of them had lasted longer than a few months, or so he'd told Stella, who had remained faithful to him through the years, much like his wife. It seemed that the two women in his life had remained with him for different reasons, however. Naomi had relished her wealth and position and wouldn't contemplate divorce for fear of scandal; not that anyone would care much these days, not since Charles and Diana divorced. If the Prince of Wales could do it, a minor lord's reputation would not be tarnished in the slightest. Stella Harding, however, had stayed with Roland Everly for a completely different reason. She had actually loved that selfish, preening wanker who turned out to be Simon's natural father, and hoped that if she remained loyal and loving, Roland would do something for his youngest son.

Simon never did understand why his mother's employer had offered to pay for his education and gave him a monthly allowance, but now everything made sense at last. He'd been shocked and angry when his mother had first come clean, but now, several months later, Simon was coming to terms with his new status. He still had no wish to live at Everly Manor but had managed to access the business accounts and keep the museum and the estate going from his London flat. He'd only come down to Surrey once since his mother's confession, leaving Stella Harding to supervise everything while visiting Naomi at the nursing home daily and watching her condition deteriorate, until her heart finally gave out last week.

The coffin was lowered into the yawning hole, and the mourners began to disperse, walking or driving back to the manor house for refreshments and a bit of a chinwag before getting back to their daily lives and dismissing Naomi Everly from their thoughts. Simon desperately wanted to get into his car and drive back to London, but he'd promised his mother that he would stay for the wake and help her clean up afterward.

Heather had promised to come along, but had bailed on him at the last minute, citing work commitments she couldn't get out of on such short notice. Simon strongly suspected that his girl-friend simply had no wish to attend the funeral of a woman she'd never met but despised by osmosis and would much rather just go to a pub with her friends or spend a quiet night on the sofa watching *Downton Abbey*. He couldn't really blame her; he had no wish to be here either.

Simon still wished on a daily basis that Max would come back from wherever it was he'd disappeared to and take this responsibility off Simon's shoulders. Simon was happy with his life, and had no desire to play lord of the manor; that was Max's job, and Max had relished it, which made his disappearance all the more strange and sinister. Simon might be wearing a fine suit and driving a flashy car, but deep down he was still Little Simon, the housekeeper's son who was always underfoot annoying Lord and Lady Everly and tagging after Max.

For some reason, Simon didn't believe Max to be dead. He'd worshipped Max when he was a child, and Max, in turn, had treated Simon like a little brother. They hadn't spent much time together since Simon had left for university, but had met for a drink or dinner from time to time in London, and the old bond was still there. They were brothers after all—not that either one of them had known. Perhaps Max had guessed, since he was older and more aware of what was going on between the adults. Was that why he'd never told Simon to sod off despite the differ-ence in their age and social standing? Simon wondered.

*I'd know it in my bones if Max were dead*, he thought as he turned away from the grave and followed his mother through the church gate. He opened the car door for her, eliciting a small smile of gratitude as she got in. She looked harsh in her unrelieved black, but she was still a good-looking woman. Simon had seen the doctor eyeing her across the open grave, despite his wife standing stiffly next to him and staring straight ahead from under the wide brim of her hat. His mother and the doctor had been friends since grammar school, and Simon had always suspected there might have been more to that relationship. There was a time when he'd thought that David Lomax was his father, but that theory had turned out to be rubbish. He honestly couldn't say if he would have preferred to be David's son. At least David Lomax was still alive, so he might have had a chance of a relationship with him. It was too late to get to know Roland Everly, and too late to be a brother to Max. Simon often wished that he'd had a sibling, and he might have had, had his mother ever wised up and found someone who was willing to share his life with her. Perhaps it wasn't too late for her to find love, even if it was too late to have more children.

Simon would have no objection to Stella finding a companion; a subject he'd brought up to her only yesterday as he'd helped her prepare quiches and crudités for today's wake. She had scoffed at him, but he'd give it a little time and bring it up again. Naomi had remained alone after her husband's death, and where had that gotten her? Rather than enjoy what was left of her life, she'd driven Max to distraction and badgered him with never-ending demands for grandchildren. It was sad really, that she never lived to be a grandmother, Simon mused as he drove through the manor gates, the tires crunching on gravel as he turned into an available parking spot.

Stella got out of the car and hurried inside, but Simon lingered in the car park for a few moments to smoke a cigarette, preoccupied with his thoughts.

Naomi had claimed until the very last that Max was still alive; perhaps she knew something the rest of them didn't. But now that she was gone, and Max was God only knew where, Simon was, for all intents and purposes, the new Lord Everly, although a very reluctant one.

Simon gazed up at the massive stone façade of the house as he stubbed out his cigarette. "If needs must..." he mumbled to himself as he squared his shoulders and marched up the steps.

# THIRTY-THREE

## APRIL 1686

### Aboard the La Belle

For the first few days of the voyage, Max just sat on deck and enjoyed the sunshine, a fresh briny breeze, and the intoxicating feeling of being alive and free. He'd forgotten what it was like to be master of his own time and not have to do backbreaking work for twelve to fourteen hours a day, stopping long enough only to eat and sleep. He still had to remind himself every morning that this wasn't a dream, and he was actually on his way back to Europe.

Max had to admit that it was ironic, given the circumstances, but he'd never been happier. Coming so close to losing one's life and then losing one's freedom, had a way of putting things into perspective and making him appreciate what he'd taken for granted for so long.

Max closed his eyes, oblivious to all the activity around him. He heard Banjo's squeal of delight as the boy was allowed to climb up the rigging with one of the sailors and look out over the sea, which sparkled in the morning sun and was as flat and still as an unrolled bale of blue silk.

Banjo seemed to be enjoying himself. He'd quickly gotten over his shyness and fear and was running around, exploring the ship to his heart's content, and visiting the galley in the hopes of getting something to eat. The sailors treated him like an adorable pet, and Banjo was enjoying the kind of attention he'd never gotten before. Even the captain seemed to have taken to the boy. He invited him up on deck and allowed him to steer the ship, which sent Banjo into raptures.

Captain Benoit expected to dock in Le Havre in the first week of June, so Max didn't feel any immediate pressure to make decisions—not that there were many decisions to make. He could either go on to Paris with the captain or find a vessel bound for England, offer to work for his passage, then hitch a ride with some farmer to Surrey, and hopefully return to his own time.

Max's rational side told him to concentrate his energies on going home, but his emotional side wouldn't let his grudge against Hugo rest. The captain had no idea whether Hugo's offspring was a boy or a girl, but it really didn't matter. Even if Hugo had a daughter, the course of history had already been altered, and there was nothing to stop him from having a son, which would leave Max nothing to come back to once he returned to the twenty-first century.

Would he remember any of this, or would he go back to a life he hadn't known before entering the passage in the crypt? Was that even possible? Max wondered as he stared out over the expanse of water. Would all his memories be wiped out if the succession had been altered and he was no longer Lord Everly when he returned?

Max leaned back against the solid oak of the mast and watched a lone seagull circle above before it dove in to catch its prey and came up with a fish flapping it its beak. *That's what I must do*, Max thought, *circle my prey until I know for sure that it's the right moment to strike*. The thought made Max feel suddenly more hopeful. He couldn't possibly take on Hugo outright, but if he devised a clever plan, perhaps Hugo Bloody Everly could just fall into his trap, and Max could reset history by getting rid of the man once and for all.

Max smiled as Banjo catapulted from the cargo hold and came to stand in front of him, grinning from ear to ear. He was wearing a red kerchief around his neck, no doubt given to him by the sailors, and a straw hat which was way too big for his head and would be blown off by the first gust of wind. He really was a cute little tyke, and had an endearing way about him which appealed to Max.

"Can I sit with you, massa?" Banjo asked, using the form of address the slaves used for their masters.

"Of course you can sit with me. And stop calling me by that ridiculous name; I'm not your master, Banjo," Max chided the boy good-naturedly. "Just call me Max."

"Yes, massa," Banjo answered automatically as he plopped down next to Max. "Are you watching the birds?"

"I am," Max replied with a chuckle. He supposed there were worse things he could be called, although the name made him feel uncomfortable, especially after what he'd witnessed over the past few months. He didn't want Banjo to associate him with cruelty and oppression, but he doubted the boy gave the title much thought. It was simply what he was used to, and since Max was no longer a slave, he saw him as a master, as he didn't know what category to place him in.

Max shrugged in resignation and turned to Banjo, who was staring open-mouthed at a large pelican that was perched on one of the crossbars of the mast, its wings folded, and its head held regally as it surveyed the calm waters of the Caribbean in search of its next meal.

"Why don't you get some stale bread from the galley and maybe we can feed the birds together," Max suggested, enjoying the boy's company. "I don't think pelicans eat bread, but there are plenty of seagulls about," Max called after Banjo as he ran off happily.

Max had never given much thought to having children despite his mother's nagging, but he always knew that at some point he would, and at thirty-five, he realized that he was ready for a family. Perhaps men had a biological clock as well, although theirs was more emotional than physical. Children had seemed like a burden and a drain on one's time and finances only a few years before, but by the time Max had reached his mid-thirties, he'd started to long for a child of his own, and a woman who would be more than a sexual partner or someone to spend time with when he was in the mood for female company. Of course, his mother wished him to have a son to carry on the family name and inherit the title, but Max had to admit that the thought of having a daughter was just as appealing. There was something so precious and vulnerable about little girls. He wanted to be his daughter's hero, her protector and mentor. But a boy would be just as nice, Max mused.

Spending time with Banjo had been an unexpected treat, and Max suddenly felt a tightening in his chest at the thought of all the things he'd missed out on so far. He had a brief vision of himself playing with a toddler as Neve looked on happily, her hand on her swollen belly.

*Why can't I just let her go?* Max thought angrily. He'd never even slept with her, but her face haunted him as if she'd been the great love of his life. Had he actually gotten to be with her, he might have tired of her, or found her to be too clingy or too distant, but not having known her in that way, Max had put her on a pedestal and painted her as the perfect woman; the one who got away. How had Hugo snatched her away from him when they might have been happy together? Neve should have —and would have—chosen him had she had more time to get to know him, to love him; Max was sure of it. She'd enjoyed spending time with him, and he'd seen the beginnings of affection in her eyes when they went out together, but now it was too late. She'd married Hugo and given him a child—a child who would change the future and rewrite the past.

Max shook his head to chase the image away. She was Hugo's, at least for now. *Her happiness will be short-lived, if she is indeed happy living in exile with a traitor and a cheat,* Max thought. Perhaps she'd like to go back with him and forget Hugo. The "charms" of seventeenth-century life must have worn off somewhat by now. After all, this was hardly Wonderland. Perhaps he could play on Neve's homesickness and possible regrets to win her back. He'd even be willing to adopt her child, take it back to the future, and raise it as his own. He resented Hugo, but having spent time with Banjo was sure that he could grow to love a child for itself, despite its parentage.

After all, Max had loved Simon like a brother, despite the fact that he was only the son of the housekeeper, and missed him very much, especially now when he needed a partner in crime. Simon would have loved an adventure and would have been practical enough and clever enough to keep Max out of trouble. Simon was always so carefree, so irreverent—unlike Max, who was more structured and rigid.

Max felt a bitter wave of homesickness as he recalled some of the more colorful outings with Simon while he was still at the university. If ever he got back, he'd make more of an effort to be a part of Simon's life, Max decided as he was distracted from his thoughts by the appearance of Banjo.

# THIRTY-FOUR

## MAY 1686

### Paris, France

I stood patiently while Sabine stuffed, laced, pinned, and tucked me into my new gown, ordered specially for the outing to Versailles. Louis XIV decided to celebrate the arrival of fine weather by hosting a three-day event. It began with a hunt and would finish today with the garden party which would culminate in supper, a performance of *L'Amour Medicin*—one of Louis's favorite Molière plays—and a display of fireworks. Last night, we had been treated to a ballet, which, to my surprise, had been rather good. I'd been amazed to find out that Louis XIV was a great admirer of ballet, and had been quite a talented dancer in his youth, performing in numerous productions himself. I hoped that he wouldn't be performing in the play tonight. I was actually looking forward to it. It'd been a long time since I had been to the theater, so this performance would be something of a treat, since it would be staged by professional actors for the king's pleasure.

I couldn't wait to leave and return to Valentine. Elodie's sister, who had a six-month-old baby, had agreed to stay at our

Paris residence and act as wet nurse to Valentine, but I still fretted non-stop that the baby wasn't well looked after or not getting enough to eat. I would have happily declined the invitation, but one didn't just say no to the king of France, especially when one was a disgraced exile in desperate need of the monarch's favor. I'd mentioned my reservations to Hugo, but he just shook his head before I'd even finished the sentence, letting me know that my objections were futile.

Strangely, Frances had been invited as well, so I was glad to at least have an ally in the strange universe of the Court. Frances had been nearly speechless with the grandeur of it all and not a little subdued, having spent most of her life in one form of isolation or another, but she had been welcomed by Louis's courtiers with something akin to wonder, and I was happy to see her enjoying herself.

Luke was there as well, so Frances had a ready escort and friend. As an admirer, Luke was expected to pay court to Frances and be within her orbit most of the time, but as my husband, Hugo was expected to converse and socialize with others and ignore me almost completely. To speak to one's own wife was the height of bad manners, which left me to fend for myself.

I'd managed to survive the first two days without incident, mostly because I'd been able to escape to our room for short periods of time and go for walks in the lavish grounds, but today would be the hardest since the festivities would last all day long, and I would have to spend hours in the company of Louis's courtiers.

The prospect of leaving in the morning lifted my spirits, so I graciously permitted Sabine to powder my hair and apply some rouge before allowing Hugo to escort me to the terrace, where liveried servants were dispensing glasses of champagne and various hors d'oeuvres. I gratefully accepted a glass and watched with some amusement as one of the ladies made a face of horror as the bubbles went up her nose. Champagne was a relatively new experience for them since it hadn't been served at Court for long, having only gained popularity in the past few decades.

I took a sip and looked around. The manicured gardens were decorated for the fete with flowers, ribbons, and colorful lanterns, which would be lit in the evening. Each lantern had a little candle inside which would make it look like a firefly once it got dark and the flame flickered inside the colored orb. Tables had been set up outside, and a makeshift stage had been erected for the performance of whatever masque was to take place for the guests' entertainment before the play. Gaily dressed courtiers walked among the trimmed hedges, their vibrant attire a nice counterpoint to the greenery all around them.

I regretfully let go of Hugo as he was approached by several men who wished to speak to him and walked toward the fountain where a number of people were congregating. I had no desire to speak to any of them, but to wander around by myself would be seen as standoffish.

I was taken completely by surprise when a deep voice called to me from behind.

"Madame Everly, what a pleasure to see you looking so lovely. Are you enjoying the gardens?"

I turned around to find myself facing Louis himself, accompanied by two ladies, one of them Madame de Maintenon, who was rumored to be Louis's secret wife. She was a charming brunette with wide dark eyes that showed intelligence and humor. Out of all the courtiers, she had been kindest to me, and I returned her smile, which seemed surprisingly genuine in a place where every gesture and glance was open to interpretation.

"Your Majesty," I replied as I sank into a well-practiced curtsy. "The gardens are just breathtaking, as is the rest of your palace. Lord Everly and I are honored by your invitation."

Louis gave a wave of the hand as if it was of no consequence and regarded me solemnly. "Making the acquaintance of your husband has been illuminating," he drawled, making me wonder what he was referring to. "He's a man of great depth and principle." A small smile played about Louis's lips and I wondered if he was referring to Hugo's secret Catholicism or his well-documented part in Protestant Monmouth's rebellion.

"Indeed he is," I agreed, feeling out of my depth.

Madame de Maitanon saw my dilemma and chimed in, "Your ward is such a lovely girl. I think she's gathered quite a few admirers among the young men."

Frances was currently surrounded by three young fops who were vying for her attention and plying her with compliments and shameless flattery. Frances was blushing prettily but seemed to be enjoying all the attention. I noticed Luke scowling at the young men from a group of courtiers he was talking to a few feet away, desperate to reclaim Frances for himself, but unable to get away without appearing rude.

"Yes, she is. She's enjoying herself tremendously," I replied, grateful for the change of subject.

"Do bring her again," Louis added absentmindedly, his gaze already on someone else. He drew Madame de Maintanon away, leaving me alone on the path.

It took less than a minute for me to be accosted by several courtiers who wanted to be near anyone singled out by the king. I made polite responses and smiled, wishing desperately that I could be alone for a while.

* * *

I breathed a sigh of relief as the first stars appeared in the lavender heavens, their light feeble compared to the hundreds of lanterns which were now lit and swaying gently in the May breeze. Dusk was settling on the gardens, and an army of servants was busy setting up for supper. A few couples had disappeared into the wooded pathways that offered more privacy than the exposed ornamental gardens.

I thought it might be a good idea to take a little walk before sitting down to supper, which would last for several hours, with course after course being served to guests who could barely eat another bite. I veered away from the garden into the park and strolled along a narrow lane. It was darker in the park, but I didn't mind. Feeling invisible for a few minutes after being scrutinized for three days seemed very appealing at the moment.

I inhaled the fragrant spring air and lifted my head up to look at the darkening sky. A few more hours and this would be over. I couldn't wait. How I wished I could call home and check on the baby, but there was no way to send a message or receive one back without actually sending someone back to Paris, which would take hours. I suppose Archie would have gone had I asked him, but it seemed unfair to make him ride there and back when we would be going home in a few hours' time. I'd hardly seen anything of him since we'd arrived, but I was sure he was making the most of the opportunity and having a good time with the rest of the men-at-arms and grooms.

I was happy to come upon a wrought-iron bench and sat down gratefully, eager to take the weight off my feet. I'd been standing and walking for hours in thin-soled shoes and felt the shape of every pebble in my aching feet. It was bliss to sit in solitude for a few moments, away from the bustle of the Court.

A couple was coming toward me, walking back to the palace from what might have been a lovers' tryst. They were talking softly and giggling, so I leaned back, hoping they wouldn't notice me as they passed by. I didn't recognize the man, but I thought the woman might be Marie Anne Mancini, one of the Mazarinettes, as the nieces of Cardinal Mazarin, the chief minister to Louis, were referred to by members of the Court.

She was an attractive woman and was the youngest of the sisters who were famous for their intrigues and affairs.

"She's absolutely divine," the man said with a wistful sigh. "If I were a few years younger, I'd make a play for her myself. No wonder he couldn't resist her, but I must admit that keeping one's mistress in the same house as one's wife is rather daring, especially for an Englishman."

"He wouldn't be the first man to make a fool of his wife," the woman replied haughtily. "The stupid cow just had a baby and is rumored to be taking care of the infant herself. No wonder he's seeking pleasure in the arms of a beautiful young girl. Who wants a wife who's nursing her own child like a peasant? It's absolutely barbaric."

"But what of the rumor that he's encouraging the match between Mademoiselle Morley and Luke Marsden?" the man asked.

"Probably just to throw his bovine wife off the scent. Or perhaps he's tired of the girl already and wants a new mistress. Of course, it could be that his intentions are more political than personal," the woman replied, her voice shrill in the silence of the park. "And they say the French are depraved. The English are no better than animals, or Huguenots," she added with disgust.

I held my breath as the two passed, unsure of whether they had seen me and chose to humiliate me or were so caught up in their conversation that they hadn't noticed me sitting there. Either way, I was enraged. Now I understood why Frances had suddenly been invited to Court despite her lack of title or fortune. We were part of the entertainment, a love triangle—or so they thought—to be observed and ridiculed. I suppose that Hugo was the hero in this scenario since he was thought to be keeping a mistress under his wife's nose; Frances was the beautiful ingénue, and I was the stupid cow, as dubbed by Madame Mancini.

I knew it was time to return to the terrace, but I simply couldn't find the strength to leave my sanctuary and face all those people, particularly since I now understood why everyone had been watching me so intently. I felt hot, angry tears sting my eyes, but I wouldn't cry, wouldn't allow them to have their victory, even if they weren't there to see it. I didn't believe for a moment that Hugo was romancing Frances, but everyone at Versailles did, and they were all sniggering behind my back.

It was nearly dark now, the glow of the moon the only light in the otherwise pitch-black park. I knew the way back, but wanted to delay by a few minutes more before going back to that snake pit.

I saw a dim outline of someone walking briskly down the path and drew back, not out of fear, but out of a desire to remain invisible. It was only when the silhouette got closer that I realized it was Hugo. His face was pale in the moonlight; his eyes haunted as he glanced from side to side, obviously searching for me in the darkness. Relief flooded his features when he spotted me, and he sat down next to me and drew me to him before asking any questions.

"We must go back," he said gently. "Supper is about to be served."

"I can't eat. My stomach is in knots," I replied, debating whether to tell him what I'd heard. I felt humiliated and out of place, and I suddenly wondered if Hugo could see how much I didn't belong here. I felt like an ugly duckling among beautiful swans who would peck the duckling to death at the first opportunity and carry on as if nothing had happened.

*You are being a bit overly dramatic*, I thought to myself angrily as I leaned my head against Hugo's shoulder.

"Neve, it's only a few more hours, and then we can go home to Valentine. I know how difficult this is for you, but we've got no choice; we must play our parts."

"And your part is that of the lover, is it?" I exploded despite my better judgment. I hadn't realized how angry I was until the words spilled out, my fury directed at Hugo since I couldn't take it out on anyone else at Versailles. "Are you enjoying the admiration bestowed on you for sleeping with a fifteen-year-old while your wife is too busy nursing a baby like a cow?"

Hugo sighed, his shoulders sagging as he rested his elbows on his thighs and lowered his head into his hands. "You've heard." It wasn't a question, but a statement of fact, and he sounded miserable.

"Yes, I've heard. Did you know all along that this is what was being said about us?"

"I've known since the hunt," he replied, his expression inscrutable in the darkness.

"And you didn't think to put an end to the rumor?" I shrieked, suddenly feeling a coldness seep through my soul. Was he enjoying this? Was there any truth to what was being said? I knew I was being hysterical, but I was so emotionally overwrought that I would have believed anything at the moment, wallowing as I was in self-pity.

"Darling, I couldn't deny it outright because that would just fuel speculation and make them think that I was trying to cover up my liaison with Frances. There's a way to defuse such rumors, and it must be done with finesse."

"Really? And how does one handle this with finesse?" I demanded, hands on my hips as I stood above him, fuming.

"One plants a different rumor but does it so subtly that whoever hears it immediately believes it to be true. It's all a game, Neve—a nasty, dirty game." Hugo got to his feet and pulled me to him, despite my protests. "Please tell me you don't believe that I'm sleeping with Frances," he whispered in my ear. "You can't possibly think there's any grain of truth to what's being said."

"No, I don't believe it," I conceded grudgingly, "but it still hurts to hear it."

Hugo kissed me gently and held me for a moment, his lips against my ear. "Neve, I'm not a man who goes from woman to woman; I think you know that. It's not easy for me to give my heart to someone, but when I do, I do it completely. You are my love, now and forever, and I will cherish you till the day I die. You are the only person I trust, and I hope you trust me. I would lay down my life for you and Valentine, and would be glad to do it if it were required. Now, please, give me a smile and tell me that I'm forgiven."

"Forgiven for what?" I asked suspiciously.

"Forgiven for putting you in this unbearable situation. Having known modern life, I can only imagine how foreign all this is to you, but it must be endured for the sake of our future. Just a little longer, my sweet."

"All right, you are forgiven," I relented as I tried not to smile, but couldn't help it; he looked too forlorn. "And how in the world do you plan to quash this malicious rumor?"

"It's already done," he replied sheepishly. "It just needs a few hours to take root. In the meantime, let's give them something to talk about. Adjust your skirts and pat your hair just as we approach the terrace," Hugo instructed.

"Why?"

"Because they will think that I just took you behind a bush. No husband wants to have an assignation with his own wife, so tongues will wag," he added with a grin, happy to be forgiven.

"I hate this world, Hugo," I said with feeling as I took his arm and allowed him to lead me back toward the palace, which looked magical in the colorful light of a thousand lanterns.

"Me too."

But I wasn't so sure that he wasn't enjoying the game just a little.

# THIRTY-FIVE

Frances took the proffered seat and gazed down the length of the table to where Lady Everly was sitting between two middle-aged gentlemen. Neve appeared calm, but her back was rigid, and her eyes glassy as she stared at the still empty stage with forced concentration, which led Frances to believe that Neve was upset about something. She was missing Valentine desperately and longed to go home, so by this last stretch of the festivities Neve was likely vibrating with frustration. Frances wished that she could offer Neve words of comfort, but there was little she could do for Neve from her end of the long table. Hopefully, the play would help distract Neve and get her through the rest of the evening. Neve had mentioned earlier that she was looking forward to the performance. Frances had never been to the theater, so this would be her first exposure to the dramatic arts, but, at times, she found watching the people around her more entertaining than anything the actors could dish up.

She allowed her gaze to slide over the table. Lord Everly was talking quietly to a beautiful brunette seated next to him. The woman was only a few years older than Frances, but she had a well-practiced sensuality about her, which led Frances to believe that innocence was something the woman could barely recall. She was nothing more than a courtesan, if gossip was to be believed, no doubt seated next to Lord Everly for the sole purpose of eliciting a reaction of some sort. After only a few days at Court, Frances realized that nothing was random, and every seating arrangement, every performance, every look was intentional and well thought out by someone working behind the scenes. What happened onstage was only part of the entertainment; the best bits took place offstage.

Hugo was nodding politely and smiling at something the lady said, but his eyes were on his wife; not quite worried, but watchful. Neve had not had an easy time of it these past few days, but Hugo couldn't afford to show sympathy or support openly, especially since he was purposely kept away from Neve at all times. The barely noticeable tension in his shoulders and the tightness in his jaw allowed Frances a glimpse into how worried he really was, and she felt a wave of tenderness toward her guardian, knowing that he was struggling behind the smooth façade. He loved Neve with a fierceness that left Frances hoping that someone would love her like that, but even with her limited experience of men, she knew that kind of love was rare, especially among the nobility, where most marriages were arranged based on rank, wealth, and social position. Neve had come to Hugo with nothing, but he didn't seem to care. He only wanted her.

Frances's eyes drifted down the table toward Luke. He was conversing with an older woman who seemed to be hanging on his every word. Luke's eyes met Frances's for a moment, and he smiled just for her before turning his attention back to his dinner companion. Frances looked away, and tried to focus on what the heavily rouged and bewigged gentleman next to her was saying. He was asking her something about the plays of Molière, but she'd never even heard of the famed French playwright until today, so just pretended to be interested, when her mind was really on Luke and their earlier encounter.

Frances was glad when the meal was finally at an end and barely suppressed anticipation rippled through the guests. The candles were blown out by the numerous lackeys, and all conversation ceased as the curtains parted to reveal the stage, the play starting at last. Frances tried to concentrate on what the actors were saying, but her French was still rudimentary, so she was quickly lost interest, failing to grasp the meaning of the double entendres.

Everyone seemed to be enjoying the performance, which was eliciting gasps and bursts of laughter. The king seemed to be enraptured as he gazed at the stage, clapping like a child when he was pleased. Frances continued to look at the stage, but with no conversation to concentrate on, she allowed her mind to wander.

* * *

With Lord and Lady Everly both occupied, Frances had more freedom than she'd ever had in her life, which was as frightening as it was liberating. All these people were fawning over her, paying her compliments, and inviting her to walk and talk with them, join them for a game of cards, or simply for a gossip. She knew nothing of Court affairs, but tried to be as polite and charming as she could. Of course, Luke had been her savior. He was always on hand; ready to help her out when she was out of her depth. Frances was grateful for his timely interruptions and invitations to take a stroll through the gardens. Only Luke had his own agenda, as Frances soon found out. A stroll in the ornamental garden had turned into a walk in the wooded park where privacy could be found if one were looking for some. Luke had drawn her off the path and into the trees, where they could be completely alone for the first time since their acquaintance.

"I've dreamed of being alone with you since the moment I first saw you," Luke confided as he smiled into her eyes and moved closer to her, forcing Frances to take a step back. "I feel as nervous as a boy," he said with a shy smile as he took her hand in his. "You're cold."

"I'm nervous," Frances replied, meaning it. She was terrified. She hadn't been alone with any man besides her husband and Archie, and she wasn't at all sure how to behave. She liked Luke, and she trusted him, but although Luke was still his charming self, something had changed in the past few weeks, something that put Frances on her guard. Perhaps she was being overly sensitive, but she'd been courted by Lionel, who had been a perfect gentleman while he'd wooed her but had turned into an abusive, cruel master as soon as they were wed. Frances had learned the hard way that trust was not to be given lightly.

Luke was gazing at Frances with undisguised adoration, but she drew back ever so slightly in a subconscious attempt at self-preservation.

"Please, don't be afraid, Frances. I only want to make you happy. If you wish to go back to the terrace, we can go right now," Luke offered, but his eyes were pleading with her to stay, and she gave in to his boyish charm. If Lord Everly trusted Luke, then she had no cause for concern, Frances concluded as she allowed some of the tension to leave her body.

"No, let's wait a few minutes," Frances said, gratified to see the joy in Luke's eyes. "To be honest, I'm a little overwhelmed by all those people. I feel as if they are staring at me as if I were a curiosity of some sort."

"But you are. You are the most beautiful woman here, and they are green with envy," Luke replied.

Frances wasn't sure if he were being honest with her or still playing the role of the simpering courtier. Flattery was the most valuable currency at Versailles, and the better flatterer you were, the more you could hope to gain in terms of favor and sexual conquests.

"There are plenty of beautiful women out there, Luke,— Lady Everly being one of them," Frances answered a trifle too defensively. She'd heard the comments about Neve and felt an overwhelming desire to punch anyone who said anything disparaging about her friend.

"Neve is very beautiful, but she's taken, and you are not. Are you?" he asked, suddenly serious.

"You know I'm not. Why would you ask such a thing?"

"I've heard some disturbing rumors," Luke replied seriously. "People are saying that you are Hugo's mistress."

Frances just gaped at him, amazed that he would give credence to such a blatant lie, especially since he was one of Lord Everly's oldest friends. "How dare you?" she fumed, stomping her foot in anger. "Hugo Everly is the most honorable, brave, and caring man I've ever met, and he would never—you hear me—never do anything to dishonor Lady Everly. He genuinely loves her, something you clearly know nothing about. Take me back this instant," Frances demanded, but for some reason she hadn't moved.

Perhaps she wanted to hear Luke beg for her forgiveness, or perhaps she was suddenly too mortified to return to a gathering where everyone believed her to be a cheap strumpet who would sleep with her guardian right under the nose of his wife, who was her closest friend in the world, and the woman who had made her believe that it was possible to make one's own choices for the future. Frances would sooner die than do anything to hurt either Neve or Hugo, but she supposed Luke had no way of knowing that. There was much she kept from him, so all he saw was the image of innocence she projected to the world, and especially to him.

"I'm sorry, *cherie*," Luke murmured, drawing her closer. "I was just overcome with jealousy. Forgive me. Please," he breathed into her ear, making her forget her outrage. "You are so incredibly beautiful that any man would be mad with lust if he had to share a house with you, even Hugo, but I know that he is an honorable man and would never stoop so low. It's just that I know so little about you. You are an enigma to be solved."

Luke's gaze was full of expectation. Did he expect her to just blurt out some shameful secret? Frances wondered as she looked at him. She supposed he had a right to know something about her if they were to continue their courtship, but Lord Everly had warned her to reveal as little as possible. What had happened to her in England was no one's business, and although Hugo never said so outright, her past experiences diminished her value on the marriage market a great deal.

But Luke was so kind to her, and so trusting. Perhaps he had a right to know a little more.

"Luke, this is not common knowledge, but I was married before," Frances murmured.

She expected him to be shocked, but Luke just stood there with his head tilted to the side, watching her intently and silently.

"I hope that doesn't change the way you feel about me," Frances said, thinking she should have just kept quiet.

"Is your husband still living?" Luke asked carefully. His expression was inscrutable as he continued to watch Frances.

"No, he's dead, so I am free to marry again," Frances replied, watching Luke for any sign of disappointment. He expected her to be a virgin, so her revelation could very well have just put an end to their courtship, but Luke didn't appear shocked or disgusted. Instead, there was relief in his eyes, which Frances didn't quite understand. It was as if he already knew and wanted to hear it from her.

"Nothing can change the way I feel about you, Frances,"

Luke replied softly. "You have every reason to be apprehensive, but I swear to you that should you accept my suit, I will be the most attentive and devoted husband you could ever wish for. I would never lay a hand on you in anger, or treat you with disrespect. I have asked Hugo for your hand in marriage, but he doesn't wish you to rush into anything. I will wait as long as it takes as long as I know that I have a chance. Do I dare hope?"

Frances averted her eyes for a moment, suddenly unsure of the answer. To tell Luke that he had hope was as good as agreeing to marry him, but although she genuinely liked him, it was Archie's face she saw before she fell asleep at night, and Archie's voice she listened for when she woke up.

But Archie didn't want her; he'd made that clear enough. Nor would Lord Everly approve of Archie as a potential suitor. He wanted better for Frances: a man who would give her financial security and social standing. Lord Everly was the closest thing she had to a father, and he seemed to favor Luke. Did she dare to disappoint him?

"Yes, Luke, you may hope, but I need some time," Frances finally replied.

She knew she was doing the right thing, but she still felt unsure. Her answer bought her time, which is what she needed most. She was only fifteen, for the love of God, she fumed to herself, not ready to sign her life away once again. For the first time in her life, she felt safe and cared for, a part of a loving family. Agreeing to marry anyone would tear her away from the people she loved, and she wasn't ready to leave the Everlys, not yet. Hugo wasn't putting any pressure on her to marry; in fact, he was advising her to wait, so there was no reason to accept Luke's proposal just yet.

Frances gazed up shyly at Luke, who seemed satisfied with her answer. The sun filtered through the trees and dappled his face with light, making it almost glow with happiness. Luke bent down and brushed his lips against her ear, then moved down to her neck. His lips were feather-light against her skin, tasting and kissing her at the same time. He held her loosely, so she wouldn't feel threatened, and continued his sensual exploration. Frances gasped as Luke kissed her breast, running his tongue along the top of her stiffened bodice. She shivered with pleasure, instinctively arching her back to lift her breasts higher.

Luke kissed the other breast and lifted his face to kiss her in earnest. The kiss was tender, almost worshipful, which made Frances lean into him and wrap her arms around his neck for a deeper kiss. Luke didn't disappoint. He crushed her against him and slid his tongue into her mouth, exploring her with a passion that was no longer held in check.

With anyone else, Frances might have been scared, but she trusted Luke, so she gave herself up to the moment, savoring the kiss and mentally comparing it to Archie's. The two men were different physically and emotionally, but she recognized the same intensity in Luke as she had felt in Archie. It was a barely suppressed longing, held at bay only by the rules of propriety and the constraints of time.

Luke suddenly broke the kiss and bent down, sliding his hand beneath her voluminous skirts. Frances stiffened with shock as his fingers caressed the bare flesh above her beribboned stockings and then slid further up to the cleft between her legs. She wanted to push him away, to chastise him for taking such liberties, but her knees buckled as Luke expertly stroked her, and she rested her forehead on his shoulder, moaning with unexpected pleasure. No one had ever touched her like this, and although she knew it was wrong, she liked it, and wanted more.

"Luke, please," she whispered, unsure of what exactly she was asking for.

"Please more or please stop?"

Frances could see the seductive smile as his fingers slipped inside, nearly making her swoon with the intensity of the feelings he was evoking.

"Please stop," she breathed. "I can't take it."

"Has no one ever touched you like this, *cherie*?" Luke was watching her now, his eyes probing her soul, her memories.

"No, no one."

"Not even your husband?" he suddenly asked.

Frances pushed him away as she felt a tightening in her chest. She didn't want to think of Lionel, or remember anything he'd done to her, but her face must have betrayed her because Luke suddenly looked contrite, realizing he'd gone too far.

"I'm sorry," he pleaded as he tried to pull her back into his embrace, but Frances just pushed him away, harder this time. Angry tears ran down her cheeks as she turned to flee.

Frances ran toward the path, but Luke caught her before she had a chance to reach it.

"Frances, please, I'm sorry. Why are you so upset?"

"My husband hurt me every day of our marriage. He nearly beat me to death. I wouldn't be here if Lord Everly hadn't intervened, so please, don't ever ask about him again. He's dead, and I'm glad. I thank God every single day that he can no longer get to me and claim me for his own. Now, let me go."

Luke didn't let her go, but kissed her hard, pulling her against him until she felt his arousal through the many layers of fabric between them. "I will never hurt you," he whispered. "Never."

Frances ignored her instinct to run away and surrendered to Luke's kiss. She needed to feel loved and wanted, and Luke intuitively felt her vulnerability and knew it was the chink in her armor. He didn't slide his hand under her skirts this time for fear of upsetting her, just kissed her and held her until she began to relax and allowed her anger to dissolve.

"Frances, let me come to you tonight. It's our only chance to be alone together before you go back to Paris. Let me show you how much I love you."

"I don't know," Frances replied stubbornly. "What if Lord Everly finds out?"

"He won't. It will be our little secret. I promise you won't be sorry. Don't you want to know what it feels like to be loved by someone who worships you? Say yes, sweetheart," he pressed.

"All right. Yes," Frances had whispered, sealing her fate.

# THIRTY-SIX

Frances had been allocated a small bedroom at the back of a dim corridor. It was sparsely furnished, and not much bigger than a garderobe. She'd gotten out of bed several times over the past hour, first unlocking her door, then locking it, then unlocking it again in anticipation of her rendezvous with Luke. She almost wished that Lord and Lady Everly were just down the hall, which would make Luke's visit impossible, but Hugo and Neve were on the other side of the building and overlooking the gardens. Their chamber was dominated by a large four-poster with hangings of golden-yellow silk elaborately embroidered with flowers and birds. They would have no inkling of Frances's transgressions, unless some busybody made it their business to tell them.

Sabine was quartered on the upper floor with the rest of the servants, forced to share a room with three other lady's maids who snubbed her at every opportunity. They were employed by French nobility, not some English upstart and his dowdy wife. Despite the frosty reception, Sabine wasn't upset in the least, since the prestige of having been to Versailles would give her much-desired cachet and elevate her standing among the other servants at the Everly residence. It would also help her secure a better position once the Everlys no longer had need of her. She wasn't around to offer Frances guidance and moral support, but she would wholeheartedly approve of Frances's assignation if she were.

Frances's hands shook with nerves as she heard stealthy footsteps in the corridor and watched in trepidation as the handle slowly turned. She wasn't afraid for her reputation, although she would hate to cause Lord and Lady Everly any distress; what she feared most was the actual lovemaking. She knew Luke was nothing like Lionel and would never intentionally cause her pain, but would she be able to respond to him? Frances had managed to endure a year of marriage with a man who cared nothing for her well-being or happiness, but was she ready to open up to someone who did? The thought of being touched intimately frightened her despite enjoying Luke's caresses in the park earlier. What if she froze? What if she were unable to please him? What if all she felt was revulsion? She so desperately wanted to love and be loved, and to enjoy that which brought everyone so much pleasure, but was it possible that her experiences with Lionel had broken something within her, and made her incapable of ever giving herself to someone without fear?

Frances felt a little less panicked when she saw Luke's sheepish smile as he quietly entered the room. Gone were the wig and the elaborate suit of clothes which Luke had been wearing earlier. His face was scrubbed clean of powder, and his natural hair was thick and wavy with a stubborn forelock that kept falling into his eyes. He was wearing breeches and a shirt that was open at the throat to reveal a mat of curly hair. His stockinged feet made no sound on the wooden floor as he slipped into the room and gave Frances a conspiratory smile as he set down his candle.

Frances held her breath as Luke turned the key in the lock

before slowly approaching the bed. Now that he was here, she was glad that she had worn her prettiest nightdress and had brushed out her hair and arranged it artfully around her shoulders. Some women wore rouge on their cheeks and lips, but Frances didn't need any; her lips and cheeks were rosy enough, especially now, since she was blushing. Sabine said that her former mistress even put rouge on her nipples before her lover arrived, but Frances thought that was just silly. She suddenly remembered how Lionel had forced her to use belladonna drops in her eyes to make them look wide and guileless, but pushed the memory away, annoyed with herself for allowing him to violate even this private moment. It would take her a long time to forget him, but she would be damned if she allowed him to ruin every good thing in her life.

"May I join you?" Luke asked as he climbed onto the bed next to Frances.

She just nodded, momentarily unable to speak. Lord Everly would be very displeased if he ever found out that she'd taken a man to her bed, but she was a grown woman; a woman who'd been married and had borne a child, Frances told herself defiantly. She had a right to shape her own destiny, and she wanted to know what it was like to have a lover; one who actually wanted to make love to her, not brutalize her. Luke claimed to love her and had offered marriage, so it wasn't wrong.

Luke cupped Frances's cheek as he looked into her eyes. "Frances, I will leave if you ask me to. I can't bear to see you looking so frightened. It's as if you are having an internal argument with yourself, and losing," he observed. "Are you that unsure of your feelings for me, or are you worried about the impropriety of the situation?"

Frances was surprised by how accurately Luke assessed her thoughts. He knew her better than she realized, so she felt she owed him honesty. "I'm not concerned with impropriety, but I am scared."

"Of what?"

"Of being physically hurt, for a start, and of being unable to overcome my fears. There are times when I wish I never had to marry, so that no man could ever lord it over me again or have the power to hurt me."

"Oh, Frances, how you must have suffered in your marriage to feel this way," Luke said sadly as he pulled Frances into his arms. "If you put yourself in my hands, I will show you that there is no reason to fear. I will show you how love is meant to be. Will you trust me?" he asked as he lifted her chin with his finger and forced her to look at him. "I will stop any time you wish."

"All right," Frances whispered. "I will trust you."

Luke didn't reply but kissed her lightly, his lips brushing hers in a manner which was completely nonthreatening as he pushed her down onto the bed. Frances expected him to undress, but Luke kept his clothes on. He was in no hurry. He kissed her for what seemed like an hour, his lips drinking her in and caressing her flesh until Frances felt as if she were floating above the bed, intoxicated with Luke's kisses. All tension fled from her body, replaced by a delicious languidness which seemed to permeate both body and mind. She barely noticed when he untied the ribbon on her nightdress and kissed her exposed breast, making her moan with pleasure.

Frances opened her eyes in surprise as Luke's mouth suddenly vanished. "Be right back," he whispered.

Frances experienced a moment of doubt while Luke shed his clothes but told herself she was being silly. Instead, she focused on Luke. He had a lithe, strong body, and his skin felt warm and soft against hers once he climbed back into bed and kissed her tenderly.

Frances felt a twinge of alarm when Luke pushed up her nightdress and slid his hand between her legs, but he whispered words of love as he picked up where he'd left off that afternoon, caressing and probing until Frances was ready for him.

"Ready?" he finally asked.

"Yes," Frances murmured, suddenly feeling anything but.

Luke slid into her and began to move slowly and deliberately, his eyes never leaving hers. She'd expected pain, a sense of violation, and the usual wave of humiliation to wash over her, but all she felt was her tender flesh stretching around him. It wasn't unpleasant, but not pleasurable either.

"Allow yourself to relax," Luke murmured. "Enjoy it." He kissed her lips, but then broke the kiss as he began to move a little faster, thrusting harder, and making Frances stiffen with fear. Was this the part where he would hurt her? Frances wondered frantically. She was no longer languid, but tense and uncomfortable, wishing only that he would finish and leave her alone. "You're holding back," Luke whispered. "I can feel it. Let me in, sweetheart."

Frances tried to do as he asked, but she couldn't let go. She wanted to cry as her hands came up against his chest. She tried to move her hips away from him, but Luke slid his hands beneath her buttocks and lifted her hips to meet his, making resistance impossible. Frances stopped fighting and just went limp, as she so often had with Lionel, in the hope that he would be done soon. Luke finally spilled himself into her and released her, panting as he rested his head against France's forehead. He cupped her cheek and pushed a stray curl out of her face as their eyes met.

"I know you didn't enjoy it, but it will be better next time, you'll see. You just need to allow yourself to relax."

"Yes," Frances mumbled, desperate for him to leave. She just wanted to be alone. She didn't want to think about what had just happened or contemplate the next time. She wanted to curl up like a shrimp and think of nothing at all until, hopefully, she fell asleep. They would be going home tomorrow morning, so she wouldn't have to see Luke or even speak to him until she was ready to face him again.

"I love you, Frances," Luke whispered as he planted a sweet kiss on her nose. "I can't wait until we are married."

Frances averted her eyes so that Luke wouldn't see her tears, but Luke was already pulling on his breeches and reaching for his shirt. Frances turned her face away, waiting for the sound of a closing door.

# THIRTY-SEVEN

The day was uncharacteristically gloomy for May; a dreary mist falling outside, and a chill seeping into every room of the house and forcing the maids to lay fires in hearths that had been cold for weeks. Even the birds were unusually silent, feeling no urge to sing when the skies looked as if they were about to open up and drench the city in a cleansing downpour. A merry fire blazed in the library, driving the chill away, but the house was hushed, as if everyone in it was responding to the weather and refusing to feel cheerful. Neve was upstairs with Valentine, and Frances had hardly left her room since they had returned from the country, claiming a mild indisposition and lounging in bed. Even Archie seemed out of sorts and had retreated to the stables to commune with the horses, followed by Jem, who was bored and restless.

Hugo didn't actually mind the somnolent atmosphere. After three days of whirlwind activities at Versailles, and a long ride back in a stifling carriage with two women who were sleep-deprived, hot, and cranky, Hugo was enjoying the silence.

He looked up from his book as Luke stormed into the library; his cheeks blotched by red spots of anger. Hugo gestured toward a chair, but Luke refused to sit down and just paced in front of Hugo like a caged beast, trying to catch his breath before blurting out whatever it was he'd come to say.

"So, which is it, Hugo? Is she your daughter or your mistress?" he finally spat out, his eyes blazing with fury as he stood over Hugo, who was still seated, his legs crossed and the book now in his lap.

"Which would you prefer?" Hugo asked solicitously, smiling up at his irate friend.

"As of Friday, rumor had it that you were bedding Frances under your wife's nose, but by Sunday, it seems that everyone had it all wrong, and she is really your love child with Morley's wife. Which is it? I have a right to know," Luke roared.

Hugo set aside the book and got to his feet. He didn't like to feel at a disadvantage when speaking with an angry man. And angry Luke was. Love was obviously having an adverse effect on the poor man. Perhaps Frances had rejected him while they were all at Versailles, or maybe Luke was having problems with Sir Trumbull. Hugo didn't know the man well, but his temper was legendary.

"First of all, you have no rights when it comes to my private life," Hugo replied calmly, "and second, neither one is true, as I am sure you know. What's really got you so upset, Luke?"

"If it isn't true, then why did you tell Monsieur Devereaux that you had been inordinately fond of Frances's mother? He's the biggest gossip at Court," Luke demanded indignantly, maddened by Hugo's knowing smile.

"Luke, someone started a mean-spirited rumor about Frances and myself, clearly meant to punish me for worming my way into Court. Something tells me that Sir Trumbull might have had a hand in it, given his obvious loathing of me. The gossip distressed and humiliated my wife, tarnished Frances's reputation, and didn't do me any good either. The only way I could find to quell the speculation was to imply that Frances is my ward because she's really my child," Hugo explained patiently. "Unless the idiots at Court are depraved enough to suggest that I'm romancing my own daughter, the rumor is now dead."

"Did you know her mother?" Luke asked belligerently, unwilling to drop the subject.

"Never met the woman, but I hear she was a beauty, just like her daughter," Hugo quipped in an effort to deflate Luke's anger.

Luke sank into a chair and smiled sheepishly. "I'm sorry, Hugo. The thought of you and her just sent me over the edge. I suppose I wanted to believe that she's really your spawn to alleviate my jealousy. I've tried to call on Frances since we got back, but she has refused to see me."

"You have nothing to feel jealous of. Frances is not mine, but I care for her as a daughter, nothing more. I love my wife, unlikely as it may seem to a courtier, and wish to spare her any more distress. Neve wasn't brought up to this life; she's out of her depth in this cesspool of gossip and malice. I simply wish to protect her."

"I understand," Luke conceded. "Were you also protecting Frances by not telling me she'd been wed?"

Hugo's expression grew hard as he surveyed his friend. "And who told you that, pray?"

"Trumbull."

"Yes, Frances had been married. She was viciously abused by her husband, Lionel Finch. Remember him?"

"Good God," Luke breathed, suddenly making the connection. "She was married to that Finch?"

"Yes. Mercifully, he's dead."

"Poor girl," Luke breathed. "I heard what he'd done to that girl at Madame Nelly's. It was unspeakable. They said she lost her sight and hearing after the beating he gave her."

"Thankfully, Frances can still see and hear, but she'd

suffered greatly, Luke, and if you so much as look at her the wrong way, I will nail your bollocks to the wall. Is that clear?"

"Crystal," Luke replied, suddenly eager to take his leave.

Hugo closed his eyes as Luke left the room, feeling strangely worn out despite the early hour. He'd grown up at the Court of Charles II, and had frequently visited the Court of James II, but in his view, and perhaps he was being naïve, no Court was as vicious as that of Louis XIV. Hugo was a seasoned courtier, but Neve was a woman of the twenty-first century, a woman who valued honesty, respect, and friendship. She was baffled by the goings-on at Versailles, and rightfully disgusted with the energy and fervor the followers of Louis XIV devoted to scheming and intrigue. She wanted nothing to do with that life, and he couldn't blame her, but their very future depended on remaining in Louis's good graces, which meant visiting Versailles, or any number of other palaces, when invited. Hugo couldn't afford to reject Louis's hospitality, nor could he refuse the summons of de Chartres, who needed an opportunity to see Hugo without meeting in private and risking exposure. Talking for a few minutes at Versailles would raise no eyebrows or connect Hugo to de Chartres in any way, which was precisely what the spymaster wanted in order to keep Hugo from becoming compromised.

It was a bit early in the day, but Hugo threw caution to the wind and poured himself a large brandy before settling back in his chair by the fire. He rarely gave in to homesickness, but there were moments, like right now, when he wished for nothing more than to be back in Cranley, away from all this scheming and gossip. He wanted Neve to be happy and safe, and his daughter to grow up on land which belonged to her family. He wished he could play a game of chess with Brad and share his concerns with his friend. He was desperate for someone to talk to, someone he could trust, someone who understood the position he was in and not judge him too harshly. Neve would support him, of course, but she simply couldn't understand the game he was playing or what was at stake, now and in the future.

He also wished that he could speak to Clarence face to face, and visit Jane's grave. It wouldn't change anything, but maybe his soul would feel a little lighter when he thought of the sister who'd committed the ultimate sin by taking her own life. Would he ever feel indifference when he remembered her, or would there always be this anger and hurt which threatened to consume him? Not a day went by that Hugo didn't replay the events of last fall in his mind, still searching for answers and arguing with a woman who was long gone in an effort to understand what had driven her to such extreme measures.

Hugo allowed himself a moment of self-pity before putting Surrey out of his mind and returning to the problem at hand. He had to earn his keep, which meant providing de Chartres with some intelligence, and soon. At this moment, the only means he had of learning anything was through Bradford Nash's letters and Luke's unguarded observations, but Gideon Warburton might prove a useful ally. The man had no place at Court, but he was well-informed, highly observant, and deeply involved in the politics of England through his profession. Perhaps it was time to renew their acquaintance, Hugo decided as he reached for paper and quill.

# THIRTY-EIGHT

Frances pulled the bed hangings closed and curled into a ball, enjoying the feeling of sanctuary that being cocooned in her bed gave her. There were nights when she still dreamed that Lionel was in her room, grabbing her by the ankles and dragging her to the edge of the bed, a twisted smile on his face as he enjoyed her terror. The dreams came less often now, but sometimes, Frances woke up with a scream on her lips and cold sweat on her brow. It took a few minutes for her to remember that she was in Paris, alone in her room, and safe.

Frances finally relaxed out of her fetal position and lay on her back, staring at the indiscernible pattern on the canopy. She heard Neve's voice in the corridor, talking to the baby as she passed Frances's room, and was overcome with a storm of emotions, ranging from smugness to deep regret. The regret was about deceiving Lord and Lady Everly. Frances wished that she could confide in Neve and talk to her as she used to, but she had found herself keeping her distance since the baby was born, unable to share in the joy when her own heart broke every time she thought of the baby she'd lost. She knew it wasn't Neve's fault, and she had done everything in her power to help her, but the pain was still there every time she saw the smiling, gurgling baby.

Of course, had Gabriel lived, Frances would be facing different kinds of problems. She would have no money, no place to live, and no desirable future, since the only way that her son could claim his rightful place was if she were to return to Lionel. Gabriel would have either grown up a pauper or fallen into the clutches of his father and suffered whatever cruelty Lionel decided to dish out as punishment for Frances, since she would have suffered deeply if her son had been abused. Perhaps Lionel would still be alive if she hadn't lost the baby or asked to leave England with Lord Everly, but whatever might have happened, no hardship in the world was as soul-crushing as losing a child. Strangely enough, Frances never thought of Gabriel as being Lionel's. He was hers, and hers alone. Frances said a prayer for Gabriel's soul, as she did every night, and turned her attention to more current issues.

Once safely back home, Frances had had time to analyze her feelings for Luke. What had happened at Versailles had not been his fault. Luke had done everything right; he'd wooed her, offered her a secure future, and made love to her gently and respectfully. A beautiful little package had been delivered the day after they had returned from Versailles, containing a pair of dangling sapphire earrings set in gold and encrusted with tiny diamonds. The earrings were the most beautiful thing Frances had ever owned, but she was reluctant to put them on, feeling the weight of responsibility at accepting the gift. Did Luke believe them to be secretly engaged?

Frances wasn't ready to commit to Luke, but she had felt that she owed their courtship another chance. Now that she knew what to expect, she had to try it one more time to see if things got better. Luke promised to be patient, and now that she'd already gone to bed with him, she had nothing to lose. Perhaps he was right, and she just needed to relax.

She'd gone out to meet Luke under the pretense of taking the air in the Gardens de Tuileries with Sabine. Sabine dutifully walked around while Frances joined Luke in his carriage, which was parked on the south side of the park just behind the Terrasse du Bord de L'eau.

Frances nearly changed her mind when Luke drew her into the carriage and into his arms, his hungry mouth devouring hers as she nestled in his lap.

"I was afraid you wouldn't see me again," Luke said as he planted feather kisses on the tops of her breasts. "You seemed so distant after we made love in Versailles."

He sounded like a petulant child, but Frances could understand how he felt. He needed to be reassured, and she had turned her back on him. Well, she was here, wasn't she, ready to try again.

There wasn't enough room in the carriage to lie down, so Luke unlaced his breeches and pushed up Frances's skirts, impaling her on him. Frances closed her eyes and willed herself to relax, trying to focus on the excitement of their secret rendezvous. Sabine thought this tryst was absolutely delicious, giggling all the way to the park and giving Frances helpful suggestions.

Luke grabbed Frances's hips and began to move within her; his eyes closed in concentration. Frances wasn't frightened or tense, but try as she might, she felt nothing other than discomfort and impatience. Luke pulled down her bodice and buried his face in her breasts, then caught her nipple between his lips.

*Any woman would enjoy this*, Frances thought frantically, but all she wanted was to flee.

Luke shuddered as he came, and Frances got off his lap and carefully adjusted her skirts.

"I must go," she said as she reached for the door.

"Frances, when will I see you again?" Luke called after her, but Frances was already out the door, running down the path.

She met Sabine, who was growing impatient, and treated her to a cup of chocolate at a nearby brasserie.

Frances had been pensive, and now she felt sure that she couldn't marry Luke. Luke was a good man and deserved a woman who loved him. He needed someone who felt more for him than tolerance, and at this point, Frances was sure that she could never bring herself to truly want him. She'd tried, she really had, but as much as she enjoyed being kissed and caressed, she couldn't bear having him inside her, and if she couldn't bear Luke, she probably couldn't bear any man. The thought of someone having rights to her body terrified her. Even someone as patient as Luke would become a despot if she rejected him again and again. He would demand that she allow him to exercise his marital rights and would probably take her by force if she refused.

She tried talking to Sabine, but the maid had different ideas about love and sex. She was practical and levelheaded, but then again, she'd also never been truly hurt, not like Frances, or lost a baby.

"Sabine, are you in love with your Pierre?" Frances asked as they sipped their hot chocolate. Sabine hardly ever spoke of her lover but escaped to see him whenever circumstances allowed.

"Of course not," Sabine replied indignantly. "I enjoy his company and he pleases me in bed, but I am most definitely not in love."

"How do you know?" Frances persisted. "If you enjoy his company and his lovemaking, why don't you love him?"

"Because loving leads to promises and heartbreak, or worse, weddings. I am not ready to settle down and spend my days cleaning some mean little house, cooking, washing, and taking care of screaming babies. I like being a lady's maid. I got to visit Versailles, for the love of God. How many women of my station can make that claim? Besides, men change once they become husbands."

"In what way?"

"They lose interest since the thrill of the chase is over. You must always remain out of reach, *ma petite*, in order to keep a man's attention. Pierre is always going on about marrying me, but I tell him every time that I will not marry him. Not now, not ever," Sabine said smugly, her dark eyes dancing with merriment.

"But, are you not afraid of losing him?" Frances asked, confused.

"When you become afraid of losing a man that's when you know you are truly in love. That's the one you marry. Are you afraid of losing Luke Marsden?"

Frances grew thoughtful, trying to imagine Luke with another woman or back in England. She felt a twinge of jealousy at the thought of being replaced, but the twinge quickly vanished. She liked Luke, but the thought of losing him didn't cause her any pain.

"No, I don't suppose I am," Frances finally replied.

"Then you are not in love. Isn't it delicious to have a lover?" Sabine asked, her pouty lips stretching into a sly grin.

Frances smiled back at Sabine. The idea had been delicious, but the reality was quite different. Frances felt ashamed, confused, and disappointed. The stickiness between her thighs was only too real, and she suddenly jumped up, desperate to get home and wash away any remnants of Luke.

"But I am not finished with my chocolate," Sabine whined as Frances tossed a coin down on the table.

"Yes, you are," Frances threw over her shoulder, already halfway to the door.

# THIRTY-NINE

## MAY 1686

**Aboard the La Belle**

A lashing rain beat against the windows, leaching all daylight from the captain's cabin. The ship rose and fell as it rode the swells that had seemingly come out of nowhere within the past hour, making Max a little nervous about the vessel's ability to weather the storm. Gone was the blazing sun and the turquoise waters of the Caribbean, replaced by the gray vastness of the Atlantic, which was heaving and churning as if some great beast had stirred to life within its depths and was now roaring and writhing in fury.

It was around noon, but it was so dark that a brace of candles had been lit, and the captain, who normally spent his days on the bridge, was hiding out from the storm and indulging in a game of chess with Max while the first mate manned the bridge. Max could have defeated Captain Benoit several times over, but he purposely made clumsy moves in an effort to prolong the game. He didn't get to spend much time alone with the captain, so this was an opportunity to drink some good wine, practice his French, and try to further his own interests, despite the gnawing fear that roiled in Max's stomach every time the ship listed precariously to the side. It was tossed about on the waves like a child's toy, but the captain seemed unconcerned, which gave Max a measure of comfort.

The captain's eyes twinkled as he surveyed Max over the rim of his cup, his lips moist with claret. "You are letting me win, Lord Everly," he drawled, partially annoyed and partially amused by Max's tactics. "Is it because you think me so dimwitted that I can't possibly win on my own, or because you hope to placate me before asking me for something?" the captain asked, a knowing look in his eyes.

Max was caught red-handed, so he could either play dumb or be honest, which he felt was the wiser course of action when it came to the captain. He was a shrewd man, and a brave one, so Max had to give him his due and treat him with the respect he deserved.

"You are clearly not that dimwitted, or you wouldn't have discerned that I'm letting you win, nor ascertained the reason for my generosity," Max replied, enjoying their banter. The captain would be more generous if he were in a good mood.

"What is it that you want of me, milord?" the captain asked with an indulgent smile, curious what his passenger might ask for given that he was hardly in a position to offer anything in return for a favor.

"My kinsman, Lord Hugo Everly and I, have some—shall we say—unpleasant history. I would like to pay him a visit when in France, but not as a pauper. My downfall would give my cousin great satisfaction," Max stated, watching the captain to see if he might offer any helpful suggestions, but Captain Benoit remained mute, forcing Max to go on. "I need to find some sort of employment which would allow me to set myself up as a gentleman of my rank would do."

"Such as?" Captain Benoit asked, clearly amused. "Gentlemen of your rank don't have employment; they sit back and spend their sizeable inheritances while others break their backs to make sure those inheritances don't dwindle, but grow with every passing year."

"As would I, had I not been sentenced to deportation," Max replied smoothly. "I cannot simply return to England and claim what's mine, so I must bide my time, and France is as good a place as any." Max took a sip of claret in order to gather his thoughts. When he'd had the conversation with the captain in his mind, he'd foreseen the captain instantly offering him some kind of solution, but the captain seemed reluctant to commit himself to helping Max, despite their mutual respect and budding friendship.

"True," Captain Benoit replied thoughtfully, "But what is it you are really asking me, milord?"

"I've given the matter some serious thought, and it would appear that the only employment I might be suitable for is that of a tutor. I am well-educated and can teach mathematics, philosophy, and English." Max had thought long and hard about what type of skills would be in demand in seventeenth-century France, but he had no knowledge of Latin or Greek, could hardly teach physics or chemistry since he had no idea what was actually known and accepted in this time period, and knew very little about astronomy.

"Hmm, that's a thought. Are you well versed in Greek, Latin, and theology?" the captain asked with a chuckle, already knowing the answer.

"No, but I can teach English, which can be useful to someone with political aspirations or mercantile connections to English-speaking countries. It won't be long before there's brisk trade with the American colonies, and English will become the language of commerce."

Captain Benoit tilted his head to the side, deep in thought. "People who wish to trade with France should learn to speak French," he finally said, but the idea had been planted, and

Max had to be patient. The captain was a businessman, one who made a living by smuggling and piracy. Perhaps he could find some use for Max's talents, especially if he hoped to branch out.

"Another game, *mon capitaine*?" Max asked as he surveyed the captain over the board. The captain had won, but they both knew his victory was a false one.

"Only if you play fair this time, milord," Captain Benoit replied as he refilled their cups. "I would rather lose after putting on a brave show than win unfairly. I might be a pirate, but I am an honorable one," he added with a wink.

Max bowed in acquiescence, ready to take the captain at his word and defeat him in under ten moves.

Thunder cracked outside, and a flash of lightning momentarily lit up the cabin, illuminating the space in a bluish hue and making everything appear like a still from a black-and-white film. If they survived this storm, they'd be docking in less than a week. The thought made Max's stomach clench with anxiety. While aboard the ship, he felt a certain sense of security, knowing that he couldn't do anything until they arrived in Europe, but now the moment was almost upon him, and he had to find a way of putting his plan into action.

# FORTY

## MAY 1686

**Paris, France**

William Trumbull quivered with rage as he reread the letter from England. He had been reluctant when His Majesty King James II had appointed him as Envoy Extraordinary to France, but had accepted nonetheless, and had done his best to make his time in France meaningful. But this latest assignment was an absolute slap in the face. Trumbull was well aware that his anti-Catholic views had garnered him enemies, particularly at the Court of Louis XIV, and his attempts to better the conditions for French Protestants after the Edict of Fontainebleau had raised a few eyebrows, but he was convinced that the final straw had been his unwilling association with Hugo Everly. Sir Trumbull tried his best to avoid Everly at Court, but to blatantly ignore a man who'd been welcomed by Louis with open arms was an insult to the monarch and a testament of his own feelings, which he wasn't allowed to have, at least not in public.

Sir Trumbull had been forced to welcome Everly to France and to speak to him for at least a few minutes every time their paths crossed, despite the fact that he would have liked to

throttle the man with his bare hands. The nerve! The absolute
nerve of showing up like that. And how in the world had he
managed to escape from Barbados? That was a question that
tormented Sir Trumbull, who secretly believed that the wrong
man had been sentenced after all. That poor wretch who
claimed to be a cousin or some such had paid the price for Everly's sins, and was now toiling on some plantation, while Hugo
Everly was sipping champagne and enjoying the best that life
had to offer, with two women by his side, if the gossip was to be
believed. What a contemptible libertine, Sir Trumbull fumed as
he crumpled the letter and threw it across the room in sheer
frustration.

The new assignment was a punishment, Sir Trumbull was
in no doubt about that, and it was to the last place on earth he
wished to go. Being surrounded by Catholics was difficult
enough, but in Constantinople, where he was being sent effec-
tive immediately, he would be surrounded by Mussulmen; men
whose Saracen religion was abhorrent to him and defied everything he'd been raised to believe. To make matters worse, his
dear wife would have to endure life in Topkapi Palace, if that's
where they were quartered, and come into possible contact with
the women of the sultan's harem. What an insult to a good
Christian woman to have to witness such degeneracy, Trumbull
raged as he refilled his wine glass.

However, to refuse was unthinkable, so he would just have
to find a way to make the new posting bearable. At least Luke
Marsden would be coming with him. Unlike himself, Luke was
a charming young man who often added great social value to a
situation. He managed to smooth ruffled feathers in a way that
was so subtle as to make the subject of his efforts regain good
spirits, without ever realizing that they were being skillfully
manipulated. Of course, Marsden would have to give up that
little strumpet of his. That was actually for the best, because the
younger man was clearly besotted despite the girl's association

with Everly and Sir Trumbull's warnings. Nothing he said had made a dent in the man's ardor, not even the rumors about the chit and Everly.

What was wrong with young men these days? Why could they simply not marry a comely, God-fearing woman of their parents' choice as he had? Sir Trumbull had never lusted after his wife, nor felt any undue sentiment, but they had a good, solid marriage; the type of marriage a gentleman should have, rather than this sordid, lustful union Luke was so intent on. Sir Trumbull performed his husbandly duties once a week, but the few minutes it took were never less than chaste, with his wife fully covered, and himself wearing his nightshirt. In all his years of marriage, he'd never seen his wife unclothed, and he liked it that way. He was able to show her respect and deference— something that might not come easily had he ever viewed her as an object of sexual desire. And there had been a few in his youth, but that was all behind him now. Desire had no place in his life.

Trumbull pinched the bridge of his nose and sucked in some air in an effort to calm himself. He would have to tell his dear Elizabeth of the new post and offer her the option of returning to England. She could wait for his return in the country of her birth where she wouldn't have to be exposed to the depravity and unchristian principles of the heathens who populated the Ottoman Empire. Elizabeth was a devoted wife and would likely offer to come with him, which he actually hoped for, but he had to give her the choice nonetheless. No Christian woman should ever be forced to go to such a barbaric country, and should only go willingly if she were a missionary, devoted to spreading the word of God.

Finally managing to regain some control, Trumbull penned a quick note to Marsden, asking him to call at his earliest convenience. Seeing the look on Marsden's face would actually be something of a treat, if William were honest with himself. Luke would do his duty, just as the Trumbulls would; he had little choice.

Trumbull sent off the note with a servant and resumed his pacing, his blood boiling once again at the insult King James had issued him for recognizing that traitor Everly. Yes, Trumbull would make the voyage to Turkey and put a good face on it, but he would be damned if that reprobate benefited from his disgrace. Whatever Everly had done to avoid deportation to the West Indies would not help him now. There were discreet ways of getting rid of someone, and people who were only too willing to accept the task with the minimum amount of questions.

William Trumbull finally stopped pacing and sat down at his desk. He had letters to write, lists to make, and an assassination to plan.

# FORTY-ONE

Luke tried to still the hammering of his heart as the carriage stopped by the Jardin des Tuileries. He'd gone over his speech a hundred times during the short ride to the gardens, but it didn't sound any better. The news had come as a shock, and he secretly agreed with Sir Trumbull that it was a form of punishment rather than an opportunity to further his political aspirations. Luke wouldn't have minded going to Constantinople if it weren't for Frances. How would she take the news? He thought he was finally on his way to winning her heart, but now he felt as nervous as a small boy waiting for his father to mete out punishment for some transgression and fearing the worst.

Frances gave him a wan smile as she ascended the carriage steps and sat across from him, as if desperate to put distance between them. Her eyes darted nervously toward the closed door, but she remained seated, waiting to hear what he had to say. On any other day, Luke might have wondered what had cooled her ardor since their last meeting, but today his mind wasn't on making love. He wanted her as much as ever, but couldn't bring himself to perform when he was in such turmoil. The conversation had to come first.

"Frances, there's been a development," he began as he reached for her hands, fooling himself with the illusion of his ability to keep her close. Frances allowed him to take her hands in his, but they were cold and limp, even when he tried to thread his fingers through hers.

"What kind of development?" Frances frowned at him, clearly taken aback by his tone. She might have been expecting a renewal of his proposal, despite their agreement to wait a while, so the tension in Luke's voice made her nervous, and she drew her hands away and folded them in her lap.

"Sir William Trumbull is being recalled from his post in Paris. He's being sent to Constantinople, and I am to go with him. Do you know where that is, my sweet?" Luke asked carefully.

"Yes, I do. Lord Everly has been teaching me geography. I quite like it," she added, still gazing up at Luke with an air of expectation.

"Do you understand what this means, Frances? I'm leaving Paris in a few weeks, after I've completed the arrangements for Sir Trumbull. He's leaving next week. He will first go to England with his wife, then travel to Constantinople on his own. His wife has refused to accompany him," Luke added as he watched Frances nervously, praying that she wouldn't use Elizabeth Trumbull's refusal to accompany her husband as an example.

Frances smiled at Luke warmly. "It will be very exciting, don't you think? It must be a terribly exotic place."

"Sweetheart, I want you to come with me. We can be married before we leave Paris, and you'll come as my wife. Just think of all the wonderful experiences we can have. It will be a great adventure. Please say yes, Franny."

Luke hadn't realized he was holding his breath but had to eventually suck in some air because Frances was taking too long to answer. She was studying him as if he were some unknown specimen, her face going through a myriad of emotions right before his eyes.

"Frances?" Luke prompted, desperate for her to agree.

Frances reached up and cupped his cheek, her eyes moist with unshed tears. "Luke, I care for you, I really do, but I can't go with you."

"I will take good care of you; I promise. I won't be like your husband. I will be kind and loving, and make your happiness my priority," Luke pleaded, but he could see that the girl's mind was made up.

"I know you would be a wonderful husband, Luke, but I simply can't bear to be separated from the only family I have. I'm too frightened to put myself at the mercy of a husband again, not without a family to turn to. Lord and Lady Everly are the only family I have, and I won't be parted from them, not ever. Being with them makes me feel safe and loved, and I can't agree to follow you to the other side of the world on nothing more than a promise of love and kindness. I hope you can forgive me," she added meekly.

"So, you don't trust me then?" Luke spat out, suddenly angry. "You give yourself to me, compromise your reputation, but you don't trust me. You think that I would hurt you without the protection of your adopted father. Well, have you ever thought that you might be a burden to him, and he might be happy to marry you off?"

"Is that what you really think?" Frances asked, her face going pale.

"No, I don't," Luke grudgingly admitted.

"I know I'm only fifteen, but I am not as naïve as you believe me to be. I know that Hugo would like to see me married, but I very much doubt that he would want to see me travel thousands of miles to accomplish that. Lord and Lady Everly plan to return to England, and I would like to return with them, and live close to them once I have my own family.

I've been alone for far too long, Luke, and I won't be alone again. I won't allow anyone to decide for me, not Hugo, and not you. I'm sorry if you are hurt, but I must do what's best for me."

With that, Frances bolted from the carriage, leaving Luke torn between anger and acute pain in the vicinity of his heart.

# FORTY-TWO

I covered the chamber pot with a towel to contain the smell and handed it to Marthe before turning my attention back to Frances. She was white as a sheet, her forehead clammy to the touch, and her eyes hooded with fatigue. Frances lay back on the pillows and focused on breathing, as I'd instructed her to do to keep the nausea at bay. Her hand went to her stomach as another wave assaulted her, but she managed not to be sick. She didn't have anything left to vomit, since she couldn't manage to keep anything down, not even broth.

When Frances had first begun to feel unwell a few days ago, I'd assumed that something hadn't agreed with her, but if this were a case of food poisoning, it would have passed by now, and no one else in the house was sick. Frances seemed to feel better by midmorning, but ill again by the time she woke up. I could see the tension in her face and the fear in her eyes. She knew what I was thinking, and judging by her expression, I had every right to be concerned.

"Frances, when was your last monthly flow?" I asked carefully. I tracked mine carefully, but wasn't sure if Frances did the same. Young girls were sometimes very sloppy about that kind of thing.

"It was in the middle of March," Frances replied, wincing with worry.

"You're late." I stated unnecessarily.

Was it really possible? Hugo had made sure that Frances was chaperoned at all times. When and where could she have found the opportunity to be with someone?

*Of course, she hadn't been as closely watched at Versailles,* I thought, suddenly realizing that Luke must have taken advantage of the situation. I didn't think that Frances would have initiated any kind of tryst; she was still too scarred from her experiences with Lionel Finch and the loss of her baby, but if the right amount of pressure were applied, I could see how she might have succumbed.

"Yes," was all that Frances said before she turned away from me.

"Frances, look at me. Are you with child?" I asked sternly, praying that Frances would tell me that there was absolutely no chance she could be pregnant. Sometimes there were unexplained delays caused by anxiety or a change in diet even when there was no chance of pregnancy.

"Yes," she said again. "I believe I am."

"Who is the father, Frances?" I asked, horrified. "Is it Luke?"

Frances kept her face turned away from me, her lips compressed into a thin line. She didn't wish to tell me, but she would tell Hugo. She worshipped Hugo and wouldn't be able to hold back from telling him.

I sat by her side and waited patiently until the morning sickness passed, leaving Frances looking considerably better. Her color had improved, and she seemed to be hungry. She reached for her forgotten breakfast tray, eating the buttered roll in two bites and drinking the now cold chocolate.

"Frances, come downstairs with me, please," I said, rising to my feet.

"You are going to tell him, aren't you?" she asked, all hope gone from her voice. "He will be so angry," she whispered as she turned her back to me to have her laces done up.

"I have no choice. Hugo is the head of this household, and he will decide what's to be done."

"I'm really sorry, Neve. You must believe me. I never meant for this to happen."

"I know, love." I couldn't be angry with the girl. She looked so young and frightened that my heart went out to her. I'd never thought to educate her on ways of avoiding pregnancy, or even how babies were made. I suppose she knew the basic facts, but it would never have occurred to her to ask her lover to ensure that there were no consequences, although that in itself was a risky game. Many a woman had gotten pregnant anyway.

Hugo was in the library, composing a letter to his nephew. He'd written to Clarence several times, but still had not had a response. Hugo worried that Clarence blamed him for his mother's suicide and was willing to do anything to regain the boy's trust. At the moment, the quill was suspended in midair, Hugo staring out the window at the glorious May morning rather than actually writing. He put down the quill and smiled brightly when we came in, but his expression quickly changed to one of dismay when he saw the solemn expression on our faces.

"What is it? What's wrong?" he asked as he jumped to his feet. "Is it Valentine?"

"No, Hugo, the baby is sleeping in the garden. Elodie is with her," I hurried to assure him. He was always terrified that something would happen to Valentine, since the daughter he'd had with his first wife had died in infancy before he ever saw her. She'd been passed off as his wife's second husband's child, but Hugo knew the truth, and grieved for the child he'd never met.

Hugo looked from me to Frances and back again, waiting for one of us to speak. Frances wasn't about to do it, so I took it upon myself to share the news.

"It seems that Frances is with child," I said quietly, wishing I could just take back the words and the fact.

Hugo looked stricken as he stared at Frances. "Is this true?" he breathed.

"I haven't seen a midwife yet, but I think so," Frances mumbled, all color draining from her face again. I hoped she wouldn't be sick again since I had nothing to shove in front of her face should she vomit.

"Frances, who is the father?" Hugo asked calmly. I knew what it cost him not to lose his temper, but he spoke softly, so as not to intimidate the girl. He could see how frightened Frances was; she looked like she wished the floor would open up and just swallow her so she wouldn't have to face Hugo's anger.

"I can't say," Frances replied. She was clearly terrified but was holding her ground.

"Frances, I need to know who the father is so that I can put this right. You must tell me."

"I can't," Frances said again. She went even paler, and her eyes were downcast, but she wouldn't be intimidated.

I saw the change come over Hugo's face as he reacted to what Frances was saying. He clenched his fist, but forced himself not to say something he would regret.

"Sweetheart, has someone hurt you?" he asked gently. "Has some man forced himself on you?"

Frances shook her head miserably. She obviously hadn't expected Hugo to come to that conclusion, but given her answers, it was obvious that he'd think she either didn't know the name of her assailant, or didn't want to marry a man who'd assaulted her.

"No, Lord Everly, no one hurt me. I was a willing participant."

"So why won't you give me his name?" Hugo asked, exasperated. "Is it because you don't wish to marry him?"

Frances just stared at the floor, seemingly rooted to the spot. Whatever her reasons, she wasn't talking.

"The child is mine."

I whirled around to see who was behind me and was shocked to find that Archie had entered the study and was standing in the doorway, his face set in hard lines as he faced Hugo across the room.

"Frances, is that true?" Hugo asked, still watching the girl.

Frances gave a barely perceptible nod, which nearly sent Hugo over the edge.

"You dog," he spat out at Archie, his eyes blazing with fury. "How dare you take advantage of this girl after what she's been through? I should have you horsewhipped, but I owe you too much to see you debased that way. Get out of my sight. I will deal with you later," Hugo roared.

Archie turned on his heel and strode from the room, but not before I saw the expression on his face. I was sure that he was lying, but whatever had made him claim responsibility wasn't for me to question. Perhaps the child truly was his. After all, he and Frances spent time together unchaperoned, and they had ample opportunity to meet since they lived under the same roof. All Frances would have to do is sneak out of her room after everyone had gone to sleep and go to Archie's bedroom on the third floor. No one would have paid any attention, and even if they had, they'd keep silent.

"Frances, please return to your room," Hugo said calmly, but I could see the tremor in his left hand as he hastily balled it into a fist. "I'd like to speak to my wife alone."

Frances didn't make eye contact as she scurried from the room; her head bent, and her eyes fixed on the floor. I couldn't tell if she was relieved to be dismissed or burning with shame and regret. It was ironic to think that teenage girls were the same in every century; except, in this time, they had fewer options. I tried not to think of a future in which Valentine was a defiant teenager, driving us to the brink of madness the way Frances was doing now, and she wasn't even our own child. What would it feel like if it were our own daughter who'd dropped this kind of bombshell on us?

I closed the door behind Frances as Hugo sank back into the chair, his mouth drooping at the corners. He was upset rather than furious, which was probably a good thing, but I suddenly felt an overwhelming tenderness toward him. I walked around the desk and stood behind his chair with my arms around him. "I'm sorry," I said.

"I tried so hard to keep her safe, to give her a chance at a better future. And now she's gone and ruined it all," Hugo sighed. "She could have had a good life with Luke, but he won't have her now, will he? Besides, Luke is preparing to leave for Constantinople. Did you know that?"

I hadn't, but now wasn't the time to be shocked by the news. "I'd hate for Frances to leave us," I said. "We'd likely never seen her again if she went with Luke, and Turkey might not be the best place for a girl like Frances. She would feel completely isolated unless she struck up a friendship with some other diplomat's wives."

"You're probably right, but she could have just rejected his offer rather than getting herself with child by Archie." Hugo pulled me around and settled me on his lap. "I just don't understand it, Neve. Archie is a good man. He's always liked women, but he's never involved himself with anyone who wasn't willing and understood the ramifications. I've never known him to go with young maidens. Archie doesn't want that type of commitment; he's always said so. What would possess him to bed Frances?"

"Hugo, have you seen them together?" I asked, suddenly realizing something that had eluded me all this time. "He barely looks at her when she's in the room for fear of his feelings showing in his eyes. And Frances has been avoiding him for about two months now. Perhaps they succumbed to a mutual passion and then realized their mistake and tried to stay away from each other. I do think he loves her, though," I mused.

"Well, it doesn't much matter now. He'll have to marry her. At least I know he'll be good to her, and she won't have to leave us after all."

"No, I suppose not, but I have a feeling there's more to this story."

"Perhaps Frances should see a physician before any decisions are made. Could she be wrong about this?" Hugo asked hopefully.

"She could, but I think she probably isn't. Women tend to be more fertile after getting pregnant the first time, so her body might have been ripe. And she wouldn't know how to avoid pregnancy."

"But Archie would," Hugo protested. "I've never known him to get a woman with child. Or maybe he just never told me," he conceded. "What a dreadful mess this is." Hugo suddenly looked stricken as he looked at me, his eyes opening wide. "Oh dear God, Neve, is this what we're going to have to worry about once Valentine gets older? I'd never realized what it was like to have a daughter. I swear I'll kill any man who so much as touches her hand," he swore. "First Jane gets herself pregnant, and now Frances. Why can't these girls keep their legs crossed until marriage?" he fumed.

"I was pregnant before we got married," I gently reminded him.

"Yes, but I would have married you in a heartbeat had the circumstances been different. I was always going to take responsibility for you and our child, you know that."

"I know, love," I replied soothingly. I wrapped my arms around Hugo's neck and pulled him down for a kiss. His lips felt stiff against mine, but he began to relax and returned the kiss as he wrapped his arms tighter around me.

"I'm sorry," he finally said. "I was just taken unawares."

"Weren't we all?"

*Archie most of all,* I thought.

# FORTY-THREE

Frances found Archie in the stables, brushing down his favorite horse as he murmured endearments to the chestnut mare. He seemed to drop his gruff exterior around animals and children, allowing himself that which he couldn't quite express to adults. Even Jem, who could drive the calmest of people to distraction, frequently got a kind word and a pat on the back from Archie, which was a feat.

Archie didn't turn around as Frances came in, but she could tell he was aware of her presence by the tensing of his shoulders and the defiant lift of the head. Archie stopped talking to the horse but didn't face her.

"Why did you do it, Archie?" she asked. "Why did you tell Lord Everly that the baby is yours?"

"To protect you," he replied without turning.

"Protect me from what?"

"From whatever it is you are afraid of. You have your reasons for not revealing the father, so either you are frightened of him, or you just don't want to compound your mistake by marrying him. By saying that the child is mine, I've given you a way out," Archie replied.

"I don't understand," Frances remarked, her frustration mounting. Archie was talking in riddles, as usual.

Archie finally turned around and faced her across the dim confines of the stable. "Frances, by coming forward as the father of your child, I've given you options. You can keep the child without marrying the father and later on claim that you'd married in France and your husband died. No one would be the wiser once we returned to England," Archie explained patiently.

"So, you weren't offering to marry me?" Frances asked, going from confusion to hurt. For a brief moment, she thought that Archie was declaring his feelings for her, but he was simply doing a favor for a friend, nothing more. He didn't think that Lord Everly would approve of a marriage between them, so he was in no danger of ruining his own life. Hugo's anger would subside eventually, and they would all go back to normal—except Frances, who would be pregnant and alone once more, her life no longer her own.

Archie looked momentarily confused by the question, as if the thought had never occurred to him. Was she really that repugnant to him?

Frances leaned against the side of the stall, suddenly feeling like her legs wouldn't hold her up for much longer. It was as if all the air had been sucked out of the stables, leaving her in some kind of vacuum with this man who wanted no part of her and had made a gallant gesture knowing there would be no long-term repercussions to himself.

Archie was by her side in a moment, lifting her into his arms in case she fainted and carrying her out of the stall toward a bale of hay by the door where the air was fresher. Archie sat down on the hay and settled Frances on his lap. He brushed a strand of hair out of Frances's eyes and finally looked her full in the face. The truth of what she was feeling was finally starting to dawn on him, and he lowered his eyes for a moment to compose his reply, likely one which would be a rejection coated in pretty words.

"Frances," he began patiently, "I would marry you tomorrow if that's what you truly wanted, but I'm a decade older than you, have dallied with a string of women, and have nothing to offer you other than a life of uncertainty and hardship. Why would you want to marry the likes of me, unless you simply wanted a father for your baby?"

"You would marry me tomorrow?" Frances repeated, a shy smile spreading across her face.

"That's the only thing you picked up on from what I just said?" Archie asked, his eyebrows shooting up with incredulity.

"Yes," Frances replied simply. "Why? Why would you marry me, Archie?" she demanded.

"Because I love you, you stupid girl," he exclaimed, unable to hold back any longer. "I've loved you since the first time I saw you when you fainted in my arms the day Hugo abducted you from your husband. You were battered and bruised, and barely conscious, and all I wanted to do was to hold you and look after you—and love you. I felt a damn fool, panting after someone else's fourteen-year-old wife, but there you have it."

"Why have you never said anything?" Frances asked, bemused. She was no longer pale and faint but flushed and glowing with happiness.

"When was I supposed to say it?" Archie demanded. "When you had just lost your baby? Or when you were so frightened of me you were ready to walk to Portsmouth rather than ride on the same horse? Or when I was chaperoning your outings with a prospective suitor who could offer you a life of safety and comfort? There was never a right moment, and I was grateful for that, for what I had to say to you had no business being said in the first place."

"I came to you, Archie. I offered myself to you," Frances argued, now really annoyed. Why were men so obtuse?

"Yes, you did. You wanted someone to practice on, someone to use. I couldn't do that, Frances. If I'd allowed myself to touch you, I'd want to claim you for my own, and it wasn't me you wanted. You wanted to be ready for the likes of Luke," Archie retorted.

"You daft fool," Frances cried, overcome by his inability to see what she'd really been offering. "I came to you because you are the only one I trust, and you are the only one I care about. You rejected me, you humiliated me, and you took away my hope. And now I'm carrying another man's child, and everything is ruined."

Frances fled from the stables, tears streaming down her face as she ran toward the garden. She just wanted to be alone, to lick her wounds, and rage at the utter stupidity of the situation. This was just like the Greek mythology that Hugo was so fond of teaching to her and Jem, where gods sat atop Mount Olympus and played with the fates of man for their own amusement. Well, she hoped the gods were amused, because there was no way out of this situation. She could marry Luke and go to Constantinople with him. Luke would be happy, and her child would have a father, but she would be miserable yet again, married to a man she didn't love and torn from the only family she knew. She could stay here, try to work things out with Archie, and expect him to raise another man's child, which was not something she had any right to ask of him, even if he was up for it. Or, she could just have the baby alone, and pretend she was a widow once they returned to England, in the hope that perhaps one day she might meet someone who loved her for who she was, and not give a fig about her past transgressions.

Frances fought back as Archie caught up with her and pulled her into his arms.

"Leave me alone," Frances cried. "There's nothing more to say. I will tell Lord Everly that you lied to protect me. There's no need for him to be angry with you. I will handle this on my own, as I always have."

"Franny, I meant it. I will marry you tomorrow, and I will be a father to your baby. I will love it as my own and never, ever hold its paternity against you. I was too blind to see what you were feeling, and I've made a mess of things, but I will do anything it takes to fix it between us. Will you let me?"

Frances shook her head against his chest. "Oh, Archie, it's too late. This is no way to enter into a marriage. This is all wrong. We are all wrong." She wrenched herself away from him and ran into the house, leaving Archie to stand in the middle of the garden looking hurt and confused.

# FORTY-FOUR

## JUNE 1686

**Aboard the La Belle**

The day was warm but overcast, the sun hiding behind thick clouds as the *La Belle* finally came within view of land. Max stood on deck watching the distant shore grow closer, his heart thumping against his ribs. He thought he'd be thrilled to see Europe again, but all he felt was apprehension. What was he to do now? He had no money, no friends, and no skills which would enable him to make enough to live on while saving for his passage back to England. Had this been the twenty-first century, he'd just whip out a credit card and get on the first flight to London, but here, he needed real coin, earned by real labor. Max's ordeal was far from over.

Banjo stood next to Max, perched on a coil of rope that enabled him to see over the rail. "Is that it? Is that France?" he asked.

His voice was small and filled with dread. The fun of the voyage was nearly over, and he would go to his new life, to new masters, who might, or might not, be kind to him. No matter how frightened Max was at the prospect of being on his own, he knew that Banjo was far more scared. Max couldn't imagine being five years old and already alone in a world of strangers, dependent entirely on their goodwill and compassion. Banjo was being awfully brave. Had this been a five-year-old Max, he would have cried and hid away somewhere on the ship, in the hope that the crew would take him along on their next voyage.

"Will you be coming with me to Paris, massa?" Banjo asked, his voice full of hope.

"Yes, I will go with you as far as Paris, but then you will go on to your new home," Max replied, moderating his tone to sound encouraging. The child didn't need to feel his apprehension; he was scared enough already.

"Will you go to yours?" Banjo asked. "Can I come and visit you?"

"In time, but first I will spend some time in France," Max replied uncertainly.

"Will you come and see me?" Banjo asked.

"I don't think I will be welcome, Banjo, but I will look out for you. Maybe I will see you one day, riding in a fine carriage, dressed in silks and velvets, and smiling with contentment." Max felt a catch in this throat but attributed it to the dampness in the air.

He laid his hand on Banjo's head, and the boy leaned against him. They stood like that for a few minutes until Captain Benoit came upon them on his way to the bridge.

"Run along, Banjo," he said kindly, and gave the boy a slight shove in the direction of the quartermaster, who was waving for him to come up on the bridge.

Banjo's mood instantly lifted, and he ran along, eager for a turn at the wheel. It would be his last time, so he wanted to make the most of it.

"So, how does it feel, milord?" the captain asked with a sly smile. "You are about to disembark as a free man."

"Yes, a free man with no money, no contacts, and no home

to go back to," Max replied, suddenly feeling sorry for himself. Where was he to go once he got off the ship? Perhaps he could get some work on the docks, loading and unloading vessels, and get a room in one of the shorefront taverns. They were bound to be cheaper than anything in the center of town since they catered to sailors and stevedores.

"I've been considering what you said a few days ago," the captain began, his eyes fixed on some distant point on shore. "The dynamics of trade are changing now that the American Colonies are a player, so perhaps learning English could benefit me in my trade."

"But you already speak English," Max replied.

"My English is not very good, but it serves my purposes," the captain agreed. "However, I have two boys, aged seven and eleven. I hope they will join me one day. I fancy having a fleet of ships at my disposal," he confided with a wistful smile. "It would serve my boys well to know English, especially if it will be the language of commerce, as you so eloquently stated."

The captain chuckled at such a fanciful notion before continuing.

"I will offer you a position in my household. You will have room and board, and a modest wage, which will go a long way toward paying for your passage home. You can tutor my boys in English, mathematics and astronomy. They will need to learn to navigate once they go to sea," the captain elaborated as if Max might wonder why children would need to learn those subjects. "I must admit that I find philosophy, Latin, and Greek to be something of a waste of time in my line of work. The only time a captain gets truly philosophical is when there's a chance of his ship going down, and the oaths that pour from his mouth are rarely in Greek. So, let's give it a few months and see how things progress. What do you say, milord?"

"Do you live in Le Havre?" Max asked, suddenly dismayed. He needed to be in Paris where the Everlys were, but he supposed staying in Le Havre for a few months would not make too much of a difference. He needed to have some money before he undertook any decision.

"My wife hates Le Havre," Captain Benoit snorted. "She says it's dingy, ugly, and utterly devoid of culture. My family lives in Paris. It's not a very fashionable neighborhood, but we have a comfortable house and several servants. I think you'll find it to your liking. And, you will be close enough to visit family," he added with a touch of sarcasm.

"I accept with pleasure," Max said as he held out his hand to the captain. "I just hope your wife doesn't object."

"My wife does what I tell her to," the captain replied, surprised that Max would even worry about his wife's reaction. But, then again, the man wasn't married, so he wouldn't understand a wife's devotion and obedience. "I'm expected on the bridge," the captain said as he turned to walk away. "We'll speak more later on, over supper at the tavern. They do a fine oyster stew, and their claret is not half bad. Don't worry, *mon ami*, supper is on me. You can pay me back by being good to my boys."

Max stared at the fast-approaching shoreline as a slow smile spread across his lean face. He'd suffered greatly over the past eight months, but things were finally looking up. The stars were aligning at last, and he would make the most of his newfound fortune. A roof over his head, meals, and proximity to Hugo and his family were all he needed.

# FORTY-FIVE

## JUNE 1686

**Paris, France**

"You are a silly, silly girl," Sabine said as she surveyed Frances, hands on her hips. "Why did you not tell me right away? I would have helped you avoid all this"—she waved her hand in the air while searching for the right word—"drama."

"And how would you have done that?" Frances asked, irritated by Sabine's attitude of superiority. What right did she have to scold her like this? She was only a maid, for God's sake, not a member of the family. Frances was too tired to even care. Her world was falling apart once again, and she just couldn't bear to deal with the consequences of her own foolishness. If she had never succumbed to Luke's caresses, she wouldn't be in this predicament. But then, she also wouldn't know how Archie truly felt about her. What a mess this was turning out to be.

"I have gotten with child twice," Sabine confided in a low voice, although they were quite alone. "I have taken care of the problem, and no one was the wiser."

"How?" Frances asked, intrigued. Sabine was a wealth of

information when she wanted to be, so Frances swallowed her irritation and gave Sabine all her attention.

"Frances, you really are a babe in arms, you know that?"

"Yes, I suppose I am. I know there are ways of avoiding unwanted pregnancy, but I have no idea what they are."

"Well, you might have asked before you tumbled into bed with Luke Marsden. Besides, considering that you are not married or even betrothed, he might have used his wits and taken care of things himself," Sabine fumed as she paced the room.

"Is it up to the man then?" Frances asked innocently. No wonder Archie never got anyone with child. He clearly had more "wits" than Luke.

"For the most part, yes. There are some decoctions women can take, but they are not always reliable. If the man loves you, he will take measures to protect you," Sabine droned on. "He can greatly reduce the risk of pregnancy by pulling out just before he finishes, but most of them are too damn selfish to want to interrupt their pleasure, which brings us back to the problem at hand."

"It does, doesn't it?" Frances mumbled to herself, wishing she was anywhere but here, anything but pregnant.

"There are ways to get rid of an unwanted child, especially early on in the pregnancy. How far along are you?"

"Over a month," Frances replied miserably.

"Do you want it or not?"

"I haven't really figured that out yet."

"Well, do, and when you decide, let me know."

With that, Sabine left the room, carrying a pile of dirty linens, her head held high as if she were a noble lady and not a lady's maid. Frances really did like her spirit and wished that she had half the fire the older girl had.

She climbed into bed and hugged her knees to her chest. She'd told Sabine the truth; she wasn't sure if she wanted the baby or not. Gabriel's death had left a gaping hole in her heart, and she thought that having another baby might fill it, at least partially, but she didn't want to have a baby by a man she didn't love. And she didn't love Luke; she knew that now. She liked him very much, but what she felt for him wasn't love. The idea of Luke leaving had taken her by surprise but caused her no great emotional upheaval. She had said goodbye to him only a few days ago, but already he felt like a distant memory, a pleasant dream that had dissipated with the coming of dawn. Perhaps she should feel guilty for allowing him such liberties, but after Lionel, she felt she deserved a little bit of affection. And now that affection had led to another baby, a baby she didn't really want. Of course, she hadn't wanted Lionel's baby either, but she loved Gabriel fiercely once he was born.

Frances closed her eyes and tried to imagine Luke's child. It would be a beautiful baby, of that she was sure, maybe another boy, but the imaginary child in her arms had red hair and bright blue eyes. That was the child of her heart—Archie's child.

Yes, she wanted another baby, but not this one. She wanted to marry Archie, if he'd still have her, but not while carrying another man's child. Archie said that he would never hold it against her, but in time he would, especially if the child were a boy and looked like Luke. Archie was only human, after all, and a constant reminder of his wife's liaison with another man would haunt him day and night. Archie might have an easier time adjusting to a girl, but it was not as if she could choose. It was a gamble—one she wasn't too eager to take.

Oh, what she wouldn't give for a miscarriage.

Frances leaped off the bed as a wave of nausea assaulted her, and she retched into the chamber pot. Her insides were churning, and so was her mind.

She angrily pushed the pot under the bed and crawled under the covers, pulling the blanket over her head. There was no one in the room, but she still felt ashamed of her tears.

# FORTY-SIX

Hugo rose early, unable to sleep. Neve was still asleep, her face shadowed in the confines of the great bed. She looked remarkably peaceful, enjoying the well-deserved sleep of one who's often woken during the night. Valentine was sleeping for longer stretches now, but she still woke up for a feeding at least once a night.

Hugo gazed adoringly at the baby before pulling on his clothes and letting himself quietly out of the room. He needed some air, and the morning was too fine not to take advantage of. Had he been in Surrey, he would have gone for a gallop through the countryside, but Paris was no place to go galloping. He would have to either ride in the Jardin de Tuileries, which wasn't open enough for what he had in mind, or go beyond the city limits toward Fontainebleau. A brisk walk would have to do.

"Where are you going, my lord?" Jem asked. He was sitting on the bottom step, munching on a freshly baked roll smeared liberally with butter and honey. His face was sticky, and he was licking his fingers with grim determination. Jem was normally the happiest when he was eating, but this morning he looked forlorn and dejected, his eyes veiled with sadness.

"Why are you sitting here, Jemmy?" Hugo asked as he lowered himself next to Jem and accepted the bite of roll which Jem generously offered.

"Cook threw me out of the kitchen. Said I'm always underfoot. I just like watching her make things. Is that so wrong?"

"Do you have aspirations of becoming a great chef?" Hugo asked with a chuckle. Jemmy's love of food could be the path to a lifelong career.

"No, I just like to watch. And eat," Jem confided. "And there's other stuff."

"What kind of stuff?" Jem offered Hugo another bite, but he politely waved the roll away, not wanting to take it away from the boy.

"No one is ever happy anymore," Jem grumbled. "Frances is in her room crying her eyes out; Archie looks like he'd like to punch someone, and you and Lady Everly are always busy with the baby and going off to Court. No one wants me around," Jem said, his eyes filling with tears. "Where are you going anyway?" Jem asked.

"I thought I'd take a walk by the river. I need some air, and the women in this house are driving me insane," Hugo replied, lowering his voice to a confidential whisper.

"I know just how you feel," Jem replied, licking the last of the honey from his fingers. "Can I come with you? I can use a break from the women too."

"Of course you can. We need man time. Why don't you bring some stale bread, and you can feed the birds, if you like."

"Should we invite Archie? I think he's borderline crazy too," Jem offered.

"Normally, I would invite Archie, but at the moment he's contributing to my bout of insanity, so let's leave him at home, shall we?"

"All right," Jem conceded. "Can I have a cup of chocolate after our walk? In that café I like?"

"Of course. And a pastry. It wouldn't be a proper walk without stopping for a treat afterward."

"Frances will be so jealous," Jem whispered happily, his good humor restored.

Jem bounced happily off the step and ran along to get his hat and coat by way of the kitchen. Hugo heard Cook berating him in rapid French as he grabbed some bread for the birds and returned to the foyer ready to go. Hugo couldn't help feeling a twinge of sadness as he remembered that he might be parted from the boy in the coming months. He hadn't said anything to Jem, but eventually Nicholas would either write or come in person, at which point Jem would find out the truth. Hugo sighed and followed Jem out the door.

The morning was too fine to remain in low spirits. The sun warmed their shoulders and sparkled on the water, making the Seine glow like a ribbon of silver. Cotton-ball clouds dotted the azure sky, and the smell of the river, cut grass, and freshly baked bread permeated the air. Several fancy carriages rolled by, taking their occupants home after a long night of debauchery, and wagons rumbled down the streets, delivering fresh milk and produce to taverns and shops.

Before long, Hugo and Jem were watching boats on the river, feeding the ever-hungry birds, and eating hot crepes bought from an old woman who made them right on the banks of the Seine, and chatting like magpies. Jem was happy to have Hugo's undivided attention, something that had been in short supply over the past months. Hugo wondered if he should tell Jemmy the truth of his paternity, but decided to wait. Jem was so happy just being with him that he felt a piercing stab of guilt at not paying more attention to the boy. He was just a child; he couldn't understand the complexities of Hugo's situation, or the all-consuming needs of a baby. Normally, Archie stepped in when Hugo was unavailable, but Archie had his own troubles of late, if Frances's pregnancy was anything to go by. Decisions would need to be made, but for now, Hugo just wanted to enjoy Jem's company.

"I'm sorry I haven't spent more time with you, Jemmy," Hugo said as they sat on a bench and watched the traffic on the river. "I've been somewhat preoccupied."

"That's all right," Jem replied, his eyes never leaving the little boat that had just appeared from behind Île de le Cité. "My mam was always preoccupied. That's just the way adults are, isn't it? Archie used to take me out and show me things, but now he's preoccupied too. I don't ever want to fall in love, not ever," Jem said hotly. "It makes you all muddled and moody."

"Is Archie in love, do you think?"

"Ach, he's been in love with Frances for ages, simply ages. Any fool could see that," Jem replied matter-of-factly.

Hugo made a mental note that he was clearly a fool since he'd been oblivious to the passionate love affair brewing right before his eyes. He supposed that he was so used to Archie's lone-wolf ways that he never imagined him to actually fall in love with any one woman, especially a fifteen-year-old child-bride. He supposed it was unfair to call Frances a child since she'd endured more than most grown women had in a lifetime, and deserved some happiness at last, but he hadn't envisioned that outcome with someone like Archie.

Perhaps Archie really did love her, but would he be able to finally settle down and be with one woman? Archie liked his sport and was never short of female companionship. Would Frances be enough for him? Would he be enough for her? She needed someone with infinite patience, someone who treated her with kindness and understanding. Archie was a good man, but he could be rough around the edges, and less than patient. He'd also been scarred by the loss of his nieces, nephew, and brother-in-law, who had all died the same week and sent his sister into a downward spiral, which had ended with her taking the veil and shutting herself away from the outside world.

Would he be capable of loving Frances in the way she needed to be loved, or would he keep her and their child at arm's-length for fear of losing them? Hugo should know the answers to all these questions, but he didn't. He'd neglected everyone in his quest for recognition and financial independence, and would have to pay greater attention to the women in his life, particularly Valentine. He wanted to be the kind of father he'd seen in the twenty-first century; a father who was involved with his child in a real and hands-on way, not one who saw his offspring for an hour a day and had no idea what they were thinking or feeling. Valentine was, of course, too young for conversation, but he did talk to her when no one was around, or in the middle of the night when Neve was asleep.

Hugo felt silly talking to the baby when someone was in the room, but when they were alone together, he poured his heart out to her. Valentine stared at him with those round, brown eyes as if she understood every word. Perhaps she did. Neve said that babies understood a lot more than people gave them credit for, and even if she didn't understand the words, she instinctively understood the tone. Neve had even suggested that it was time to start reading to her, which was something Hugo felt more comfortable with. He liked holding the baby in the crook of his arm while he read poetry to her, and watched her lashes begin to flutter as she fell asleep in his arms. His daughter was obviously not ready for such romantic sentiments, but he liked the feeling of bonding those quiet moments gave him, and looked forward to them every day.

"Time to go back, I think," Hugo said as he rose from the bench and stretched his back. "Lady Everly will wonder what's become of us, and I'm still hungry, truth be told. I can use a good breakfast."

"No, she won't. She's too busy with the baby," Jem replied

angrily, making Hugo smile. "But I suppose a second breakfast would be nice," he conceded as he jumped off the bench.

Hugo began walking along the river with Jem trailing behind him reluctantly, not quite ready to go home. Hugo couldn't help wondering what his life would be like if Nick came to get him. Would Nick be a loving father, or would he take in Jem simply because he needed an heir? His wife wouldn't be too pleased, or would she? Taking in a child who had been conceived years before would probably be less painful than watching her husband fall in love with someone new and father a child she could never give him. Perhaps she would take to Jem. He was such a sweet, animated boy.

Hugo suddenly realized that Jem was no longer walking next to him. He'd probably been distracted by another boat, or a nice pair of chestnut horses drawing a carriage. Having spent time with Archie, Jem had a real appreciation for good horse-flesh, and never failed to stop when he saw a beautiful horse. Hugo began to turn around when he heard Jem's terrified shout and saw him hurl himself at a man who was pointing a gun straight at Hugo's chest. The man looked like an ex-soldier but, judging by his disheveled dress and greasy hair, had been out of the army for some time.

The shot was deafening when it rang out, everything seemingly taking place in slow motion as Jem tackled the man, who tossed him off, and took off at a run. Hugo felt a terrible burning sensation in his chest. It was as if a hot poker had been thrust through his flesh, searing everything in its path, the pain all-consuming as it spread toward the heart.

Hugo looked down, his mind still refusing to comprehend what his body already knew. A large bloodstain bloomed just over his heart. He felt an overwhelming dizziness, as if life were draining out of him as he sank to his knees, his eyes still focused on Jem. The boy seemed to be screaming, but Hugo couldn't hear a thing. His ears were ringing, and his blood roared in his veins as it whooshed through his body. He hit the ground hard, falling on his side. The pain exploded like a firework, taking his breath away and blinding him with its intensity. Hugo tried to hold on, but it was too strong for him, too powerful. He saw Jem running toward him as he lost consciousness.

# FORTY-SEVEN

I was just finishing getting dressed after feeding the baby when I heard the stomping of feet and screams coming from down-stairs. This wasn't the usual commotion that was the result of Frances getting into a spat with Jem, or the maids seeing a mouse out of the corner of their eye. I yanked on my laces and raced from the room, hoping that Valentine wouldn't be awak-ened by the ruckus. She had just fallen asleep, and I had been hoping for a peaceful breakfast before all hell broke loose.

I nearly fell as I slipped on the slick floor of the foyer as I raced toward the salon where the wailing was coming from. I thought it was water but was stunned to see blood on the hem of my skirt. A sob tore from my chest as I threw open the door and burst into the room. Marthe was kneeling by Hugo, keening, with her face in her apron. Hugo was lying unconscious on the settee. His shirt was soaked with blood, and Elodie was wiping his face with a damp cloth. She wasn't crying, but she was white to the roots of her hair as she fought for control of her emotions. Jem was crouched behind the settee, crying silently, his face contorted in agony, his hands over his ears to block out Marthe's screams.

Frances came running in after me, her eyes huge with shock.

"What happened?" I cried. "Please, someone tell me what happened." My heart was thumping painfully against my ribs, and my hands shook badly as I approached my husband. My mind managed to register that Hugo was breathing, which was a relief, but the breaths were shallow and labored.

"Someone shot milord by the river," Elodie whimpered. "Jem managed to get help and bring him home. Archie's gone for the doctor."

I kneeled by the settee and took Hugo's limp wrist. I could feel his pulse, but it was weak and erratic. His skin was ashen. Hugo's eyes twitched beneath his eyelids as if he were having a nightmare, but he wasn't lucid. I felt a wave of hysteria wash over me but forced myself to breathe evenly and concentrate. I was Hugo's only chance of survival. A seventeenth-century doctor could do more harm than good, so I had to retain my wits and try to remember everything I knew of wounds, which wasn't much. Hugo had been shot on the left side, but if the shot had penetrated the heart, he'd have been dead before Jem could even call for help. There was hope; there had to be.

"Marthe, stop wailing and bring me a cup of spirits," I ordered.

"Now is not the time to get drunk," she grumbled.

"It's not for drinking."

I carefully slid my hand beneath Hugo's back and pulled it back out. There was no blood, which meant that there was no exit wound. The bullet was lodged in Hugo's chest. I was fairly certain from watching medical programs on television that an exit wound would have been preferable, but I wasn't sure exactly why. Perhaps because the wound would heal cleaner. Or maybe because it couldn't begin to heal until the bullet was removed. If the bullet was close to the surface, it might not be too difficult, but it could be lodged deep inside, making the extraction very dangerous and painful.

I carefully pulled the shirt away from Hugo's chest, revealing the ragged hole just above his chest. It wasn't large, and the bleeding seemed to be minimal since Hugo was lying on his back. But what if Hugo were bleeding internally? I fretted as I tried to remember all I could. What then?

I grabbed the cup of brandy from Marthe and began to disinfect the area, allowing a few drops of alcohol to slide into the wound. Hugo moaned with pain, but I continued to do my work. Focusing on something practical kept me from going completely mad with worry and fear, although my hands were shaking badly.

"Jem," I called, "please come out and stay with me. I need you."

Jem crawled out from behind the settee. His face was white as a sheet, his eyes black holes in his frightened face. "Will he die?" he whispered. "I did my best. I screamed for help until the men came and lifted his lordship into the wagon. They were kind, and one of them gave me a sip of brandy. They told me not to cry," he mumbled apologetically, as if crying was cowardly. He looked so small and frightened standing there that even Frances was moved. She wrapped her arms around the boy and kissed the top of his head in a motherly gesture of comfort.

"Jemmy, you saved Hugo's life. If not for you, he'd be dead by now, lying on the riverbank until the life bled out of him. You were very brave. Very brave," I repeated as tears spilled down my cold cheeks.

Hugo could still die, could still bleed to death if the doctor didn't come soon. And even if he did, his abilities and resources were minimal compared to what a modern-day hospital could do. Even if he managed to extract the bullet, the risk of infection was very high with nothing to kill the bacteria. Hugo would need antibiotics, and possibly morphine for the pain.

"Hugo, love, can you hear me?" I pleaded. "Please open your eyes. Please, Hugo, hold on. The doctor is on his way. He will help you." But what if there was nothing the doctor could do? my mind screamed hysterically.

I sank to the floor with Jem pressed against my side. We just sat like that, drawing comfort from each other until Archie finally ushered the doctor into the room. He was a small man in his sixties with a kindly face and a brisk manner. My eyes flew to his hands, which were, thankfully, clean. His clothes were fastidious, his wig carefully coifed. I prayed that this man understood the benefits of cleanliness in healing but couldn't be sure until I saw his instruments.

"Please, move aside, my dear lady," the doctor said as he set down his bag and tried to approach Hugo. "My name is Fabrice LeGrand," he added as he took Hugo's pulse and pulled up his eyelids.

"Will he live?" I moaned as I moved out of the way, but still hovered over the doctor's shoulder.

"Please, clear the room, milady," the doctor replied as he set down his case and pulled out a wooden tube which was the present-day equivalent of a stethoscope.

I ushered everyone out of the parlor except for Archie, who refused to leave. He was too nervous to sit down, so he leaned against the wall and forced himself to be still so as not to distract the doctor, who removed his coat and tossed it carelessly across a nearby chair. I sank into a chair, feeling that my legs wouldn't hold me up for much longer.

The doctor paid me no mind as he examined the wound, then checked Hugo's back for an exit wound and listened to his heart. I could hear garbled noises coming from the foyer. Everyone was milling around outside, waiting for news.

"Please, Doctor LeGrand," I pleaded. "Tell me if he will live."

The doctor finally set aside his tube and turned to face me. He didn't take a seat, but stood over me like a specter of doom, his curly wig nearly blocking out the light from the window. I focused on his eyes, which were kindly and soft. He didn't look like a person who was about to deliver terrible news.

Doctor LeGrand sighed and took my hand as a gesture of comfort, which was meant to disguise the checking of my pulse. He seemed satisfied that I wasn't about to keel over before finally answering me.

"Lady Everly, your husband was gravely wounded, but he was very, very lucky. The bullet entered a little above his heart. Slightly lower and he would have been dead. Your boy saved his life when he threw himself at the assassin. Your man here told me what happened," he added by way of explanation. "Now, the bad news is that the bullet is still lodged in his chest, and we need to extract it before healing can begin. Milord is healthy and strong, so I have every confidence that he will recover, but we must act quickly. I will require a flat surface, such as a table, to work on. I cannot operate on the settee. I will also need clean towels, hot water, and a quantity of linen bandages. And why does he smell of brandy? It seems to be coming from the wound."

"Alcohol is a disinfectant, *monsieur*. I cleaned the wound to keep it from festering," I replied, knowing that the man would think me mad.

"I see," was all he said, gazing at me with sudden interest. "Shall we begin?"

I ran for the door, ready to command my troops. Within ten minutes, the dining-room table had been covered with a sheet and several jugs of hot water waited on the massive sidebar. A stack of towels was next to the jugs, and Frances and I were ripping a sheet into strips to use as bandages.

Doctor LeGrand rolled up his sleeves in preparation for

surgery and washed his hands, per my request. He looked skeptical, but didn't object, which was surprising for a seventeenth-century physician. At least he wasn't a barber-surgeon like the ones I'd seen in Blackfriars, pulling teeth, amputating limbs with rusty saws, and cutting out ill humors with filthy knives. I was amazed that anyone ever survived after seeing one of those for their complaints.

"May I?" I asked the doctor.

He opened his mouth to reply, but just gave me a brief nod. I dipped a towel in brandy and wiped all blades and forceps, thanking the Lord that the doctor didn't throw me out of the room for my impertinence.

"Do you have some medical knowledge, milady?" he asked as he chose a pair of forceps that looked like pliers.

"No, but I believe that unsanitary conditions aid the spread of infection," I replied carefully.

"An interesting notion," the doctor replied, clearly intrigued. "I happen to agree with you, although many medical men would ridicule me for this opinion."

I hoped that Hugo would stay insensible for the procedure, but he chose this moment to come around. His lips were dry and his eyes mere slits, but he was lucid. "What happened?" he whispered.

"Young man, you have a bullet in your chest. I'm going to extract it. It's going to be painful, but if you remain immobile, it will go faster. Can you do that for me?"

"I'll try. Can I have something to drink?" Hugo murmured. He was pale and clammy, but his grip on my hand was strong, which was a good sign.

I lifted Hugo's head and held a cup of brandy to his lips. He drained it and tilted his head back as the doctor gave him a leather strip to bite down on. I shuddered at the imprint of tooth marks on the leather, but kept my mouth shut. Hugo bit down obediently and closed his eyes. He knew what was coming, but managed to lie still, his face fairly relaxed for a person who was about to be tortured.

The doctor came around the table until he was facing the window rather than standing with his back to it. He had the benefit of daylight, which was much brighter than candlelight and would make it easier for him to see what he was doing.

I held Hugo's hand firmly and sucked in my breath as Doctor LeGrand inserted the instrument into the wound. Hugo went as rigid as a board but remained quiet as the doctor rooted around for the bullet. After a few moments, Hugo was panting with pain; sweat was running down his face as the doctor went deeper, searching for the bullet. Crimson blood leaked out of the wound, making it more difficult for the doctor to grab the slippery ball.

Hugo turned an alarming shade of white and then went limp like a rag doll.

"Is he in shock?" I cried, alarmed.

"Yes, but I got it." The doctor held up the little ball triumphantly and dropped it into a waiting bowl. The skin around the opening was puckered and red, and blood still oozed slowly, but not as much as before. The doctor asked me to hold a towel to the wound while he withdrew a metal stick with a small square attached to the end from his satchel. I had never seen one of these instruments before, but I had a pretty good idea what it was for. He was going to cauterize the wound. I prayed that Hugo would remain unconscious, but he seemed to be coming around again, his eyelids fluttering as he regained consciousness.

"Did you get it?" His voice was hoarse.

"Yes, I did. I have to close the wound to stop bleeding and prevent festering. It's going to be painful, but it must be done. Would you like more brandy, milord?"

"Yes."

I poured Hugo nearly a half-cup of brandy, hoping it would dull the pain. I couldn't begin to imagine the agony of having a red-hot iron pressed to my skin and held down until the flesh began to sizzle, but as far as I knew, cauterization worked, and was still used in some instances in the twenty-first century. I averted my eyes as the doctor withdrew the heated instrument from the fire.

"Hold his hand, but turn away, madam," the doctor advised. "It's best if you don't watch."

I felt a wave of nausea as Doctor LeGrand held the iron to Hugo's chest. Hugo let out a roar of pain as he crushed my hand in his. The stench of burning meat filled the kitchen, making me gag as bile rose in my throat, threatening to choke me. Hugo's hand was the only thing that kept me from fainting. I held on to it for dear life, giving him my support, and receiving his in return. He was no longer screaming, but his eyes were closed again, and his breath was ragged.

"We need to move him to a bed after I bandage the wound," the doctor said as he packed away his instruments. "I will give him a tincture of laudanum for the pain. If the wound doesn't fester, he should begin feeling better in a few days. Call me immediately if there's any sign of fever, putrefaction, or excessive bleeding. Someone should stay with him at all times. He's not out of danger."

"Thank you, Doctor," I mumbled as I let out my breath.

"You need to calm down, especially before you nurse your baby," he said. "Your milk might sour."

"How did you...?" I asked.

I would have blushed crimson had I not been terrified for Hugo when the doctor's eyes traveled to my bodice, which was soaked with milk. Big, wet patches covered my breasts, but I didn't care; I was still shaking from the shock of what I had just witnessed. The whole thing had been barbaric, from start to finish, but if it saved Hugo's life, I had to be grateful. This was the best medicine that was on offer in seventeenth-century Paris, and had we been poor, even this wouldn't have been available to us.

"Here," the doctor said as he added two drops of laudanum to a cup of water. "Drink this. It won't put you to sleep, but it will help you calm down. Go feed your baby, and then see to your man. I will come back tomorrow morning. If anything changes, send Archie."

I obediently drank the mixture and called Frances. She was just outside the door, hovering in case she was needed. "Frances, please stay with Hugo until I come back. I need to feed the baby. We'll need something flat on which to carry Hugo upstairs to our room. Maybe Archie can find an old door or a wide plank of some sort that we can lay him on."

My tongue seemed to refuse to obey me any further as the opium became absorbed into my bloodstream. Perhaps this wasn't the best time to feed Valentine, but she was hollering at the top of her lungs, her face red with fury as Elodie tried to calm her down by walking up and down the corridor with her. Valentine was picking up volume, her toothless gums quivering as she cried.

I sank onto the settee and pulled down my bodice, completely indifferent to the stares from Archie and Jem. My breast was heavy with milk and the baby latched on hungrily, finally quieting down. I leaned back and closed my eyes as Valentine nursed. The reality of the past hour began to sink in, and I was grateful for the anesthetizing numbing of the laudanum because I think I would have just gone completely to pieces.

I watched through half-closed lids as Archie and a groom from next door carried Hugo up the stairs on an old door, with Frances following close on their heels. She would make sure he was comfortable until I was done feeding the baby. Valentine's eyes rolled into the back of her head as my laudanum-infused milk entered her system. She was now sated and sleeping peacefully, for which I was actually grateful since I simply couldn't begin to rouse myself to dealing with a fussy baby. I felt done in, but I covered myself up and made my way up the stairs with Marthe carrying the baby.

Valentine was deposited into her cradle while I went to sit with Hugo. He was pale and in pain, but the bleeding seemed to have slowed down, and he was conscious.

"You look awful," he said.

"So do you."

"I hope you're not with me for my looks," Hugo replied, making an attempt at humor, which nearly made me cry again.

"Hugo, what happened?" I asked, needing to know if this was an accident.

"I don't know. One minute I was walking with Jem, the next someone was shooting at me."

"Did you see the man?"

"Yes, but I didn't recognize him. I have no idea why he'd want to kill me." Hugo reached for my hand and held it tight. "He missed, my sweet."

"No, he didn't, and he would have killed you had Jem not knocked him out of the way. He saved your life." My voice sounded tearful, but I tried not to cry.

"I know. He's a good little lad. I owe him my life."

"I heard Jem telling Archie that the man cursed at him in English. What does this mean, Hugo?"

"It means I made an enemy."

"What else is new? You are not the most popular guy." I was going for humor, but I finally broke down in sobs. I couldn't hold in the strain anymore. Hugo drew me to him, and I rested my head on his good shoulder. "I'm not letting you out of my sight," I sobbed as he tried to calm me.

"I will be all right; you'll see. Please don't cry; you'll wake the baby."

"No, I won't. She's out like a light."

"Good, so get some rest. You need to sleep for a while, and so do I. I feel very drowsy."

"It's the opium," I said as his eyes began to close again.

"I like opium," Hugo muttered as he fell asleep.

# FORTY-EIGHT

Hugo slept through the rest of the day. He looked gray in the dim confines of the bed, and his forehead was covered with cold sweat, but his breathing was even and his pulse steady. I'd fallen asleep next to him, but woke up an hour later, refreshed and ready to keep vigil.

While Valentine slept peacefully, I tried to recall anything I could about infections and fevers. I needed to be prepared in case Hugo's temperature spiked during the night. Doctor LeGrand had actually impressed me with his knowledge and bedside manner, but I needed to feel that I was doing my best to help Hugo. I kept checking him for a temperature, and woke him up every few hours to have a drink. I didn't want him getting dehydrated.

The rest of the household was quiet, people drifting in and out to check on us at regular intervals. Jem came in looking lost and frightened, so I allowed him to lie down next to Hugo for a while, as long as he promised not to disturb him. Jem curled up and went to sleep; his hand wrapped around Hugo's wrist as if he were afraid that Hugo would disappear. The poor child was exhausted emotionally and physically, the only thing keeping him from falling to pieces being the knowledge that he'd saved Hugo from certain death. I was overcome with gratitude but could do nothing more than keep telling Jem how brave he'd been.

Eventually, Jem woke up and got out of bed, but not before he kissed Hugo tenderly on the forehead. Jem came over to me and silently put his arms around me. In the perceptive way of children, he sensed that I needed comforting, and his sweet gesture nearly undid me.

I swallowed back the tears that threatened to flow again and gave him a wan smile.

"Go get some food in you; you must be starving."

"I don't think I can eat. My stomach is all in knots," Jem replied. "We had crepes just before..." He swallowed hard, forcing himself not to cry. "I'll go work on my sums. Lord Everly will check my work once he's better."

"That sounds like a good idea," I said. "He was telling me just last night what great progress you're making."

"Really?" Jem perked up a bit at this piece of news.

"Yes, he said you're a natural with numbers," I replied. What Hugo had actually said was something quite different, involving words like "stubborn" and "mule," but I decided to spare Jem the details.

Jem let himself out of the room just as Frances came in. She offered to sit with Hugo, but I sent her away; I wanted to be alone with him. Instead, I asked her to go to the apothecary and buy some willow bark. Doctor LeGrand had said that willow bark tea was used for bringing down fevers, and I was sure there was none in the house. Frances agreed immediately, happy to be of help.

Valentine slept for a record-breaking six hours and was starving when she finally awoke. I changed and fed her and asked Elodie to take her out into the garden for a little fresh air. Hugo was still asleep, so I asked for some hot water and had a quick wash. I smelled of sour milk, sweat, and fear. I felt a little better after I'd freshened up and changed into a clean dress. I suddenly realized that I hadn't eaten anything all day. I wasn't really hungry, but I needed nutrients to produce milk for the baby, so I made my way downstairs. Cook was in the kitchen, stirring something fragrant in a pot.

"I'm hungry," I said as I sat down at the table.

"Here, have a bowl of soup."

I gratefully accepted the bowl and tucked in. The soup was hot and fresh, with vegetables and pieces of beef. Cook gave me a thick piece of bread to go with it. I hadn't realized how hungry I was until Cook took away the bowl and refilled it, pushing it toward me wordlessly.

"Should I make up something for milord?" she asked carefully, watching my face.

"I don't think he can eat just yet. He's sleeping anyway."

"Well, sleep is the best medicine, I always say," Cook replied as she took the soup off the metal hook and replaced it with another pot. "And prayer. Nothing soothes the soul like talking to the Lord. I've prayed for him, and I know he will get better now."

"I wish I had your conviction," I replied, mystified by people's ability to believe so completely. I prayed all the time, but, in truth, didn't expect much help from that quarter, especially not after what had happened today.

"Have faith, milady."

"My husband was shot this morning," I rebuked the cook, irritated by her calm manner in the face of today's tragedy. My tone was acerbic, but I couldn't help myself. Ignorance didn't sit well with me, and neither did being lectured.

"And God made sure that Jemmy was there to save him," Cook replied, unperturbed.

"Perhaps God could have prevented Hugo from getting shot in the first place," I suggested, still annoyed.

"If God chose to prevent every bad thing that happens, the world would be a very different place," Cook said, "but every situation has two sides to it. You can say that God let you down, or you can say that he saved your man. I know you don't believe as I do, milady, but you will; it comes with age. You learn that in the end, there's no one there for you but the good Lord."

"Thank you for the soup," I said, pushing my empty bowl away. I wasn't about to embark on a theological discussion with the cook. I had to get back to Hugo, but first, I had to make a stop.

Archie was lying on his bed, an open book on his stomach. He wasn't reading, just staring at the ceiling as if all the answers could be found in the patterns of the cracking paint. Archie jumped up when I entered, embarrassed to have been found lounging about and worried that I had come for a reason.

"Is he...?"

"He's sleeping," I replied before Archie could finish the sentence. "May I talk to you for a minute?"

Archie sat up on the bed and leaned against the wall; his attention focused on me. I moved some clothes from the chair and sat down across from him. I knew what I wanted to ask him, but I wasn't sure I really wanted to hear the answer, so it took me a moment to begin. Archie just sat there, watching me silently. He guessed why I was there, and I could see sympathy in his eyes. Archie and I didn't spend much time alone together, but there was an unshakable bond between us born out of all the experiences we'd shared over the past two years. I knew that if I ever needed him, Archie would be there for me in a heartbeat, and possibly even lay down his life to protect me.

"Archie, why would someone want to kill Hugo?" I finally asked. Putting the question into words brought the reality home, forcing me to acknowledge that Hugo might not be out of danger. Whoever had shot him was still out there, perhaps waiting for another chance to finish what they'd started. This wasn't a simple robbery gone wrong; this was personal.

Archie met my gaze. He knew exactly what I was thinking, and appeared torn between telling me the truth and something that would pacify me and let me sleep at night. He seemed to have decided on the truth because he averted his eyes from mine, not wishing to see my distress.

"My lady," Archie began, "there are people in this world who only care about having food in their belly and a roof over their heads. And it's not only the poor people; it's also people who have something to lose. They go through life avoiding risk and danger, betting on what they believe to be the winning horse. Those types of people tend to prosper in any situation since they never declare for anyone unless they are forced to do so, and even then, they find a way to play both sides."

"Are you saying that because Hugo is not one of those people he's made enemies?"

"Yes, that's exactly what I am saying. Hugo has chosen a dangerous path, a path he knew would lead him into danger, even death. He's managed to escape execution and deportation, but there are those who want to see him pay for his actions." Archie grew quiet, but I could see that he wasn't finished. There was something else, something he didn't want to tell me.

"Tell me, Archie; I need to know."

"I heard some talk at Versailles," Archie confessed, now looking me straight in the face. "There's much speculation about why a Catholic king would allow a man who conspired against a fellow Catholic into his presence."

"What are you suggesting?" I asked, suddenly growing cold. Hugo had told me that Louis had invited us to Court out of courtesy, but Archie was implying that there was more to the invitation.

"I'm suggesting that no one—especially not the king of France, who believes himself to be God's representative on

Earth—would ever do something without getting something in return."

"Such as?"

"You'll have to ask your husband. I don't know, and I won't speculate, but I can only assume that whatever Hugo dangled in front of the king whet his appetite."

"I doubt he'll tell me," I said, suddenly feeling as if I didn't know Hugo at all. Or maybe I did. We had met because of his political wheeling and dealing, and now we were in this predicament for exactly the same reason. A leopard didn't change his spots, and neither did a man who was as passionate about his beliefs as Hugo. He wasn't the type of man who could just sit idly by and enjoy life's bounty. Hugo was a man of action, who didn't feel whole unless he was doing what he believed to be right. I had no idea what "right" was in this instance, but I now knew that he was up to something. "So what do we do in the meantime? Just sit and wait for him to be shot again?" I asked. I was angry and confused, and very tired.

"I will talk to Jem once he's had a chance to recover and find out what he can remember. Leave it with me," Archie said. "I will find whoever did this."

"Let me know when you do," I said as I got up to leave.

"My lady, what about Frances?" Archie asked. I could see the telltale flush on his cheeks. He thought Hugo was angry with him, but needed to find out where he stood, which was understandable.

"You really love her, don't you, Archie?" I asked, suddenly feeling sorry for the young man. He must have been suffering in silence for quite some time. I was sure that Frances's baby wasn't Archie's. He'd never touched her, and had never spoken to her of his feelings.

"I do, and I don't even know why," he added, bemused.

The façade of gruffness fell away, and beneath it I saw a vulnerable boy who only wanted to be loved, but was mystified by the intensity of his own feelings. He might not understand, but I did. I knew exactly why Archie loved Frances. His feelings weren't fueled by Frances's beauty or sweetness. Archie was a caretaker by nature; he needed to protect, to love. Being with willing older women gave him a physical outlet, but it wasn't until he met Frances that someone touched his heart. Frances was fragile and damaged, and Archie wanted nothing more than to take care of her and fix her. He wanted to make her whole and keep her that way for the rest of her life. Despite his many dalliances, I knew that if Archie ever married Frances, he would be devoted to her till death did them part, and I wholeheartedly hoped that they would find a way to be together.

"Will his lordship forbid us to marry, do you think?" Archie asked, his voice cracking with despair.

"And if he did? Would you just accept that?" I asked, challenging him.

Archie tilted his head to the side as he considered my question. I could see thoughts racing behind the eyes as several expressions passed over Archie's features.

"No, I wouldn't. I would try to change his mind, but I wouldn't ask Frances to elope, if that's what you are asking. I respect his lordship's authority, and I would never want to put Frances in a situation where she would have to choose."

"There is hope for you yet, Archie," I replied with a smile. "Don't worry; I'll put in a good word for you."

With that, I left Archie to his thoughts and went back to our bedroom to watch over Hugo and feed Valentine. I could hear her fussing as Elodie carried her upstairs from the garden. The girl was singing softly to Valentine, but the baby wasn't impressed. Nothing short of a breast would do.

# FORTY-NINE

The hours went by slowly. I was terribly listless, unable to settle to anything as I kept my vigil. Hugo was still asleep, but his face was drawn in hard lines since subconsciously he still felt the pain in his chest. I tried reading but couldn't concentrate and abandoned my sewing after pricking myself repeatedly and drawing blood. Archie came by with Jem, who wanted to wish Hugo a good night. In his innocence, he believed that Hugo would be cured by now, but seeing him so still and white made Jem cry.

"Why isn't he better?" Jem kept asking. He was so overcome with emotion that his voice was unusually shrill.

"It takes time. Go to bed, Jemmy. Things always look brighter in the morning," I said, hoping he'd take my advice.

"Why?" he asked.

"Because we associate darkness with evil and sunlight with good. So, when the sun comes out, good things happen."

"I never thought of it that way," he replied as he got up to leave.

"Neither did I, until now."

I noticed that Jem reached for Archie's hand as he left the

room. Normally, Jem wanted to be treated like a big boy, but tonight he needed to be a child, and feel the reassurance only an adult could give. I heard Archie offering to read to him as their footsteps echoed down the empty corridor.

I changed into my shift and unpinned my hair. There would be no more visitors tonight. It was true what I'd told Jem; I feared the night, this night. If Hugo were feeling better by morning, everything would be all right, I told myself, but we had to make it through the night.

I checked on the baby and curled up next to Hugo, conscious of his even breathing. I clasped my hands together and prayed: for him, for us, for Max, and for our child. I didn't pray often, but it felt right. Perhaps something the cook said had resonated with me.

I eventually drifted off to sleep, my body succumbing to the strain of the day's events. I was exhausted, emotionally and physically, and couldn't keep my eyes open any longer. I was dreaming that I was on a tropical beach, lying on warm sand, the sun shining brightly in the cloudless sky. Hugo was lying next to me, his body glistening in the sunlight and beads of seawater sliding off into the sand. His hair was wet and tousled. He was breathing hard, probably because he'd been surfing. A bright-red surfboard was propped up against a palm tree, the surface still wet. As the sun climbed higher toward its zenith, I got hotter. Now would be a good time for a swim. I tried to stand up but couldn't. Something was holding me back.

I woke up with a start. I was thirsty and hot, but the heat wasn't coming from me. Hugo was burning up. His breathing was labored as his body tried to fight off the infection that must have set in, despite the cauterization and sterilization. I hopped out of bed, lit a candle, and wet a towel in a basin of water. I wiped Hugo's face and gave him a drink before carefully pulling aside the bandage. The flesh around the wound was swollen and hot to the touch, and thick yellow pus oozed through the scab, but his skin felt dry, so he wasn't sweating off the fever. I put my hand to his head. I had no thermometer, but even without it, I knew that the fever was very high.

My first thought was to go for the doctor, but my scant knowledge of seventeenth-century medicine warned me that he might try to bleed Hugo. What else could he do for an infection? He had no antibiotics or fever-reducing medicines. What I wouldn't give for an aspirin.

I threw on my shawl and raced to Archie's room.

Archie jumped up like a tin soldier, his eyes wide open as he bolted from bed. "What is it?"

"Archie, I need your help."

"Should I fetch the doctor?" He was already pulling on his breeches and reaching for his boots.

"No. I want you to fill the tub with water and get a block of ice from the cellar."

Thankfully, Archie didn't ask any questions. He sprinted down the stairs and disappeared into the darkness of the sleeping house, bound for the cellar where we kept the ice.

I ran back to Hugo. He was muttering in his delirium. I couldn't make out all of what he was saying, but I thought he was talking to Jane, asking her to repent, and not condemn her soul to Hell. He also mumbled something about Jem. Hugo's eyes seemed to move rapidly beneath closed lids as he grew more agitated.

"Hugo, can you hear me?" I pleaded. "Please, wake up. I need you to help me fight this fever. Hugo?"

But he couldn't be roused. He was thrashing on the bed, muttering, and fighting unseen demons.

Archie finally returned, carrying two buckets of cold water that he upended into the tub. It wasn't enough, but it would have to do. I was afraid to wait much longer.

"Help me get him into the tub," I said as I pulled off Hugo's shirt.

"Are you sure about this?" Archie asked as he picked up Hugo carefully beneath the arms. "The cold water might be too much of a shock."

"We've got to get his fever down."

Archie lowered Hugo into the water, which covered him only to his waist. Hugo shivered as the cold water met with his overheated body. His teeth were chattering, and he was shaking like a leaf, but there was no choice. I used the pitcher to pour water over his chest and shoulders, carefully avoiding the bandages. Hugo was shaking so hard I thought he might bite his tongue, but Archie took his face in his hands and held it firmly as I continued to pour water over Hugo. The water that had been cold only a few minutes ago was already a few degrees warmer from his heat.

"Archie, bring the ice," I commanded.

Archie disappeared, and came back a few minutes later with a small block of ice, which I placed by Hugo's feet. His body convulsed with the shock, so I moved the ice away from his skin and let it cool the water instead while continuing to pour water over Hugo's burning body.

Archie put his hand to Hugo's forehead. "He's cooler," he said, amazed. "This is working."

"We can't keep him in there too long," I said. "Let's wait a few more minutes, then dry him off and get him back to bed. We'll do this again if the temperature starts to rise," I told Archie as I moved the ice against Hugo's feet again. His reaction wasn't as volatile this time, but he tried to move away from its cold grip. Hugo's skin felt almost cool now, so it was time to stop. I was terrified that the shock to his system might do something to his heart, but his heartbeat was surprisingly steady.

We moved Hugo back to the bed and sat by his side. I applied cold compresses to his head while Archie wrapped the ice in a towel and held it to his feet to draw out the fever. Hugo's breathing eased, and his color went from a mottled red to a healthier pink.

"I'm cold," Hugo muttered. "So cold."

I covered him with a sheet but left the goose-down blanket off. I didn't want the fever to take hold again.

Archie removed the ice which was melting now and soaking the sheets. "What now?" he asked.

"Now we prepare some willow bark tea, and we wait."

"Go to sleep," Archie said as he took in my disheveled appearance. "I'll sit with him. There's no need for both of us to stay up. You look done in."

"I am, but I can't sleep."

"Just close your eyes," Archie suggested, and I took his advice. I was past the edge of reason and fatigue. Soon the baby would be up, ready for her feeding. I just didn't think I could manage it in my present state.

I sank into a fitful sleep, fragments of dreams colliding and shattering, as my mind tried to process the events of the day and make some sense of the attempt on Hugo's life. I dreamed of twenty-first century London with cars whizzing by and buses rumbling past me as I stood on the curb. People were shouting to me, but I couldn't hear them over the sounds of the traffic. Somewhere, a bell was tolling, and then it was as if every bell in London was ringing at once. Someone was pushing me, pushing me hard into oncoming traffic. I woke up with a start just before a city bus came too close. Archie was shaking me awake.

"What is it?" I exclaimed as I saw Archie's face looming over mine.

"You were screaming, so I thought I'd better wake you."

"It was just a bad dream. How is he?"

"Better, I think. He's still warm, but not hot. I gave him some tea, like you said. He's been asking for you."

I looked over at Hugo. I couldn't tell if he was awake or

asleep, but his hand closed over mine in a silent confirmation that he was with me.

"I'm hungry," he suddenly said.

"Now, that's a good sign," Archie exclaimed. "Shall I go down and get him some bread soaked in milk?"

"No. He needs strength to fight this infection, and he won't get it from mushy bread. Just stay here for a few minutes; I'll be right back."

I grabbed the guttering candle and made my way to the kitchen. It was quiet and dark, everything in its place except for the small pot in which Archie had brewed the willow bark. I wasn't sure how he'd heated the water, since the fire was out, but it wasn't important. Cook would be reclaiming her domain soon, but for now, I was on my own.

I set my candle on the table and looked around. I hardly ever came down here, so I wasn't sure where anything was. I finally found a bowl with eggs and cracked three into a cup. I added two spoons of sugar, then went into the parlor and poured in a measure of brandy. I mixed this concoction and took it upstairs.

"What in the world is that?" Archie asked as he saw the slimy, yellow drink sloshing around in the cup.

I held the cup to Hugo's lips. He nearly gagged but forced himself to drink the mixture. "What is that?" he gasped.

"It's raw eggs with brandy and sugar."

Both Hugo and Archie just gaped at me, but I wouldn't be made to feel guilty. Hugo needed protein and sugar to jump-start his system. He hadn't eaten in nearly twenty-four hours, and he needed fuel to fight off the infection. The brandy was just to make it a little more palatable and give him some pain relief. He wasn't complaining, but having seen the wound, I was sure that he was in excruciating pain, both from the bullet extraction and the cauterization.

I looked out the window, surprised to see the peachy haze of the spring morning. The sun was just rising over the rooftops, its blaze reflected in the glazed windows, which lit up the skyline like a raging fire. I almost expected to see the filigreed silhouette of the Eiffel Tower, but, of course, it wasn't even built yet. There was nothing on the horizon but rooftops and chimney pots. Paris was slowly waking up; the rumble of a wagon audible in the distance, and the clip-clop of horses' hooves as a carriage rolled by, bringing some nobleman home from a night's entertainment.

"Archie, will you please go for the doctor now. I just want to be sure that Hugo is on the mend."

I waited for Archie to leave the room before allowing tears to course down my cheeks. I needed to relieve the pressure which had been building inside me for the past few hours, desperate to regain some sense of control. I turned away from the bed so Hugo wouldn't see me crying, but he knew.

"Come here, love," he said as he patted the space next to him.

I crawled into bed and snuggled next to him, feeling marginally better.

"I'm going to be all right," he promised. "I'm not that easy to kill."

"Oh, Hugo," I mumbled, "no one is indestructible, not even you. I could have lost you last night."

"Neve, I want you to promise me something," Hugo said as he turned to face me.

"No, I am not promising you anything," I retorted stubbornly, knowing that he was about to ask me to do something that I didn't want to do.

"Neve, please. I need to know that if anything happens to me, you and Val will be safe. Promise me that you will go back to your own time if I die."

"You are not going to die, so I don't have to promise anything," I insisted. I was being selfish; I knew that. He needed peace of mind, and I was denying him a small promise, but I refused to entertain the notion of him dying. Truth be told, if anything happened to Hugo, I would go back. There was nothing for me in the seventeenth century without him. Archie would look after Frances, and between them, they'd parent Jem. Sadly, I had no one to return to, but at least I would be able to give our child a better future.

I shook my head as if a pesky mosquito was buzzing in my ear. I would not think along these lines. Hugo would get better. He would not die.

# FIFTY

"You did what?!" the doctor exclaimed, his face slack with shock. "You submerged him in cold water and pressed a block of ice to his feet? Are you mad, woman? You could have killed him. His heart could have given out, don't you realize that?"

Doctor LeGrand was fussing with the clasp of his satchel, but his hand shook with agitation, and he finally gave up and faced me full on. His expression was hostile, and I drew back, suddenly aware of the risk I'd taken to save Hugo. I was desperate and scared and did the only thing I could think of to bring the fever down fast.

"I've never heard of such a thing. Cool compresses, yes, perhaps a lukewarm bath, but ice?!" he raged as he finally managed to open the bag and extract the stethoscope.

"And then she made him drink raw eggs with sugar and brandy," Archie added helpfully from his stance by the doorway. His eyes twinkled with mischief, mostly because Hugo was reclining in bed, propped up by several pillows, and looking like someone who'd been snatched from the jaws of death. His color was good, his breathing even, and his eyes alert as he followed the exchange with interest.

"What? Why? You should have given him some broth if he was hungry, or milk. Where are you getting these extraordinary ideas, madam?"

"I feel much better," Hugo chimed in as he noted the rising color in my cheeks. Perhaps what I'd done was wrong, but I couldn't stand to be berated.

"And it's a miracle that you do," Doctor LeGrand retorted hotly. "She could have killed you."

"But I didn't, did I?" I asked triumphantly. "And the fever has broken. What would you have done in my place? Bleed him?"

"Well, yes, for a start."

"And it would only have weakened him further," I protested. "He was burning up; a cool compress would only have done so much. I had to act fast, and I did. As you can see, my method worked."

The doctor ignored me for a moment and began to examine Hugo in earnest. He listened to his heart, took his pulse, and peeled away the bandage to see how the wound was healing. I turned away, loath to see the angry burned flesh beneath the linen. I had applied some honey to the wound, which left the doctor speechless with shock.

"What in the name of God...?" he cried as he bent down to sniff the wound, which smelled of honey, blood, and pus; not a pleasant combination.

My stomach heaved in protest, but I swallowed down the bile and faced the doctor like a general getting ready to do battle. I was willing to defend my methods. Since I didn't have any type of antibiotic ointment, honey was the next best thing, and anything was better than doing nothing.

"Honey has antibacterial properties," I explained patiently, watching the doctor's pupils dilate with amazement.

He opened his mouth to berate me again, but clearly

thought better of it, took a deep breath, and asked politely, "Pardon me?"

"It prevents festering," I amended. The good doctor would not know what bacteria was.

"And how have you come by that knowledge, madam?"

"From a healer I knew," I replied, trying to sound as vague as possible.

"I see."

He didn't, but decided that he had no chance of winning this particular argument. Archie had left the room a moment ago, so the doctor and I were quite alone. He looked away briefly, then turned to me, having come to some kind of decision.

"Milady, I believe in science and God. Where science ends, God begins. But sometimes there are other forces which fit into neither category, such as witchery. Be very careful what you say to me."

"Are you threatening me, Doctor?" I asked, my voice trembling with shock. I had allowed by twenty-first-century arrogance to cloud my judgement, forgetting that I was putting myself in danger. This man had the power to denounce me if he wished; he didn't seem like a malicious person, but I had driven him to the brink, and the gleam in his eyes made me take a step back and shut my mouth before I infuriated him further.

"No, I am warning you," he replied, gentling his tone in the face of my fear. "There are those who would see your methods as being guided by magic. You have helped your husband, but now you must help yourself. Don't say another word, especially in front of the servants. They are an ignorant lot, and you wouldn't want to find yourself under—shall we say—unnecessary scrutiny." The doctor took my hand and patted it in a paternal manner. "I don't mean you any harm, but others might."

"You mean like someone trying to shoot my husband?" I asked bitterly.

"Yes, like that, and more."

Hugo had remained silent during this exchange, but I saw the look in his eyes. It was telling me to be quiet, very quiet, and I lowered my eyes obediently and thanked the doctor for his advice. Frequently, I still forgot about the danger lurking all around us, in places I'd never expect. I hadn't developed close relationships with the servants, but didn't think that any of them would denounce me to a priest, but perhaps the doctor was right, and I needed to be more cautious. Marthe, in particular, had a nasty streak, and although Elodie was quiet as a mouse, still waters ran deep, or so my mother had always told me. I'd done what I needed to do, and now I had to step back and let Doctor LeGrand do the rest.

"There is something I must tell you both," the doctor suddenly said, facing Hugo with a determination born out of making a sudden decision. "I have examined the bullet with which you were shot, milord," the doctor began. I saw him waver for a moment, but he shook his head, as if chasing away his doubts, and continued. "I suspected as much when I extracted the ball, but needed to be certain before saying anything."

"Doctor, what are you trying to tell us?" Hugo asked, his eyes narrowed in apprehension.

"What I am trying to tell you is that the bullet had been smeared with excrement."

"What? Why?" I cried. What the doctor was saying was shocking, incomprehensible. Why would anyone do such a foul thing?

"Because someone wanted to make sure I die one way or another," Hugo replied calmly. "It's not unheard of for soldiers to smear bullets with shit to make sure that even if the enemy isn't killed outright, the infection caused by the dirty bullet finishes the job. Isn't that so, Doctor?"

"I am afraid you're quite right. Someone wanted to make sure that you die, and if I were a betting man, I'd say that your assailant believes that his job is done. As soon as word gets out that you survived, you will be in danger once again."

# FIFTY-ONE

Hugo wrapped his arm around the baby and pressed her a little closer to his side. Valentine was sleeping peacefully, and her solid little weight gave him a world of comfort. Neve had been apprehensive about allowing the baby to nap with him, but Hugo overrode her objections, claiming that bonding between father and daughter was medicinal. His chest felt as if someone was branding him with a hot poker every time he shifted his weight, but otherwise, he felt better. The fever had broken and, according to Doctor LeGrand, the wound was healing cleanly now, after the infection had cleared up. Doctor LeGrand had heartily disapproved of Neve's methods, but grudgingly admitted that she'd probably saved his life.

It would take at least a week until Hugo was allowed out of bed, but at least he was on the mend. Doctor LeGrand stopped by every day to check on his progress and, despite his better judgment, refrained from commenting on the poultice of garlic and honey applied to the wound by Neve. Hugo smelled like roast pork, but the mixture seemed to be aiding in the healing process and preventing the wound from festering again.

It was almost noon, and Neve had gone downstairs to talk to

Cook, which was a blessing since she was watching him like a hawk, her face taut with worry every time he so much as winced. He remembered only too well when the situation had been reversed, and he was mad with guilt and anxiety after breaking Neve out of Newgate. Sometimes being the patient was easier than being the one who loved them.

Valentine made a sweet sound in her sleep and pursed her lips as if she were having a bad dream. Did babies have bad dreams? Hugo wondered as he held her closer. The moment passed, and the baby smiled dreamily. At three months old, she was a miniature Neve, with her golden curls and wide, brown eyes. Just looking at her made Hugo catch his breath with wonder, and fear. He was responsible for this little life, and Neve's as well, and he had let them down, again.

Hugo glanced at the window, which was just visible through the bed hangings. The day was overcast; the sky blanketed in thick, thunderous-looking clouds that leached daylight from the room. It wasn't raining yet, but it was bound to. The branches of the trees outside shivered in the wind, and a loose shutter banged somewhere on the upper floor. Fat drops of rain began to fall as Hugo looked on, quickly covering the window in a film of moisture, and soaking the world outside. It was the perfect sleeping weather, but Hugo couldn't sleep, had barely slept since the effects of the laudanum had worn off. The same question went round and round in his mind, but he was no closer to an answer.

Hugo shuffled the names of everyone he'd met in France like a deck of cards, dealing the names this way and that. Who would benefit from his death? Who might want revenge for an offense, real or imagined? But he wasn't making any headway.

The only person who would benefit from his death was his nephew, Clarence. Clarence was fourteen and living with his stepsister in London. Bradford Nash had actually forwarded a letter from Clarence which had arrived only a few days ago.

The boy was trying to be brave and talked of his studies and the running of his estate in Kent, but it wasn't difficult to read between the lines. Clarence was bewildered by his mother's suicide, frightened, and worried about the future. He made sure to tell Hugo that Magdalen and her husband were kind to him, and that their two children were simply precious, which Hugo took to mean that they were little monsters. Clarence knew Hugo couldn't come home, but he could sense the boy's longing, and wished he could reassure him that everything would be well in time.

Aside from Clarence, no one would stand to gain anything from Hugo's death. If memory served, he hadn't inflicted any insults, nor had he so much as looked at another man's wife, sister, or daughter, so there could be no motive for retribution. The only name that kept coming back was that of Sir Trumbull. According to Luke, the English envoy had been reprimanded by London for acknowledging Hugo and banished to the Ottoman Empire, but Hugo couldn't, and wouldn't, believe that simply not snubbing him in front of Louis XIV was cause enough to send a man to Constantinople. Something else was at play, something he wasn't privy to. William Trumbull had a reputation for being short-tempered and at times brutally frank, but he was a career politician, one who knew when to speak and when to remain silent. The idea that Sir Trumbull might want him dead was ludicrous, especially since Hugo's death would do nothing to alter his predicament. And yet...

Then, of course, there was de Chartres. Perhaps he'd decided that his association with Hugo was proving to be less than beneficial and resolved to rid himself of an unwanted asset. Of course, there was no reason for de Chartres to want Hugo dead. He could simply tell him that the deal was off the table, but that seemed far-fetched. The Marquis de Chartres was not a man who would ever turn down intelligence, no matter how trivial it might be. Hugo couldn't give him much now, but, in time, he could become very valuable. Hugo smirked as he remembered watching some show on television when he had visited the future where spies who'd been deep undercover for years and awaiting activation had been referred to as "sleepers." Well, putting him to sleep permanently would accomplish very little.

In order to find out who'd ordered his death, Hugo needed information, but there was no one he could talk to until he was well enough to leave the house. His first port of call would be de Chartres. He wished that Luke was still in Paris, but Luke had left weeks before, dejected and angry by Frances's refusal to accompany him. Frances had refused him in person, but Luke had come to see Hugo in the hopes that Hugo might exercise his power over Frances and force the match. Hugo hadn't been sure why Frances was so reluctant to marry Luke, but now that the reason was clear, he was glad that he hadn't pressed her.

Frances and Archie. Who would have thought? Something would have to be done about those two, but he couldn't bear to think of it just now. His head hurt, and the baby was starting to fuss.

Hugo lifted Valentine with one arm and rolled her onto his chest, wrapping his arm around her. She lifted her head and looked up at him, her mouth stretching into a sweet smile.

"So, what do you think, Val," Hugo asked conversationally, "who is trying to kill me?"

The baby just cooed and reached out her hand to grab his finger, which she tried to pull into her mouth.

"You don't know?" Hugo asked. "I don't know either. But will they try again?" he mused as he made a face at the baby which made her smile. "And what should we do about Frances? Should we make her marry that rascal Archie? I can't see that union working for long."

Valentine got tired of playing with the finger and remembered that it was time to eat. Her face went from contentment to outrage in the space of a second, and she opened her mouth in preparation for an epic howl, only to be scooped up by Neve, who appeared as if by magic.

"She doesn't think Frances and Archie should marry," Hugo told Neve as she put the baby to her breast.

"Really? Did she also give you the lotto numbers?"

"What?"

"Never mind. You need to get some rest. You didn't sleep a wink last night. Don't think that I didn't notice. Would you like some more laudanum?"

Hugo was about to refuse, but his head ached dully, and the wound burned and itched, making him even more short-tempered than he already was. A few hours of sleep would be just the thing, and maybe he would be able to reshuffle his deck of suspects and see it more clearly once he was rested.

"Yes, I suppose I do."

"All right, you can have some after you've eaten. I don't want you taking it on an empty stomach," Neve answered in a no-nonsense tone that reminded him of his nanny. "And stop smiling at me like that; I will mother you until you can no longer stand it."

"I'm actually enjoying it very much," Hugo lied, making Neve harrumph with disbelief. She hadn't said anything about a possible second attempt on his life, but he knew that fear was gnawing at her, as it was at him. Were Neve and the baby safe?

# FIFTY-TWO

Max spent his first week in Paris settling into the household and getting to know the Benoit children. Saying goodbye to Banjo had been harder than he could have imagined. The boy had cried and wrapped his arms around Max's legs, before one of the servants had physically disentangled him and carried him off into the house where he would serve as a page. Max had never thought of himself as a particularly emotional man, but he knew that he would remember Banjo for the rest of his life, and always wonder what became of him. Having grown up in safety and privilege, he'd never given much thought to the suffering of others, but seeing a five-year-old boy taken from his family to be sold to someone as a pet left a mark on his heart that would never truly go away. He hoped that Banjo would have a better life than he envisioned, and have the strength of spirit to overcome his circumstances and forge some happiness for himself.

Max was given a small garret room on the top floor at the Benoit residence, next to Mathilde the cook, and Cherri the maid-of-all-work. He didn't mind. He had a bed, a small desk, and a window with a nice view. There was even a hip bath that he could use in complete privacy. After his pallet in Barbados

and his hammock on the *La Belle*, this was five-star accommoda-
tion. Madame Benoit, who'd come as something of a surprise to
Max, had found some clothes that no longer fit her portly
husband and made alterations so that Max now owned more
than one suit.

Vivienne Benoit was petite and lively, with an elfin face
which was dominated by large green eyes and framed by russet
curls. She clearly had a flair for fashion, and although modestly
dressed, used cut, color, and fabric to her best advantage. Most
of her gowns were in shades of green, bronze, and burgundy,
and offset her coloring in a dramatic and flattering way. She was
one of the most beautiful women Max had ever seen, and he
made a mental note to stay as far away as possible from his new
mistress, for fear of saying or doing something inappropriate.
He needed this job, and would do nothing to cause Captain
Benoit any offense. Had he come straight from the twenty-first
century, Max would have had a hard time suppressing his arrogance and keeping himself in check, but having spent months
on a plantation where any transgression could result in punishment, he now knew how to appear subservient and keep his
thoughts and opinions to himself.

The two boys, Edouard and Lucien, resembled their
father. They were both round-faced, a little chubby, and good-
natured, which was all that Max could ask for in potential
students. They were eager to learn, and Max found himself
enjoying their lessons. He'd had no idea where to start, but
the beginning was always a good place, so he had carefully
written out the alphabet and then proceeded to teach the children simple three-letter words that began with each letter.
They, in turn, had helped him improve his French by
babbling incessantly. The boys had a natural curiosity, which
made teaching them that much easier. Max spent half their
lessons answering numerous questions about England, the
defeat of the Spanish Armada, which they seemed fascinated

by, and the king's menagerie at the Tower of London. Max
answered to the best of his ability, and made up what he
didn't know. It's not as if they could google the answers and
call him out on his mistakes. He drew pictures of elephants,
lions, and camels, to the great delight of Lucien, who loved
animals.

Max was expected to dine with the Benoits, since Captain
Benoit thought of him as nobility, but Max would have been
just as happy to eat in his room. For the first time in his life, he
was enjoying the simple pleasures, such as a bed, a book, a walk,
and even the act of going to the privy and washing in private.

It was June, and Paris was in bloom; the city not one he
remembered from the twenty-first century, but a delight all the
same, especially since Max was seeing it as a free man. He had a
few hours of free time each day and spent them just walking
around the city, savoring the sights and sounds of Paris.

As he walked, he peered at every carriage that rolled by,
unsure of whether he was hoping for a glimpse of Hugo or
Banjo. He asked Captain Benoit about the boy, but the man put
a finger to his lips, signaling that it was time for Max to forget
about the child. No good would come of asking after him
anymore. Banjo's parents would be told that their son was
happy and healthy, and maybe, in time, receive a letter, most
likely written by the captain himself. He was no longer interested in Banjo, and it was doubtful that their paths would ever
cross, unless the new masters were unsatisfied in some way and
wanted to give the boy back for a full refund. Max hoped that
wouldn't happen, and Banjo would make a home for himself
with the family.

Max was surprised when the captain invited him to come
out with him after supper one night. The night was warm and
intoxicating, the smell of chestnut trees permeating the air and
light spilling from the windows. A full moon hung in the inky
sky, countless stars twinkling in the heavens. This wasn't the

"City of Light" that Max knew from the future, but it came damn close.

Benoit was in a fine mood, pointing out things of interest and telling Max something of the history of the city. Max was barely listening; he was just drinking it all in, his senses fully alive. He'd taken so much for granted all his life, and he would never do so again.

"Where are we going?" Max asked, realizing that the captain wasn't just out for his evening constitutional, but had an actual destination in mind.

"It's a surprise, *mon ami*," the captain replied happily. "One that you are sure to like."

Max followed the captain into a narrow building, squeezed between two prosperous taverns that were doing brisk business this evening. People were eating and drinking; snatches of song could be heard coming from the taproom, and an appetizing smell of food mixed with the stink of tobacco, spilled alcohol, and refuse coming from the alley. Max noticed in passing that all of the patrons seemed to be men. He supposed it wasn't unusual for men to enjoy a pint in the evening while the wives saw to the house and the children; this wasn't the twenty-first century, where women enjoyed equal rights and enjoyed a night out at the pub as much as the boys.

Captain Benoit rapped on the door, and a burly, middle-aged man let them in. He wasn't dressed like a servant, nor did he act like one.

"Ah, Captain, back with us, I see. Everyone will be happy to see you again," he exclaimed, giving Max an appraising look. "And who is your associate?"

"Be respectful to milord, Alfred," the captain warned as he ushered Max inside.

They walked down a narrow corridor and came into a large, well-appointed room lit by braces of candles. Several men sat in comfortable chairs, sipping cognac and brandy and flirting with the young women whose only purpose seemed to be to entertain them.

Max had never been to a brothel, had never needed to pay for sex, but this was clearly a high-end whorehouse. The girls were all fairly young and beautiful, their skin still clear, and their eyes sparkling with humor and the promise of pleasure. They weren't scantily clad as one would expect, but dressed in fine gowns and jewels, which were probably paste, but sparkled prettily nonetheless, bringing attention to slender necks and ample décolletages.

Max felt a momentary outrage on behalf of Madame Benoit. Vivienne was more beautiful and graceful than any of the girls here. Why did the captain feel the need to dishonor the vows he had made to her with whores? Of course, it was none of his business, but something of what he was thinking must have flashed across his face because the captain suddenly began to explain himself.

"I don't do this often, but I thought it was fitting to bring you here. This is my gift to you, milord. Choose anyone you like. You can have her for an hour—my treat. I, myself, prefer Lucille. She always makes herself available when I'm at home. Ah, and there she is. Good evening, my angel," the captain purred, forgetting all about Max.

A blonde young woman came floating down the stairs, her lemon-yellow gown doing little to hide full breasts and ample hips. She was the polar opposite of Madame Benoit, who was probably lying in bed, wondering where her husband was—or fully aware of his destination tonight. Max would have chosen Vivienne over Lucille any day, but the captain seemed to like blousy women who were free with their charms. Lucille was already sitting in his lap, her breasts in the captain's face, and her hand lightly brushing against his breeches in invitation. The captain seemed to be in heaven, so Max left him to it and looked

around the room. He hadn't been with a woman in nearly a
year, and if the captain was giving, he was taking.

Max's gaze settled on a girl of about twenty, with glossy
chestnut locks and wide blue eyes. She wasn't as Rubenesque as
some of the other women, but slender and short, with small,
pert breasts and a narrow waist. Her coloring was different, but
something about her reminded him of Neve. She seemed shy
and reticent, not like the other girls who were flirting with
potential clients and making suggestive comments. The girl
hung back in the shadows, probably hoping that no one would
pick her tonight. Max approached slowly, so as not to frighten
her.

"Good evening," he said. "I'm Maximillian."

"*Enchanté, mousier*. I'm Juliette," she replied quietly.

"You seem nervous," Max observed, curious about the girl.

"I'm new here," the girl answered shyly.

Max didn't dare ask if she had come to the brothel willingly,
or if she had been forced into her line of work. It wasn't his business. He wasn't here to enforce civil rights or champion
anyone's cause. Whatever her story was, it had nothing to do
with him.

"Would you like to sit down?" he asked as he took her hand
and drew her toward a settee in the corner. It was private
enough to have a conversation, but that wasn't what Max had in
mind. He simply wanted the girl to get comfortable with him
before he took her upstairs.

A serving girl brought them snifters of brandy, and Max
gratefully accepted, feeling more than ready for a drink. Juliette
cradled her glass but didn't drink.

"You are very beautiful, Juliette. Are you originally from
Paris?"

"No, *monsieur*, I come from the country. It's a small town;
you wouldn't have heard of it."

"You are probably right," Max said as he turned her hand

over and ran this thumb over the inside of her wrist. Juliette stiffened but didn't take the hand away. "I'm from a small town in the country as well, but my home is in England. I grew up in Surrey."

"Oh?" Juliette had no idea where Surrey was, but it was her job to make him feel as if anything he said was of great interest to her.

Max kept up the small talk, and she gradually began to relax. Surely he wasn't her first customer, Max mused as he studied the girl. Juliette was a little more animated now, and she finally drank her brandy with an air of one who was enjoying a last drink before facing a firing squad.

Juliette suddenly got to her feet and took his hand, pulling him in the direction of the stairs. Max followed obediently, eager to be alone with her.

The room was small but pretty and, most importantly, clean. Max went to unbutton his coat, but Juliette laid her hand over his.

"Allow me," she said.

Max stood back and allowed the girl to undress him while he drank in her creamy skin and flowery scent. She must have bathed before coming down tonight because she smelled of lilac and soap. Max prayed that she didn't have any kind of disease since he couldn't exactly ask for a condom in a seventeenth-century brothel. Getting the pox would just be the cherry on the top of the cake of his current existence, he quipped to himself with an inward chuckle.

Strange, but this would be the first time that Max had had unprotected sex. He'd always been fanatical about using protection, partly because he was afraid of disease, and partly because he dreaded finding himself in a position where some girl got pregnant and demanded that he marry her. He didn't have to worry about that with Juliette. Even if she got pregnant by him, she would take care of it. He was sure that few girls kept the bastards they conceived with their clients, otherwise there wouldn't be a whore in Paris who wasn't pregnant.

Juliette held his gaze as she removed her own garments and stood naked in front of him. She was breathtaking: young, supple, and beautiful, her skin glowing in the candlelight. Max was suddenly afraid that he would embarrass himself. It had been a long time, and he might not be able to acquit himself as a man should, but his worries were forgotten as soon as Juliette sank to her knees and wrapped her lips around him. Her eyes never left his as she grabbed his buttocks and took him deeper into her mouth, sucking and caressing him with her tongue until he came with a shudder. He'd forgotten how exquisite it was to have a woman's mouth around his cock. Juliette wasn't the novice she pretended to be. Perhaps it was all part of her act.

"I always find that it's best to get that out of the way, so that the second time can be more pleasurable for us both," Juliette said after rinsing her mouth and climbing onto the bed.

"I like the way you think," Max replied, feeling reborn. He sent a mental thanks to the captain, hoping that he was enjoying himself as much as Max was.

"Now, it's your turn, I think," Juliette said, opening her legs in invitation.

"At your service, my lady," Max replied as he slid his hand between her legs. She was more than ready, but he felt it his duty as a gentleman to satisfy her as well, rather than just take her and leave. They had time, and Max planned to make the most of it.

By the time he finally took her, Juliette was purring with desire. Max was surprised when she threw her legs over his shoulders and ground her hips against his, pushing him deeper and urging him to go faster. He tried to think of cutting cane in order to prolong their pleasure, but it was no use. He exploded into her after only a dozen thrusts, too sated to worry about disappointing her.

"*Mon dieu*," Juliette said as she smiled up at him. "I like you, but I hope you last longer next time."

"Are you always this demanding?" Max asked with a smile as he rolled off her, panting.

"I'm not demanding; I'm insatiable," she said with a little laugh. "And we still have a half-hour left. I will give you a few minutes to recover, but then I will expect you to pleasure me again."

"Your wish is my command, madam," Max replied as he felt blood flowing to his flaccid penis. Tonight he was insatiable too.

# FIFTY-THREE

Wispy clouds raced across the sky, their wooly shapes shining eerily as they passed in front of the moon and then drifted off again into the silvery quilt of the night sky. The night was warm, with hardly a breeze to stir the trees. Archie melted into the shadows as the man he'd been following came out of a nearby tavern. He was inebriated, but not falling-down-drunk. The man walked along the dark street alone, singing in a rich baritone, completely unaware of danger as he stopped for a piss between two buildings.

> *As Oyster Nan stood by her Tub,*
> *To shew her vicious Inclination;*
> *She gave her noblest Parts a Scrub,*
> *And sigh'd for want of Copulation...*

Archie allowed his prey a moment of privacy before resuming his pursuit. He hadn't been to this part of town before; it was seedy and reeked of poverty, refuse, and rot. The houses were small and mean, some of them open to the elements for lack of glazed windows. It was past 10 p.m., so most residents were already abed, needing sleep for their early-morning wake-up call. A baby cried somewhere in the distance, and several hungry-looking dogs trotted past in search of food. Archie had been trailing the man for nearly two hours now, but he was in no hurry. He would confront him when he was good and ready.

Archie had spent the past week in dogged pursuit of the man who had shot Hugo, but he hadn't had any luck until tonight. He'd questioned Jem repeatedly, trying to extract every last detail, but all the poor boy could recall was that the man was tall, whippet-thin, and had greasy light hair which hung to his shoulders. Another useful bit of information was that the man cursed at Jem in English. Archie couldn't imagine that, when taken by surprise while attempting to shoot someone, a person would curse in anything other than their native tongue.

So, he was looking for a tall, thin, blond Englishman. Not an easy task, but not impossible either. An Englishman would stick out like a sore thumb among the French. Of course, he might speak excellent French, but the French could always spot a foreigner, no matter how well assimilated he might be. The French were as wary of the English as the English were of the French.

Archie had gone back to the scene of the attack and methodically questioned everyone who worked or lived in the vicinity. There was a good amount of people who had stalls, shops, boats for hire, and windows facing that part of the Seine, but no one would talk. Archie had been met with either blank stares, hostile words, or Gallic shrugs, but he was sure he was on the right track. Most people had no idea whom he was looking for, but a few had smothered a spark of recognition before telling him to sod off. The man was known in these parts, but obviously had a reputation for violence which was impressive enough to buy him the silence of those who knew him.

It was purely by chance that Archie had spotted the man

himself only that afternoon. Archie had been coming out of the stables when he saw a man fitting Jem's description glancing up at the house from across the street. Perhaps it was a coincidence, or perhaps the man was checking to see if his victim had died as a result of his handiwork. A house in mourning wasn't difficult to spot, so all he would have to do was walk past.

Archie had raced upstairs, grabbed his dagger, shoved an extra knife in his boot, and took off. He'd trailed the man for hours, but by now he was sure of two things: the man was English, and he was well known, since several people he'd encountered either averted their eyes or shrank back in fear. The man must have bathed since Jem saw him, and his clothes, although not new, were relatively clean and not too shabby, but there was something in his eyes that led Archie to believe that he hadn't been merely strolling by.

Archie slid behind the thick trunk of a tree as the man whirled around, finally aware of being followed. The street was empty, and very quiet, so Archie couldn't stay hidden for long. It was time to strike. He waited until the man resumed walking before approaching him from behind on silent feet. Archie twisted his arm savagely and pushed him up against a crumbling stone parapet.

"What ye want? I ain't got nothing worth taking," the man grumbled in French. He was annoyed, but not afraid, which led Archie to believe that he was armed.

Archie patted him down with one hand and extracted a vicious-looking knife with a thin, curved blade.

"Give that back, ye jackal. That's a family heirloom," the man hissed, really angry now. He struggled against Archie, but only succeeded in twisting his arm further and grimacing in pain.

"I have a few questions for you," Archie said in English as he pressed the knife against the man's Adam's apple and caressed it lovingly with the blade.

"Piss off, ye red-headed sack of shit," the man spat in his native tongue, but now he was scared.

"Ah, so you know who I am. Good, we are getting somewhere. Who are you?"

"Jack."

"Jack what?"

"Jack yerself off," the man replied, chuckling at his own joke.

Archie gave him a vicious punch in the kidney with his left fist which silenced him momentarily. "Let's try again. Who are you?"

"Jack Duffy. Does that elucidate ye, *Ye Lordship?*" Jack asked sarcastically.

"Not yet, but I'll get there. Why did you leave England?" Archie asked.

The man was clearly surprised by the question, but answered, nonetheless. "It was bad for me health, if ye know what I mean. Decided to start a new life, turn over a new leaf."

"So, what is it that you do, Duffy?" Archie asked patiently.

"A little o' this and a little o' that. What's it to ye?"

"Who hired you to kill Hugo Everly?" Archie asked, knowing he wasn't going to get an answer.

"No one. I don't know what yer talking 'bout."

Archie pressed the blade harder against the man's neck. "Why did you shoot Hugo Everly last week?"

"I didn't like the look of 'im." The man tried to cackle, but it came out more like a pitiful cough.

"Let's try this again, shall we?" Archie used the point of the dagger to cut a thin line in Jack Duffy's cheek. Blood oozed from the cut, but it wasn't deep enough to do any actual damage. "Who hired you?"

"Well, I don't know, do I?" Duffy growled. "I spoke to a servant, not the master."

"Whose servant?"

"Do ye think he's daft enough to give me his master's name? All's I know is that he said I must do it after his master left the country."

"And where was he going?" Archie asked patiently.

"How should I know? All's I know is that's it's far, like Africa or something."

"Constantinople, perhaps?" Archie supplied helpfully.

"I don't know. Maybe."

"Did the servant go too?"

"Yeh, he was to follow with some other cove. He had to pay me the balance first, but I didn't finish the job, did I, so I only got half me money."

"Was the servant English, like you?"

"Aye. Can I go? I've no reason to kill 'im now. The client's gone, so I won't get paid anyhow." Jack Duffy seemed indignant, but honestly believed that their business was concluded.

"Of course you will," Archie replied soothingly. "I was sent to pay you if you finish the job."

"Ye want yer master dead too?" Jack asked with interest, licking his dry lips. He suddenly seemed more animated, eager to hear what was being offered.

"Can you do it?" Archie asked as he lowered the knife from Duffy's throat.

"'Course I can do it. I'd 'ave done it the first time if not for that meddling kid. Knocked me hand upward, so the shot went astray. How much ye willing to pay? I s'pose I should do it fer half price, given he's half dead already. Like shooting a sitting duck, 'tis."

"I'll pay you in full right now. Goodnight, Jack," Archie whispered tenderly in the man's ear as he slid his dagger beneath the ribs and straight into the heart. He felt the warm blood flow over his fingers as he pulled out the blade and wiped it on Jack's coat. The man dropped like a rock, his lifeblood oozing out of him and forming a black puddle which began to soak into the thirsty ground. Jack's eyes stared at the dark sky, the moon reflected in them, a look of surprise forever frozen on his features.

Archie dropped the knife next to the body and gave Jack Duffy one last kick before swiftly walking away. He'd got what he came for. The murder had been commissioned by William Trumbull, arranged by his servant, who had followed his master with Luke Marsden. Archie doubted that Luke knew anything about it, but he was glad Luke was gone all the same.

# FIFTY-FOUR

Frances rose unsteadily to her feet as Sabine slipped into the room. All was quiet except for the whisper of trees outside her open window and the barely audible cry of Valentine, who seemed to be fussing instead of going to sleep. The room was bathed in silvery moonlight one moment, pitch dark the next, as clouds scuttled across the shining orb of the moon, blocking out the light almost completely. Somewhere in the distance, a horse neighed, and the wheels of a carriage rattled down the silent street.

"Why are you sitting in the dark?" Sabine asked as she went about lighting the candle. A soft glow dispelled the gloom, bringing Frances's worried face into stark relief. Sabine ignored her friend's expression and handed her the cup she'd brought upstairs with her.

Frances sank into a chair in front of the cold hearth, peered into the cup, then sniffed experimentally. The mixture smelled bitter and unpleasant, its muddy brown color reminiscent of the contents of a privy. The cup was only half full, so whatever was in it must be potent. Frances's gaze slid to Sabine, who was watching her with narrowed eyes, waiting.

"Are you sure about this?" Frances asked.

"I've used it twice, and it worked a treat," Sabine replied patiently.

"What will happen?"

"You will start to feel cramping an hour or more after you drink it, then you will start to bleed. It'll be like your monthly, no worse. Then you will miscarry. By tomorrow morning, you will be free of this baby, and free of Luke Marsden forever."

"What's in it?" Frances asked. She felt a hollowness somewhere in the pit of her stomach, and her heart began to hammer uncomfortably as her body sensed her fear; the primal instinct that warned human beings of danger since the dawn of time kicking in. But she was determined to be rid of this child. No matter what happened with Archie, she would not put herself in this position. This was her chance for happiness, and she would not ruin it by having Luke's bastard.

"It's an infusion of rue. Quite safe," Sabine replied testily.

Frances had hoped that Sabine would stay with her through the night, but she suddenly wished that the maid would just leave. Sabine was growing impatient, but she wasn't the one who would be drinking this witches' brew tonight, so she had no reason to be cross. She was treating Frances as if she were a bothersome child rather than a young woman about to make a life-altering decision. Perhaps she'd gone through this twice, but that didn't give her the right to belittle Frances's fear or sense of guilt.

"I'd like to be alone for a little while, Sabine," Frances said as she set down the cup. She would drink the infusion when she was ready, and not a moment before.

"As you wish," Sabine replied, clearly offended by the dismissal. "I've prepared some rags for you, a few towels, a pitcher of water, and a hip bath. Just don't bleed all over the bed."

"Won't you check on me?" Frances asked, her panic rising.

She wanted Sabine to leave, but she assumed that the girl would at least make sure she was all right and check on her throughout the night.

"It'll look suspicious if I keep coming to your room in the middle of the night. We don't know how long this will take, do we? Abortion is a sin for us Catholics, so I don't want anyone accusing me of anything. I will check on you in the morning. You'll be sleeping like a baby. Now stop fussing and drink so that I can take the cup away and clean it."

Frances supposed Sabine was right. She was only postponing the inevitable. The sooner she drank the mixture, the sooner it would all be over. Frances obediently drank. It tasted horrible: bitter and thick. She felt a wave of nausea, but it passed after she took a drink of water.

Sabine gave her a pat on the shoulder and an encouraging smile. *"Bonne chance, ma chère,"* she said as she took the empty cup and left the room, closing the door softly behind her and leaving Frances alone.

Frances folded a few rags and inserted them between her legs before getting into bed. It might take an hour or more for something to happen, so she might as well try to rest. She closed her eyes and tried to focus on tomorrow morning. It would be all over; she would be free. She would go down and have a good breakfast, maybe even allow herself a second cup of chocolate as a treat, then go break the news to Archie. He would no longer have to marry her out of a false sense of obligation or a desire to rescue her. She wasn't a damsel in distress; she was a grown woman who could make her own decisions. Granted, the decision to allow Luke to make love to her hadn't been a prudent one, but she was taking steps to fix things, and to ensure that the rest of her life was hers for the taking. Of course, she wouldn't tell anyone that she'd induced a miscarriage. Lord Everly would not look kindly on such a thing, so she would just say that it had happened on its own. No one could fault her for that.

Frances burrowed deeper under the covers and tried to relax, but suddenly felt a wave of overwhelming anxiety. It seemed to be washing over her, making her heart beat faster and her limbs move with uncontrollable restlessness. She wasn't in any pain, nor did she feel sick, but she felt an almost uncontainable need for movement.

Frances got out of bed and began to pace the room. Being in motion made her feel better, but she felt an irrational sense of panic. She wasn't regretting her decision, but the panic mounted until she felt like she would scream just to release the tension building within her.

"Calm down, Frances," she mumbled to herself as she continued to circumnavigate the room. "Everything will be all right. It will all be over in a few hours."

Frances took a drink of water and resumed her pacing. The house beyond her door was quiet; everyone was asleep, even Valentine. Normally, Hugo liked to stay up and read or play a game of dice with Archie, but he'd been abed for the past week recovering from his wound, and even if he weren't, relations between Archie and him were strained these days.

Frances stopped pacing for a moment. She hadn't seen Archie since early afternoon, and he hadn't come down for supper either, now that she thought of it. Archie liked to eat in the kitchen, but Neve insisted that they all dine together like a family. Archie found that to be unorthodox, but complied, secretly enjoying the feeling of belonging. Tonight there were only three of them at supper: Frances, Jem, and Neve, since Archie was out, and Hugo had a tray in bed. He complained bitterly about being treated like an invalid, but Neve gave him one of her basilisk stares and ordered him to follow doctor's orders if he didn't wish to be bled. That seemed to have the desired effect and he had surrendered with good grace. Frances had barely eaten anything at supper, and Neve had only picked at her food. She had looked tired and worried, despite the fact that Hugo seemed to be recovering. Only Jem had been his usual self, tucking into his meal with relish.

Frances had decided before supper that today would be the day. Hugo was resting; Neve was too busy taking care of him and the baby, and Archie was out somewhere. No one would be the wiser, and she would be free to start her new life with Archie. It had taken them a long time to get to this point, but now their feelings were out in the open, and they could finally speak of the future. And tomorrow, that future would be assured.

Frances sat down for a moment, tired of pacing. She still felt panicky, but the feeling receded somewhat, allowing her to feel more peaceful. She climbed back into bed. Perhaps she might sleep a little before the pains came. Maybe she would miscarry while asleep and wake up to find it all behind her. Sabine said it was like menstruation, and she slept through that all the time.

Frances began to drift off when she felt a tensing of her womb. It wasn't painful, just uncomfortable. Was it starting? she wondered. The tightness went away but came back again a few minutes later. It came and went for about half an hour before the tensing of the womb turned into cramping.

*Not too bad*, Frances thought as she adjusted the rags just in case. There was no bleeding yet.

Frances sat down by the empty hearth and waited, moaning quietly and bending over as each new contraction took her breath away. The pain intensified with every passing minute, reminding her of the labor pains she had suffered when Gabriel was born. Frances suddenly wished that someone was with her; she was terribly afraid. She wanted Neve, but couldn't find the strength to go down the hall. Besides, Neve would be upset with her if she realized that this wasn't a random act of nature, but a deliberate attempt to snuff out a life that bore no responsibility for the foolish actions of its mother or the carelessness of its father. A disturbing thought flashed through Frances's mind as she stifled a scream; Hugo would see this as murder.

Frances wasn't sure how much time had passed; it might have been ten minutes or an hour. The pain was becoming unbearable, and she felt nauseous and disoriented. Objects in the room began to move of their own accord, and seemed to be surrounded by an iridescent haze as if they were glowing. Frances shrieked with terror when she thought she saw Lionel lurking behind the heavy wardrobe in the corner. She drew her knees up and hugged them to her chest as wave after wave of terrible pain kept her prisoner.

*It has to be soon*, she thought frantically. Her hands were shaking, and her vision became blurred by disorientation and tears. Frances was crying hard now, and whispering jumbled prayers as she rocked back and forth in a futile attempt to ease her suffering.

At last, she felt a gush of blood between her legs. The rags were soaked in moments, forcing her to reach for the towels and stuff them between her thighs. The blood was hot and thick, coming out in clumps as her body expelled the child. Frances cried with relief, hoping it would all be over soon, but the pain continued to escalate, and the bleeding became more profuse, the towels doing little to contain the flow. Frances's lower back was aching unbearably, and her womb was contracting, one contraction blending into another. Frances was panting, but felt as if she weren't getting enough air in her lungs. She needed help; something was wrong.

Frances shuffled to the door, careful not to dislodge the towels between her legs. Blood streaked down her thighs, and she left bloody footprints as she walked. Frances pulled open the door but couldn't go any further. "Help," she called, but her voice sounded weak and frightened and came out more like a squeak. "Help me, please," she tried again.

The world seemed to tilt as Frances grabbed on to the doorjamb for support, but black spots danced before her eyes and strange lights exploded just beyond her line of vision. She slid to the floor. *It's nice and cool*, was her last thought before she lost consciousness.

Crimson blood pooled beneath her hips, seeping into the cracks of the parquet and congealing as it cooled. The house was quiet, the night silent, as Frances remained unconscious, life bleeding out of her.

# FIFTY-FIVE

Archie carefully washed his hands before making his way upstairs. He'd missed supper, and questions would be asked, so he'd have to make something up to explain his absence. He didn't want to tell Neve that he'd been stalking Hugo's attacker and had killed him in cold blood; she had enough to worry about. But he needed her to know that now they were safe. Neve had looked worn out lately, the lack of sleep beginning to tell on her face. She was living in fear, terrified that whoever had attempted to kill Hugo would try again as soon as he was well enough to leave the house. Archie wanted to run upstairs and tell her that Hugo was safe, and she could stop worrying and allow herself to rest easy, but confessing to killing a man, even if he was a hired killer, would not endear him to Neve. Being a woman, she tended to see things as black and white, whereas Archie was more partial to shades of gray. Perhaps he should leave telling Neve to Hugo. Archie would speak to Hugo tomorrow, and come clean about what he'd done. Tonight's events might help thaw the relations between them, and they could finally clear the air and move forward. Hugo would have no choice but to forgive him for his behavior toward Frances.

Archie smiled at the thought of Frances. Funny, how before no one ever cared when he took a woman to bed, but the one time he'd done the chivalrous thing, he was painted as a blackguard. It had been worth it, though. He knew now that Frances loved him, and they would make a life together no matter what. Hugo would probably insist that Archie marry Frances, and he would do so gladly. He wasn't so glad about Luke's child, but he'd made a promise, and he would keep it. He would accept the child as his own, and love it even if it killed him, for Frances's sake. The girl had suffered enough not to spend a lifetime being made to pay for her mistakes. She was young and naïve and needed his protection and guidance, not derision and guilt.

Archie wished that he could go see Frances and tell her that all would be well, but it was late, and she would be asleep. She'd looked so wan these past few days, worrying about the future and her fractured relationship with Hugo. They would talk tomorrow. As his father always said, "Good news will keep, and bad news won't leave."

He sprinted up the stairs and was just about to head to the top floor when he saw something white lying on the floor by Frances's room. He turned away from the stairs and made his way down the hall, unsure of what he was seeing, but suddenly scared.

"Oh, dear God," he exclaimed.

Frances was lying in a pool of blood, her body at an unnatural angle, as if someone had just thrown her down in a heap. She was cold to the touch, her skin almost translucent in the moonlight streaming through the window. Archie grabbed the girl's wrist and held his breath as he felt for a pulse. It was weak, but her heart was beating, so there was still hope. He lifted her off the floor, laid her on the bed, and covered her with a blanket before going for help. He'd never entered Hugo's bedchamber without permission, but he had no choice; he needed Neve.

"My lady," Archie called as he burst into the room. "My lady, please help. It's Frances," he cried. He was about to shake Neve awake, but she was already up, her eyes full of terror as she stared at Archie, trying to comprehend what had happened. He hated to frighten her, but he had no choice. Time was of the essence.

Hugo tried to sit up, but winced with pain and sank back onto the pillows.

"What's happened, Archie?" Hugo asked, his calm voice masking the worry in his eyes.

"Frances is bleeding, and she's insensible. I'm going for the doctor. Please see to her. I don't know what she's done, but she's dying."

Archie didn't wait for a reply as he flew down the stairs and into the night. His mind was desperate for answers, but they wouldn't know anything until Frances came to. All he knew was that if he hadn't come home when he had, Frances would have certainly died. She still might, but at least there was a chance. He didn't bother saddling the horse, just vaulted onto the startled animal and galloped down the empty street.

Every moment that the doctor took to get ready felt like an hour to Archie, but he remained patient, waiting for the man to get dressed and collect his medical bag. The doctor's horse had already been saddled by the sleepy groom and was waiting outside when they finally emerged. Archie wished the man would hurry, but he rode at a trot, refusing to be rushed.

"I'm going as fast as I can," the doctor said with a note of sympathy in his voice.

Archie's panic came off him in waves, but galloping down the dark streets of Paris would put them in danger of colliding with an oncoming vehicle.

Archie nearly dragged the man off his horse as soon as they got to the house. He didn't even bother to tie the horse to a post or give it some water and oats. Instead, he ran upstairs before him, unable to wait any longer.

Frances was still and white, the only spot of color the blood on her shift. Neve was pale and shaken, her hands covered in blood, and her own nightdress smeared with red streaks. She'd done her best to clean Frances up, but the tang of blood filled Archie's nostrils, nearly making him gag. He sank to his knees by the bed and carefully took Frances's hand. It was limp, but he could feel a barely noticeable pulsing in her wrist. There was still hope.

"Oh, thank God," Neve breathed as the doctor finally entered the room. She moved out of the way to allow the doctor to approach the girl. "Please, Doctor LeGrand, save her," she pleaded. "I don't know what happened, but she's lost a lot of blood."

"I will do what I can, milady. Now, please, get me some clean water and towels, and get a cup of brandy for yourself and the young man. I think he's about to have an apoplexy. And get him out of here."

Archie opened his mouth to protest, but the doctor just held up his hand.

"Leave now. This is no place for you."

Neve grabbed Archie's hand and pulled him from the room. She led him to the parlor and poured him a large brandy before taking one for herself and drinking it in one long swallow. Her hands were shaking, and she was ashen, but the brandy seemed to help.

They both turned to the door as Hugo came in. He was walking slowly, holding on to the wall for support since he was still weakened from loss of blood. His chest was heavily bandaged, and his face was pale from the effort. Hugo sank into a chair and held out his hand for a cup of brandy as well.

"How is Frances?" he asked as he drained the cup and held it out to Neve for a refill. Archie held out his cup too. Before long, they would all be falling down drunk, but emotions were running high and there was nothing to do but wait.

"I think Frances tried to abort the baby," Neve replied, watching Hugo's expression, which went from worry to shock.

"Why? Archie, did you refuse to marry her?" Hugo asked, gazing at Archie with suspicion.

"No, but the child is not mine. I lied to you to protect Frances. It's Luke's, and she didn't want it. I love her, Hugo. I swore I'd love the child, but she must not have believed me," Archie explained miserably.

"Luke's?" Hugo asked. He pinched the bridge of his nose and closed his eyes in exasperation. "Luke begged her to marry him. Why didn't she? He would have given her a good life."

"Because she doesn't love him," Neve replied. "She loves Archie."

"So, why in the name of all that's holy did she allow him to fuck her?" Hugo exclaimed, finally losing control.

"Because I wouldn't," Archie replied.

Hugo held up his hand to silence Archie. He'd heard enough. "Now I understand why everyone wants sons," he mumbled to himself as he shook his head. "It's not because they perpetuate the bloodline and inherit; it's because they are much easier on the nerves—and the heart," he added.

Neve sat down next to Hugo and rested her head against his shoulder. Everyone just waited. There was nothing to say or do.

# FIFTY-SIX

Frances was walking down a dark wooded path. She couldn't see anything between the trunks of the trees, but felt the danger all around her. Strange noises carried on the wind, and countless eyes watched her as she made her way through the forest. She had no idea where she was going or why, but she knew she had to get there. She was terrified and lost. She tried to run, but her feet barely moved, refusing to obey. She was terribly thirsty, but there was no water anywhere, just thickly growing trees with branches that intertwined over her head to block out all the light and obscure the sky. She couldn't even tell if it was day or night, but it had to be night because the darkness was almost impenetrable.

Frances heard the sound of rushing water and hurried toward it, but her progress was very slow, her limbs heavy. She saw a stream and kneeled down gratefully, but the stream was dark, blood tinting the murky water and spreading on the surface. Frances gasped and tried to turn away, but suddenly her hands were covered in blood, and a red stain bloomed on her shift just between her hips. She began to scream, but there was no one to hear her, no one to help. She fell onto the bank of the stream and just lay there, suddenly sure that she was about to die.

Something was lying next to her. It was mewling pitifully, so she forced herself to sit up and look for the source of the crying. It was a baby, tightly swaddled in a winding sheet. Frances's heart leaped in her chest. "Oh, dear God, Gabriel," she cried as she picked up the baby and held it close.

The baby opened his eyes and looked at her, his expression one of an adult, not a child. "Come with me," his eyes seemed to be saying. "We can be together again."

Frances wanted to answer, but the words got stuck in her throat. She wanted to be with Gabriel, but something held her back, something important. She couldn't quite remember what it was. She just held the baby and rocked him until he went to sleep in the crook of her arm.

Frances was so exhausted, she could barely sit up straight, so she allowed herself to lie down on the bank and closed her eyes.

Frances wasn't sure how long she remained there, but by the time she woke up, the sky seemed to have lightened, and the water was no longer streaked with red, but sparkling as it flowed by. She looked down at her hands; they were clean, and her shift was new. Gabriel was gone. It was only *a dream*, she thought groggily, *only a dream*.

She tried to pry her eyes open, but couldn't. Her body felt heavy and uncooperative, so she just allowed herself to lie quietly, listening to the wind moving through the trees above her head and to the birds who were singing now that the night was finally over. Eventually, different sounds began to penetrate her brain. She heard a male voice, but it wasn't anyone she recognized.

"Frances, can you hear me?" A warm hand rested on her forehead, and she felt the pressure of a tube against her chest. "Frances?"

"Hmm," was all that Frances could manage. She wanted to reply, but her tongue wouldn't comply. It felt wooly and too large for her mouth. Her limbs felt as if they were weighted down with iron bars, and her lips were dry and cracked.

"Will she live?"

That was Neve. She sounded so frightened.

Frances tried to open her eyes to reassure Neve that she was still here but couldn't.

"Yes," the man said.

*Doctor LeGrand, that's who it is,* Frances thought happily.

"What had she taken?" Hugo asked. He sounded furious, but Frances heard the underlying fear in his voice. He cared about her, just like a real father, she mused. She didn't want him to be angry with her.

"She's taken an infusion of rue. Many women take it to rid themselves of unwanted children, but what Frances must have taken was rue oil, not tea. The oil is more concentrated and highly dangerous; a large dose can be fatal. She suffered not only a miscarriage but poisoning as well. Rue causes an initial period of anxiety and an excess of energy, then stimulates the womb. I expect that Frances also suffered nausea, tremors, headache, and hallucinations. It would have been better if she'd vomited the poison; the effects wouldn't have been as severe. She would have most certainly died had Archie not found her in time."

"Will she recover, Doctor?" Archie asked. His voice was shaking, and Frances felt a wave of guilt for putting Archie through this torture. She'd done it for him, but now he would feel responsible.

"It will take some time, and I am not at all certain that she will be able to conceive again. She might have damaged her womb, but I have no way of knowing for sure. Time will tell. Frances is to have nothing but broth for the next few days. No solids, not even bread. Her body needs to be cleansed of the poison. She's still not fully conscious, but she will eventually wake up, and when she does, she will feel achy, disoriented, and weak."

"Dear God, I can't believe she's done this to herself," Neve breathed. "How would she even know to take rue?"

"Perhaps she learned of its properties from Sister Angela," Hugo suggested. "You did say she helped out in the preparation of medicines while at the convent."

"Yes, she did, but I can't imagine that Sister Angela had much call for rue, being in a convent."

"Rue is not just for causing miscarriages, milady," the doctor replied. "It can be used for other medicinal purposes, but in very small doses and brewed into tea. Frances has taken a large enough dose to abort a colt, not just a child."

"Thank you, Doctor," Neve said. "Is there anything we can do for her?"

"Frances is out of danger, but she is very weak. Try to get her to drink as much as possible, and don't allow her to get out of bed for at least a week. Once she's back to eating solid foods, I recommend beef and liver, to regenerate the blood she's lost. If you can get fresh blood from the butcher, mix it with a bit of milk and have her drink it at least once a day."

Frances couldn't see Neve's face, but she heard the sharp intake of breath at the mention of that particular remedy.

Neve didn't reply, but Hugo assured the doctor that they would do everything necessary.

Frances wished that everyone would just leave and let her sleep. She was so tired. Perhaps she'd dream of Gabriel again.

"I trust there will be no more life-and-death emergencies this week," the doctor said with sarcasm as he prepared to leave. "Lord Everly, back to bed with you. You are looking rather green around the gills. And you, Lady Everly, have a hearty breakfast today. You need nourishment for your baby. You've lost a considerable amount of weight since I saw you last week. I will be back this evening," he added. "I think I will go home now and have a well-deserved rest."

Frances heard the door close as everyone finally left. It was quiet and peaceful, and she drifted off again, thankful to be alive.

The sound of a door opening woke her up, but she kept her eyes closed in the hope that whoever it was would just leave her in peace. Sooner or later, she would have to face the consequences of her actions, but she simply wasn't strong enough to deal with Neve's unconditional forgiveness, Hugo's condemnation, and Archie's guilt.

"Frances, are you awake?" Sabine whispered urgently. "Frances, I know you can hear me. Don't tell anyone I gave you the rue, or I will be punished. Lord Everly is furious; he'll have me whipped. Don't tell anyone, or you'll be sorry," Sabine hissed and pinched Frances's arm.

*I'm sorry already*, Frances thought as she drifted away.

The last thing she heard was Sabine's yelp of pain.

* * *

Sabine struggled against Archie as he dragged her out into the corridor. She hadn't expected him to be standing behind the bed-hangings, unseen, but not out of earshot. He'd heard what she'd said to Frances, so there was no denying her guilt. Archie clamped a hand over her mouth to keep her from screaming, and his hand felt like a vise on her arm as he shoved her unceremoniously. Archie removed his hand from her mouth, but continued to drag her until they were downstairs, where he pushed her into the parlor and closed the door behind them.

"I knew you'd come." His voice was quiet, but Sabine shivered with fear at the menace in his tone. "Frances had an accomplice, and it had to be you."

"She asked me to help her," Sabine retorted. "I would have never suggested it."

"And how do you know about this remedy?" Archie asked conversationally.

"I heard the maids talking at Versailles. They said it works every time."

"So, you've never used it yourself?" Archie demanded.

"No," Sabine whispered. She could have lied, but she knew that Archie would see right through her. Frances would believe anything, but Archie wasn't someone you toyed with, not if you valued your life.

"Why did you give her so much?"

"Frances wanted to make sure it worked," Sabine replied.

Blaming this on Frances was her only form of defense. Perhaps Archie would only give her a tongue lashing. After all, it was not as if she'd gotten the stupid girl pregnant, she'd done that all on her own. Frances was so naïve and trusting that she'd never even asked Luke to make sure there were no consequences, and Luke was only too happy to try and ensure a desirable outcome for himself. Why did Archie care for her so much? Sabine raged. Frances was just a silly child, not even a woman.

Even in her defensive state, Sabine couldn't help noticing how handsome Archie was with his wide blue eyes and hair the color of burnished copper. She'd warm his bed any day if he asked her, but he only had eyes for that idiot upstairs who had every man eating out of her hand. Even Lord Everly couldn't resist Frances's charms. He doted on her as if she were his own daughter and would probably do no more than scold her gently for what she'd done. Sabine's own father would have horse-whipped her if she'd come home pregnant and unmarried, but no one would lay a hand on Frances. Instead, they would wait on her hand and foot until she was recovered.

"Now, you listen to me, you little bitch. You will pack your bag and leave this house immediately. You will not tell anyone you're going, nor will you get any reference for future employment."

Sabine squared her shoulders and glared at Archie defiantly. "You have no authority over me. You did not hire me, so you can't dismiss me. I only did what Frances asked me to, so don't you go blaming me. I'm not going anywhere without my wages and a good reference, so do your worst, Archibald Hicks; I'm not afraid of you." She was afraid, but she'd be damned if she let him see it. She wasn't leaving this house without what was due to her.

"My worst?" Archie chuckled bitterly. Was he actually laughing at her? "You don't want to see me at my worst."

Sabine stood her ground, ready to spar with him, but Archie wasn't in the mood for arguing. He was upon her in an instant, his hand over her mouth and his arms across her middle as he lifted her off her feet and carried her through the kitchen and to the back door. He kicked the door open with his foot and carried her out into the street, where a pile of horseshit lay steaming in the road. Archie tossed her into the dung as if she were rubbish, and rubbed her face in the horseshit until she was gagging. Tears of humiliation streamed down Sabine's face, and her mouth was full of shit.

"Come back and I will do much worse than this. Don't test me, girl," he said as he held her face down.

Archie turned on his heel and strode back into the house, leaving a sobbing Sabine lying in the middle of the road.

# FIFTY-SEVEN

## JUNE 1686

**Paris, France**

Max found his job as a tutor to be surprisingly flexible. Madame Benoit was only too happy to have the house to herself for a few hours, allowing Max to take the boys on field trips, as long as they returned in time for their dinner. The children loved the outings, during which Max pointed out various sights and taught them the English words and phrases for what they were seeing. They were happy to have a little adventure and leave the stifling schoolroom. Max, on the other hand, used the outings to familiarize himself with seventeenth-century Paris, and mentally file away useful information which would help him formulate his plan. He'd have only once chance to get it right, and this time he wouldn't be creeping behind Hugo with a rock. This time, nothing would be left to chance.

Max usually made sure that the boys were falling-down tired by the time they got home, so while the children napped, Max availed himself of the opportunity to study the Everly residence, which was a forty-five-minute walk from the Benoits' house. After a week of observation from a strategically selected vantage point, Max was disappointed to say that he'd learned very little. He'd seen a red-headed young man come and go, as well as several servants, and a boy of about ten, who strongly resembled Hugo. An older man came by once and left a short while later. Otherwise, there was very little activity of interest. Max hadn't seen Hugo or Neve, so wasn't even entirely certain that he was watching the right house. At this rate, he'd still be planning his revenge a year from now.

Max decided that perhaps he might need to change the location of his stakeout. He walked around the block; his hat pulled down low and his manner unhurried. There was no need to attract attention. He was just a respectable tutor out for a walk during his free time. Max sauntered around the back of the house. There was a sizeable garden surrounded by a tall iron fence. The garden was lush at this time of year, but Max could still see several benches placed beneath the trellis dripping with roses. A little fountain, more a birdbath, was in the center of the garden, and a path led from the door to the birdbath and to the gate built into the fence. Max gingerly pulled on the gate, but, of course, it was locked. The good thing about the garden was that it wasn't a typical, well-ordered English garden where the flower beds and neatly trimmed hedges outranked natural chaos. This garden was slightly more unkempt, perhaps because the inhabitants didn't employ a gardener. Therefore, it was much easier for a person who wanted to observe the family to stay hidden.

Max pulled out the spyglass he'd borrowed from Captain Benoit's study. The captain had departed a week before and wouldn't be home again for several months, so Madame Benoit had invited Max to use the captain's study to work on his lessons, which couldn't be better if he'd planned it himself. He trained the glass on the windows of the upper floors, hoping to catch sight of someone in the bedrooms. It was late afternoon, and the slanted rays of the summer sun reflected in the wide windows, making it difficult to make anything out, but Max remained in his position, certain that if he waited, he'd see someone. He'd positioned himself in such a way that he wouldn't be seen either from the street or from the house, hiding behind a large lilac bush. The blooms had died away, but the leafy branches offered excellent cover.

Max stepped from foot to foot, tired of standing in one spot. He still hadn't seen much after skulking about for nearly an hour. It had to be going on 6 p.m., and he was hungry and tired after spending most of the morning herding the boys around town. He'd give it another fifteen minutes, then call it a day. Max was just about to unlace his breeches to take a piss when he noticed movement in one of the upstairs rooms. He forgot all about his need and pointed the spyglass at the window. His heart nearly skipped a beat when he saw Neve. She approached the window, holding a small child. The baby looked remarkably like her, but Max couldn't tell if it was a boy or a girl since it was wearing a white gown, the type that could be worn by either sex. Children in the seventeenth-century were dressed like girls regardless of the sex until they were toilet trained, at which point their clothes resembled that of the adults.

Neve seemed to be talking to the child as she threw the window open. Max couldn't hear what she was saying, but the cadence of her voice carried, and he closed his eyes as he listened to her familiar voice. It was strange to see Neve after all this time, especially with her hair swept up and wearing a period gown, but she actually looked even more beautiful than she had when wearing a pair of jeans and a sweater, with her hair loose about her shoulders. The gown and hairstyle gave her a certain maturity, but did little to hide her natural sensuality.

Neve turned away from the window and Max lost sight of her, but it took him a few minutes to slow down his heart.

He finally relieved himself, put away his spyglass, and drifted back out into the street. He now knew several things: he had the right house; the baby was thriving; and Hugo had to be somewhere nearby. What he didn't know was why he hadn't seen Hugo or Neve leave the house, or how to go about achieving his objective. Perhaps he had to watch the house in the mornings rather than in late afternoons. Perhaps they liked to rest before supper, and that's why he'd been unable to make any progress.

Switching up the schedule with Madame Benoit would be easy enough. She was a remarkably flexible woman, probably due to the fact that she'd had to get used to living with a husband who always came and went, rather than stayed at home and ruled the roost. She liked the freedom to make her own choices, and having the boys out of the house in the late afternoon would give her an opportunity to rest after her morning chores and social calls. There weren't many, but Vivienne had a couple of friends who came by for a cup of chocolate, a pastry, and a gossip. They were all wives of the captain's associates, so they had much to talk about, and Max heard them laughing through the closed door of the parlor. At times, he envied their camaraderie. He missed having friends. He missed Simon, and even Mrs. Harding. She'd often given him a cup of tea and a biscuit when he was a boy and talked him through his adolescent trials when his own mother couldn't be bothered. It'd been a long time since anyone had cared about him, and Max felt a bone-deep loneliness steal over him, especially at night when he was alone in his room.

Max decided to watch the house several times a week, and his initiative eventually paid off. He watched with trepidation as Neve emerged into the garden with the baby. The child seemed to be ready for a mid-morning nap, so Neve positioned the baby in her lap while she enjoyed an hour outdoors. Sometimes she read, and sometimes she just sat quietly, her face turned to the gentle sun. Although her features were relaxed, Max noted a tension about her which hadn't been there before.

Neve was no longer the young woman he'd known in the twenty-first century. There was a certain wariness about her, as if she'd been through a lot and was now preparing herself for some unseen danger. Was life with Hugo not quite what she'd bargained for? Max wondered as he watched her.

A young woman joined her outside on the second day, her golden curls framing her lovely face, which, despite its classical beauty, looked wan. The girl sat next to Neve, and they chatted quietly, so as not to wake the baby. The girl must have recently been ill since she moved somewhat slowly and was terribly pale. The red-headed man made an appearance as well, smiling at the girl in a way that suggested that their relationship was something more than lady/servant, or just friendship. She rested her head on his shoulder as he sat down next to her, and his arm came around her, loosely, but with a hint of possession, nonetheless. But where was Hugo? Was it possible that he wasn't here at all?

It took Max three more days of observation before he finally spotted his prey. Hugo came out into the garden with Neve and sat on the bench. He reached for the child, and Neve carefully placed the baby into the crook of his arm. Max was shocked by Hugo's appearance. This was not the man he'd met a year ago. That Hugo had exuded physical strength and robust health, but the Hugo who sat in the garden now looked pale and drawn, and his movements were careful, as if any sudden jolt would cause him great pain.

Max trained his spyglass on the man and watched him with rapt attention. Hugo seemed in good spirits despite his physical discomfort, and Max could see the genuine affection between him and Neve. She did seem to be fussing over him, though, which made Max wonder if Hugo had been ill as well. Perhaps there'd been an outbreak of something in the house, which would explain the lack of activity and the less-than-blooming appearance of the occupants. Max turned the glass back to

Neve. She appeared to be well enough, but she appeared tired, and there was a constant look of worry in her lovely eyes. What had happened to make her look so concerned, and what was wrong with Hugo?

Max kept up his vigil for two weeks, familiarizing himself with the routine of the household. The one thing that remained constant was Neve's outings with the baby. Hugo came outside from time to time, as did the other girl, but Neve made an appearance around the same time every day. Max couldn't help noticing that both Hugo and the girl appeared to be recuperating from whatever it was they'd suffered from. Hugo was moving with more assurance, and his color was healthier than it had been two weeks ago. He was still mindful of his left side, but he was obviously on the mend, which meant that Max had to act soon. He didn't want Hugo at the top of his game.

Max returned to his stuffy garret, threw open the dormer window and took a sip of warm red wine. He'd been biding his time long enough. It was time to put his plan into action.

Strange how sometimes small, insignificant things suddenly took on new meaning based on the events currently taking place in a person's life. Max had hated visiting the Paris catacombs with his friends when he'd taken a backpacking tour of France shortly after graduating from university. He'd tried to opt out of that particular excursion, but his friends had ridiculed him for being scared, and to prove them wrong, Max had reluctantly gone along. He'd hated every moment of being submerged beneath the ground, surrounded by millions of dead eyes, boring into him as he tried not to focus on the fact that these people had once lived, loved, and suffered. The catacombs had been the ultimate oubliette—a place of forgetting—but had eventually become a tourist attraction since people couldn't stay away from the haunting experience of walking through a graveyard of bones and skulls.

Now, in the seventeenth century, the catacombs were not

yet a graveyard, but a series of abandoned mines used to extract limestone which had been used to build most of the city; a warren of tunnels which would soon be ordered to be inspected for fear that they might undermine the city above them.

No matter, the mines were as good as the catacombs. All Max needed was a secluded, dark place to carry out his plan. He hadn't taken the children beneath ground, but he'd made sure to take several walks in the vicinity of what would one day be the entrance to the *Catacombes de Paris* and find a way in. Most of the mines had been closed off, but Max eventually found one that would serve his purpose very nicely. He marked it on a crude map he'd drawn, and mapped out the quickest route from the Everly house to the entrance of the mine.

Max paced the floorboards until they groaned with protest, so he stretched out on his bed, put his hands behind his head, and went over every detail of his plan again. He needed two days to get everything in order, then it was showtime.

## FIFTY-EIGHT

I breathed a sigh of relief as Valentine finally fell asleep. She'd been crying on and off all night, and this morning I'd noticed that her gums were swollen, and two tiny white lines had appeared where her bottom teeth would be. I thought it was too early for her to be teething, but some children cut their first teeth sooner than others. I wished I could give her something to relieve the pain, but I had nothing at my disposal, save alcohol, and I wasn't going that route just yet.

I snuggled closer to Hugo, eager for another hour of sleep until it was time to get up and start the day, but the moment had passed, and I was wide awake.

Hugo turned onto his side and smiled at me. "Try to sleep. I'll get her if she wakes again."

"She's teething," I replied. "She's in pain."

"I seem to remember our nurse putting brandy on Jane's gums when she was teething," Hugo said, his eyes clouding over as they always did when he thought of his sister.

"There must be something else I can give her that's non-alcoholic. I should have asked Doctor LeGrand when he was here last."

The doctor hadn't been back for nearly two weeks, having pronounced his patients to be no longer in need of his care. Hugo still felt some discomfort, but the redness and swelling were gone, leaving in their place a small, square scab where the doctor had cauterized the wound. It pained him to move his shoulder a certain way, but he was getting better every day.

My mind still couldn't quite grasp the fact that Sir Trumbull wanted Hugo dead, but now that he was gone, and the hired gun was dead, I felt slightly calmer, if not completely at peace. Hugo hadn't been particularly surprised when Archie had told him, having already worked it out for himself, but he was relieved that Archie had been able to track down his assailant.

Frances was recovering as well. She'd refused to drink the blood, but had been eating meat and liver, as the doctor prescribed. I was sure that the meat-heavy diet would replenish the iron she'd bled out and make her feel stronger.

I knew that Hugo had strong feelings about what Frances had tried to do, but he hadn't said anything to her, figuring that the poor girl had suffered enough. Archie sat with her every day while she was abed, reading to her or just talking. Seeing them together always made me smile, nearly as much as it made Hugo frown. He still had reservations about their future, and made no secret of it.

"Will Archie and Frances wish to be married soon, do you think?" I asked Hugo, sleep forgotten. Frances was still too young to get married, in my opinion, but under the circumstances, she would be safest with Archie, who loved her and would take care of her as no one else had. She was like a wounded bird that needed all the tenderness it could get until it felt safe to leave the nest and fly again.

"I've asked Archie to wait," Hugo replied sourly. "There's no rush, not anymore."

"Is there some other reason you want them to wait?" I could

tell that Hugo was holding something back. He had that closed look that meant he was up to something.

"I didn't want to say anything until I knew for certain, but I've asked Gideon Warburton to look into Frances's financial situation. As Finch's widow, she stands to inherit it all, but her father-in-law is claiming abandonment, and is trying to have the marriage posthumously annulled. If he succeeds, Frances will get nothing, but if he doesn't, she will be a very rich woman. I think it would be best to wait and see what transpires before she remarries. Having her marry another will only strengthen the elder Finch's case."

"And how do you think Archie would feel if Frances was suddenly a rich widow?" I asked. Archie might feel emasculated by their uneven status, uncomfortable at being supported by his wife.

"Archie is no fool. He might feel a little awkward at first, but he'll learn to live with it. He would be good at running the estate."

I had to admit that a small part of me hoped that Hugo's plans would not come to fruition. I hated the thought of parting with Frances and Archie. They were part of my family, part of me. I was about to share my feelings with Hugo when there was a knock at the door.

"I'll get it," Hugo said as he gave me a kiss and got out of bed. "Get some rest while Val is sleeping.

I couldn't see who was at the door, but I heard Elodie's voice. "You have a visitor, milord. I've asked him to wait in the parlor."

# FIFTY-NINE

Hugo briefly wondered if he was making a mistake by walking into the parlor unarmed. Who would be calling at such an early hour while everyone was still abed? He wasn't expecting anyone, nor was there anyone he particularly wished to see. Everyone he loved was already there: safe and sound for the moment. He hadn't heard the sound of carriage wheels, so the visitor had either come on foot, or on horseback, which was usually the sign of the person being a messenger.

Hugo pushed open the door. A man of medium height and build was standing with his back to the room, gazing out the window, his hands clasped behind his back. He wasn't wearing a wig, and his coat was travel-stained and dusty, as were his boots. Hugo experienced a momentary sense of déjà vu as the man slowly turned, his tired face splitting into a warm smile. How many times had Hugo seen him look just like that: tired and travel-stained, but full of inner light that shone out of his dark eyes?

The man walked toward Hugo, his gait slow, as if uncertain of his welcome. At any other time, he would have been welcome, but not today, not when his arrival meant only one thing.

"Hugo," he said as he drew Hugo into a brotherly hug. "I hope you don't mind me coming so early. I just couldn't wait a moment longer. I arrived in Le Havre yesterday and have been traveling since. Where is he?"

Hugo sank into a chair, his legs suddenly weak. He knew this moment would come, had tried to prepare for it, but now that it was here, all he wanted to do was delay it.

"He doesn't know," Hugo said. "I suppose I should have prepared him, but I wasn't sure you'd come, and didn't want him to be disappointed. Sit down, Nick. Have you eaten? Why don't we have some breakfast first? How is Anne?"

Nicholas Marsden shrugged noncommittally. "Anne is the same, I suppose. Her body is broken, but her mind is as sharp as ever, and so is her tongue. I go days without seeing her; can't take her bitterness, I suppose. It's been a relief to be away from her these past few weeks."

"Does she know where you've gone?" Hugo asked carefully. Few women would be eager to welcome their husband's bastard into their household, even if they couldn't bear children of their own. A constant reminder of a torrid love affair that bore fruit would be painful to even the most accepting of women, and Anne was nothing if not temperamental.

"She does. You know I always told her the truth. She wasn't best pleased, but she understood. She'll be good to him, Hugo; you have my word." Nicholas looked away for a moment, his face suffused with color. "Luke said he looks just like Margaret."

"He does. He's the spitting image of her, but some say he looks like me," Hugo said with a teasing smile.

"What is he like, this boy of mine?"

"His temperament is nothing like his mother's," Hugo replied, trying to think of a way to describe Jem in the most favorable light. "Jem is sweet and kind, and very vulnerable. He doesn't have the same sense of self-preservation or the desire to always grab for more like Margaret did."

"Is there something of me?" Nicholas asked, his eyes desperately eager to hear that he'd made some mark on the boy even without being a part of his life.

"He's selfless and brave. And stubborn as a mule," Hugo replied with a grin. "He's loyal to a fault, and quick to learn, when he's not trying to get out of doing his lessons."

Nicholas's face split into a happy grin. "So, I did give him something of myself," he observed.

"Yes, your legendary love of food," Hugo countered. "That child would sell his soul for a treat."

"Tell me he's never been hungry, Hugo," Nicholas pleaded. "Tell me he hasn't suffered."

"No one's life is without some hardship, Nick, you know that; but Jem has been loved, and cared for. I've made sure of that, and not just for Margaret's sake."

"You knew he was mine?"

"Not until recently, but I suspected as much, despite what Margaret claimed."

"Did you think he was yours?" Nicholas asked carefully.

"Jem is not mine, but I often wished he was. I love him like a son, Nick."

"And now you have a daughter," Nicholas mused. "Our children could be promised to each other. It'd be a fine match."

"I am not even going to justify that with a response," Hugo said. He assumed Nicholas was joking, but with Nick you never really knew. Hugo could just imagine Neve's reaction to the news of a betrothal between a nine-year-old and a four-month-old baby.

"I wish to see him, Hugo. I can't eat or drink until I meet my boy."

"I understand," Hugo replied. His stomach felt hollow as he yanked the bellpull to summon Elodie.

"Did you want some refreshment, sir?" she asked as she appeared a few moments later. "Cook has some fresh buns, just out of the oven."

"No, Elodie, not just yet. Would you please ask Jem to come in?" Hugo felt as if he would choke on the words, but there was nothing he could do to stop the inevitable from happening. He had no right. His own needs did not factor in this. Jem deserved to know his father, and to benefit from all that entailed. But how Hugo would miss him.

Nicholas jumped to his feet, unable to sit in the face of deep emotion. He began pacing the room; his eyes glued to the door as if he was afraid to miss the moment when his son would walk into the room. Hugo felt Nick's elation when Jem poked his face into the parlor, his eyes round with curiosity. He inched into the room, wary of the stranger.

"Did you send for me, Your Lordship?" Jem looked tousled as ever, with a bun still in his hand, probably for later. He quickly stuffed the bread into his pocket when he noticed the stranger staring at him as if he'd never seen a boy before.

"Jem, come in. This is Master Nicholas Marsden, Luke Marsden's older brother. He's come all the way from England to see you."

Jem's expression transformed from one of idle curiosity to fear. No one had crossed the river, much less the sea, to come and see him. Why would Luke Marsden's brother take such an interest?

"Would you like me to leave you two alone?" Hugo asked. He knew he should stay for Jem's sake, but he didn't wish to witness this private moment which would change all their lives.

"Please stay," Nicholas replied, his eyes on Jem. He was drinking the boy in, his face going through a myriad of emotions as he beheld the son he never knew he had. Nicholas had always had an expressive face, like Jem, but now he looked downright overcome. He drew a little closer to Jem but refrained from getting too close for fear of spooking the child, who already looked as if he were ready to flee.

Hugo couldn't help noticing the resemblance between the two, not so much in features, but in facial expressions as father and son gazed upon each other.

"It's nice to finally meet you, Jeremiah," Nicholas said as he held out his hand to Jem.

"Likewise, sir," Jem replied politely, clearly confused.

"May I call you Jem?"

"Sure. Everyone else does," Jem replied as he took a step backward, just in case.

"Jem, I knew your mother a long time ago," Nick began. He was sweating, Hugo noticed, beads of perspiration gathering on his brow as he searched for the right words. Poor man, this couldn't be easy for him.

"I knew her too," Jem replied as he glanced toward the door, marking his escape route.

"I'm not going about this correctly," Nick said as he took out a handkerchief and dabbed at his forehead. "Jem, what I am trying very clumsily to say is that I am your father."

Jem just stared at the man as if he'd suddenly sprouted a third eye or a pair of horns. He tilted his head to the side, studying Nicholas for signs of insanity. "My father was a groom. He left before I was born."

"No, Jem, your mother only said that to keep me away because I was married to another, and she wanted to punish me by denying me my boy. Had I known you were mine, I'd have come right away. I'd have taken care of you, especially after your mother died. That's why I'm here now. I've come to take you home, son."

"This is my home," Jem protested. "I want to stay here." Jem was fighting back tears, but his lip was quivering, and his small body was as rigid as a pike. He'd given up on the door, and was moving toward Hugo, looking for protection from this man who wanted to tear him away from everything he held dear. "I want to stay with his lordship," he added in a small voice as he grabbed Hugo's hand the way a drowning man grabs a piece of flotsam, thinking it will save him.

"Jem needs a little time to think this over," Hugo chimed in. "Don't you, Jemmy? We can all have breakfast, and then you and Master Marsden can go for a walk, or just talk awhile and get to know each other. Nothing has to be decided today. Or tomorrow."

"Of course," Nicholas responded, sensing that Hugo was speaking directly to him rather than Jem. "I will stay in Paris for as long as it takes," he added.

"We have plenty of room, so you are welcome to stay here," Hugo suggested.

"May I go now?" Jem asked, his voice quivering.

"Won't you join us for breakfast, Jemmy?" Hugo asked.

"No." Jem bolted from the room before anyone could say anything more.

"Is he afraid of me?" Nicholas asked as he slumped into a chair.

"He's not afraid of you; he's afraid of change. He doesn't want to leave us, Nick. We're his family."

"I know. I will bide my time until he is ready then."

Hugo just nodded, unable to speak.

# SIXTY

Hugo found Jem an hour later, sitting on a bale of hay in the stables. The horses snorted and rolled their eyes, as if sensing Jem's agitation. Hugo noticed that Jem's lips were moving, as if he were having an argument with himself, but the boy froze as soon as the door opened, his body stiffening with tension. He relaxed slightly when he saw Hugo, but his expression remained closed, his eyes wary, as if Hugo had betrayed him somehow.

"May I sit with you?" Hugo asked as he approached Jem.

"Suit yourself," Jem answered. He wasn't normally so surly, but he was angry and needed someone to take it out on.

Hugo sat down and leaned against the rough wood of the wall. The stables were dim, and the smell of horses and hay filled his nostrils. Hugo briefly reflected that both were comforting. He also used to hide out in the stables when he was a boy and his father was angry with him. Something about being around horses brought him peace. It was Archie's favorite refuge as well. Jem normally went to the kitchen. He liked the warmth and bustle of the kitchen, and the women always took pity on him and comforted him with bits of food. The fact that

Jem wasn't hungry did not bode well. The poor boy wasn't merely upset; he was devastated.

"You knew, didn't you?" Jem finally burst out, his voice full of accusation. "You knew all along and said nothing. And now you will let him take me away. Well, I'm not going. I'll run away if I must. I survived in London, and I will survive here." Jem wiped away angry tears, loath to give Hugo the satisfaction of seeing him cry.

"Jemmy, I only found out a short while ago. I knew your mother was, eh... close to Nicholas, but I didn't know who your father was. She never told me the truth either. Your mother had her pride, and she wished to do things her own way—until the very end."

Jem looked even more crushed, forcing Hugo to realize that he'd just essentially told the boy that his mother left him to live in poverty and squalor rather than give his father the satisfaction of knowing that she bore his child. She could have told the truth before she died, ensuring that Jem had a future, but she'd remained silent, nursing her bitterness toward Nicholas and not doing what was best for her son.

"I won't go," Jem repeated, baiting Hugo.

"Jem, can we talk man to man?" Hugo asked.

"Well, I'm not a girl, am I?" Jem retorted angrily.

"That's not really what I meant. I meant that you have to put aside your childish hurt and talk to me like an adult. You are nearly ten, and I wish to speak to you as I would speak to a grown-up."

"All right then—speak," Jem relented. He turned to face Hugo. His shoulders were squared and his eyes downcast, but the defiance of a few minutes ago was gone, replaced by silent resignation.

"Jeremiah," Hugo began, "you are almost a grown man, and so you must learn to think like one. A child thinks of the here and now; a man thinks of the future and the consequences of his actions. I know that you are happy with us, and we love having you as part of our family, but you must think practically, as a man would. You know that you will always have a place with me, but you are not my natural-born son, so I cannot offer you anything more than a position in my household. I cannot bestow my title on you, nor leave you my estate. I must save those privileges for my own son. You have a father who is a gentleman, and who's traveled here to meet you as soon as he learned of your existence. All he asks is that you give him a chance to love you and give you what's yours by birth. Nicholas is not titled, but he is wealthy and well-connected. He will give you a good education, a comfortable life, and a secure future. You will inherit his estate, and, in turn, bequeath it to your own son. Now, isn't that better than being my secretary?"

Jem raised his eyes to meet Hugo's. "I don't understand," he mumbled. "Master Marsden wasn't wed to my mam. He said so himself. So, how can he claim me as his son?"

"Master Marsden can legitimize you. It's what he wants."

"What about his own family?" Jem asked. He was clearly worried about displacing other children.

"Jem, Nicholas's wife had a riding accident some years ago. She's an invalid who can't bear children. You are Nicholas's only child, and he wants you as his son and heir. But please don't think that this is his only goal. He loved your mother, and he wants to love you. He needs you, Jem."

"What about you? You don't need me?" Jem asked, his voice breaking.

"Jemmy, I love you and need you, but it would be selfish of me to deny you a chance at a better life. I give you my word that I will always be there for you. I will visit you once I return to England, and you will always be welcome in my house. Perhaps we can ask Nicholas to make me your legal guardian should anything befall him before you reach majority. Would that make you feel safer?"

Jem nodded. He wanted to rage at Hugo and protest, but he knew that what Hugo said made sense and couldn't deny it.

"Jem, will you give Nicholas a chance?"

"Yes, I will," Jem agreed, but his expression was still mulish. "I will think like a man, and consider my future prospects, but I wish I had a choice in the matter. Sounds to me like you've decided everything between you, and my feelings don't matter much to anyone."

Hugo gathered Jem into his arms. The boy tried to push him away, but Hugo just held him tighter until he began to relax. Jem buried his face in Hugo's chest; his shoulders finally slumping in surrender.

"Jem, your feelings have always mattered to me, and nothing will change that. They matter to Nick as well. He's just so overcome by finally meeting you that he's not thinking very clearly; he wants to make up for lost time. Take as long as you need. Nicholas will wait until you are ready to go. And try to think on the bright side," Hugo added.

"Which is?"

"That now you will have two families. You will always have us, and now you will have a father and stepmother, who is very eager to meet you from what I hear. She's longed for a little boy all these years, and now she'll have one."

Jem raised his face and gave Hugo a quizzical stare but didn't say anything. He was still trying to figure out these convoluted adult relationships and his place in them, but he'd been placated for the moment.

"I've asked Nicholas to stay with us, so you can have time to get to know each other. Perhaps you can show him something of Paris; he's never been. I wager Nicholas would love to see some of your favorite places, and I know he has a fondness for sweets, just like you. You can take him to that brasserie that you and Frances love. What do you say?"

"All right," Jem replied as he slid off the bale. "I'll go talk to him."

Jem was surprised when Hugo held out his hand. Jem took it and shook his hand, making him feel extremely grown-up.

"Thank you, Your Lordship," Jem said as he smiled up at the older man.

"For what?"

"For not treating me like a baby."

Hugo patted Jem on the shoulder. "Jem, you saved my life. You are a man in my eyes, and a man deserves to be treated with respect."

Jem smiled and pulled Hugo down to his level. He gave him a warm hug and kissed his cheek. "Can a man say that he loves you?" he asked as Hugo hugged him back.

"Always."

# SIXTY-ONE

I adjusted my bodice after feeding Valentine and hoisted the baby onto my shoulder. The day outside was simply glorious; a June morning that lifted the spirits and made the heart sing. Valentine's eyes were already closing since it was nearly her nap time, so I grabbed a book from my dressing table, and made my way to the garden. The house was usually quiet at this time, with Frances still in bed, Archie tending to the horses and any other little things that he perceived needed doing, and Hugo spending an hour with Jem in an effort to teach him some Latin. I'm not sure who was more frustrated with these efforts, but they both appreciated the time spent together, especially now that Jem's prospects had so radically changed.

Nicholas thought it best not to interfere with Jem's routine, so he went out for a walk along the Seine. He'd arrived only yesterday, but already it felt as if Nicholas Marsden had been a part of our lives for much longer than a day. Nicholas was a few years older than Luke, and darker in his looks, but he had the same easy charm and good humor, which made it easy for him to fit right in. I was struck by the similarities between him and Jem when I finally saw them together. Hugo thought that Jem favored Margaret in looks, but since I'd never met the woman, I could only see Nicholas in him. There was no doubt in my mind that Jem was truly his son. I didn't need a paternity test to see that they shared blood. What I found intriguing was the obvious similarity in mannerisms in two people who hadn't met until yesterday. It reminded me how much stronger nature could be than nurture. I had no doubt that once Jem and Nicholas got past the awkwardness of getting to know each other, they would grow very close and develop a bond that would be rock-solid.

Jem would be leaving us soon, and losing him would be the equivalent of having a limb amputated, especially for Hugo. Jem was such a part of our lives, such a fixture. I couldn't imagine a life in which Jem was no longer there. Nicholas promised to give their relationship time to develop, but I could see the impatience in his eyes as he looked at his son. He wanted to take Jem home, to start teaching him about the life he was born to and familiarizing him with the running of the estate. In my modern eyes, Jem was still a child, but by seventeenth-century standards, he was practically a man. Had Margaret lived and Jem remained in Cranley, he'd already be doing an apprenticeship of some sort to prepare him for the life ahead and enable him to learn a skill which would support him and his future family.

Even Clarence, who was now fourteen, was already taking on the running of his estate in Kent, and the responsibility for all the people on it who were dependent on him for their livelihood. Childhood was short and often grim in this period in history; innocence and naiveté quickly extinguished as the realities of life set in. One only had to look at Frances to see the contrast. How different her life might have been had she been born in the future. Funny, I'd always thought that my life had been extremely complicated, but compared to the uncertainty and hardship I'd endured over the past two years, my life in the twenty-first century had been a walk in the park.

I put aside my grim thoughts as I emerged outdoors. The garden was bathed in soft sunshine, the bees droning lazily as they made their way from fragrant bloom to fragrant bloom. I settled Valentine on a blanket in the shade of a chestnut tree and sat next to her with my book. I'd have loved a good thriller or even a titillating romance, but I had to settle for a well-read volume of Shakespeare's sonnets since there were hardly any books in English in the house, and I felt that I was speaking French enough as it was.

I turned the dog-eared pages to my favorite sonnet, which I reread at least a few times a week.

Let me not to the marriage of true minds
Admit impediments. Love is not love
Which alters when it alteration finds,
Or bends with the remover to remove:
O no; it is an ever-fixed mark,
That looks on tempests, and is never shaken;
It is the star to every wandering bark,
Whose worth's unknown, although his height be taken.
Love's not Time's fool, though rosy lips and cheeks
Within his bending sickle's compass come;
Love alters not with his brief hours and weeks,
But bears it out even to the edge of doom.
If this be error and upon me proved,
I never writ, nor no man ever loved.

I closed my eyes, having recited the poem out loud to myself. It never failed to bring me pleasure. I turned my face up to the gentle sunshine, enjoying its golden warmth. It was vulgar for a gentlewoman to have anything resembling a suntan, but I took off my wide-brimmed hat for a few minutes a day, telling myself that it was a good source of Vitamin D, and therefore necessary to my good health.

I smiled as a shadow fell on my face and blocked the rays of the sunshine. "Sit down, I'll read to you," I said without opening my eyes. Hugo frequently joined us in the garden after his lesson with Jem, and having struggled with the boy for an hour, enjoyed a few moments of peace as I read to him.

"Thank you, but I have other plans for the rest of the morning."

The voice was pleasant, but not quite right.

My eyes flew open to see a dark shadow in front of me. It took a moment for my vision to adjust, but it was long enough for my heart to register what my mind was already screaming. The man in front of me wasn't Hugo, but Max, and at that moment, I was actually glad to see him.

Max looked remarkably well for someone who had survived the ordeal of being sent to the West Indies for indentured labor. His clothes were not fashionable, but well-made and of good quality, as were his shoes. He was leaner, but stronger, if the bulge of his biceps beneath the velvet coat was anything to go on. His hair was longer than it had been in the twenty-first century, and he wore a goatee, which only accentuated his lean cheeks and the remains of a deep tan.

But what had changed the most were his eyes. The Max I had initially known, before his ill-fated attempt on Hugo's life in a moment of pure lunacy, had warm brown eyes, full of humor and light. They were the eyes of a man who knew his place in the world, and was pleased with his prospects. The Max who stood before me now had eyes that were hard and cruel, but crinkling with a mirth which came from a place of cynical irony rather than humor. My joy at seeing him alive quickly dissipated, leaving in its place a nagging fear.

"My God, Max, I'm so glad to see you alive," I said carefully as I watched his face for any indication of his intentions. "What are you doing here? How did you manage to escape from Barbados?"

"So, you know all about that, do you?" he asked pleasantly. "Neve, please take the child and follow me," Max requested calmly.

"I'm not going anywhere," I replied as my mind whirred frantically. I didn't want Max to see Hugo, especially since Hugo was still not fully recovered, but I needed help to thwart whatever Max had in mind. The only person who could take on Max was Archie, and he'd gone out after breakfast and wasn't back yet. I was on my own.

Max withdrew a pistol from the waistband of his breeches and pointed it straight at my heart. "Please, take the child and follow me," he repeated. "I know you think that I won't shoot you, but, believe me, I have nothing left to lose, Neve. I don't want to harm you, but I will if I must." Max deliberately moved his arm, pointing the gun at the sleeping child. "Now, *milady,*" he added, his voice dripping with sarcasm.

I grabbed Valentine and walked in front of Max as he maneuvered me toward the little-used gate in the back wall. He must have forced the lock because, as far as I knew, no one had the key to that gate; it'd been lost years ago.

I tried to glance back at the house, but Max pushed the barrel of the pistol against my back, urging me on. "Don't even think of screaming. It will do you absolutely no good, and wake up the child, which will only complicate matters."

A closed carriage waited in the street, the horses stomping nervously as if they sensed that they were involved in something nefarious. Max pushed me into the carriage and locked the door from outside before he jumped onto the bench and took up the reins. The carriage rolled away at a stately pace as if the occupants were just out for a leisurely ride rather than being abducted by a madman who'd risen from the dead and was intent on some kind of twisted revenge.

I saw the streets of Paris pass by outside the small window of the chaise. It was hard to orient myself without any major landmarks, but I suspected that we were heading south. Why? What was there? Perhaps Max wanted to take me to wherever he was staying, but why? What did he want with me? And how was it possible that he was here in Paris after being sent to Barbados six months ago? How had he managed to escape, and how had he known we were here? Someone must have helped him, but who? Who could Max possibly know in seventeenth-century France, and why would he not try to make his way home to his real life? Had I managed to escape captivity, my first thought would have been of returning to my own place and time. My only chance of getting out of this situation was to understand what Max was about and try to somehow talk him out of it. I couldn't take him on physically, so my only weapon was reason, but having seen the gleam of insanity in Max's eyes when he pointed the gun at Valentine, I wasn't sure if reason was something that could still reach him.

I tried to remain calm as I cradled the sleeping baby in my arms. "We'll be all right, my darling," I cooed to Valentine, but I was really trying to convince myself. How long would it take Hugo to notice that we were gone, and how would he know where to look for us? "Oh, God," I moaned as memories of another carriage ride, one that took me to Newgate Prison, welled up inside me, turning my anxiety to terror. Max had tried to kill Hugo once, but perhaps he'd hit on another tactic of getting at him, through his wife and child.

I shivered with apprehension as the carriage finally came to a stop and Max opened the door, inviting me to step out. I wasn't sure exactly where we were, but this part of Paris didn't look respectable. It was a slum. There were no houses nearby; and the ones I could see in the distance were no more than tumbledown shacks. The ground was uneven, covered with withered-looking tufts of grass and litter. I noticed a broken shard of pottery; a few planks which had rotted and turned brown, and several pieces of metal, which at some point might have been tin cups or some kind of tools, which were now nothing more than rusted wands poking out of the ground.

Max took my elbow and pulled me toward a dark opening gaping in the barely noticeable hillock. A wooden lintel indicated that at some point this entrance might have been used for something, but right now, it looked completely deserted. The narrow passage descended steeply into the bowels of the earth, where an old ladder protruded from what appeared to be a hole in the ground.

I looked at Max, wondering if pleading might help, but he just shook his head. "Get down," he said.

"I can't; I've got the baby."

It wasn't particularly cold in the cave, but I was shivering uncontrollably, my mind racing as my terror mounted. What was Max's plan? What if he simply took the ladder and left me and Valentine to die? Did he, in some twisted way, blame me for his predicament? I had nothing to do with his arrest or deportation, but perhaps he didn't see it that way. He'd suffered, that was clear from the look in his eyes, but why did he want to punish me? What had I done? Did he blame me for finding the passage, or for choosing Hugo over him? I'd never made any promises, but for some reason, Max had taken it for granted that we had a future together. Had I led him on in some way?

And then it dawned on me, and I nearly fainted as a blinding light of clarity assaulted my senses. Max had attempted to kill Hugo because he feared for his status as Lord Everly. Hugo had been meant to die in 1685, but instead, I'd saved his life, and had brought him to the future to escape arrest for treason and execution. And now, I was Hugo's wife, the mother of his child, the woman who had altered the past, and therefore, the future. Max didn't know what he would be coming back to if he allowed me and my child to live. The life he left behind might not be the life he returned to if the succession had been altered.

The birth of Valentine changed everything, and if Max chose to leave us to die in this hellhole, Hugo would never know what happened to his wife and child, would not be able to remarry or father another legitimate heir unless they found our remains, and would therefore still leave everything to Clarence, allowing Max to eventually inherit as he was meant to.

"Max, please, don't make me go down there," I pleaded, but Max barely paid any attention to me as he took the baby and pushed me roughly toward the ladder.

"You can climb or you can fall; the choice is yours," he growled.

I grabbed on to the ladder and made my way down, feeling for the next step in the darkness. The opening above grew smaller as I descended, the darkness more oppressive. Max watched as I made my way down, then followed with Valentine. It was easier for him to hold on with one hand since he didn't have long skirts to deal with. He handed the baby back to me after finally reaching the bottom, and motioned for me to step away from the ladder.

Several lanterns sat on a wooden plank, and Max lit them, illuminating the deserted mine. It was relatively wide, with a low ceiling supported by old, rotten beams. I prayed that he wouldn't force us to go deeper since the mine seemed to disappear into the darkness, the damp breath of the earth reminding me that it might go on for a mile or more. I nearly screamed as I saw a grinning skeleton propped up against one of the walls, its head tilted to the side as if it were watching us. Several more human bones were scattered around, probably by animals who'd burrowed their way into the tunnel.

Max ordered me to go a little further into the shaft, but allowed me to stop before descending deeper. There was a makeshift bench, which he graciously invited me to sit on. I clutched the baby, hoping she wouldn't wake up just yet. I needed my wits about me, and a wailing child would prevent me from thinking rationally.

"What do you think of this place?" Max asked conversationally. "In two hundred years or so, this will be a major tourist attraction—The Catacombs of Paris. Thousands of skeletons will line the walls, creating a macabre draw for people who are fascinated with death. Most of them will just walk through the tunnels, taking it all in without ever really thinking about the people whose skulls stare at them in mute horror. But all those people had lived, had loved, suffered, and feared death as much as you and I. Will you be one of those people, do you think?"

He was enjoying himself; I could see that. This wasn't something that he'd just thought of on the spur of the moment; this was a well-conceived plan, and a prepared speech. He was trying to scare me, to intimidate me, and, God in Heaven, was it working. I knew I had to try to talk to him, to reason with him, but my wits had deserted me. I was numb with fear and panic, but I had to think of something to say. I had to save my baby.

"Max, why have you brought us here?" I asked, hoping my voice wasn't dripping with accusation. My only chance of escape was in talking him around and infuriating him wouldn't help.

Max sat down opposite me, placed the pistol on the wooden plank, and planted his hands on his thighs. "I suppose I owe you an explanation," he replied, smiling at me as if we were about to order dinner at some restaurant and he was apologizing for being late.

"Yes, you do," I replied, hoping it would be a long one. Hugo had to realize that we were missing by now. I tried not to think of the fact that Max had left no trace of where we'd gone; Hugo would have no idea where to search for us.

"As you know, I was arrested in place of Hugo and sent to the Tower of London, where I was beaten, tortured, ridiculed, sentenced to death, and eventually sent down to Barbados for seven years of indentured labor because some mysterious benefactor bribed the judge."

"Hugo was your mysterious benefactor. He paid for Gideon Warburton. We tried to help you, Max," I cried, seizing the opportunity Max had just provided. Perhaps if he knew that we hadn't abandoned him, he'd give up on this crazy plan.

"Well, that was most kind of Hugo, I'm sure," Max replied, as if I'd just told him that Hugo sent his regards. "You wouldn't believe what I went through to escape, and I won't bore you with the details. You see, my initial plan had been to just make my way to England and return to my rightful place. You have no idea how much I miss home," he added.

"What changed your mind?"

"I happened to learn, quite by accident, mind you, that you and Hugo were in Paris, and that you've had a child. Imagine my surprise," Max said theatrically, his eyes growing wider. "By the way, is it a boy or a girl?" he suddenly asked.

"It's a girl."

"Hmm, shame for Hugo. I suppose he wanted a son, but I am all right with having a daughter," he shared with me as if it were a great secret.

"What are you saying?" Horror crept up my back like cold fingers; caressing me as it threatened to choke me.

"Neve, I have no wish to harm you; I love you, and I will love your child. You have my word. We can have the life we were meant to have, you and I. I know you won't go quietly without your baby, nor will you forgive me if anything happens to her, so I will make sure you're both safe."

"I don't understand," I replied, feeling hysteria begin to well up inside me. He was really scaring me, especially with his calm and jovial demeanor. Had he lost his mind?

"Neve, I brought you here in order to lure Hugo to his death. After I kill him, we will make our way back to England,

and back to our own time. You will be free to marry me, and I will adopt Hugo's child; I owe him that much. She will grow up calling me 'Daddy.' I love the irony of that, don't you?"

"I will not go anywhere with you," I hissed, really terrified now.

"What reason would you have to remain here if Hugo were dead? He can be one of the first skeletons to grace this place, along with this handsome fellow. Hugo won't even receive a proper Christian burial, which I know would be important to him, so I'll punish him even in death."

"Hugo has done absolutely nothing to you; he tried to help you; he risked his life for you," I shrieked, but Max remained unmoved.

"Neve, I freely admit that Hugo is an honorable man, one who deserves your love. However, your child is a threat to my future, as are any other children you might have. If I allow Hugo to live, he might father a son, which would leave me disinherited. I would have nothing to go back to, and I couldn't bear that after what I've been through. I don't hate Hugo; as a matter of fact, I even admire him, seeing what he risked, doing what he felt was right, but that doesn't change my intent. Hugo must die, and you must come with me. History will be set to rights; Clarence will inherit, and everything will be as it should have been. I really do love you, Neve. I realized that after I saw you with Hugo. You tore my heart out."

"You love me?" I gaped at him. "You don't do this to people you love. And the only reason you want me is because I love him, and not you. You want his life for yourself."

"Yes, I suppose I do," Max agreed, nodding to himself as if the idea had only just occurred to him. "It pains me that you chose him over me, but I can see why you would. He's a real man, not a preening, self-absorbed peacock who only cares about posturing and gain. I will be the man you want, Neve. I've learned much in the past, and I will make you proud," Max said, his gaze suddenly earnest. "I will become worthy of your love, and worthy of our daughter."

"Max, do you honestly believe that a man who would kill my husband can ever be worthy of my love? Please, let me out of here. I will go with you willingly, but leave Hugo alone. He's suffered enough."

"I'm sorry, but I can't do that. Hugo cannot be allowed to reproduce. Shall I castrate him, do you think?" Max asked with a twinkle in his eye. "Would he prefer life as a gelding to death as a man? I suppose that's an option, but I doubt he'll submit."

I was staring at Max, my heart pounding with fear. He was mad. His captivity had turned his mind. He must have been through hell, I'd grant him that, but he was talking like a madman. Did he really believe that I would love him after he killed Hugo, and allow him access to my only child? Did he really believe that Hugo wouldn't put up a fight to save us?

"How will Hugo know where to find us?" I asked, praying that Archie would be on hand when he did.

"I sent a note to the house, telling him that I have you and to come alone and unarmed, or I will kill both you and the child. That should bring him running. What's wrong with him, by the way? He looked a bit sickly the last I saw him."

"Hugo had been shot," I replied tersely, not wanting to give Max any more ammunition.

"He does tend to make enemies, doesn't he? I'm surprised Lionel Finch never killed him. He certainly wanted to; I saw it in his eyes at that mockery of a trial."

"Finch is dead. Hugo killed him, and he will kill you," I spat out, "as he should have when you tried to brain him with a rock. He was merciful."

"Hugo could afford to be merciful; I was no threat to him, but he is to me," Max explained patiently.

I drew back in apprehension as I heard something coming from outside. Would Max try to shoot Hugo as he descended without even giving him a chance to defend himself? I had to distract him somehow. But Max was onto me as I tried to divert his attention when I saw a pair of boots coming down the ladder. He got behind me, with his pistol trained on the opening.

Hugo jumped off the ladder and faced Max, his hands held up.

"I'm not armed, Max, as you requested," he said soothingly. "Neve, are you all right?"

I tried to answer him, but all that came out was a desperate sob. In a few moments, Hugo could be dead, and I couldn't do anything to stop it. Max held all the cards, and Hugo and I were at his mercy.

"Hugo, I know you tried to help me while I was in the Tower, and I am grateful for that; I want you to know that. I do admire you, really, but I'm afraid you must die. You have made a mess of my future, and I must set things to rights before I return to my rightful place. Sorry, old man, but sometimes sacrifices need to be made. I just want you to know that I will take good care of your wife and child. The least I can do is give you that little bit of peace."

"Let Neve and the baby leave, Max. They don't need to watch me die."

"Oh, but they must," Max replied calmly. "Neve must know for sure that you are dead, or she will never be able to move forward. I intend to marry her, old boy. We will be a proper little family."

"She'll never love you," Hugo replied, his voice laced with fury.

"She will in time. I am the only person who will be able to understand what she's been through, and it's not as if she has much to go back to—no family, hardly any friends. I will happily provide for Neve and the baby, and, in time, they'll forget you ever existed. The child doesn't even look like you, so not like her looks will be a reminder of dear old dad."

"You truly are mad," Hugo said as he looked at Max's gleeful expression.

"Yes, I suppose I am, but there's method to my madness. Now, shut up; I've heard enough from you."

I tried to meet Hugo's gaze, but he looked utterly shaken by Max's revelations, the shock evident in his eyes as he stared at his sister's descendant. Hugo's face was gray in the feeble light of the lanterns, and his lips moved as if he were praying. He leaned against the earthen wall of the tunnel for support, closing his eyes momentarily as he breathed deeply to combat whatever he was feeling.

Max stood back, watching Hugo with interest, obviously in no hurry to fire the gun. He was enjoying this too much to let it end quickly. He'd had months to plan this, to envision how it would all play out, and now that it was a reality, it was too intoxicating to just terminate mid-performance.

Hugo doubled over, his arm across his middle as if he were going to be sick. I hoped he was stalling until Archie got there, but there was no sign of reinforcements. Max had demanded that Hugo come alone, and he did, too afraid to jeopardize our safety. It was just the four of us, and only three were coming out alive.

"Kneel," Max ordered, pointing to a spot before him with the pistol. He was going to kill Hugo execution style. "Don't make this any more difficult than it has to be for your wife."

Hugo's eyes finally met mine. They were full of love and longing. He didn't say anything, but his expression said it all. He was saying goodbye.

"Max, I beg you for his life," I pleaded. "I will do anything, anything at all."

"I would gladly take you up on that, Neve, if it were possible, but you know the situation. Hugo must never have another child, biological or even adopted. The line of succession must not be altered. History must be reset."

"Hugo," I cried as I tried to go to him, but Max pushed me back.

"See to your daughter, Neve. I think she's waking up."

Valentine was fussing in my arms, her eyes fully open now, gazing around at her strange surroundings. She smiled when she saw her father, revealing her two emerging bottom teeth.

"I love you both," Hugo said as he sank to his knees in front of Max, his hands folded as if in supplication. Why wasn't he fighting? Did he think he was protecting us? Is that why he was going to his death like a sacrificial lamb? I wanted to scream at him, urge him to fight, to resist, but Hugo looked up at Max, daring him to shoot. Their eyes held each other in thrall, the moment frozen in time just before all hell broke loose.

Max lowered the gun, ready to shoot. I closed my eyes, unable to watch as my husband met his end at the hands of someone I had once liked and trusted. I was shaking all over, which made Valentine giggle. She thought I was playing with her. I pressed her closer to my body for comfort and squeezed my eyes tighter. I was expecting to hear a gunshot, and I did. It sounded like an explosion in the small space, and a shower of dirt rained down on my head, causing me to open my eyes in alarm. A sound of animal agony tore from Max as he collapsed to his knees in front of Hugo. I had no idea what had happened, only that Max had fired upward and was now screaming and clutching his middle.

Hugo was on his feet in seconds. He grabbed Max's gun and stuffed it into the waistband of his breeches before dragging me toward the ladder and pushing me up as I struggled to hold my skirts and the baby at the same time. I climbed out of the hole, followed by Hugo, who took Valentine away from me since I was shaking so badly I was about to drop her. He grabbed me by the elbow, and half dragged me toward the nearest street.

Archie was waiting with the carriage, his arms crossed over his chest, and a look of ferocious anger stamped on his features. He gave us a quick examination before flinging open the door and helping me into the carriage.

Hugo climbed in and put his free arm around me, drawing me close. I could see that he was in pain, but he just shook his head as I tried to take the squirming child away from him. Valentine was howling with terror, having been frightened by the shot, but Hugo held her close and whispered to her until she began to calm down. She grabbed onto his finger and began to gnaw, the pressure easing the pain in her swollen gums.

"I don't understand," I stammered. "What just happened? I had my eyes shut; I couldn't bear to watch. I thought this was it."

Hugo shook his head, giving me a look of pure astonishment. "Did you really think that I would allow myself to be executed?" he asked, pretending to be hurt. "You know me better than that, I think. I needed an element of surprise, sweetheart. I know you were frightened, but it's all over now."

"What did you do?" I asked again as my mind began to accept the fact that we were now safe. "You were unarmed."

"I grabbed a piece of a broken bone when I leaned against the wall," Hugo explained. "I saw it protruding and needed an excuse to get close to it. I knocked Max's arm upward just before he fired and drove the bone fragment into his stomach."

"Oh, dear God," I gasped. "You stabbed him in the gut?"

Hugo smiled guiltily, but I could see that he was quite pleased with himself.

"Hugo, why did you not finish him off?" I was angry now, the fear having morphed into aggression. "Why did you let him live after what he was going to do? This is the second time he's tried to kill you."

Hugo shook his head, as if trying to clear his thoughts. I could see the emotions playing over his lean face, the regret, the sorrow, the loss. "Neve, I don't want to be the one to take Max's life. He's the only living descendant of Jane; he's the only thing left of my sister. I know that she deserved what happened to her, but I still feel responsible. Perhaps there's something I could have done to save her from her fate. To kill Max in cold blood would be like killing Jane, and I couldn't do it. If he dies, let it not be by my hand. His injury is severe enough; he's not likely to survive."

"But if he lives, he'll find us. We'll never be safe," I wailed, suddenly scared.

"He won't find us," Hugo replied.

"How can you be so certain?"

"Because we are leaving."

"Where are we going?" I asked, shocked.

"I don't know. That's the beauty of my plan. No one can betray us if they don't know where we've gone. I will decide once we get there."

I opened my mouth to ask another question, but shut it again, suddenly overcome by fatigue. I was emotionally drained, and Hugo would take care of things; he always did. I felt guilty for doubting him down in the mine, but who could blame me? I'd been terrified.

Hugo helped me into the house and made sure I had a large brandy before going to lie down for a bit. I was still shaky, my mind unable to process what had just happened to us. I'd never wished anyone harm, but at that moment, I hoped Max would bleed to death and vanish from our lives forever. I needed to know that we were safe.

# SIXTY-TWO

**Surrey, England**

Simon Harding let out a growl of exasperation as he pushed away a pile of bank statements. He'd been at it for nearly three hours and had accomplished very little. Max's affairs were a mess, to say the least. Simon had always assumed that Max's fastidiousness extended to his business affairs, but he had been wrong to presume anything. There was an accountant in the village who saw to the quarterly filings and year-end taxes, but, for the most part, the accounts were appallingly disorganized.

Simon had put off the task as long as he possibly could, but he'd had some vacation time coming to him, and this was as good a time as any to tackle the business at hand. Max had been gone for just over a year now, and although it had taken months to get a court order to allow Simon to access Max's business accounts, Simon was only now getting started. He'd taken care of paying the employees, making retirement fund contributions, and approving whatever repairs were necessary, but the bulk of the paperwork had been left until a later time.

Truth be told, Simon wouldn't even be there if he and

Heather hadn't had a blazing row last month and decided (well, actually he decided) to slow things down a bit. Heather was starting to drop very obvious hints about marriage and leaving strategically placed adverts for engagement rings and honeymoon destinations.

Simon liked Heather, enjoyed her company, and more often than not shagged her without the benefit of picturing someone else, but the thought of committing to her for a lifetime sent him into a tailspin of pure panic. Would he still want her five, ten years from now? Would he still find her attractive, witty, or even bearable? Was he ready to settle down with one woman and start a family, because that's exactly what the next step would be? He was only twenty-seven, for the love of God. What was the rush? At twenty-three, Heather was hardly deafened by the tolling of the biological clock. They had time, why couldn't they just enjoy it and see where their relationship took them?

Simon had tried calling her about twenty minutes ago, but the call went straight to voicemail. She was avoiding him in the hopes of making him wonder what she was up to, and coming to the inevitable conclusion that he would lose her to another man if he didn't put a ring on her finger with the utmost urgency. Simon pondered the notion of Heather with another man. Was he jealous? Did he care? He supposed it would hurt to know that she'd moved on so quickly, but he would recover, probably sooner than Heather thought. How much had they even had in common besides the sex? Granted, the sex was good, but nowadays, women were as talented as porn stars, having the benefit of years of aimless shagging and online tutorials. Practice made perfect, or so his mother always said, but, of course, she wasn't referring to sex.

Still, he would hate to lose Heather. They were a good fit, when all was said and done, and he'd need to smooth Heather's ruffled feathers before too long. He wasn't ready to marry her, but perhaps he could ask her to move in. His flat was big enough for two, and living together would be a good prelude to marriage. Maybe Heather would see what a slob he was and change her mind about marrying him. She wasn't the type to spend the rest of her life picking up after him and keeping the house tidy.

Simon sighed and dialed Heather again, then disconnected the call when it went to voicemail and threw his phone on top of the pile of statements. He opened the bottom drawer of the desk to see if there was anything else inside. A battered-looking notebook came out; the pages yellowed with time and the ink faded to a dull brown. The date on the first page caught Simon's eye. The entry had been made over a century ago. Well, anything was better than looking at all this boring paperwork.

Simon began to read, quickly getting absorbed into the story.

The church clock struck midnight by the time Simon finally set aside the notebook and stared off into space. It had been a fascinating account, a work of fiction better than some bestsellers he'd recently read. He'd heard of the author, of course; heard the story of his disappearance and subsequent "rest" at an asylum for the mentally disturbed. Simon had never cared much about what had happened to Henry Everly, but hearing his voice in the narrative made him real, and surprisingly sane.

Simon replaced the notebook in the drawer, shut off the lights, and went up to bed. He was bone-tired, and his eyes burned from lack of sleep. The night before he'd gone to a stag party, one that Heather wouldn't want to hear about given the "friendly" nature of the Eastern European stripper. Simon had not partaken, but his friends had and seemed to enjoy the experience. If anyone ever mentioned anything, Heather would never believe that he was innocent, when, in fact, he was.

Simon undressed, brushed his teeth, and climbed into bed, ready to sleep, but his brain was going full speed despite all his attempts at slumber. Henry's voice was still speaking in Simon's head, his teenage observations surprisingly poignant and honest. The boy must have had a very active imagination to come up with such a tale, or...

Despite Simon's love of science fiction and fantasy, the idea of time travel had never entered his mind. It was the stuff of romance; an entertaining diversion so frequently relied on in films and novels to capture the imagination. Sure, he'd seen every episode of *Doctor Who* at least half a dozen times, but that was just fun.

Simon flipped onto his back and threw off the covers, suddenly hot. His thoughts were taking a ridiculous turn, but once he opened that door a crack, it had blown wide open. Max had gone without a trace. There was no sign of a struggle, no witnesses, and no body. His car had been in the drive, his wallet on the bedside table. There had been no internet, mobile, or banking activity since the day of his disappearance, so where was he? Surely, if he were dead, his body would have been discovered by now, unless he'd been abducted by aliens, which was an interesting theory as well, to be analyzed at a later date.

Of course, no one in their right mind would ever suggest that Max had traveled through time, but there was Henry's journal, Max's unexplained absence, and the bizarre disappearance of that woman—what was her name?—Neve Ashley. She had vanished under much the same circumstances, and then showed up a few months later in the company of what his mother claimed was the twin of Max's seventeenth-century counterpart. So where was Neve Ashley now? Perhaps he could speak to her, have her tell him that he was barking mad and put an end to this ridiculous speculation.

Simon suddenly sat up in bed, having been struck by a thought. If Max had indeed traveled through time, he might have done something to alter the course of history, and in this wonderful day and age of the internet, Simon might even be able to find his footprint. It was a long shot, but he had to try, or he'd never get any rest.

He booted up his laptop and entered a search for Maximillian Everly. Pages and pages of relevant hits popped up, most of them dealing with Max's disappearance, and before that, his political aspirations. Simon scrolled through all of them, his hopes dwindling. There didn't seem to be anything of interest. He was just about to check his Facebook page since he was up anyway, when an entry at the bottom of the umpteenth page caught his eye. He clicked on the link and was brought to some middling historian's blog, discussing the aftermath of the Monmouth Rebellion. The man went on and on. God, he could have bored for England if there were such a category in the Olympics, but a paragraph at the end was gold. It read:

The last conspirator of James Crofts, the Duke of Monmouth, Lord Hugo Everly, was tried in October of 1685, having eluded authorities until then. The fascinating thing about this particular case was that up until the very end, the accused claimed his arrest to be a case of mistaken identity, swearing on the Bible that he was Maximillian Everly rather than Lord Hugo Everly, for whom the warrant had been issued. Perhaps it was simply a gambit for freedom, but the accused had legal representation, which was virtually unheard of at the time, and actual physical evidence presented to the court meant to disprove that he was Hugo Everly. George Jeffreys, who presided over the trial, dismissed the evidence out of hand, and sentenced the man to death by beheading, which was commuted to deportation to the West Indies. Presumably, a sizeable bribe helped him see a way to being merciful, but the unfortunate Maximillian/Hugo Everly died shortly after arriving in Barbados, possibly of yellow fever.

---

Simon stared at the paragraph in awe. Was this a coincidence? There could have been other Maximillians along the line, but he'd never heard of one. Was this actual proof that Max had gone back in time and been arrested in lieu of his ancestor? He did bear a striking resemblance to Hugo Everly. Did this mean that Max was dead?

Simon felt the hot sting of tears behind his eyelids. He'd grown up idolizing Max, had worshipped him as an older brother, only to find out that Max *was* his older brother. If the blog entry was correct, then Max had been dead for centuries, but was there anything Simon could do to help him? Was there a way to prevent the injustice which had claimed Max's life? Simon gave up the idea of sleep and padded downstairs. He needed a sandwich and a cup of tea before he began to tackle this insane idea.

# SIXTY-THREE

## NOVEMBER 1686

**Rouen, France**

I snuggled against Hugo, lost in that shadowy world between wakefulness and sleep as a blissful peace settled over me. Valentine, who was now thankfully sleeping through the night, was warm and snug in her cradle, Hugo was fully recovered and stretched out next to me, and Frances was just down the corridor, still unwed, but secure in Archie's love and happy for the very first time in her life.

We'd been living in a sprawling farmhouse a few miles outside of Rouen since we'd left Paris last June, and I had to admit that I had never been happier. The constant worry, intrigue, and uncertainty had been replaced by safety, a comforting routine, and the feeling of serenity. Hugo had chosen Rouen because of its proximity to the port of Le Havre, and we had all the benefits of living close to a large city without actually being a part of it.

There was a moment each morning when we remembered that Jem was gone, and wouldn't be sitting in the kitchen, swinging his feet to and fro as he stuffed his face with whatever was on offer. Saying goodbye had been one of the hardest things we'd had to do, but Hugo had solemnly promised that we would see Jem as soon as we returned to England, and I knew that promise would be kept, no matter the cost. The knowledge that Jem had left willingly went a long way toward making us feel better. Once he'd gotten over his reservations, Jem had grown fond of his father, and the notion of becoming a gentleman and a landowner didn't displease him too much either. He'd gone to a better life and a more promising future, and that was all we needed to know for now to deal with our grief at losing him.

Leaving Paris had helped me find peace and contentment. For the first time in our married life, Hugo and I weren't hiding, running, or scheming. Our life now was simple, and beautiful, but Hugo was restless, and I knew the idyll wouldn't last. In exactly two years, the winds of change would sweep through England as the Glorious Revolution dethroned James and put William and Mary on the throne, starting a new dynasty and altering the future of England forever. Hugo would finally be free to return home but would have to bend the knee to a Protestant monarch and live in the knowledge that his dream of religious freedom would not come to fruition during his life-time. I hoped that he would be able to adjust to this new reality, but there was a part of me that knew Hugo wouldn't just roost at his country estate and keep out of politics.

From time to time, I still dreamed of Max, and woke up bathed in a cold sweat, crying in terror as I imagined myself in that dark mine, praying for Hugo to come, but knowing that he would be walking into a trap. It saddened me to think that Max had died alone, in the dark, and with no one to bury or mourn him, but it was a fate he'd chosen for himself. I couldn't help remembering what he'd said about the sightless eyes of numerous skulls grinning at the tourists and shuddered at the thought of Max being one of them. How different his life might have been if he'd never followed me through the passage in the crypt. He might have won that seat in Parliament, and could even have had a family by now, which is something I thought he longed for.

Hugo slid his hand over my belly as I began to drift off to sleep. He'd noticed that I'd missed my period, and was silently asking me if I might be pregnant again. I wasn't sure, but I suspected I might be. The idea no longer frightened me as much as before, and the joy we had from Valentine made up for the pain I had endured. I covered his hand with my own before my thoughts turned to dreams.

# EPILOGUE

## DECEMBER 25, 1686

**Paris, France**

The aroma of roast goose filled the house, mingling with the smell of pine and the pleasant scent of burning wood coming from the roaring fireplace. The table was set for Christmas dinner, but the house was silent, except for the sounds of activity coming from the kitchen where the cook and the skivvy were putting the finishing touches on the meal. The Benoits would be home from church any minute, their cheeks rosy from the cold and their stomachs growling after the lengthy sermon.

Max carefully made his way down the stairs, wishing that he could have just remained in his room during the festivities, but Vivienne wouldn't hear of it. He wasn't partaking in the spirit of love and forgiveness, although he had every reason to be thankful. Not a night went by that he didn't revisit that morning in the mine, when Hugo had outsmarted him once again, and left him for dead. Max had lay sprawled on the cold, dirt floor of the mine, his blood seeping into the ground as he grew colder and more disoriented. The candles in the lanterns were burning low, and soon they would gutter and die, leaving Max in complete darkness and buried alive. He still wasn't sure where the last reserve of strength had come from, or how he had managed to drag himself up that ladder, but he'd made it back to the road to call for help. The last thing he recalled was giving some farmer the Benoits' address before passing out from loss of blood.

Max had needed a hospital, but what he got was Vivienne Benoit. She had nursed him back to health despite the odds. Max had drifted in and out of consciousness for days, but once he finally came around, what he learned was that the bone Hugo had used to attack him had perforated his intestine, creating a puncture which refused to heal properly, and leaked gastric fluids into his abdominal cavity. Even now, six months later, he could barely keep down solid foods, and suffered from acute pain any time he ate anything that was difficult to digest, such as meat.

Max put on a brave face as the Benoits exploded through the door: happy, spiritually uplifted, and ready to eat. He joined them at the table, drooling at the sight of the goose he couldn't eat, and the wine he couldn't drink. The cook put a plate of mashed turnips in front of him and a cup of milk to wash them down with. Max lifted his cup in a silent toast as Captain Benoit wished them all a *Joyeux Noël*. It was Christmas after all, and it was almost the New Year, a year in which Max would heal, and start planning his return to England.

# A LETTER FROM THE AUTHOR

Huge thanks for reading *Sins of Omission*, I hope you were hooked on Neve and Hugo's epic journey. It continues in book four, *The Queen's Gambit*. If you want to join other readers in hearing all about my new releases and bonus content, you can sign up for my newsletter!

www.stormpublishing.co/irina-shapiro

If you enjoyed this book and could spare a few moments to leave a review that would be hugely appreciated. Even a short review can make all the difference in encouraging a reader to discover my books for the first time. Thank you so much!

Although I write several different genres, time travel was my first love. As a student of history, I often wonder if I have what it takes to survive in the past in the dangerous, life-altering situations my characters have to deal with. Neve and Hugo are two of my favorite characters, not only because they're intelligent and brave but because they're fallible, sensitive, and ultimately human. I hope you enjoy their adventures, both in the past and the present, and come to see them as real people rather than characters on a page.

Thanks again for being part of this amazing journey with me and I hope you'll stay in touch – I have so many more stories and ideas to entertain you with!

Irina

Printed in Great Britain
by Amazon